RATTLESNAKE FEVER

RATTLESNAKE FEVER

Lorie Blundon

iUniverse, Inc.
Bloomington

Rattlesnake Fever

Copyright © 2012 by Lorie Blundon.

All rights reserved. No part of this book may be used or reproduced by any means, graphic, electronic, or mechanical, including photocopying, recording, taping or by any information storage retrieval system without the written permission of the publisher except in the case of brief quotations embodied in critical articles and reviews.

This is a work of fiction. All of the characters, names, incidents, organizations, and dialogue in this novel are either the products of the author's imagination or are used fictitiously.

iUniverse books may be ordered through booksellers or by contacting:

iUniverse
1663 Liberty Drive
Bloomington, IN 47403
www.iuniverse.com
1-800-Authors (1-800-288-4677)

Because of the dynamic nature of the Internet, any web addresses or links contained in this book may have changed since publication and may no longer be valid. The views expressed in this work are solely those of the author and do not necessarily reflect the views of the publisher, and the publisher hereby disclaims any responsibility for them.

Any people depicted in stock imagery provided by Thinkstock are models, and such images are being used for illustrative purposes only.
Certain stock imagery © Thinkstock.

ISBN: 978-1-4759-3001-6 (sc)
ISBN: 978-1-4759-3002-3 (hc)
ISBN: 978-1-4759-3003-0 (ebk)

Library of Congress Control Number: 2012910034

Printed in the United States of America

iUniverse rev. date: 06/12/2012

*This book is dedicated to my grandmother, Lois Isabel Roberts,
who taught me strength, determination, and courage,
and the meaning of what family should be. Love you, Gram.*

Thank-Yous!

Thank you to my husband, John, and our children, Wesley and Rebecca, for all their love and support and for putting up with this crazy lady. Thank you for listening to me constantly and going on adventures to help me find the answers. You understood and encouraged me when I wanted to give up, because you knew it was something I needed to do. I could not have done this without you. I love all of you so much!

Thank you to my dear Aunt Luella, the strongest woman I know with the biggest heart in the world. Remember to do for you, too! You deserve it. You are loved more than you know.

Thank you to my special Toronto archivist for never giving up and all your help. You are the best!

Thank you to the Cobourg Court House for all your assistance in making this book a reality.

Thank you to all my friends and angels for the guidance you have given me on this difficult journey that needed to be told.

Last but not least, an extra special thank-you to my Grandma R and Great-Grandma V, for watching over me and guiding me.

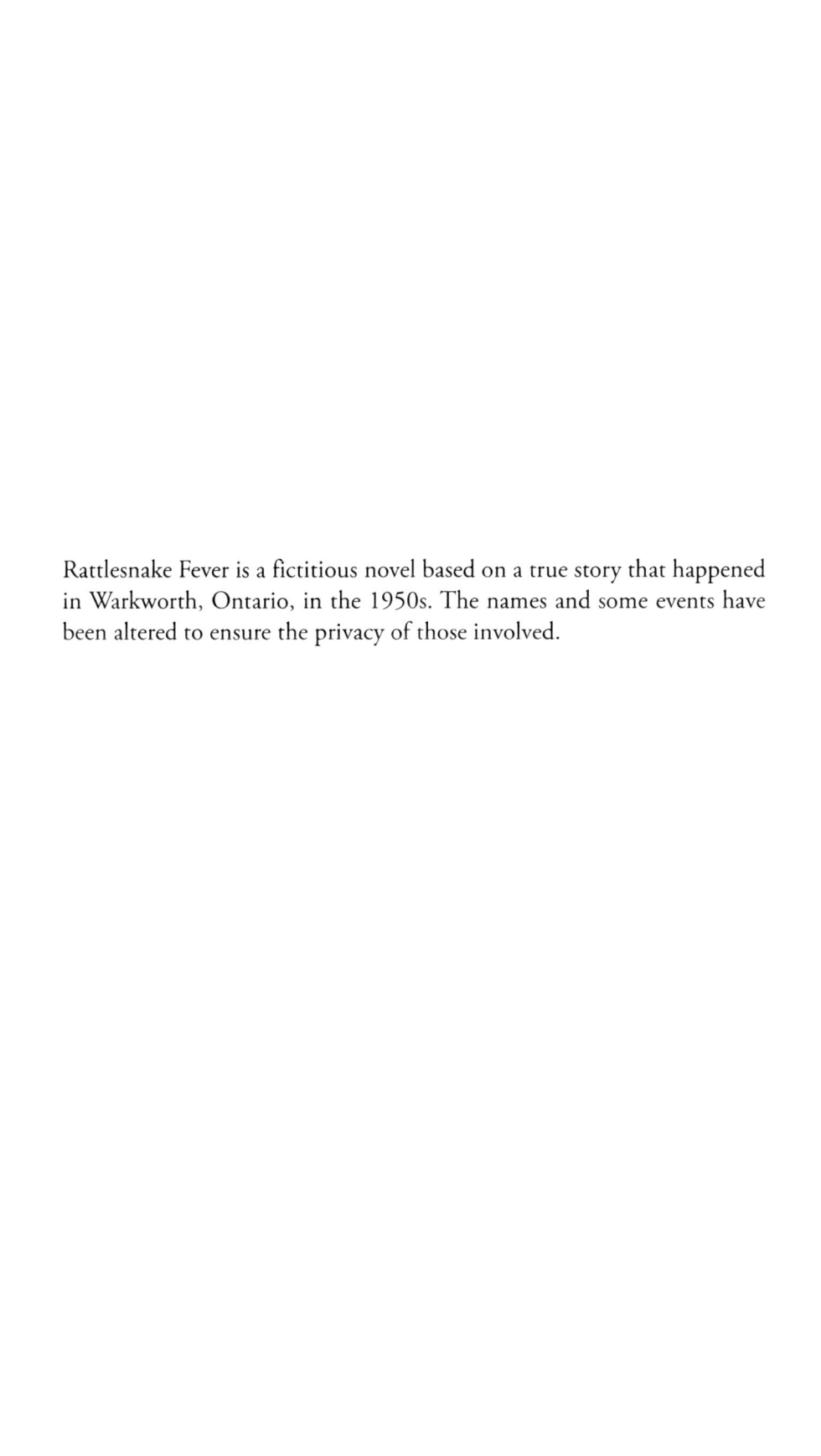

Rattlesnake Fever is a fictitious novel based on a true story that happened in Warkworth, Ontario, in the 1950s. The names and some events have been altered to ensure the privacy of those involved.

We must become the change we seek in the world.

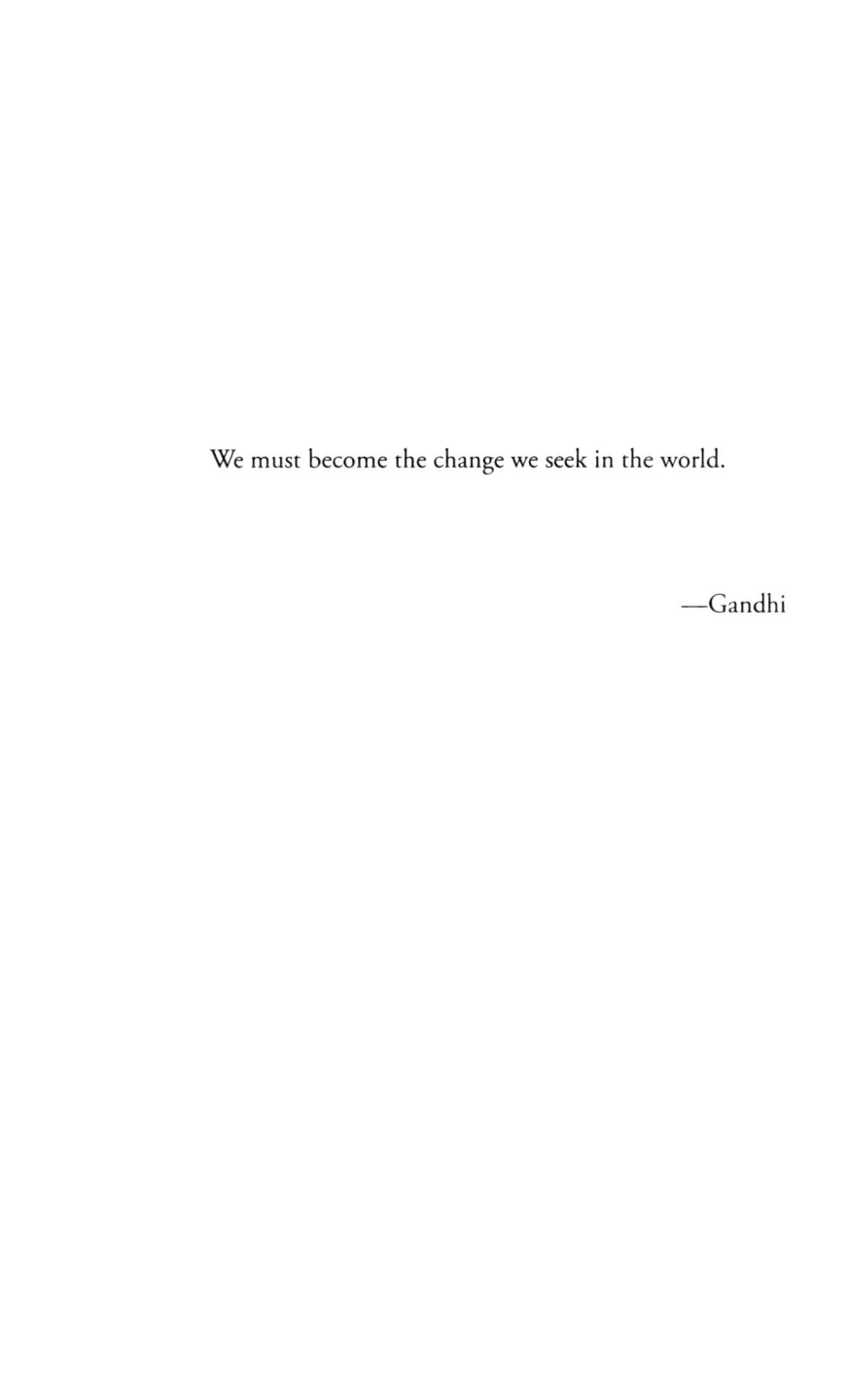

—Gandhi

Foreword

Sometimes we get so caught up in surviving life that we forget to live it. Family is so important, yet it becomes overtaken by jealousy, greed, and misperceptions. People tend to become what they see, and this is not always a good thing. Although we may feel that our destiny is already chosen for us, the journey we make is one of our own choice. We have the power to be in control of our own lives, and the only person who can choose to make a change is *you*. Make that change when necessary and do not repeat the unspeakable past.

One

At around 4:30 p.m. at work, Malorie received the call from her cousin about her grandmother's passing on Monday, June 2, 2008. Her grandmother was 87. After hanging up the phone, Malorie sobbed at her desk. She took the train home as she always did—she worked in downtown Toronto—and she could not stop thinking about her grandma and their last visit together. She had just been with her grandma the weekend before, and she had felt like the worst babysitter in the world. She had offered to help out Aunt Georgie, who had to go out for the day and could not leave her mother alone. She had been named after her Aunt Georgia.

When Malorie had tried to get her grandma up, the older woman had said she wanted to sleep. It was May, but it was quite warm outside. She let her grandma sleep, but when she went in, again she noticed the bed was wet; Grandma had been sweating. Malorie told her grandmother that she had to get up so she could change her. Despite the fact that she had lost a lot of weight, she was still solid, and Malorie definitely got her workout for the day because her grandmother was unable to use her legs; they were dead weight. She and Grandma laughed as Malorie called her grandma "farm girl" and tried to get her all washed up and dressed in new clothes.

Malorie washed her face and body down with soap and water, and she rubbed some baby powder on her skin. Then Malorie combed Grandma's hair, hoping the elderly woman would feel better. Once Grandma was all dressed and ready to go, Malorie rolled the wheelchair out to the living room and got her a drink. Malorie always brought lime soda pop and butter tarts, but she could not find lime pop anywhere before she came to visit that day. Malorie got her a glass of Sprite and told her she was going to put the laundry on and would be right back.

When Malorie came back upstairs, she asked her grandma if she wanted something to eat, but nothing seemed to appeal to her. Malorie got out some banana yogurt and told her grandma she had to eat something. She put the spoon in her grandma's hand and the yogurt in the other hand. Her grandmother's hands were crippled by arthritis, but she could still feed herself. She had lost her sight years before, after cataract surgery. Malorie then ran back downstairs to put the fabric softener in the rinse cycle, and when she went downstairs, there was a huge flood. "Give me a break!" Malorie yelled, but not loud enough that her grandma would hear.

Malorie quickly ran back upstairs to check on her grandma, walked in very nonchalantly, and advised in a calm voice that she would be right back and she was just taking care of a minor technical difficulty. Grandma asked her what was wrong, and Malorie confessed that she had a flood downstairs. Malorie tried to act calm and in control, but Grandma Annie perked up right away with a worried look on her face. "Don't worry, Grandma, everything is under control. I will be right back," Malorie assured her. That was a lie—it was totally out of control downstairs.

Malorie quickly called Aunt Georgie at the number she had left her in case of an emergency. Malorie advised her Aunt Georgie that there was nothing to worry about, but she just wanted to confirm if the drain in the laundry room was under the washer. Aunt Georgie said it was. Malorie didn't want to ruin her aunt's time away because she rarely, if ever, had time for herself.

Malorie went back downstairs and began to move the washer out. She was not a very pretty blonde-haired girl, and despite her short height, she was built like a man and was able to lift like a man, which at times like this came in handy. She turned the water off and tried to unplug anything electrical. The drain wasn't there, so she started to soak up the water with towels and wrung them out in the sink. She heard her aunt come in the back door. Malorie yelled, "I'm downstairs." As her aunt entered the room, Malorie began to cry and confessed that she was the worst babysitter ever and wouldn't blame Aunt Georgie if she never let her come back again.

The sweat was pouring from Malorie's head, and she wasn't sure if it was from the heat or the stress. The water was up to her ankles, and her shoes were soaking wet.

Aunt Georgie smiled and giggled. "Malorie, don't worry, it's nothing that can't be fixed. I bet the lint hasn't been cleaned out; it happens all the time. Come on upstairs, and we will have a cold drink."

As Aunt Georgie turned to go up the stairs, Malorie yelled out, "Aunt Georgie, Grandma didn't seem to want to eat anything." Malorie was worried about her.

When Malorie went upstairs, Grandma Annie was sitting up and eating away. Malorie was relieved. Aunt Georgie could see how worried Malorie had been. "Mother, you had Malorie scared to death."

Grandma had a grin on her face and said, "No I didn't. She looks fine to me." They all laughed. Malorie had to head home to get her daughter from work, but before she did, she gave her grandma a big hug and kiss and told her as she always did, "I love you, Gram, and I'll see you soon."

Malorie heard the conductor announce her stop and got off the train. When she arrived home, she went directly to the phone to call Aunt Georgie and make sure she was okay. Malorie told her aunt she wished she could have been there for her grandmother. Grandma Annie had asked for her, but Malorie had been in Ottawa that weekend looking for an apartment for her daughter, Rorie, who would be heading off to university in the fall. Her uncle had tried to call her but had not left a message. Of all weekends! Malorie would have been there in a heartbeat had she known her grandma was sick.

Malorie got off the phone, put on her pajamas, and crawled up in her comfy chair with a box of tissue. She was happy to know her grandmother was no longer suffering and was with Grandpa Seth, but Malorie was already missing their visits. They would chat, or Malorie would read to her grandma while she ate the butter tarts. There was always something to do. Grandma would tell Malorie that they were the best butter tarts, complimenting her on how flakey the pastry was. One time the butter tart had fallen on the ground, and Grandma was quite adamant that there was a five-second rule and it was not to be wasted. Malorie had felt quite proud that her grandmother felt that way about her tarts, and she had told her grandma it was the one on the floor, but she had actually replaced it with a new one. Aunt Georgie would come up behind Malorie and eat the one that had fallen. She laughed and said, "Mother is right—we can't waste that." Malorie wondered for whom she would make her butter tarts now.

Now all that had come to an end. As Malorie sat in her comfy chair and reminisced, the doorbell rang. Aunt Georgie's daughter had driven her to Malorie's house because Georgie was worried about her niece. Aunt Georgie hugged Malorie tight. and they both cried, "Aunt Georgie, I wish I could have been there."

It all happened so fast. Aunt Georgie was shocked; she had just taken Annie to the hospital because she had a cold, and they were supposed to come home. Aunt Georgie said her mom had wanted her bed propped up a bit. She then began rocking back and forth as though she was in a rocking chair, saying the Lord's Prayer. She was humming, "Jesus Rock Me Home," and before Aunt Georgie knew what was happening, her mother had passed away. It was too soon.

Aunt Georgie told Malorie that Grandma had made all her arrangements before she'd passed, and she was going to call the funeral home the next day and arrange the date for the viewing and the funeral. She was thinking that perhaps having it all at once would be good. There was too much family drama and this day was for Grandma Annie; there was no room for airing dirty laundry or having the last say. The less time available for this, the better. Uncle Gary had wanted the granddaughters to be the pallbearers, and Malorie agreed for her grandma's sake.

Malorie was more nervous about having to see her estranged father. She had been embarrassed and upset when she had learned about her father's deceit toward his own mother . . . yet for some reason, she wasn't surprised. She had placed her father on a pedestal when she was a small child, but he had plummeted to the ground over the years. Malorie now saw her father for what he was.

The funeral was not going to be until Friday, and it seemed like the longest week of Malorie's life. There was too much sadness; this was the end of her Sregor family lineage. She no longer spoke to her father, and it was as though a part of her history had now died. Aunt Georgie had always felt she was a black sheep, too, and she and Malorie had a bond. They were kindred spirits. Malorie had joked a couple of times with her aunt to say she was like a mother to her, but Aunt Georgie never said much to that. She was always there for Malorie, though—Aunt Georgie was there for anyone who needed her, no matter who they were. She was an angel on earth, but make no mistake, if someone was out of line, she had no problem putting him or her in place. Malorie greatly admired her aunt and was very thankful to have her in her life.

Two

Malorie's grandmother, Annie Sregor, had lived on a farm in Warkworth. Malorie's grandfather, Seth, had passed away when she was five. She had been very close to him and missed him terribly. Even though she had only known him for a few short years, he had left an impact that would last a lifetime. Grandma Annie had since met a man and had been living common law with him for quite a few years. Grandma Annie was a stocky but good-looking woman with piercing blue eyes and red hair. She was a strong woman, someone with whom no one would want to tangle.

When Malorie was young, she had overheard a conversation between her parents and Grandma Annie. Her grandmother had told her parents that she would never love Malorie. At the time it had hurt Malorie to hear those words; she couldn't understand them. As she grew older, she needed to know why her grandma would not love her. What had she done? She was so young—what could a child do that was so bad that one would not love her? It was her own flesh and blood. When she asked the question, her grandma looked a little miffed. "Of course I love you," she said, her eyes watery. Grandma Annie told her that after her grandfather died, some of the children and grandchildren would come to visit and stay for a night or two, but when they left, it was like losing Grandpa all over again. The pain and the loneliness was too much for her, so she tried to put up a wall and love no one. She said she thought, *If you don't love, you cannot feel pain.* Grandma Annie realized that by trying to avoid being hurt, she was hurting others, those she loved. Things had changed greatly since that day.

A few years later, Malorie's grandmother stood before her and gave her a great gift. What Malorie had only heard about over the years was now hers to keep: the transcript of the preliminary hearing for the murder of her great-uncle, Troy Sregor. As her grandma handed her the transcript, she had only one stipulation. "Malorie, I want you to have this because I know you love to write, and this story needs to be told . . . but not while I am alive. I don't want to re-live it ever again. I don't think I could survive it a second time." Grandma Annie smiled, but it was not a smile of happiness; it was one of love for her granddaughter as she passed the pages of family history on to the next generation.

"I promise, Grandma. Thank you so much. I will treasure this forever," Malorie said as she took the sacred treasurer, and she hugged her grandma tightly. Her grandma always gave the best hugs in the world. Malorie was surprised that she was the grandchild chosen to receive this gift. She felt honoured that her grandmother trusted her enough to bestow this upon her. She would honour her grandma's wishes. She took the transcript home, put it in a safe place, and left it there even though she was always thinking about it, reflecting on the stories she had heard her father tell time and time again of the murder of Troy Sregor. Once in a while she couldn't help herself and would look at some of the newspaper clippings that had accompanied the family treasure, but she would always quickly put it back. She was true to her word.

It had been over 22 years since her Grandma Annie had given her the transcript and newspaper clippings, which had remained tucked away in a safe place. It was a long time ago, but it seemed like only yesterday.

One afternoon Malorie and her grandma had been sitting around chatting, and the topic of Troy's death had come up. Grandma Annie then began talking about Malorie's father, Ken, and how she was so upset at how he had stolen money from her. "If he had just asked me, I would have given him the money. All he had to do was ask," cried Grandma Annie. Malorie was ashamed and embarrassed by what her father had done.

Ken had brought an investor to her house to talk about Annie's GIC investments. There was one for $50,000. She had trusted her son, and given Grandma Annie's blindness, he was also her power of attorney. He had told Grandma Annie that she needed to sign a piece of paper for reinvestment purposes. In the end it was to fill his own personal bank account. He was not the only one—her daughter Tina had also taken $50,000, but there was a rumour that Grandma Annie knew this was to put towards a new house. Some had written this off as "Once the favourite child, always the favourite child." But the worst one was her son Harry. He had taken Grandma Annie to a lawyer and promised that if she signed papers to sign over her house to him, he would take care of her for the rest of her life. She was scared, vulnerable, and unfortunately very trusting. She had lost her home and a place to live.

Malorie mentioned to her grandma that she couldn't understand why her children, Malorie's aunts and uncles, had not learned from Troy's death that greed was a terrible sickness. She reassured her grandmother that she would not write about Troy's death until the time was right. Her grandmother had told her very tenderly that she could start writing about it then if she liked. Malorie didn't realize it at that time, but now she realized Grandma Annie knew her time was coming to an end. Grandma Annie had given birth to seven children, four boys and three girls. She had spent her last couple of years confined to a wheelchair. She had worked hard for many years on the farm, and her body had paid the price. She was smart as a whip and her memory was great, but as old age took over, it had taken her eyesight and her mobility, and it severely deformed her hands. Now as Malorie sat listening to the minister speak, she realized that not only had she lost her grandmother, whom she had become very close to in the last few years, but also a great deal of family history knowledge.

Grandma Annie died without a cent to her name. She had been very blessed to live out her last years with her eldest daughter, Malorie's Aunt Georgie. Grandma Annie had actually launched a lawsuit against her son Ken at one point out of principle, but Aunt Georgie had put an end to it when she saw the turmoil it was having on her mother. Georgie couldn't stand to see how it was affecting Annie's health, and she had promised her mother she would always take care of her. Aunt Georgie incorrectly assured her that she still had her house that they could sell, which would give her mother some money of her own.

But when they went to sell the house, they found out what Harry had done. Aunt Georgie felt sick when she found out that her brother Harry, the second oldest son, had basically stolen it out from under Annie's feet. Harry was not a bright man and truly believed that the wrestling on television was real. He had been part of a biker gang for a while and was always getting into trouble. Despite being married, he had two women pregnant at the same time. He had five children in total that Malorie was aware of, but three of them never knew their father. He was never there for them emotionally or financially. He had lied, cheated, and stolen his way through life, and he had no boundaries—stealing from his mother made that clearer than ever.

When Aunt Georgie had found out, she looked into what she could do, but everything had been done "legally." It may have appeared legal, but it was definitely wrong.

Some of Annie's children had got what they wanted, and there was nothing left. Grandma Annie had cried and screamed at Aunt Georgie because she had made her drop the suit against Ken, and now Harry had taken her house. Aunt Georgie held her mother's hand and said, "Don't worry, Mother, everything will be okay. I will take care of you," and she whole-heartedly meant it. Her hatred toward her brothers was stronger than ever, and it broke her heart to see her mother in so much pain. No mother should have to endure betrayal and deceit from her children.

Aunt Georgie had taken her mother in and given her unconditional love and care. Her mother could be quite abusive, but Aunt Georgie took it. Sometimes when Aunt Georgie would try to put her socks and shoes on her mom's feet, Grandma Annie would address her as Ruth or Tina, beat on her back with her fists, and call her names. The anger coming out was not meant for Aunt Georgie. Malorie always tried to remind her aunt that people only hurt the ones they loved the most, the ones they knew would be there no matter what. For Annie, that was Aunt Georgie.

Aunt Georgie had dreaded the day her mom would pass on, but she felt comfort in knowing that her mom and dad would be together again. Aunt Georgie had been closest to her father, and over 40 years later her heart still ached for him. He had been her best friend, and although she had not felt that same bond with her mother, she had always promised her father she would take care of her mom. Once the money was gone, it was as though her children had no reason to visit, except for her eldest son, Gary. Gary did not like all the family drama and tried to keep his distance. He took great pride in one of the lessons his father, Seth Sregor, had taught him: "Leave the knife at home in the drawer."

Uncle Gary was very tall and handsome, with a rather high-pitched voice. Sometimes when he would call, Malorie would start off by saying, "Hi, Aunt Georgie," and she would go through all her aunts' names before she embarrassingly realized it was Uncle Gary. When Uncle Gary was born, Grandma Annie had said that the first born would be hers, to help her in the kitchen. Uncle Gary had grown up to be an amazing cook, baker, and seamstress. He would make leather goods and crochet, but he was also great with the outdoor chores such as gardening and farming. And if that wasn't impressive enough, he was also a musician and had learned everything he knew by ear. He could play the piano and the accordion. The family did not have any money for lessons, and yet he had picked it up.

Uncle Gary had lived with Malorie's parents when they were first married. Malorie's father used to say her real father was her Uncle Gary, because she had brown eyes like him. There had been many a day when Malorie had prayed and actually begged her mother to tell her that Uncle Gary was her real father. He was always so kind and caring; his brown eyes were warm and sincere, a reflection of his soul. Malorie had always thought it was odd that he was the only son that didn't have any children. It was disappointing because he would have made a wonderful father. Uncle Gary's wife had passed away from cancer; he never left her side. While he was technically single, Malorie knew he would never remarry because in his heart he already was.

Grandma Annie's youngest son, Rick, had passed away in 2005 from cancer. Malorie and her grandma had talked about it, and the pain was unbearable for Annie to have lost a child. Malorie had two children of her own: a 19-year-old and a 21-year-old and she could only imagine the pain her grandmother felt. Children were to bury their parents, not the other way around.

Despite Malorie's sympathy for the loss of her grandmother's son, she was embarrassed by Uncle Rick's actions; there was no love lost there. A year before his death, he'd had a heart attack. When he didn't return home, a woman identifying herself as his wife called the police department to file a missing person's report. The police advised that he had been taken to the hospital in Kingston after suffering a heart attack and that he was in a coma. She arrived only to be confronted by his first and legal wife, Lucy, to whom he had been married for over 30 years. Rick ended up making the front page of the Peterborough newspaper—not because of anything heroic, but because he apparently had other wives and children. There were apparently 14 other children, or so the story went. Malorie was not sure what the attraction was because he was average weight and height, with balding red hair and a curly moustache. His body was so hairy that he reminded her of a human Chia Pet.

When Rick finally came out of his coma, the doctor had apparently advised him that things did not look good and had asked him about the "do not resuscitate" clause. Uncle Rick was unable to speak but had nodded that he did not want them to bring him back should something happen. But at his daughter's wishes, his legally married wife overruled his decision. Malorie had often thought if it was her, she would bring him back so she could kill him—with kindness, of course. Malorie's Aunt Lucy had stood by his side until the very end, because that was how it was done: "Until death do you part," and "Thou shall not bear judgment on thy husband as you were to honour and obey." Malorie gave her Aunt Lucy credit for honouring her wedding vows, and she thought Lucy was a better woman than her to be able to forgive Rick.

Grandma Annie's children were all very different, and she had accepted the good with the bad. She may not have always been a perfect mother, but she did the best she could with what she knew and what she had. Times had been different when she was raising her children.

Three

On the day of the funeral, the viewing was in the morning, from 10:00 to 12:00. Malorie tried to be the bigger person and went up to give her condolences to her aunts on the loss of their mother. These were the two aunts who had been very rude to her only a couple months prior, because Malorie had been listed as one of the contacts in case of an emergency when Grandma had to go into respite care. Despite the fact that there had been seven children, if Aunt Georgie had to go away to visit her son in Nova Scotia or her mother-in-law in New Brunswick, none of Georgie's siblings would offer to take Annie or come and stay with her. Malorie had offered, but it was not so easy with her working and with Grandma Annie needing constant care and attention. As a result, Aunt Georgie had to put Grandma Annie into a nursing home for respite care, but she did so for as short a time as possible. This one particular nursing home was not the best, and they had all referred to it as the filming location for *One Flew over the Cuckoo's Nest*, but her stay was for a short time and there were no other options. Grandma Annie was safe and well taken care of, but the other patients were a little odd.

Aunt Georgie had not advised her sister Ruth because she thought she still had power of attorney and had free access to the information. Aunt Georgie did not realize that Ruth had actually removed herself, and so when she called the social worker to find out where her mother was, they would not give Ruth the information. The company had the Privacy Act to adhere to. The social worker had called Malorie because she was the emergency contact; then Malorie could advise Annie's daughters.

Malorie was actually surprised when she got the call, but she took the information and wrote it down. Malorie actually thought about whether or not she wanted to tell her aunts. They didn't come to visit, and when they did, Grandma Annie always seemed so upset afterward. Malorie's intuition was telling her not to call, but she decided they were her daughters and had a right to know, so she called them. Besides, Aunt Georgie would have wanted them to know. The minute Malorie called them, she wished she hadn't. They felt that because Malorie's parents had divorced, she was no longer family. "Why would *you* be the contact?" one of her aunts questioned.

"Look," Malorie said, "I am just giving you the information." And with that she hung up. That aunt had called back the next day to give her another go, but Malorie did not bite; she wasn't interested in being part of this tangled web.

That Sunday, Malorie went out to visit her Grandma Annie and ran into one of the sisters. Malorie said hello to her Aunt Tina and was very courteous and professional. Malorie was there to see her grandma, and that was it. Aunt Tina began to continue where Aunt Ruth had left off w(hen she'd phoned earlier in the week). Tina made Malorie feel like she was nothing and had no place in the Sregor family. Malorie was a little shocked because she had always thought of Aunt Tina as a rather quiet, mousey person with no backbone and her thoughts really came from others. This sounded more like her Aunt Ruth talking.

At first Malorie thought she was going to cry; all she wanted to do was visit her grandma. Instead, Malorie decided this was her opportunity to share with her aunt how she perceived the family and the reasons she felt they were such a dysfunctional family. Again there was the "Why you?" Malorie was offended; now Aunt Tina was just making her mad. Malorie made it quite clear that although she had hoped and prayed she had had a different father, one thing was true: she was the granddaughter of Annie and Seth Sregor. All she wanted was to spend time with her grandma, and she had no wish to be part of the family debacle.

She told her aunt in front of her grandmother that parents do not set out to intentionally cause trouble for their children, but they can only do what they know. Malorie told Tina that from the outside it was very clear to her that they had all been played against one another, and it was up to them as adults to see past this and communicate with each other. Malorie revealed that her father had done the same with her and her sister; as a result they were not close, and Malorie doubted that they ever would be. Too much damage had been done that could never be fully repaired; once trust is broken, one can never mend it.

Malorie reminded her aunt of the death of Troy Sregor, and how it was a result of land and greed. Malorie was disappointed that the family had not learned from this and was instead repeating history. Her aunt's only response was, "Well, I hardly think we would kill each other."

Malorie shook her head. All she could think was, *They probably thought the same things about Great-Uncle Troy, but things have a way of getting out of hand. If someone can steal from their own mother, what else are they capable of?* Malorie told Aunt Tina that she had been through too much in life and was not prepared to continue this path of destruction. If it made them happy, she would no longer see her grandmother. Malorie stood up, hugged and kissed her grandmother for one last time, and whispered in her ear, "I love you, Grandma, but this has to be good-bye."

Malorie walked down the hall of the nursing home to the elevator with tears streaming down her face. She could hear her grandmother calling her name, but she just couldn't be a part of this. Enough was enough. Malorie drove off and sat in a Tim Horton's parking lot, sobbing. She called her husband, Anthony, her anchor, and he was able to calm her down. Her sobs had been out of control. Anthony said he was worried about her because she had an hour's drive home. Malorie gained composure and told him that she would be okay. Malorie hated to cry; her father had taught her that crying was a sign of weakness. The one person she could always cry in front of, and who never thought badly of her, was Anthony. "Be careful, Sweetpea. I love you," Anthony said before they hung up the phone.

When she had told her Aunt Georgie later about what had happened, Aunt Georgie was furious at how the other aunts had treated Malorie.

She let Malorie know that this was not what Grandma Annie wanted; the old woman missed Malorie's visits. Malorie began her visits again and was glad she had. Malorie had thought that by staying away, it would make her Grandma Annie's life easier, but Grandma Annie felt differently.

Four

On June 6, when they were celebrating Grandma Annie's life and helping her to make her journey to heaven, Malorie tried to remind herself that the past was the past and had no place in the present. Grandma Annie looked peaceful and beautiful in her black lace dress as she lay there sleeping. Her hair was done beautifully, and she had soft pink lipstick on her beautiful, smiling, wrinkle-free face. Her hands were no longer curled but perfectly straight, the arthritis and pain gone from her body. Grandma Annie looked years younger as she lay in a beautiful cream-coloured coffin. There were beautiful pink pin roses imprinted on ivory on the corners of the coffin. The inside was lined with a pink satin lining and embroidered roses on the inside of the lid. Malorie knew her grandma was finally at peace, no longer in pain, and in such a beautiful resting place.

As Malorie sat at the end of the row of chairs in the parlour with her husband, Aunt Georgie walked down the aisle and whispered as she walked by, "Your father and Leeza are here."

Malorie continued to talk to her husband and children as though nothing different was happening; her back was to them as they walked down the aisle. She had thought her father had said, "There's the man" while looking at her son Seth, who had been named after her grandfather and was his spitting image. He also resembled her father, and Malorie was constantly telling her son to be careful he didn't get the deadly Sregor promiscuity gene.

Malorie stood up. As she leaned forward with her arms open to give him a hug and her condolences, he flinched and moved back. The hatred in his eyes was something she would never forget. Keeping her emotions intact, she held out her hand and said, "I'm sorry about the loss of your mother."

He did not extend his hand and responded with only, "Why?" Ken Sregor was a man full of anger and hatred, but it went deeper than that.

Ken was a great storyteller. He had grown up with three brothers and three sisters on a farm in Warkworth, Ontario. He was over six feet tall, with sparkling blue eyes and brown hair that was slicked back. He was always clean-shaven, nicely dressed, and extremely charismatic. He was like a magnet where women were concerned. When Ken and Malorie's mother met, he moved to Scarborough, but she always knew he missed the farm life. He reminded Malorie of a modern-day Tom Sawyer, with his stories of when he was a boy on the farm. At night when he would get home from work, they would sit at the kitchen table while he told her stories of his childhood. No matter how many times she'd heard them, each time was like the first time. There was one particular story he would tell over and over again, and yet she never tired of it. It was the story of a family feud over land that led to his Uncle Troy's death. Some said it was an accident, but Malorie's father always referred to it as a murder.

Malorie had not seen her father in a long time, ever since he had left Malorie's mother for Malorie's friend. But watching him now, Malorie could tell he was mentally disturbed. He looked the same, and even though his hair was a bit greyer, she knew he still had the ability to have women lining up and drooling over him. He could be very charming and entrapping, which she had witnessed time and time again. He was ashamed to have Malorie as his daughter; he referred to having only one daughter, and she was not the one to whom he was referring. He had not changed at all. Malorie was now able to see him through adult eyes.

Malorie could sense her children's upset from behind her, and she knew her focus needed to be with her family. Ken went up to the coffin; behind him followed what Malorie referred to as her "Sleezy Wicked Stepmother." Leeza had been her best friend, and their sons had been best friends. But when Malorie's father had left her mother after 30 years of marriage for Leeza, Malorie's mother and sister had blamed Malorie and had never forgiven her for introducing Leeza to the family. Malorie never really blamed her dad for leaving her mother because she never thought her parents should be together, but his lack of respect for her mother and his total disregard for his children and grandchildren had sickened Malorie. He had chosen Sleezy over blood. A lot of people had suffered as a result of his behaviour.

Malorie looked back and realized her daughter Rorie had disappeared. She was worried because she knew her daughter could be quite feisty despite her five foot two, 100-pound frame. Malorie quickly located her in the bathroom. Rorie was upset at how her grandfather had not only ignored her and her brother, but how he had looked at her mother and what he'd said to her father. Malorie had not heard what Ken had said to Anthony; it was probably better she hadn't. It was not the place for her to express her anger, and had she heard it, she would have defended her husband to the death. Anthony had worked hard all his life, and his body was paying the price. Back surgery had not been as successful as they'd hoped, and Anthony now walked with a cane. When Ken had approached Anthony, Anthony had not stood up given the difficulty of doing so, and Ken had made a rude comment about not being a real man. Malorie apologized to her husband but told him she could not say anything because this was her grandma's day. He fully supported her, and they both spoke to the kids to ensure they also ignored it. Rorie and Seth adored their parents and would do anything to protect them. Malorie and Anthony were lucky and proud parents. They were grateful for the bond they shared with their children.

Ken did not stay for the funeral. He had really only come to try and cause trouble. People had been invited to write down a few words that they would like the minister to read, or they were welcome to say it themselves. Malorie had actually written something and given it to the minister. She had wished she could say the words herself. Public speaking was part of her career, but she just didn't feel strong enough under these circumstances.

The pallbearers had been seconded to a room to be given instructions on the process to be followed. Malorie had asked the 90-year-old funeral director how much he thought the coffin weighed; she was worried when she saw all the ivory. He gave a snotty response back. "Well, if you can't lift it, why are you doing it?" Malorie ignored him and thought to herself,

Buddy, if you don't watch it, there's room for two at that gravesite. He looked like he had risen from the dead and she was in no mood for any lip.

Malorie ran quickly to the bathroom. When she returned, the pallbearers were dropping like flies, too upset to carry Grandma Annie. Malorie asked if she could be on the right because that was her stronger arm, and her left knee sometimes gave out. They had gone from eleven granddaughters to five who were willing to carry the casket. Malorie had asked her son Seth to stay close in case they needed help; she knew they had to tackle stairs going out and a big hill at the gravesite.

They all proceeded into the sitting area for the service to begin. As the minister began to speak, Malorie looked around the room. She couldn't believe her father had not stayed for his mother's funeral; that was disgusting. She had decided earlier in the day that not only was she burying her grandmother, she was also burying her father in her mind. She was ashamed of him. She found out later that day that Ken had also dropped off words that he would like to have shared, but after the minister had reviewed them prior to the service, he had been very disturbed and had returned Ken's words to Malorie's Uncle Gary, never to be discussed again. As she sat trying not to cry, she heard the minister say he wanted to read something written by Annie's granddaughter, Malorie Londen.

Malorie reflected on the close call prior to the minister beginning to speak. Just before the gathering of pallbearers, Malorie had run outside to grab a bottle of water from the van. It was a scorcher of a day. Malorie had worn a navy blue suit and was sweating like a pig on a spit. When she was outside, she started talking to some of her cousins. Malorie had never fit in with them and always felt uncomfortable. They started talking about birthdays. Malorie had always been proud to think she was the oldest granddaughter and Craig was the oldest grandson; she felt she had a special place. But as they all began talking and noting their birth dates, Malorie was shocked to discover that she was not the oldest granddaughter—her cousin Lesley was. Suddenly not only was she the black sheep, but she felt as though she had no place at all. She was not special; she was just one of many granddaughters. She immediately ran to find her Aunt Georgie as soon as she heard this, because the letter she had written and given to the minister had started off by referring to herself as the oldest granddaughter. Malorie found the Minister and had him change it. He was not too friendly about it, but Malorie thought that a man in his position could show a little compassion given her devastation. But at least she was able to fix the situation before it was too late.

As Malorie sat there listening to the minister begin to read what Malorie had written, she realized he had chosen it to be the eulogy. Malorie was the only grandchild that had written anything. Malorie sat there as he read the words that she had written just days before.

> As one of the granddaughters of Seth and Annie Sregor, I have been truly blessed to have known both of them and shared a part of their lives. For all of the grandchildren and great-grandchildren, as your cousin I wanted to share some of my memories with all of you so that you can forever carry a memory of them from the early years in your hearts.
>
> When I was very young, I could not wait to go to Grandma and Grandpa's farm in Warkworth. There would always be lots of family around, and Grandpa loved it. Family was the most important thing to him. The uncles and my dad would sit around the table, sometimes playing cards and other times just shooting the breeze. Those young cousins that were around always tried to steer clear of Uncle Tim's spittoon of chewed tobacco. The aunts and Grandma would be busy in the kitchen.
>
> I was only 5 years old at the time, but I remember dancing to the country and western tunes on the old record player, and going with Grandpa to feed the pigs, cows, and chickens in the barn. I remember riding on the back of the tractor in my overalls while my dad ploughed Grandpa's field, and I thought I was a real country girl. I remember gathering milk pods with Grandpa from the nearby woods and then sitting on the back porch and blowing on the seedlings as they flew everywhere. My last memory of Grandpa was a week before he passed away. We were driving down in the car from Toronto, and my mom had packed a whole bunch of bananas. I loved bananas and

could never get enough of them. My parents had told me I could not have any more, and I curled up disappointed and went to sleep. When we arrived at Grandma and Grandpa's, I went running in to the house to see Grandpa, and what was before me but the biggest dish of bananas that I had ever seen. I had hit gold. Grandpa was lying on the couch, and I ran over and snuggled up beside him. "Would you like a banana, Malorie?" Grandpa asked. My eyes shone, and I had a big smile on my face as Grandpa passed me one. He then looked at me and told me he would put the rest away for next week, when I came to visit. That was the last time I saw Grandpa alive, and the last time I ate bananas.

When I was young, I mostly remember Grandma being in the kitchen cooking. I remember she was always peeling potatoes and filling the pig pail with potato peels and scraps, which we would take out after dinner to feed to them. I remember being eye level with the gas stove and being scared when Grandma would light it with a match. She made cooking for all those people seem easy. There are certain parts about Grandma's cooking that I always remembered. Dinner was usually a ham or pork roast with corn still in its liquid, potatoes, and real butter. Then there was always the glass full of ice water. At Christmas I remember the red Santa boot filled with a variety of candies. The pantry in the basement was full of preserves, and Grandma was always working hard at something. I remember wondering how she had seven children, and I was convinced that she had taken a moment out of working in the fields to give birth to her baby and then headed back to the field to keep working with the baby on her back. In the lingo of today's kids, "To me, Grandma was a tank. She was the strongest woman I knew and she seemed bullet-proof." She was the strong and silent type who gave the best hugs in the whole world. When she hugged you, you felt safe. I could never get enough of them.

When I was 20 and it was about two weeks before my wedding, Grandma and I were sitting together by ourselves at the kitchen table at our house in Scarborough. She knew that there had been a lot of negativity about my upcoming marriage, ranging from the age difference between my fiancé and me to religious issues and a whole bunch of stuff in between. Anything that could go wrong did. In my heart of hearts, I knew it was right, but the odds were against us. Grandma leaned back and said that as an Orangeman she should be putting a stop to my future marriage. I was shocked. Then she leaned forward and said, "But I am not going to, because as long as you are happy, that is all that matters." I threw my arms around her neck and gave her a big hug and thanked her. She had a glimmer in her eye and smiled at me.

A couple of years ago, when Aunt Georgie had a birthday party for Grandma, it reminded me of when I was little: all the children were running around and having fun. It was wonderful, and Grandma had a permanent smile on her face. I leaned over to Grandma and said, "Look at all of us—this is all your fault." She giggled. I told her Grandpa would love to see this. She smiled, nodded, and said "He sure would."

But in the last few years, Grandma and I actually had many opportunities where we would just sit and chat. I would always try to bring her butter tarts and her favourite lime pop, and then we would chat about how we would solve the world's problems, or the phenomena of Sylvia Browne and astral dreams. We would talk about gardening and blueberry bushes, all kinds of farm things. We talked about when she and Grandpa met, their courting days, and how he swept her off her feet. He had his eye on her from across the room at one of the barn dances; that was the beginning of all of us. We chatted about the hard times and the good times. Grandma was proof that those things that did not kill you only make you stronger.

In my 40 plus years, I have been a daughter, granddaughter, mother, sister, and wife, and the one thing that I have learned is that as we get older, each decade our thoughts and perceptions change. For those of you that have not turned 40 yet, I am here to tell you that each decade only gets better. The most important thing in life to me is my family. As a parent, I always wanted to be the perfect parent, but that is not a realistic expectation because we're all human. One day my doctor said something to me, and it was like a light bulb went off. She said as parents we do the best we can; there are no manuals, instructions, or courses that come with the birth of our children. Our intentions are to be the best we can. Being a parent is the hardest job in the world, but it can also have the biggest rewards.

One of my more recent memories was when Grandma had had a dream the night before our visit that she thought was real. It was all her children as the adults they are now, sitting around the dinner table and eating together as a family, and she was so happy to see all of them.

During our afternoon chats we would talk about her mom and dad, her brothers and sisters, and she would tell me about the dreams she had. In her dreams she said that everyone was happy and there was no bad feelings among any of them; the past was the past, and life was too short to hold on to those things. She smiled and was at peace. I had always thought that Grandma was more quiet and reserved with her feelings; she may not have expressed herself the same way I remembered Grandpa did, but what was very clear was that she loved her children, grandchildren, and great-grandchildren, and this love was unconditional. A true mother's love.

I am sure that all of us have our own memories of Grandma that are near and dear to our hearts, and it is important to keep these memories alive through our children and grandchildren and for future generations to come. As Grandma now joins Grandpa, I am sure they are pretty busy making up for lost time. I hope that now as the torch passes to the next generation, we will continue on the path that they set out on January 11, 1940, to build a family with a good foundation and a home full of love. There is nothing more important than family.

Grandma, until we meet again, please keep visiting me in my dreams so we can have our chats. I will bring the lime pop and butter tarts. I love you, farm girl!

Malorie was sitting behind her fellow pallbearers, and she could hear her cousins in front of her making fun of what she had written. Later at the reception, some of the cousins had actually told Malorie how they had made fun of her and did not believe she had carried her fair share of the casket. Malorie was not the one who had called for a coffee break halfway up the hill to where Grandma would rest with Grandpa. Malorie just ignored their talk; it had always been that way since she was a child. One of her cousins must have thought she was a donut as a child. Malorie knew she looked like a Pillsbury dough baby, but it didn't give that cousin the right to chomp into her with her teeth and never want to let go. That cousin was definitely a biter. As hurtful as they had been over the years, Malorie just felt sorry for all of them.

Malorie stood listening to the Minister's final words, *"Ashes to ashes, dust to dust . . ."* She then noticed her Uncle Rick's name on the headstone together with her grandparents. He too had been quite wealthy at one time but had died poor. Malorie was sad for a variety of reasons, but she was also too old to play these childish games. Malorie had done the best she could, and there was nothing more she could do. It had been a beautiful day for her Grandma Annie, and that was all that mattered.

After the service and the reception, Malorie, Anthony, and their children went home. Malorie was exhausted and felt as though a piece of her life was gone forever. She was so sad. Even when she slept, she didn't dream anymore—she hadn't since her grandma had passed away. Malorie had counted on her dreams because they quite often brought her messages.

With Rorie going off to university, Malorie was able to keep herself quite busy with that preparation. Although she didn't seem to be getting messages in her dreams anymore, her messages began to take a new form. She was now about to begin an unbelievable journey.

Five

In July, Malorie and Anthony decided to take two weeks for vacation. It had been a rough year, and it was only half over. They spent time doing things around the house. Malorie made a stained glass window for over the fireplace. She had taken a course the previous December and found it very relaxing. She made her famous strawberry and raspberry jam. Her raspberry jam took forever to make because she sieved all the seeds out. Seth and Rorie were home in the evenings, but during the day they were working at their summer jobs. Malorie and Anthony took advantage of their alone time together, relaxing and enjoying each other's company.

On the last Saturday of their vacation, they decided to go blueberry picking. Seth was at work, but Rorie wanted to join them. The three of them set out on their journey to Wilmot Orchards. Malorie had looked up the directions on the Internet, but of course they got lost. A 30-minute drive took almost two hours, and they had their blueberries picked in 20 minutes. Her shortcuts had a way of always taking much longer. It didn't matter, though, because they had lots of fun together and enjoyed the afternoon drive in the country. The scenery was breathtaking, and the blueberries were scrumptious, the best they had ever tasted. They were heading home to make blueberry jam and freeze the rest for homemade pies and muffins over the winter.

As they drove back, Malorie mentioned how one of her uncles who had been present at the tragic death of Great-Uncle Troy apparently lived somewhere around there. There were rumours in the family when Malorie was growing up that he and his wife had had something to do with it.

Malorie said that he was supposed to live on a sheep farm and for everyone to keep their eyes open.

Anthony was driving along, and all of a sudden Rorie yelled out, "Mom, there's the sheep, and that's him!"

It was a one-lane road, and it was pretty busy, but Malorie told Anthony to turn around and go back. "Where am I supposed to turn here?" Anthony asked, but he was such a trooper. He would do whatever he could to make his wife happy. After all, Malorie was his sweetpea.

After he made the U-turn, Malorie asked him to pull over. Everyone felt awkward and stalker-like, but she wanted to get a good look. He looked exactly like the newspaper clipping. He was 52 years older, but even his hat looked similar to the picture in the newspaper. Together with his work clothes and the profile of the side of his face, it was definitely William Booker. Willy, as most people knew him, had once been over six feet tall with a slim build, but he now walked with a slight limp and appeared a little shorter. He had a thin, long face with a strong and debonair nose. He wore a fedora-style hat. But as they sat on the side of the road, Malorie felt as though they looked into each other's eyes for a brief moment, and she felt locked into his soul. They did not seem like the eyes of a murderer.

Although Malorie had promised that she would not do anything with the transcript while her grandma was alive, she was tempted to start now. Still, she thought that it was too soon to begin doing research; that would not be respectful of her Grandma Annie. It was only a little over a month since her grandmother had passed away. Malorie was not ready, despite this uncanny discovery. As they were driving home, she remembered that she had not heard back about an inquiry she had made with the Toronto Archives earlier that year.

―∞―

In January of that year, Malorie had been looking at the court transcripts because she was concerned they were beginning to deteriorate. She wanted to make sure they were safe and the information was written down somewhere in case something happened to her hard copy. Malorie kept it well protected, but one never knew. She did not want to take any chances with photocopying, so she began to type the pages when she had time. She had come across a section about a lawyer in Oshawa and wondered if perhaps this lawyer might have some information, if he still practiced law. Malorie wanted to be true to her promise to her grandmother, and she did not start writing, but she did not think asking a couple of questions would hurt anything.

When she contacted one of the partners at the Oshawa law firm, he advised that they did not practice criminal law; estates and real estate transactions were their speciality. He further stated that they had acted for Virginia Booker and that in the January following her brother's death, she had come and taken all the files, so there were no copies left. Malorie was more certain than ever that Troy's death had something to do with her great-grandfather, James Seth Sregor. This was Troy's father and her great-grandfather. She believed she needed to get a copy of his will; this would give Malorie the answer and maybe even lead her to the real murderer.

This mission led her to the Toronto Archives. She had spoken to the archivist a couple of times since January and had given as much information as possible in terms of names and dates, but there was nothing. The archivist agreed that given his will had been probated, there should be a copy somewhere. She decided that she would follow up on the Monday when she got back to work.

Anthony was driving as Malorie gazed out the window, daydreaming and wondering what all of this meant. It was probably nothing and just her imagination running wild. Malorie poured all of her energy into working hard at making blueberry jam and preparing berries for freezing. She became more self-absorbed in the fact that their vacation was over and she had really enjoyed the last two weeks with her husband. It was time to go back to the old grind. She loved the people she worked with, but she loved spending time with her family and working in her garden more. It was the relaxation she loved and needed.

On Malorie's first Monday back after vacation, by lunch time she was exhausted. She wasn't used to getting up until almost noon, and now she had already been going strong for six hours. She stayed focused and was thinking about lunch. For Malorie, food was comfort and a stress reliever, until of course she gained weight from eating . . . but that was a whole other story. Malorie had always struggled with a weight problem, and her short height did not help. She was trying to be good now that her vacation was over. She had just finished a bag of raw carrots. Of course the sauce she put on them was counter-productive, but at least she would be able to see in the dark from all the carrots she ate.

Something was nagging at Malorie. She decided to contact the Toronto archivist just to see if he had been able to find anything. He answered the phone on the second ring. He was extremely puzzled as to why he could not find anything. He had tried every lead he could based on the information Malorie had given him. She began to mention Havelock as a possibility, and then she remembered she was on the wrong side of the family. "I am sorry, I'm just making matters more confusing by giving you the wrong information. I just need to know if there is a relationship between my uncle Ted Sregor's land in Warkworth . . ."

"Wait a minute, I remember seeing those names, Ted Sregor and Warkworth. I just have to remember where. I am going on vacation in two days, but when I get back, I will look into it more." The archivist sounded almost as happy as Malorie.

"Thank you so much. I really appreciate the time you are taking on this file. I can't explain it, but I feel like I am being pulled to keep searching."

When Malorie got home that night, she told her husband about her conversation with the archivist. She was sure her great-grandfather's last will and testament would help answer some questions.

Malorie knew it sounded silly, but she felt as though her Grandma Annie was sending her messages; there was something that needed to be told. The truth was out there, and Malorie was supposed to find it. She wasn't sure how yet, but she trusted that in time she would be guided to where she was meant to be.

The next day was Tuesday. When Anthony was at work, one of the girls he worked with had written her name down on a piece of paper for Anthony to give to Malorie. This girl was going to be writing a certification exam in the fall that Malorie had proctored in the past, and she had hoped Malorie would keep an eye open for her.

That evening as Malorie sat in her comfy chair sipping coffee, Anthony came up and sat on the coffee table beside her. Anthony began to expand on what had happened during the day at work. Anthony handed Malorie a piece of paper with the name on it. Both of them looked at each other in astonishment, and Malorie's jaw dropped. "I know, that is exactly how I felt when I saw it," Anthony said, dumbfounded.

The girl at Anthony's work was named Julie Booker-Smith. "Is she related to Willy and Virginia Booker?" Malorie asked Anthony.

"I didn't dare ask. I was shocked when I saw it and didn't know what to say. All I could do was tell her I would give the piece of paper to you." Anthony was quite excited by this discovery.

"Wow!" was all Malorie could say. Malorie believed in angels, spirits, and receiving messages from the universe through signs. Even though Anthony claimed to support her, she knew he didn't believe as she did; she would always just laugh it off and call him a good Catholic boy. He had gone to Catholic school as a small boy but had been unable to further his education because he needed to work three jobs to help take care of his family. He had eventually saved enough money and moved to Ontario with the hope of finding more secure work. Anthony had always dreamed of being a chef, and thought his dream had not come true, Malorie thought she'd died and gone to heaven because he was a magnificent cook.

As Anthony continued cooking another marvellous dinner, Malorie climbed up on the chair by the counter and watched. They just looked at each other and smiled. Was it possible this woman was actually Malorie's cousin? What did all of this mean?

Malorie had heard that her Aunt Virginia had died. She knew years ago that Virginia had been at the nearby mental institute, and Malorie thought maybe she would try to do a bit of detective work. The next day, Malorie decided to call the hospital and told the receptionist that she wanted to have flowers delivered but wanted to make sure she had the right hospital first. She asked if that was the right address for Virginia Booker. The person on the phone was very helpful and advised that she was not there at the moment and was in fact an out-patient, coming and going when needed. She even told Malorie the year Virginia was born to ensure they were talking about the same person. Malorie thanked her.

Virginia Booker was alive—she was not dead as people had said. The family rumour had always been that she had killed her brother because of the dispute over land and their father's will. Malorie's Grandpa Seth had often referred to her as a rattlesnake, and how fitting to have the name Virginia, after the Virginia rattlesnake. Sometimes her bite would be full of venom, and other times she would slither away and not bother anyone. One could never be sure how she would react. She was a beautiful woman, a little over five feet with blonde hair and big brown eyes. She had a nice figure and would make many a man's head turn, but she could also knock a person dead with the poisonous venom from her mouth—and, if the rumours were true, also by her frightening actions.

Malorie's Grandpa Seth was the oldest of 10 children. His parents, James and Elizabeth Sregor, also had a son John who died at 7 from scarlet fever. Then there was from oldest to youngest, Alice, Ted, Ethel, Bethany, Troy, Daniel, Virginia, and Joan. Virginia was the second youngest.

The next morning Malorie woke and began her journey to work. She couldn't get the last week's events out of her head. She knew it could be dangerous ground she was treading on, but she just had to know more. Again there was this push and pull all in one. She needed to find the answers, and she didn't know why, but she was feeling a strong pull to return to the Town of Warkworth and see if she could find the house where Troy Sregor had been murdered.

Malorie kept searching the Internet but kept coming up empty handed. She could not find a rural address to go with the lot and concession address listed in the court transcripts. Then she saw the Warkworth Library and decided to e-mail them. She wanted to know where Troy's grave was located, and she needed an actual address to go with the concession address she currently had. Of course with it being a small town, it was a one-stop shop. The librarian very kindly provided Malorie with a name and number that she could contact for both inquiries, advising Malorie that if anyone knew, Lee-Anne Mitchell would.

When Malorie called Lee-Anne, it turned out that Lee-Anne's husband, Bueler, was the caretaker at the cemetery and knew exactly where the grave was. Lee-Anne herself knew Troy's name because she had gone to school with one of his daughters. She also tried to assist Malorie with the house location, but she was young at the time, and despite it being a small town, during the last 52 years it had grown and changed a great deal. Lee-Anne told Malorie that it should actually be located on the concession behind her house, but to confirm she gave her a name and phone number at the township for her to call. Lee-Anne told Malorie that Bueler would put an orange peg as a marker in the ground by Uncle Troy's grave so that Malorie could easily find it. Malorie was very grateful, but she also realized that if she kept digging, others may become upset. It was a small town, and Malorie was confident that she would hear something if she touched a raw nerve.

When Malorie called Molly at the township, her fear was further confirmed. Molly had initially told Malorie that this information would be in storage boxes offsite, given the length of time that had passed, and it would probably take a while to find the information. Malorie explained more about her family and her grandfather, and the description of the house from what she could remember. Malorie remembered it as a big, beautiful white farm house up on a hill. Malorie laughed as she told Molly about it, because though it seemed big as a child, it may not be as big as she remembered. Molly laughed too, and Malorie thanked her for her time before she hung up the phone. It had already been 52 years; what were a few more weeks? Malorie was late for a meeting at work and ran off with her notepaper and pen.

When Malorie returned from her meeting, there was a voicemail message from Molly at the township office. Malorie returned the phone call thinking there was more information she required. Molly answered on the second ring.

Malorie replied, "Hi, Molly, that was fast," and she giggled. Oddly enough, Molly did in fact have the directions and information already. It turned out that one of the gentlemen she worked with actually knew the Sregor family and the exact location of Malorie's great-grandparents' house. But now Molly's voice did not seem as friendly. "Who did you say you are again?"

"My name is Malorie, and Troy Sregor was my great-uncle, my grandfather's brother."

"Well, a relative of the Sregor family works here," stated Molly.

Oh crap, thought Malorie. *Darn these small towns.* She wasn't sure if it was polite to ask or what she was supposed to say, but what did she have to lose? She was who she said she was, and yet she was feeling as though Molly did not believe her. Malorie tried to explain a bit more about her family tree and then asked how this person was related, and if she was able to share their name with her. She wasn't sure if Molly was at liberty to share that information, but Molly didn't hesitate to tell her that Tim Slan worked for the town, and his wife was related. His wife advised that Malorie's great-grandfather's wife had just died. Malorie was now confused because she had passed many years ago, the day before Malorie's 18th birthday. But Molly was actually referring to Grandma Annie, Grandpa Seth's wife. Malorie was still missing her grandma dearly and knew she always would.

Malorie came back from thoughts of her grandma and said, "No, that was my grandfather, Seth Sregor's wife, who just died. Tim Slan's wife is my Aunt Tina." Tina was the same aunt that had confronted Malorie at the nursing home, and Malorie really didn't want any further words with her.

"Well, I am a little confused as to why you would call us and not just ask your aunt and uncle directly. I'm sure they could help you," said Molly.

"Do you have to tell them I called? I would rather they not know. I am doing some family searching, and I come from a very dysfunctional family and would prefer not to involve them if at all possible," begged Malorie.

Suddenly Malorie could almost feel the warmth and friendliness through the phone. "Say no more," said Molly. "I know what family is all about. I will have the clerk from our office fax you a property plan, and hopefully this will help you." Molly also gave Malorie the directions to her great-grandparents' white house on the hill. Molly wasn't sure though if this house had been torn down, and the land divided and two new houses built in its place. Malorie knew she had to go and see for herself no matter what. She didn't know why or what she was looking for, but the pull was like a magnetic force, and it wasn't going to end until she made the trip.

Malorie continued on her journey, and she felt that as some doors closed, others would miraculously open. When Malorie got home that night, she couldn't wait to tell Anthony about the day's events. As she began to tell him, he couldn't keep it in anymore. "I have something to tell you, too." He looked like he was going to burst.

"You go first," Malorie conceded.

"I'm pretty sure the girl I work with is actually related to Willy Booker."

"What makes you think that?" Malorie was puzzled.

"She said Booker is her maiden name, and she said she grew up on a sheep farm in north Oshawa. I'm sure it's not just a coincidence."

"Well, it must be his granddaughter or great-granddaughter. She would be my cousin, then." Malorie's wheels were turning in her head. Anthony had mentioned that he thought the girl he worked with was in her early 30s.

"Should I tell her who you are and that you might be her cousin?" Anthony questioned.

Malorie was afraid. Whenever she had asked questions of her father, she had always been told, "Leave it alone!" Was she treading on a dangerous path? Again there was that pull, and she couldn't let it go. The girl may not even know who Malorie was, or Willy for that matter. It would just be a very casual kind of comment. Besides, they didn't know she had the transcript or that she was looking into the murder of her uncle after 52 years. A man had gone to jail for the murder of Troy Sregor, but in Malorie's heart of hearts, she always believed he was innocent. One of the men who had been part of the preliminary trial had died, and she was not sure of the man who had gone to jail, but she felt that whether they were alive or dead, the truth needed to be told. Their families needed to know, and if they had both passed on, they needed to be able to rest in peace. Malorie was counting on receiving the right signs to lead her to the truth.

The next day Anthony asked Julie, the girl at work, if she knew Willy and Virginia Booker. Julie looked shocked and puzzled at the same time. It turned out that Julie was Willy's daughter from his second marriage. She said she had a half-sister named Veronika, or Ronnie for short, and that she had grown up with her from her father's previous marriage, but that her father's first wife, Virginia, had gone a little loopy, and he had divorced her. Julie also had one brother.

Anthony proceeded to tell Julie about Malorie and her relationship to Ronnie; they were cousins. He also explained that Grandfather Seth was Virginia's brother. That would make Ronnie first cousins with Malorie's dad, Ken. This was a lot for everyone to digest.

The long weekend in August had almost arrived; it was definitely needed for Malorie and Anthony. It was Friday night, and Malorie called to let her husband know that she was on her way to catch the train. She was getting out of work on time for once, but she had a lot of running around to do. She had to pick up her grandmother from her mother's house, pick up Anthony's birthday present, and then swing back and pick up her daughter Rorie at the train station. It was pizza night, so that would at least save her some time. *One job ends and another begins,* she thought. "Anthony, I should be home around eight o'clock."

"I have some news to tell you," said Anthony.

"Now what?" said Malorie.

"Your cousin Ronnie was very excited to hear about you and wants to meet you," Anthony said with some hesitation, as if he wasn't sure how Malorie would take this.

"Oh, really? And she knows who my grandfather is?" questioned Malorie.

"Yes, and she is going to call you on Monday night and arrange a time when you can get together and meet. Are you still there?"

"Yes, I'm here. Let's talk more when I get home. I'm just not sure about this, Anthony. I'm a little worried. Not to mention, how odd is this? The daughter of the people I think may be possible murderers wants to meet me? Maybe she wants to silence me?" Once again Malorie's imagination was running wild.

Malorie had a vivid imagination, and at times it had a way of getting the best of her. While they had been on vacation, Malorie had been working on retyping the transcript. It was a Friday night, and their phone lines to their house were not working. It was just Anthony and Malorie home, and after Anthony went to bed, Malorie kept typing; she was at a really good part of the transcript and did not want to stop. While she was typing, she watched an episode of *CSI*. Oddly enough, on the show the phone lines had been cut, and this serial killer was going in and killing the families. Wouldn't it figure that together with their own phone not working and the scary show on TV, Malorie was at the part where Willy Booker and his brother-in-law Marty Morgan had cut the phone lines to the house in which Troy Sregor was killed in the next day.

When Malorie went to bed that night, she locked her bedroom door, hugged her bat, put a big rock on her end table, and put the covers over her head. She awoke to her husband trying to get out of the bedroom to go to the bathroom. "Anthony, I was watching *CSI,* and I was at a scary part in the transcript, and . . ."

As he looked over and saw Malorie lying in bed, clutching the bat, he tried hard not to grin and be stern. "That's it, no more *CSI* for you. Besides, I was sleeping right beside you; what if you had hit me with that bat or rock by accident?"

"Well . . ." Malorie said with a wince.

Anthony finally got the door unlocked and ran to the washroom. As he ran down the hall, he yelled back "No more!"

For the next little while, every spare minute that Malorie was able to get, she would continue retyping the transcript.

There was a loud horn honking in the background. "Are you okay, Malorie?" Anthony could hear it through the phone.

Malorie came back from her daydreaming, "Oh, yes. I'm fine. Sorry, I'm just jaywalking and trying to catch my train. Wouldn't that be awful to get killed on a Friday night?" Malorie chuckled and told Anthony she would see him soon, "Love you."

Now all Malorie had to do was wait until Ronnie called her.

Six

Another week had gone by. It had been a long and interesting one, but now it was Friday night. Anthony was sleeping and the kids were out with friends. Malorie curled up in her comfy chair with a glass of wine to reflect on the week's events. She glanced around the room and felt so warm and safe there. Her couch and love seat had a Victorian look to them, and the tapestry was of burgundy, gold, and sage-green colours. The imprint of flowering almonds and peonies, together with big comfy pillows, made the room feel cozy. The windows were covered in gold drapes that Malorie had made with pearl tie backs. Above the fireplace was the stained glass window that Malorie had made herself. She was aiming to make it plain and simple with a heart in the middles, but it ended up looking like a heart with angel wings. It turned out much better than she could have imagined.

Her family of animals were around her. Tweak, a yellow cockatiel, was the newest addition. Boo was a beautiful flame point Himalayan cat, and he was snuggled up on the back of her chair. Oliver was a huge orange tabby, bigger than their smallest dog Molly, a 14-year-old Shih-tzu. Oliver was curled up on a pillow on the loveseat, and Molly was in her bed near the fireplace with her stuffed blue teddy bear, which was bigger than she was. Sprawled out on the floor of the living room were Sydney and Tess. Tess was a beautiful black lab and golden retriever mix. She was getting up there in age, and her hips didn't always work the way she would like them to, but she adored Malorie; Tess was definitely her dog. Then there was Sydney, a boxer and great Pyrenees mix, but she looked more like a great dane. Malorie and Syd had not always seen eye to eye, but they had grown to love each other.

While she stared at the television and its black screen, she found herself shifting her eyes and staring into the blue and red flame of the fireplace, daydreaming. It was August, but it was cold and damp, and the fireplace helped take the chill off. That week, Ronnie had called her, and they had chatted on the phone for about an hour. It was as though Ronnie thought she was telling Malorie about a family Malorie didn't know. Ronnie was graciously taking Malorie under her wing as the black sheep that she was. Malorie had not said anything about her book, and Ronnie assumed Malorie was just family tree-searching like she was. But Malorie did know a lot about their family and thought that she might actually know more about her mother than Ronnie did.

Ronnie told Malorie how her mother, Virginia, had been institutionalized for about 20 years. She told Malorie about their Aunt Ethel, who was Grandpa Seth's sister, and how she was the keeper of the family Bible with all the family tree information. She was also Ronnie's mother's sister. What a family tree! Despite the fact that Ronnie and Malorie were second cousins, Ronnie was actually younger than Malorie. Ronnie would actually be first cousins with Malorie's father, Ken.

Malorie was very intrigued to find out that they were apparently related to two past United States presidents, and that their family had come over on the *Mayflower*. In addition, a few generations before, their grandfather had actually drowned while trying to escape the natives. Their grandmother at the time had been pregnant, unknown to both of them when she was captured by natives. She gave birth to Joshua, Ronnie and Malorie's grandfather, a few generations back. Joshua ended up being raised by Natives until he was much older. When Malorie heard this, she had teased Anthony that she was betraying her ancestors by sleeping with the enemy; Anthony's ancestors were from the Mi'kmaq tribe. They could laugh about it now, but in reality, had her grandmother not been pregnant, she would not even exist. Funny how one little thing could possibly change history and future events.

Ronnie seemed so excited to find a cousin, and Malorie was excited too, but she was also nervous and a little bit afraid. They decided that they would meet in person later that week at a coffee shop.

Malorie arrived early and decided to get a cup of coffee and a good view of the doorway where her cousin would enter. When Ronnie walked into the Tim Hortons, Malorie knew immediately it was her. She had told Malorie what she would be wearing, that she would be bringing her youngest son Robert with her, and that she would know them because he always ordered a sprinkled donut. But without even ordering the donut, Malorie knew. She was the spitting image of her Aunt Liza, Ronnie's father's sister.

When Ronnie sat down, Malorie could tell she was also nervous and afraid. Ronnie could not believe how much Malorie looked like her half-sister Julie even though there was no blood relation between the two. Robert was such a handsome young boy, so sweet and polite. He began to talk about his Grandpa Willy having some surgery, but Ronnie had stopped him quick and said that was family business. She had been so open on the telephone, but now there was a bit of a wall. Ronnie had told Malorie that their cousin Joseph, who was Troy's son, had conned her mother's trustee out of a lot of money by saying that he was like a son to her. She said Joseph had also tried to kill her at one time and tried to find her a few times, which explained why she was probably a little nervous. Malorie had been confused at first because she kept calling him Troy, but for some reason Joseph had taken on his father's name. He was a very young boy when his father was murdered, and Malorie could only imagine the effect that must have had on him and his two younger sisters at the time.

Ronnie told Malorie that she would call Aunt Ethel and see if they could come to visit and see the family Bible and go through all the family pictures she had. Malorie was very excited about this, and she did want to learn about the family tree . . . but there was so much more she wanted to know. Ronnie said she would be in touch, and they departed.

When Malorie arrived home, the kids were out and Anthony was sleeping, so she poured herself a drink. As she sipped her wine, she wondered if she would hear from Ronnie and where this journey would take her next.

SEVEN

As Malorie continued retyping the transcript, she remembered back to when she would visit her Grandpa Seth and Grandma Annie on their Warkworth farm. They had owned a tobacco farm years ago, and the tobacco houses still existed in the field. They had married in 1940, when Annie was 19. They had met at a barn dance before Christmas and were married a year later. When they were older and ready to retire, they had kept a small piece of land for themselves to the east end, and they set up their own house and barn with a small field to farm. The countryside of Warkworth was beautiful, with rolling hills and green pastures. There were different forks in the roads that would take you in and out of Warkworth; visitors could enter from the north, south, east, and west. Grandpa Seth used to tell stories about how when convicts would escape from the Warkworth Penitentiary, they would pass through his property as part of their escape route. He would give them a warm meal in exchange for them working in the fields and helping with chores that needed to be done around the farm. Then they would disappear as quickly as they had appeared. Seth had very little education and couldn't read or write. He had lived through the Depression and the Second World War, and he had seven children to feed and raise. He was an incredibly hard worker, yet he was open to any help he could get on the farm. He would help out whomever he could, giving others food to eat, a warm place to sleep, and the shirt off his back. His motto was, "The more the merrier." He also felt that if one had a living room, one had an extra room for someone to sleep.

Although some things may have seemed a little unethical, such as getting an escaped convict to help with chores in exchange for a meal and a place to sleep for a night, or stealing corn to feed his children from nearby fields, one thing was for sure: Seth was a family man, and there was nothing more important to him than his wife and children. He would do whatever he had to do to protect them and take care of them. He may have been uneducated, but he was not stupid and did not suffer fools gladly. He was a manly man.

Seth Sregor was about five foot six and 320 pounds. He had dark brown eyes and curly hair that he wore slicked back. He was stocky and strong and was known for his white T-shirt, bib overalls, and cap. If he did have to get dressed up with dress pants and a shirt, there would be suspenders attached. His voice was deep, and he had a warm yet mischievous smile. When he laughed, it was a hearty laugh, right from the deep pit of his stomach. He would do what he could for anyone, but it was wise not to take advantage of him or do wrong to him or his family, because it would awaken the beast within.

As Malorie continued to type, she tried to take herself back to 1956 and visualize the events through the words of the evidence being produced. At the preliminary trial for the murder of his brother, Troy Sregor, Seth had been the first to testify. Troy was Seth's second youngest brother. Seth was the oldest, and there were many years between the two, yet from a distance or from the back, many thought the two were twins. They even dressed the same, from the bib overalls right down to their linen ivy tam cap, which was similar to a newsboy's cap.

Troy's death was a tragedy, a needless and senseless death. Malorie began looking at the newspaper clippings that had accompanied the transcripts Grandma Annie had given her. The headlines in the newspaper the day after Troy's murder read that two youths had been charged with the murder of Troy Sregor, who was 29 and the father of three children. It stated that the shooting was a result of an ongoing family argument. The preliminary hearing was held in the Magistrate's Court of the Province of Ontario before J. T. Butler, Magistrate for the Province of Ontario in Brighton, and it began on October 31, 1956. BJ Barry, Q. C., represented the Crown; R. J. B. O'Neill, Q. C., and C. Fitzgibbon, Esquire, were representing the accused Stanley Blake; and Leonard Karl, Esquire acted on behalf of the accused Jasper Billings.

The police had been holding the two accused in jail until their preliminary trial. Stanley Blake was 18 and was a boarder at the home of Seth Sregor. Jasper Billings was 24 and had worked for Seth on his farm. Jasper was a rather tall man at almost six feet, with a long, oval-shaped face that was very clean-cut. His black hair was shaven close on the sides, and his hair was longer on the top and was slicked back. He had worked very hard for Seth and became a part of the family over the years.

Stanley Blake had messy, short, curly, dirty blonde hair and was about two inches taller than Jasper. Jasper had hung his head in shock and disbelief when he was put in the police cruiser, but Stanley almost had a slight grin. His dark brown eyes were very close together, and the inserts of his pupils were small and round, almost like that of a mouse. He had no problem holding his head up, but there was something odd and different about Stanley. When one first met Stanley, one could tell there was something different about him, but it was hard to put a finger on it. He had been a foster child and moved from house to house, never really having an actual home. He almost seemed a bit simple-minded.

They had been in jail since the murder, without the option of bail. When they came out to sit by their lawyers for the preliminary trial to commence, they were both dressed in suits. Annie and Seth had brought the clothes to the courthouse the night before so that they would be presentable for court. Annie and Seth supported them entirely and believed in their innocence.

BJ Barry represented the Crown. He stood before the court and made a request of the Magistrate. "In this matter counsel have agreed that the Crown might amend, and it doesn't matter which information, to add the other accused to the information so that the accused can be tried jointly. If Your Worship would simply added the phrase, 'together with Stanley Blake.'"

The Magistrate responded, "The two of you are charged jointly that you, Jasper Billings, together with Stanley Blake, on the 27th day of August, 1956, at the Township of Percy, in the County of Northumberland, did unlawfully murder Troy Sregor, contrary to Section 206 of the Criminal

Code. This is a preliminary hearing to determine whether you should be committed for trial on this charge."

BJ Barry sought confirmation. "It is my understanding that counsel again are agreed the witnesses should be excluded in this matter."

Justice Butler called out to those present, "All those called to give evidence in this matter will please leave the courtroom and remain outside during the hearing."

One further request was made by BJ Barry: "It has further been agreed that Corporal Brown may remain, Your Worship, as well as Inspector Fancy."

Eight

Braden Joseph Barry, known as BJ Barry, was the Crown Attorney. He had been born and raised in Warkworth, and he was pretty familiar with everyone around town. He was of medium height and build; a good man who came from a long-time farming family. He had been the first to go to university and had accepted the position as Crown Attorney in Brighton upon graduation from law school. He wanted to have each witness testified separately, so that there could be no corroboration with the evidence and testimonies.

The first witness that BJ Barry called was Seth Sregor. After being sworn in, the questions began.

"Where do you reside?"

"Township of Percy," replied Seth.

"And you are the brother of the late Troy Sregor? Is that correct?"

"Yes, sir."

"And a brother also of Mrs. Virginia Booker?"

"Yes, sir."

"Do you know either of the accused, Jasper Billings or Stanley Blake?"

"Yes, sir."

"Dealing firstly with Billings, how long have you known Billings?"

"Oh, approximately about four and a half years."

"And where does he live?"

"He lived with me."

"And was he employed by you?"

"Yes, sir."

"In what capacity?"

"Well, on this farm, more or less on a share basis."

Justice Butler interjected to clarify Seth's response. "On your farm?"

Seth looked at the Magistrate. "No, on my brother's farm, the one I rented."

BJ Barry looked a little puzzled. "Seth, let us understand that you say *not* on your farm?"

"Well, I more or less share basis on all the farms, on the work, but more or less this one farm."

"Which farm do you mean?"

"The farm I leased from my brother, Ted."

"And what about Stanley Blake?"

"Well, I don't know whether you would call it working for me. He was just staying there for a portion of time. He came down to work on the pea-vining."

"That is where you first knew him?" questioned BJ Barry.

"No, I met him up at my aunt and uncle's before that."

"But he came into the Warkworth area to work on a pea-viner?"

"Yes."

"When would that be?"

"Sometime in July."

"Of this year?"

"Yes."

"When did he first come to your place?"

"Sunday night."

"Do you remember when?"

"No, Saturday night or Sunday night; I couldn't recall the date."

"Would it be in July?"

"I imagine it would."

"What were the circumstances under which he came to your place? On invitation from you, or did he suggest it himself?"

"Well, more or less we were talking—he was talking about getting a job, and I don't know if I told him, or Stewart Fine told him, that he could get a job on the pea-viner."

"Do I understand when he was working on the pea-viner, he was living at your place?"

"Yes."

"And when did he start working on the pea-viner?"

"He was only working two days or nights."

"And did he remain at your place?"

"Yes."

"And what was the wage arrangement?"

"Well, I wasn't giving him very much, because I couldn't offer to pay very much at that time until I got my grain threshed."

"And he was living at your place?"

"Yes."

Justice Butler intercepted, "This year?"

"Yes, sir," answered Seth.

"This last summer?" BJ Barry asked Seth.

"Yes, sir."

"Well, to go back to this farm that you say you rent from your brother, Ted. As I understand it, that was a farm originally owned by your father?"

"Yes, and sold to my brother Ted approximately 15 years ago."

"Did your father take back any security in connection with the sale?"

"I don't know; I never seen any papers."

"Did you ever hear of any such arrangement?"

"Well, according to the will, a mortgage was taken back."

"I take it you mean your father's will?"

"Yes, sir."

"There was a mortgage taken back in favour of your father?"

"Yes."

"Have you any idea what was owed under that mortgage at the time of your father's death?"

"Approximately $500, I take it."

"And in the distribution of your father's estate, what became of that mortgage, do you know?"

"I do not know," Seth replied.

"Have you ever heard what became of it?"

"Well, as near as I can make out, Virginia was supposed to get the mortgage on my father's death, or through my father's will."

"That is Mrs. Booker?"

"Yes, sir."

"So, to get that mortgage—and she did in fact get the mortgage under the distribution of the estate?"

"I don't know about that."

"In any event, following the distribution of your father's estate, when did that take place, Mr. Sregor? When was that matter finally settled?"

"Last fall, in October."

"That would be October of 1955?" BJ Barry asked.

"October or November."

"And at that time was your brother, Ted, working that farm?"

"No. He had wheat on it that summer of '55."

"And had you any arrangement at that time in October 1955 with your brother, with relation to this farm?"

"Yes; I had it rented."

"For what period?" Barry asked.

"For approximately five years, and if I was satisfied with it in five years, I could keep it for 10."

"When was that arrangement entered into?"

"September."

"That was September of 1955, was it?"

"No, I had the agreement drawn up—that would be in August, early part of August, I would say."

"Where was this agreement drawn?"

"The first agreement was drawn just to give me the okay to go ahead, and drawn in my house."

"By whom?"

"My wife."

"And that was for how long?"

"No definite length of time."

"Just to let you go on the property?"

"Just to give me permission to go until we got a further paper drawn up for the length of time we were supposed to keep the place," Seth clarified.

"Was another paper drawn up?"

"Yes, sir."

"When was it drawn up?"

"Just a very few days afterwards the other paper was drawn up."

"Where was it drawn up?"

"Back at my father-in-law's."

"What is his name, please?"

"Ken Garvey's."

"Who drew that paper?"

"My wife."

"And that was a lease for how long, Mr. Sregor?"

"For five years."

Ryder O'Neill, the solicitor for Stanley Blake, spoke. "This is more or less secondary evidence of a written document. I can produce the document."

"Perhaps it would be just as well if it was produced," BJ Barry said as he held up a document. "Will you look at this document, Mr. Sregor, and tell Justice Butler if that was the arrangement entered into at your father-in-law's place?"

"Well, I can't read what is on there. I know my signature and my brother, Ted's signature."

"That is your signature and your brother's signature, isn't it?"

"Yes, sir."

"Where does your father-in-law live?" questioned Justice Butler.

"Havelock. Warkworth is where the place is," Seth said. "My brother was working at that time back at the Blue Mountains, and boarding at my father-in-law's. Mrs. Booker and Willy came in and caused a disturbance among my two boys that was ploughing; we went back and had this paper drawn up very quickly."

"I suggest if the witness can't read that I can read it to him and ask him if it is the terms of his understanding." BJ Barry knew that Seth could not read or write, but needed clarification. "This read in this fashion, Mr. Sregor. 'Warkworth, Ontario, August 8, 1955. This is to certify that Seth Sregor on this date rents from Ted Sregor Ted's farm consisting of 135 acres, Lot 13, Concession 2 and Lot 13, Concession 3 in the Township of Percy, for a period of approximately five years, farms known as the Old Home Farm and Cassidy Farm. Ted Sregor is to receive one dollar ($1.00) and one-third of the price of the grain after sold by Seth Sregor. Grain to be sold as soon as possible after threshing. Seth Sregor to have full possession of all buildings, except a house on Old Home Farm which Ted Sregor keeps for his own personal use. If Ted Sregor does not use said house on Old Home Farm, Seth Sregor can rent same and collect rent if so desired. Seth Sregor does not keep any buildings or fences in repair. Seth Sregor is to have all straw and hay. Term ends December 31, 1960. Signatures, Ted Sregor and Seth Sregor.' And below the signatures, 'Note: if Seth Sregor is satisfied with renting at the end of 1960, he can continue on until December 31, 1965, under the same terms.' Signed again, Seth Sregor and Ted Sregor."

"Yes, sir."

"This is exhibit one," stated Justice Butler.

BJ Barry held the lease. "Will you look at this piece of paper, Mr. Sregor, and tell Justice Butler if that was the first lease entered into?"

"Well, my name and Ted's name signed it," responded Seth.

BJ Barry pushed further. "And it reads this way, 'Warkworth, Ontario, August 6, 1955'—this is to say, two days before the lease, exhibit one, was entered into—'This is to certify that Ted Sregor and Seth Sregor make bargain on this date for Seth Sregor to work land on shares. Farm where Ted Sregor lives and farm known as Cassidy Farm. Ted Sregor to receive one-third and Seth Sregor to receive two-thirds; grain to be divided at threshing. If Ted Sregor wants grass seed sowed, he will furnish seed for Seth to sow. Signed Ted Sregor and Seth Sregor.' Was that your understanding of that arrangement?"

"Yes, sir."

"Please note this as exhibit two," Justice Butler said as he held the lease up.

BJ Barry continued. "At any time, Mr. Sregor, did you have a third arrangement about this farm which was for a period of one year?"

"No, sir."

"There was no such arrangement, you say?"

"No, sir; this is all the papers we have."

"Then did some dispute arise between you and your sister, Virginia Booker, about the possession of this farm?"

"No, not definitely. This William Booker and Virginia Booker came in and bothered the boys from ploughing."

"Go ahead."

"Well . . ." Seth paused.

BJ Barry tried to remind Seth where he was/ "You say they came down and bothered the boys. What boys?"

"My two boys, Ken and Harry Sregor."

"Your two sons?"

"Yes, sir."

"When was this?"

"Well, I wouldn't just say the date, but just a few days after we had leased the place."

"That is, in the fall of 1955?"

"When we were doing the ploughing to put in the fall grain."

"In what way did they bother them?" Barry asked.

"They came and told them to get off the place. Virginia said it was her place, so I met William Booker and my sister, Virginia—"

"William Booker is your sister's husband?"

"Yes. After they just came away from interrupting the boys, I told them I had it rented for an indefinite length of time. I didn't tell them how long, and I warned them to stay off the place and to keep their cattle off the place."

"That was in the fall of 1955, was it?"

"Yes, sir."

"And did they stay off the place?"

"No, sir, they never did," Seth said.

"When did they come back on?"

"In the spring of '56 they put cattle—no, in the fall of '55 their cattle, Booker's cattle, pastured my wheat."

"You mean wheat on the Ted Sregor's farm?" questioned BJ Barry.

"Yes, sir."

"Was anything done about that?"

"I put the cattle in the barnyard and told William Booker and Mr. Duberg to stay off the place, that I was taking the cattle in pound, that they had done enough damage last fall, and they was taking the grain all fall, this grain I had sown. I said I was going to get Canova's Transport to truck them to pound. When I was gone, the cattle were led out of the barnyard and taken across the fields down to their place where I had tracked."

"What happened in the spring of '56?"

"So then I went to Mr. Hurman, and I had Mr. Hurman write Bookers a lawyer's letter demanding $100 in damages."

"Then did you have a reply to that letter from Mr. Hurman?"

"I don't remember whether I did or not."

"Then what happened in the spring?"

"Mr. Hurman, if he did, would have a copy of it in his office. In the spring they put cattle—well, they kept on pasturing the wheat until it froze up, and in the spring they put three head of cattle and a calf in the barnyard—or a couple of calves. I couldn't say, but I think just one calf in the barn."

"And during this time, Mr. Sregor, was anybody living in the house on the place?"

"No, sir. I wasn't going to rent it because I didn't know what time my brother Ted would want to go back there and live, so I just left it over."

Confused, Justice Butler asked, "Where was Ted?"

"Some of the time with my mother, and some of the time up with me. He spent different times with me," Seth replied.

"In the spring they put cattle back in the barn?" BJ Barry asked.

"Yes, sir."

"And what was done about that?"

"I was up to the farm, and young Troy came to me first and said, 'Do you know Bookers has cattle in your barn there?' And I said, 'No, Troy, I didn't know.' And he said, 'They have cattle up there.' So I went up and I looked around, and sure enough there were three cattle and one calf—could have been two calves, but one I am sure—in the barn, and there was no hay or nothing in the barn, only some of Timothy's threshing hay. The cows were very thin, so I left them then for a day or two and went back again, and I met Mr. Henry Booker."

"That is your sister's . . . ?"

"Father-in-law. And when I approached him, he was pumping water at the pump. I asked him what he was doing there, and he had a three-pronged, short-handled fork, and he told me not to come too close. I said, 'Listen, Mr. Booker, I have this place rented, and I want you to take your cattle and toddle on down the road.' He said, 'They are not my cattle; they belong to the Dutchman, and they are in Oshawa.' Well, I said—"

"When he said the Dutchman, who did you understand him to mean?"

"This Morgan, who married my sister Joan," stated Seth.

When Morgan talked, he sounded like his mouth was full of marbles; he killed the English language. When he was in school and told the teacher he was going to get his lunch box, it sounded like he said he "was going to get a Dutchman." The kids laughed and teased him. At a very young age he had received the nickname of Dutchman. Many had thought his family was from Holland, but that was not the case.

It was now noon, and Justice Butler called for a break. "We will continue in one hour at one o'clock."

Nine

After the break, Seth continued with his testimony. "So I asked him what he was going to do with the fork, and he said, 'I just got it for my protection, and if you come too close, you will get it,' so I told him to make an awful good job when he done it."

"Was anything further said?" asked BJ Barry.

"He told me about them working in Oshawa, and I said, 'We will leave them here till Saturday, but I want them out by Saturday.' Saturday came and, the cattle wasn't removed."

"So what did you do?"

"I left them there. I thought maybe they would be down later on, so I stopped in on the way down and seen Mr. Booker and said, 'Mr. Booker, I want them cattle out of there. I had to make a bargain for the place, and if you want to put cattle in there, I think it is fair for you to make a bargain to put them there, not to steal the rights and put the cattle in the barn.' So nothing was done about it."

"Were the cattle left there?"

"Yes, sir. So Sunday after we had our dinner, I drove up—"

"When was this, can you tell us?"

Seth scratched his head. "I think my wife can tell you about the time, because she wrote all these agreements down."

"I see. But it was in the spring, was it?"

"Oh, I would say approximately the first of March, somewhere in there, or April—in the spring."

"What was the final upshot? Were the cattle moved?"

"I took the cattle from the barn I think on Sunday afternoon, approximately two o'clock, and drove them out and down to the top of the hill. Then this Morgan and my sister, Joan, was coming up the road in a red Chevy truck, and I met them on the hill. She said, 'Seth, they are my cattle.' I said, 'Joan, this is right, but I didn't know whose cattle they was when I first seen them, and I told Mr. Booker the least they could do is have some permission to put them in the barn.'"

"So what became of the cattle? Were they taken back or taken to the Morgans'?"

"They were taken down to Booker's."

"And what happened next in connection with the farm, Mr. Sregor?"

"Well, it went on for approximately sometime in June—pretty sure sometime in June—and the cattle was taken off the pasture and drove over my place on a Sunday."

Justice Butler interrupted, "You mean your place?"

Seth clarified, "Taken off my brother's farm. I had eight head of yearlings."

"Let us qualify this. Were they your cattle?"

"Yes, sir."

"Taken off your brother Ted's farm, and taken to your own farm?"

"Yes, sir."

"They were your cattle?" repeated Justice Butler.

"Yes, sir."

"And that left no cattle pasturing on Ted's farm?"

"Every day I went over and watered these cattle at the pump on my brother Ted's farm that I had leased, so anyway they was drove over to my place on a Sunday, and I was pretty vexed about it."

"I am sorry, what happened on a Sunday?" the Judge asked.

"Drove over—"

"These cattle were driven from Ted's place to his farm," Judge Butler interrupted as he was trying to understand the sequence of events.

Seth replied, "About a mile and a half, and Virginia Booker and William Booker—"

"Did you see them?"

"Yes, sir, Henry Booker, Liza Duberg, and Joe Duberg, I think."

"This would be when?"

"This would be in June."

"And I take it of the accused, only Billings was at your place at that time?"

"Yes, sir."

"Blake was not there at that time?"

"No. Stewart Fine was at our place that day, and he seen the cattle, and I was pretty mad and was going to give them a flogging in the road."

"What do you mean by that?"

"I was going to chew them all up on the road, and my wife grabbed the braces of my pants and broke the braces, and that stopped—"

The Judge said, "And I suppose at that time there was some hot words exchanged, were there?"

"No, I told them I was going to Mr. Hurman and was going to sue them for stealing cattle off the place."

"And what they had done was bring them from Ted's place to your place?"

"And Ted was there at the time they were brought down."

Confused, Judge Butler asked, "At your place?"

"Yes, sir," Seth said with a nod.

"And what happened following that?"

"I went to Mr. Hurman, and Mr. Hurman wrote a letter to them, to the Bookers, to Cosgrove in Oshawa."

"Mr. Cosgrove is solicitor for your sister, Virginia Booker?"

"Yes, sir."

"Had he replied to Mr. Hurman's previous letter?"

"I couldn't say that. I don't understand what you—"

"You said you had a letter written by Mr. Hurman demanding $100 damages?" Judge Butler was trying to clarify things for Seth.

"Yes, sir."

"Did he get an answer to that letter?"

"I don't know whether Mr. Hurman did or not."

"The only reason I suggest it is that in order to know to write to Mr. Cosgrove, he must have had some previous contact with him."

"Mr. Cosgrove wrote down to say to take the cattle off the place, that we had no right to have the cattle on the place, and we were doing petty thieving and that kind of stuff on our own premises."

"I take it what Mr. Cosgrove was saying in effect was that Virginia Booker was the person entitled legally to possession of the farm. Is that about what the sense of his letter was?"

Ryder O'Neill tried to assist. "Do you want the letter?" He placed it on the bench.

"I don't suppose you recognize that?" BJ Barry asked Seth.

"I don't know anything about that," responded Seth.

"It is addressed to you and dated June 14, 1956. Did you get a letter from Mr. Cosgrove?"

"Oh, I could tell you maybe it was read to me."

"It was apparently addressed to you at Warkworth?"

"Yes, my wife read me the letter."

"This is your proper address, Warkworth?"

"Yes, sir."

"And your wife read you the letter?"

"She read me a letter from Mr. Cosgrove, and we took the letter to Mr. Hurman and took our agreement to Mr. Hurman, and he replied to the letter, and then we wasn't bothered for quite a definite length of time from that time. That was after the cattle were removed."

"All I want to establish at this stage is the contents of this letter were made known to you by your wife, and you took it into Mr. Hurman?"

"Yes, sir."

"Exhibit three, please, Your Worship," BJ continued. "On this occasion you say you went back to Mr. Hurman, and he wrote another letter to Mr. Cosgrove?"

"Yes, sir. But the first time that I had Mr. Hurman to write to Bookers, they didn't write to Mr. Cosgrove. That was—"

"Directly to the Bookers?" questioned BJ Barry.

"Yes, sir, about the cattle pasturing," replied Seth.

"And that letter was sent by Mr. Cosgrove on behalf of the Bookers?"

"I don't think so. I don't think there was any—" Seth did not get to finish his sentence when BJ Barry began talking again.

"To go back to this incident in June, what was the upshot of the exchange of letters between Mr. Cosgrove and Mr. Hurman?"

"We never was bothered any more, until I started cutting the grain, and then the sheaves—the bands were all cut on the one field of grain of wheat and a stove put in the house."

"What happened to that stove?"

"I put it out on the doorstep."

"Is it the one on the doorstep this morning?"

"Yes, sir."

"I noticed the boiler is full of bullet holes."

"Yes, sir."

"How did that happen?"

"I put them there," Seth said.

"What was the reason for that?"

"We had a .22 up there, and I wanted to see how good I was to shoot, so I was seeing if I could put two bullets in the same hole."

"Whose stove was it?"

"I don't know."

Justice Butler interrupted, "You didn't put it in the house?"

"No, sir," Seth said.

BJ Barry seemed confused. "It wasn't your stove?"

"No, sir."

"Did you know whose it was?"

"No, sir."

"You didn't even suspect?"

Seth paused. "Well, I didn't know whose it was, and I didn't bother inquiring because I figured the stove had no right to be there."

"You moved it out and shot the reservoir full of holes?"

"Yes."

"Just to clarify, did you move it out first, or shoot it there?" asked Justice Butler.

"No, I moved it first."

"When was that done?"

"Oh, that was on a Monday morning."

"What Monday would that be?"

"That would be in August."

"The latter part of August?"

"Yes, sir."

"Was anybody with you when that was done?"

"Yes, I think Jasper Billings and Stanley Blake."

"They were there?"

"Yes."

"And this rifle you had at that time, where had it come from?"

"Well, there were two rifles there that belonged to my brother Ted."

"Where were they?" BJ Barry asked.

"At my place."

"At your own home?"

"Yes."

"Had you taken the rifle up with you to the other place?"

"No, the boys had the rifle. They stayed in the house on a Sunday night; stones were thrown through the window—"

"I am not talking about that occasion. I am talking about the occasion when you shot the reservoir in the stove."

"That would be a Monday morning. The boys stayed in the house on the Sunday night, when the stones were thrown through the window."

"We have gotten this far, as I recollect, to a point where Mr. Hurman and Mr. Cosgrove had exchanged letters about this trouble, and that was apparently in June, according to the date of that letter?"

"Yes, sir."

"What next happened after that when there was some difficulty between yourself and your sister?"

Seth said, "Well, we put locks on the door at the house, and we had put up the telephone, and batteries were stolen out of the telephone."

"When did that happen?"

"That happened in June, and ground wire was cut on the telephone. We were up there working—the reason I put it up was I could call over home and call the wife to bring me stuff, binder twine and that, and the three sets of batteries were stolen out of the phone, and so then we put a lock on the door, and the lock was busted off the door."

"When did that happen?"

"That was in June or July, one or the other, and so we put no trespassing signs on the house after the cattle was removed, and brother Ted was with me the day we put the lock on the house and put no trespassing signs on the house, and we stepped back, and I took some pictures of the no trespassing signs on the house. I took a picture of my brother Ted too while the cattle was there watering, and that was before Doc Magee was there. After Doc came, he put two sheets of steel down the roof and a sheet of steel on the door. So it was before then that the pictures were taken, and my cattle and my brother Ted was there the day we put the no trespassing signs on the house, and I took pictures of my brother Ted, and Ted had one picture with him."

"Did anything else happen in connection with that particular house until the weekend of August 25-26?"

Seth started, "Well, Dr. Magee came to me on a Sunday afternoon—"

"When would that be?" BJ Barry asked.

"That would be on the Sunday before the shooting took place."

"When did Dr. Magee go into occupation of that place?"

"Oh, I couldn't tell you. There is an agreement to that effect some place."

"Do you know when about that was?"

"Sometime in July or August. I wouldn't commit myself on the date."

"I have had produced to me a document dated July 13, 1956, which reads as follows: 'On this date Simon Magee rents house on Lot 13, Concession 2 in the Township of Percy, known as Ted Sregor's house on Old Home Farm for the sum of one dollar ($1.00) per month. Simon Magee to take possession July 16, 1956. This agreement is in connection with the agreement between Ted Sregor and Seth Sregor on the farm.' And it is signed Simon Magee, Seth Sregor, and Annie Sregor?"

"Yes, sir."

"And underneath is written, 'Received rent for twelve months.'"

"Yes, sir."

"Who wrote it up?"

"My wife."

"Exhibit number four, Your Worship. And you say Dr. Magee went in there on the 16th of July?"

"Yes, sir."

"Did he stay there all the time, Mr. Sregor?"

"Oh, part of the time. He was away doctoring and I don't know what. I am quite sure he stayed there at night."

"Had he any other place to stay?"

"He was in Campbellford; he had a home in Campbellford by the canal, but there was no doctor in Warkworth, and Warkworth should have a doctor there, so I rented him the place more or less to see who came there and to see who was meddling around the farm."

"That was the reason you rented the farm to Magee?"

"Yes, sir."

Ryder O'Neill, the defence counsel, interrupted. "The farm?"

BJ Barry corrected himself. "I am sorry, the house?"

"Just the house," answered Seth.

BJ Barry continued with his questioning of Seth Sregor. "And what happened after Dr. Magee?"

"The ploughs were broken, and the flaps where you turn over from wheat to oats on the seed drill, they disappeared, and a casting broke on the disc plough. So I figured it was time to have somebody in there to see what was going on, because I lived about a mile and a half or two miles from the place, and Bookers lived in between, and every time I go down they know I have left."

"And what next happened? You harvested your grain, I think you told me?"

"Well, next we went to thresh the grain by the drive shed or the garage, and the bands was cut on the wheat. It wasn't very tall wheat, and the—"

"You mean the binder twine that goes round?"

"Yes, sir, and it made it very hard to thresh."

"When was that?" BJ Barry asked.

"Well, that would be sometime in July. Well, it was after Dr. Magee went there, for he seen Mr. and Mrs. Booker in there—"

"We will have to let him tell us what he saw, but what next happened?"

"Next happened was we was threshing, and Virginia Booker come up and said to me, 'I want to see this grain threshed.' I said, 'You go down town and you hire whoever you like to come up and see this grain threshed, but after all you have done to me, you can't stay on the place.'"

"And when was that?"

"That was shortly after Dr. Magee came; I couldn't just say the date. My wife has the date, I think."

"What did Mrs. Booker say to that?"

"Oh, she wasn't going. She started to count up the number of bags of wheat, and I said, 'You don't have to do that; there is a weigher on the machine.'"

"Was she alone at this time?"

"Her husband and this Dutchman."

"Mr. Morgan?"

"Mr. Morgan, that's right, on the road. They never came in while I was there."

"Did she have anything further to say at that time?"

"Oh, she done quite a bit of cursing and swearing, and Stewart Fine told her to go down the road and mind her own affairs because he was there attending to the bushels."

"Was either Blake or Billings there?"

"I think Billings and Blake was up in the field, and I and my son Gary and Ken and Harry, I think, was at the separator. Gary and I were taking turns feeding the separator, and I hired Stewart Fine to look after the bushels."

"What happened next, following the threshing incident?"

"I told her to leave the place, and the boys got a pail of water and throwed it on her and told her she was getting pretty hot, and to get on her way."

"Who throwed it on her?"

"I think it was Harry."

"One of your boys?"

"Yes."

"And you were there?"

"Yes, and I said, 'If you are not going to go, I am going to call the police.' I came home and left her there and sent up for Harry, and one of the boys went up to get Jasper and Stanley from the field, and I went home and I called Campbellford for Mr. Bigelow. He was on his holidays, and so we called Peterborough and nobody came. We called to Brighton to Corporal

Lowe on the telephone, and I asked him to come up because we were having some trouble, but he never came, nobody came."

"You are sure of that, are you?"

"Well, I didn't see anybody."

"Then what happened following that? What was the next trouble you had?"

"Well, the next trouble we had was we was threshing down the other place—"

"What do you mean, 'the other place'?"

"The Cassidy place and the home place."

"Where did this first trouble take place?"

"At the home place where Dr. Magee was, and Mr. Beattie and Troy came in, and I was threshing there, and Mr. Beattie said he brought Troy up and there was some trouble over the grain."

"Of what nature?"

"Troy was supposed to get some grain. I told Mr. Beattie, "Look, we have no papers with Troy whatsoever on the grain. I have all my agreements with Ted.'"

"Is it correct, Mr. Sregor, that Troy apparently had some deal with Ted that he was to get Ted's portion of the grain?"

"I seen no papers whatsoever. He told me the time before in the wood shed at our place that he had bought the place from Ted, and he was supposed to get the place from Ted."

"You are talking about the Cassidy place, not the place where this matter occurred?" BJ Barry asked.

"Yes, sir, and he was supposed to get Ted's share of the grain, so I said to Troy, 'You get Ted and you bring him to me, and we will draw up an agreement. Ted signs it and we will pay you the money, but you bring Ted to us, or we will go to your place and draw up this agreement, because it will be a lot easier for me to give you Ted's grain than handle it and take it to Peterborough and sell it.' So the paper never came, and I asked Ted about it, and he said he had nothing to do with the grain; he and I made the bargain."

"When was that that Corporal Beattie and Troy were at the Cassidy place? Do you remember what date that was?"

"I couldn't recall the date; Annie has it down."

"Would it be in August?"

"I imagine it would be."

"Then what happened after that?"

"Well, I got the grain threshed, and they went away when I told them I had no papers whatsoever and wasn't being bothered. I didn't want to be bothered because I had the grain to thresh, and it was rainy weather and I wasn't going to be bothered. If they wanted to get a hold of Ted and get the paper, all right, but I had an agreement with Ted, and I was going to fill the agreement."

Barry asked, "What happened next after you got finished with that threshing?"

"Well, there was nothing happened—oh, yes, I had a chunk of ground rented from Mrs. McKibbon. She has a life lease off the Cassidy place, and my brother Troy and I went in and ploughed that, and that wasn't being made any harder, so we went back to the other place."

"You are talking about the home place where this matter occurred, are you?"

Seth said, "Yes, and I went up there one day, and Mr. Booker and Virginia was ploughing in the corner field."

"That would be what date? Was that on a Friday immediately before this matter?"

"Just a few days before this accident."

"Was it on a Friday, do you remember?"

"I wouldn't commit myself on the date; could be Friday, could be Thursday, could be any day."

"You went up there, and what was going on?"

"Well, in the meantime I had the 10-gauge shotgun down at Ron Ward's getting a trigger fixed on it, and I had put that shotgun in the truck. I went up there to Booker's, or went up to my place, and William Booker—"

"What do you mean, 'my place'?"

"The place I had rented from my brother."

"Is that the same thing as you refer to as your brother's?"

"Yes, and they were ploughing—Virginia Booker and William Booker."

"Did they each have a tractor?"

"Yes, they had Mother's tractor for one and Booker's tractor for another."

"What time of day would this be?"

"Oh, that would be maybe two o'clock in the afternoon, maybe three o'clock."

"Was anybody with you?"

Justice Butler interrupted. "It is now four o'clock, and I would like us to reconvene tomorrow morning at nine o'clock. Mr. Sregor, I want to remind you that you should not discuss this case or your testimony with anyone outside of this courtroom." Justice Butler rapped his gavel and got up and left. Jasper Billings and Stanley Blake were then escorted by the court officers back to their jail cell. Everyone then got up and left the courtroom.

Ten

It was beginning to get colder outside now that November was here. Seth had already been up for a while feeding the chickens and tending to his other livestock. Everyone had re-entered the courtroom. Stanley and Jasper were at the front of the courtroom as Seth proceeded to the witness box.

The court reporter repeated back the last line from the day before: "Was anybody with you?" Seth was now back on the stand and knew he was still under oath.

Seth began to answer the question from the day before. "No, not at that time. Canova had come to truck up some of the grain, and my wife came shortly afterward to tell me Canova's truck was there to take the grain. I went over to tell William Booker and Virginia Booker to please get off the place and mind their own affairs, because I had it leased, and they started backing up with their tractor to run over me. So then I went and got the old 10-gauge shotgun out and shot it in the air, and I told them to get off the place, and they backed up with their tractors and dared me to shoot them, so I put the shotgun in the truck and came home and went to Mr. Beattie, and I told him."

"You just happened to have this shotgun with you?"

"Yes, sir. I had it fixed at Ron Ward's, so I had one of the—"

"And you just happened to have some ammunition for it?"

"Yes, just in the truck."

"Where were you when you fired this shot?"

"I was at this end of the field."

"And they?"

"At the other end."

"How far would they be away?"

"Oh, they would be across a six-acre field."

"How far would that be?"

"Oh, as far as from here down to the corner."

"Did you see where the shot hit?"

"It was bird shot."

"Did you see it hit?"

"No, it wouldn't go more than twice as far as the length of this room."

"And you got in your car and drove away?"

"Yes, sir. The wife got away in the car, and I drove away in the truck. They had no notion of leaving, and they were going to back over the wife, and I told them if they did there was going to be real trouble, and they both backed the tractors, one Ford and one Ferguson, towards the wife. I said, "Don't touch her," because I was getting pretty angry at that time."

"Did anything further happen on that occasion?"

"No. I went away, and after supper I came back up to say something to the Doctor, and they was ploughing another field. So the next morning after that I went in to Mr. Hurman's office, and Mr. Hurman was not in. I was going to see Mr. Hurman and lay a charge against them for bothering me.

Mr. Hurman did not get in his office until the Tuesday after the shooting took place, I think."

"Is it your recollection that this incident of the ploughing and discharge of the shotgun occurred on Friday, the Friday prior to the day your brother was shot?"

"Could have been, sir."

"What was the next thing that occurred with relation to these premises?"

"Well, on a Saturday night there was a load of straw going off the top of the stack on the upper place behind Doc Magee's house."

"You mean taken?"

"Yes, sir, by a dual-wheeled truck."

"When did this incident of you going up and finding the stove in the premises and shooting it out take place?"

"The stove had been out on the veranda at the time Doc Magee moved in there."

"When did you shoot it?"

"That would be on a Monday; the boys stayed in on the Sunday night."

"You mean the same day your brother was shot?"

"Well, the boys went in on a Sunday night, and I picked them up on a Monday morning."

Justice Butler was a little confused. "Did they stay in two different Sunday nights?"

"Sunday night, see, so on a Saturday night the stones was thrown through the window." Seth was a bit frustrated.

"That wasn't this last time?" Justice Butler questioned.

"Yes," Seth said firmly.

BJ Barry understood what each was trying to say. To try and assist, he confirmed, "As I understand the sequence of things, that Saturday night the stones were thrown through the window of the place?"

"Yes, sir," Seth answered.

"On Sunday Billings and Blake went up and stayed there."

"Yes, Sunday night."

"On Monday your brother was shot?"

With a quiet and sad voice, Seth hesitated and then responded, "Monday night." Seth missed his brother and blamed himself for not being there to protect his sibling.

"That is the sequence of events? Is that correct?"

"Yes, sir."

Again Justice Butler queried, "They must have stayed there another Sunday night?"

"No, sir," said Seth.

BJ Barry referred back, "But you have said this stove was out on the veranda before Magee moved in, and Magee moved in sometime in July."

Seth went through the sequence of events again, "The stove was out on the veranda, and the boys stayed there on a Sunday night. On a Monday morning I picked them up, and they had their guns with them, and I took one of the guns—I don't know which one it was—and I said, 'I will see how good I am on the shooting,' for I never done very much shooting. I held it up and thought I would try on the old stove because I was going to take the stove for junk, and so I tried to see if I could put two bullet holes in the same hole."

Justice Butler asked, "This was a Monday morning that your brother was shot?"

"Yes, sir," replied Seth

Justice Butler and BJ Barry seemed to keep taking turns. BJ approached the bench where Seth was sitting. "You say you were going to take the stove for junk?"

"Yes, sir."

"Was it your stove?"

"No, sir. It was no good whatsoever."

"Certainly no good when you finished with it," BJ Barry said as he turned and walked away from the bench.

"It was no good before. If you looked inside, there was no grates in it."

"You say there was an incident occurred on the Saturday night, when stones were thrown through the window and the window was broken?"

"Yes, sir."

"Did anything else occur that night?"

"Well, Doc Magee came over to me about—"

"When did you first learn that had occurred?"

"Oh, around 4:30 maybe, Sunday afternoon."

"And whom did you learn it from?"

"Dr. Magee."

"And you and Dr. Magee had a conversation about it?"

"Yes, sir."

"And as a result of that, what happened?"

Seth replied, "I said I would like to find out for sure who was doing all this trouble, and I said so, and the wife said, 'No, don't you go. Your place is home with me and the family.' So I didn't go, and Annie asked Jasper and Stanley if they would like to batch it for a night, to see who was interfering around the place. I think it was Annie, or one of the others. And they said, 'Sure we will go up and stay there until we can get in touch with Mr. Hurman and have them sued.' They stayed there to hold the place, so we had gone to Cobourg I think on a Monday, and Mr. Beattie . . ." Seth did not get a chance to finish what he was saying.

"Just a minute—they went up and stayed there on a Sunday night? Is that correct?"

"Yes, sir."

"On that occasion, did they take rifles with them?"

"Yes, sir."

"How did it come about they took rifles?"

"Well, they stayed there on a Sunday night and asked me if they could take the rifles, and I said, 'Stand guard; take the old 10-gauge shotgun, if you want.'"

"Was there any conversation between you about what was to be done with the rifles?"

"No, sir."

"Were any instructions given to these two boys?"

"Not that I know of. I didn't say anything; I said just to see who come there and find out who was there."

"They were more or less to find out who was there?"

"Make sure, because we told Mr. Hurman, and he said, 'You can't guess on it.'"

"I am talking now about the Sunday."

"That is what we put them there for, to see who was there."

Justice Butler followed BJ's questioning. "You said Mr. Hurman told you . . . ?"

Seth turned his head towards the Justice as he sat in the witness box. "We was going to sue them before, the time we sent the letter to them about the cattle."

"You had to have proof of what?" asked the Justice.

"Of what they were doing, who was doing it. The same time they buggered up my seed drill and broke the ploughs with a sledge hammer, and he said, 'You can't sue somebody; you have to find out who is doing it.'" It seemed pretty clear to Seth.

BJ Barry began questioning again. "You went up and got them on Monday morning?"

"Yes, sir."

"And that was when the stove was shot?"

"Yes, sir."

"On the Sunday, was any arrangement made for them to return on the Monday and spend Monday night there?"

"Dr. Magee asked them to go back and stay Monday night, and he gave Jas or one of them the key, but we threshed that day, and we didn't get up there the time we were supposed to, because we had just finished threshing and were a little late. We met Dr. Magee by burying ground, and he gave one of the boys the key."

"What was your purpose in going there?"

"To take the boys up."

"For what purpose?"

"To see who was there, and Dr. Magee was to call later to see who was cutting the telephone wires and causing the trouble."

"Did they on that occasion have rifles?"

"Yes, sir."

"Where did these rifles come from?"

"As near as I can make out, they are both Ted's. Ted told me he had two rifles."

"Where were they kept ordinarily?"

"I guess they were kept upstairs."

"Upstairs where?"

"In my house. Jasper looked after the rifles; I didn't have anything to do with them. The only time I had them in my hand was the time I shot the holes in the stove."

"Where had the ammunition for the rifles come from?"

"The boys had that."

Leonard Karl, Jasper's lawyer, stood up with a confused look on his face. "What boys?"

"Jas—" Seth said.

"Billings and Blake?" asked BJ Barry.

"Yes."

BJ Barry continued questioning. "Where did they get it?"

"I don't know. I was not with them when they got it."

"You have no idea where they got it?"

"Stanley had a box of ammunition when he came down."

"You mean Blake, when he came to your place? Did he have a rifle when he came down to your place?"

"I don't think he did. I don't know."

"On the Sunday, do you know people by the name of Jennings?"

"Yes, I met Mr. Jennings sometime in June."

"But did you see him on Sunday, the 26th of August?"

"Yes."

"The day before your brother was shot?"

"Well, before I met Mr. Jennings first, my brother Troy came to me."

"When was this?"

"Sometime in June, and he told me that the Jennings' was going to rent the upper place."

"You mean Ted's place?"

"Yes, sir. And I said, 'They can't rent the place, because I have a lease on the place, and they can't rent the house or any part of the place.' He said, 'I know it, Seth, and that is the reason I am here. Would you want to go over to Jennings, and we will tell them, and I will make you acquainted with them.' He knew them. 'And we will show them a copy of the agreement.'"

"Did you go over to Jennings?"

"Yes, sir, with Troy."

"When was that?"

"Before Dr. Magee rented the place, and we learned from Jennings that Virginia had already rented the house to Jennings and paid 20 dollars."

"You mean they had paid Virginia 20 dollars?"

"They paid Virginia 20 dollars, so my wife showed Mr. and Mrs. Jennings a copy of the agreement, where the original agreement was at Mr. Hurman's."

"And what was the final upshot of that?"

"And we told them she couldn't rent the place. Then she wanted to rent it from me, and I said no."

Justice Butler looked at Seth. "Who do you mean by 'she'?"

"Mrs. Jennings wanted me to put the hydro in. and I said I wouldn't spend one dime on the place outside of just keeping, and wouldn't put the hydro in or water in. She said there is a cistern in, but I said, 'Yes, but no eavestroughs on the house and no pumps of any kind.' There are pipes, but it will be no good for you because you have a lot of electrical appliances.' She said, 'Virginia told me she would wire the house up, and I could have it the first of September.' I said, 'We can't rent it to you.' So that was the final of that."

BJ Barry was curious. "Did you see the Jennings again on the 26th of August?"

"Yes, sir, I might have after the shooting occurred."

"Did you not see them before any of that occurred on Sunday the 26th? I am not talking about the 27th, but the 26th."

"I think the Jennings was at our place just before Dr. Magee came, and they wanted me to buy Dr. Magee off so they could have the place."

"And what was said then?"

"I said, 'No, I rented the place to Dr. Magee. This Dr. Magee would sell off, and we couldn't rent the place a second time.'"

"Were any figures mentioned?"

"Not right at that time. So then we went up to Mrs.—we went up to look at the straw stack or one up by Troy's, and we see Jennings go into Troy's. After that we got in the car and went over to tell them, after Doc Magee came, that if they wanted to pay Dr. Magee for moving out there, and one thing and another. he was getting pretty fed up, and if they would pay Dr. Magee for moving out there, and one thing and another, it would be around $70-75 for the trouble that he had. Why, then they could move in that way."

"You told that to the Jennings?"

"Yes, sir."

"That was on Sunday?"

"Yes, sir, and after that I told her about the hydro, and when we left there, we left with the impression we had told them they had hydro in the house and everything, and the best thing was to stay where they were. When we left them, we had the impression that they wasn't going to bother us anymore."

"But you did tell them if they squared up with Dr. Magee, they could move in?"

"I told them if they would give $75, if Dr. Magee was satisfied with the amount of money, then we would see them again and we would let them move in. But they said—she swore an oath and said, 'Where will we get $75?' And I said, 'That is the way the situation is. If you haven't got the money, you don't move in.' So the impression was left with us that night that they were going to stay where they were, and I told them that was the best thing to do."

"That was a Sunday, and the same Sunday night Billings and Blake went up and stayed there."

"Yes, sir."

"And on Sunday night they had guns with them?"

"Yes, sir."

"They were .22 rifles?"

"Yes, sir."

"On Monday, when did they go up again?"

"Well, it was quite late. We drove them there. It was quite late. We had had supper, and I would say it was after seven o'clock when we, when they went up there, and we met Doc Magee there, and he gave Jas or Stanley the key."

"Where did you meet?"

"Right along by the burying ground."

"What instructions were given to them on the Monday night?"

"Just gave them the key, and Doc Magee told them where to put the key if they happened to leave before he got back, or if something happened to leave the key under a plank."

"Did you drive up there?"

"Yes, sir."

"Who was with you?"

"My wife."

"What time did you leave them there?"

"Well, I would say when I left them, it was a very short distance from there to the corners, and I turned the lights on to go down the back road. So I would say it was something after eight o'clock, somewhere in there."

"Before you went out to the farm, did you go into Warkworth on your way out?"

"I don't know right offhand whether I did or didn't."

"I would like your best recollection of it, Mr. Sregor."

"I don't know whether I did or whether I didn't go into town."

"Did the boys take any food with them?" BJ Barry asked.

"Yes."

"When was that?"

"I think we went downtown, and Annie got some meat or stuff for them to take up, or some tea or something. I don't know."

"Was anything else obtained at that time?"

"I couldn't cover myself what I done at that time."

"Was anything else obtained at that time?"

"Not that I know of; I didn't see anything."

"Did you give either Billings or Blake any money at that time?"

"I don't know whether I did or not. I had given them money different times. I wouldn't commit myself whether I gave them money at that time or not, or if the wife gave them money."

"Do you know if either of them bought anything at that time?"

"I don't know; I wasn't with them. I don't know if they bought, or what they bought."

"Did you give them any instructions when you left them at the farm?"

"No. All I told them was the same as Doc Magee: hold the fort, and we would be out in the morning, pick them up, and come through and see Mr. Hurman to have them sued."

"You said to hold the fort?"

"Yes."

"What did you mean by that?"

"Well, stay in the house."

"That is what they were to do?"

"Yes. Doc Magee told them to hold the fort, and so I just used his words."

"Was that all you told them?"

"Yes, sir, that is all I remember."

"And then where did you go?"

"I got in the car and I went down to . . . I guess I told the boys I was going down to see if the other straw stack was drawn away, or if it was like the straw stack at the house. So I drove down to see the other straw stack, and the other piece of wheat was coming that we hadn't cut, and it was too dark to see much about the wheat. We turned the lights on in the field, and there was a bunch of cattle in the wheat we hadn't cut, and we went down to Mrs. McKibbon's and stopped there."

"How far would it be from Mrs. McKibbon's to where you looked at the wheat?"

"I would say it would be approximately . . . well, the wheat is on the way down to Mrs. McKibbon's."

"How far would it be?"

"It would be approximately a mile from concession to concession, I would say."

"From the wheat to Mrs. McKibbon's?"

"No, that is on the same farm where Mrs. McKibbon lives."

"And you had left Billings and Blake with the impression you were going down to look at the wheat?"

"Yes, sir."

"What time was it that you got to McKibbon's?"

"It was dark."

"Have you any idea of the time?"

"No. I would say maybe nine o'clock, maybe half past eight, maybe half past nine. I wouldn't say offhand."

"What was the first you knew of this matter?"

"We were sitting talking to Mrs. McKibbon, and a knock came to the door."

"Who was present with you when you were talking to Mrs. McKibbon?"

"My wife."

"Anybody else?"

"Just Mrs. McKibbon. A knock came to the door, and Mrs. McKibbon said, 'You go to the door.' I went to the door, and it was Stanley, and he said, 'Troy got it.' I said, 'Troy got it?' 'Yes,' he said. 'He went to take the gun from me, and in the commotion the gun went off and shot him in the stomach.' So I said, 'What?' By that time Annie was out there, and we told Mrs. McKibbon we had to go because there had been some trouble, and we left."

"Did Blake have anything with him?"

"Yes, he had the .22 with him."

"Who left the McKibbon farm?"

"I did, the wife, and Stanley."

"That is Blake?"

"Yes."

"And where did you go?"

"We left and went directly up to my brother Ted's place."

"Did you have any talk on the way up?"

"I don't think so. We moved along quite quickly, and I don't think we had anything to say—I didn't, anyway."

"You didn't say anything?"

"No, The wife asked Stanley if he had anything in the gun before we got in the car to take it out of the gun, and Stanley was very upset. He was just about—"

"And then you went back to the farm, did you?"

"Yes, sir," Seth replied.

"Who did you see there when you got there?"

"I seen Mr. and Mrs. Jennings, and it was dark. I couldn't see who was in the back of the car."

"Where did you stop the car when you got back?"

"I pulled it off to the side on the south side of the road, I think."

"And where were the Jennings?"

"They had their car—the garage is here, and they had their car at approximately two feet from the garage."

"Were they in the car or out of the car?" BJ Barry asked.

"I would say they were in the car when I went there, so the first I met was Jasper, and Jas said—"

"Jas who?"

"Billings. And he said, 'I think Troy is dead. This is awful.' So I went then, and Jennings got out and said, 'This is my place.' I said, 'Your place is on the road, and get there and get there awful fast, because you have caused enough trouble without sticking around here.' Jennings said this was their place—"

"Where was Blake at this time?"

"I don't know just where Blake was at that time, because it was very dark."

"What was he doing, do you know?"

"I couldn't see Blake until when we walked around in front of the lights."

"Did you see him in front of the lights?"

"Yes."

"What was he doing? Before the Jennings left, did he say anything or do anything that you saw?"

"No. He was shaking pretty much, and I think he said that he was going down to the barn to shoot himself, but the wife said that I am wrong, that he said he was going down to hide the gun. I asked him if he shot Troy intentionally, or if it was an accident. He said, 'Seth, I didn't mean to shoot your brother.' I said, 'If you didn't mean to shoot my brother, you have nothing to worry about, so don't run away. Keep your gun and come back up, and the police will be here. But if you did mean to shoot Troy, this is going to be too bad for you.' And he said, 'Seth, I didn't mean to shoot him.'"

"And where did you go?"

"I stayed there for a few minutes, and I heard noises in the house and said, 'He is not dead.' And maybe they have called a doctor and maybe they haven't, and maybe they have called the police and maybe they haven't. So I struck for Campbellford to see if I could get a doctor and the police awful fast."

"Did you go alone?"

"I went alone."

"And you left your wife and Blake at the farm?"

"Yes."

"And met Corporal Beattie on the way down?"

"Along this side of Hoss Edwards' I met Constable Beattie, and Dr. Burger was coming this way, and I knew Dr. Burger was the coroner."

"So what did you do?"

"I went over to Campbellford, and I got along by Meyersburg and ran out of gas."

"Did you continue on into Campbellford after you got some gas?"

"Yes, I went on to Campbellford, because I didn't have no money with me, and I got my car filled up at the gas station on my credit card."

"In Campbellford, did you see Dr. Magee?"

"I saw Dr. Magee and told him what happened."

"And did you go back to the farm?"

"Yes, sir, directly back to the farm."

"Between the time going to the farm from the McKibbon place and going to Campbellford, were you in the house at all?"

"No, sir. I was going to go in the house, and I heard noises in the house, and it seemed to be upstairs, it seemed to be in the kitchen part, and it seemed to be in the front room and all over the house. I said, 'That is him thrashing around in there trying to get up, and I am going to get him.' The wife said, 'No, don't go in because with what's happened around here tonight, you will be in bad trouble.'"

"Was there anybody else in the house you knew?"

"Not that I know of. The first I see go in the house and the first I see come out of the house was the police."

"The Jennings had left by this time?"

"Yes, sir; I told them to leave."

"How many cars were there when you got there?"

Seth replied, "One car."

"And how many persons were in the car when it left?"

"I couldn't see. I knew there was two and could have been three people. I think there was three. Liza Booker Duberg, but as to my seeing Liza, I couldn't swear to her in the backseat of the car."

"And you left your wife and Blake and Billings on the premises?"

"Yes, sir."

"And were there other people in the house?"

"I don't know, sir. I couldn't say; I wasn't in the house."

This concluded the examination-in-chief of Seth Sregor.

Eleven

After a short adjournment, Seth Sregor returned to the box with a stick in his hand. The people in the courtroom stared at Seth with shock and disbelief.

Justice Butler questioned Seth, "What is the purpose of the stick?"

Seth had a point to make. "This is the stick, Your Honour, on a Friday before the shooting took place that Mr. Henry Booker was going to use on me, and Stanley Blake I think will back up that Mr. Booker sat on a fence with this stick down like this, and when I came up, he pulled the stick up and said, 'Don't move any closer.'"

"Did you bring it with you?" asked Justice Butler.

"Yes, sir, and I picked up a couple of stones, and I told Mr. Booker to clear off the premises, which he did, and he pulled the stick up and hit Stanley on the boot or somewhere, and Stanley threw a stone through the fence, and this is the stick I picked up."

Ryder interrupted. "Is this the Crown's exhibit number five?"

Braden, the Crown Attorney, responded, "I have no knowledge of the exhibit."

"Perhaps in view of the fact that it was put in by the witness himself, we will mark it people's exhibit." As Ryder spoke, he looked at Braden and then back at Seth Sregor.

"Well, just set it down in the corner," Justice Butler said, pointing at the stick and then gesturing for Seth to put it over at the side.

Seth stepped out of the witness box and put the stick in the corner of the courthouse. He then returned to the box to continue his testimony. Ryder O'Neill, solicitor for the defendant Stanley Blake, cross-examined Seth.

Referring to Seth's statement about the stick, Ryder wanted to confirm to whom Seth was referring. "That was Mr. Henry Booker?"

"Yes, sir," replied Seth.

Ryder continued with the cross-examination. "This occasion you have just discussed occurred on the Friday before your brother was shot?"

"Yes, sir, I am sure of that. And on a Saturday night Stanley Blake went to town to get some tobacco, and he came home, and Mrs. Henry Lester was at the premises about around ten o'clock, somewhere as that way. And Stanley Blake came home, and I don't know what he came through—the screen door—but the next morning the screen door was in pieces, and he was very afraid and said, 'Those black buggers chased me home.' We went round the table twice, and Mrs. Lester, Jill Lester, and Laura Lester was there and stayed at our place till approximately twelve o'clock that night. I never let on I had seen Stanley, and Mrs. Lester drew my attention to Stanley being so scared and the way Stanley was acting."

"This was the Saturday before?"

"Yes."

"He came home afraid?"

"Yes."

"Were there any cross-pieces in?" asked Justice Butler.

"Yes," responded Seth.

"He had gone through that, too?"

"It was all tore to pieces, so I imagine he had gone through the screen door. I don't know if he bust it or not, but he had come in with the tobacco."

Ryder continued with the questioning. "How old was your brother Troy?"

"Well, he would be 30," said Seth.

"And was he something of your build?"

"Yes, very short and stout. He was, oh, I would say, about five feet six."

"How much did he weigh?"

"He would weigh around 200 pounds."

"Was he in good health?"

"Yes."

"Was he strong physically?"

"Very strong and stout."

"And what about his temper?"

"Oh, he had quite a temper. If it was somebody with—if a bunch was with him, he would show off quite a bit."

"Was he inclined to use violence at all?"

"Oh, yes, but not with me."

"With smaller people?"

"Yes. He was more or less afraid of me."

"But with smaller people I understand he would be violent?"

"Oh, yes."

"Were there ever any occasions in which he beat up on smaller people?"

"Just he had homeboys there, and I used to feel sorry for the homeboys. He would give them a flogging, and I have stuck up for them when I was round there. There were no hard feelings between Troy and I. I worked with him in the summer and gave him five loads of hay, and I lent him the truck, and the only time was when I felt I shouldn't give him the grain. I told him I shouldn't give him the grain, and he wasn't there to do me any good."

"Troy was aware of the making of this agreement, exhibit two, was he not? The agreement between you and Ted for the five-year lease?"

"Yes, Troy was at our place, and Annie read the lease to him, and I think the first day we read the lease to Troy, and the first we knew he said he bought it was in the spring, and he was sitting up on the fence at the Booker's house balling at Bookers because he said he had lost a sheep."

"Yes, well now, you had told the court earlier that Troy came to you one day and mentioned the Jennings' were coming, and you and Troy went to see them?"

"Yes, definitely," Seth said.

"And you took with you a copy of the agreement?"

"Yes."

"Was it a copy of . . . ?"

"That one."

"Exhibit one?"

"Yes."

"That is the one made on August 8?"

"Yes."

"So Troy knew of that agreement?"

"Annie read it to them."

"Now then, these rifles, they were around your house although they belonged to Ted?"

"Yes."

"And I suppose Jasper Billings and Stanley Blake used them from time to time?"

"Oh, I think so. They were out rabbit hunting at different times with them."

"Shooting at whatever young people shoot at with .22s?"

"Oh, sure."

"And shooting at targets?"

"Yes, they had targets around there, sure."

"It was quite a normal thing for them to take the rifles around with them?"

Seth explained, "They have them around with them. I have a name on the side of the truck, and they were trying to hit the "O" in "Sregor," and different things they had been shooting—oil drums and one thing and another."

"The Monday morning you shot at the stove, were they shooting at targets and things around the place?"

"I think so. I think Stanley shot at the stove, too."

"And an old pump there?"

"My brother gave that to me, a gas pump."

"There was a pump shot at?"

"That was the gas pump that was not used."

"And they shot at the shed, didn't they?"

"I don't think—I don't know if they shot at the shed that time. We didn't stay very long. I just thought—I had seen the .22s, and I wanted to see how good a shot I was, and so I shot at the reservoir on the old stove."

"Where is Ted now, by the way?"

"I do not know, Air."

"And Liza Duberg—you mentioned at the end of our evidence she is a sister of yours?"

"No, she would be a daughter, a sister of William Booker."

"Oh, yes, and the Booker's farm is right next to the Home farm you rented from Ted?"

"Kind of parallel with the home farm, one farm here and one here. I think they are both intended to be long hundreds and parts sold off—a hundred acres, we call them down there long hundreds and square hundreds."

"And the cattle that were in your grain on the Saturday night, I think it was the Saturday night—not the same night as the shooting, wasn't it—do you know whose cattle they were?"

"No, I didn't bother going to see, because I had 45 acres of grain, and before that I didn't collect $200 after paying the pasture, after ploughing it, and so on, and threshing. I didn't get $200 for 45 acres."

Ryder said, "Now, before I forget, in connection with this agreement, you said something about Mr. Hurman writing to Mr. Cosgrove?"

"Yes, sir."

"Was that the agreement, exhibit one?"

"Yes, sir."

"You gave that to Mr. Hurman so he could send a copy to Mr. Cosgrove?"

"Yes; he kept it the rest of the summer. It was with him all the time. I thought it was with him all last fall from the time we rented the place, but he said no, so I was mistaken."

"Did you notify the police of the cutting of the telephone wire and the stones through the windows, which occurred on the Saturday night before the shooting?"

"Dr. Magee did. I wasn't there, but that is what he told me, and he stated the police were up there on Monday afternoon."

"No doubt that will come out in their evidence. Now, when Stanley Blake came to Mrs. McKibbon's place after the shooting, what state was he in?"

"Oh, he was in a very—I never seen anybody in that kinds of state in my life."

"How would you describe it?"

"He was in a very . . ."

"What was he doing? Crying, or—"

"Oh, he was just trembling, shaking. He was in a very bad state of mind."

"Very nervous?"

"Oh, yes. I couldn't word just the way."

"Frightened?"

"Yes."

"And upset?"

"Oh, yes. He couldn't stand still, he was so scared, and said Booker was there after—"

"That was the Saturday night, was it?"

"Yes."

"I am thinking of the time after the shooting."

"Well, he was very scared, sure, and Annie talked to him more than I did because he called Annie 'Mother,' see."

"And he was very frightened that night?"

"Yes, very frightened. He was very frightened the night that he came home to our place—"

"I was asking about the time after the shooting, Mr. Sregor."

"Yes."

This concluded the cross-examination of Seth Sregor by Ryder O'Neill. Seth Sregor was then cross-examined by Leonard Karl.

Karl stated, "One or two things, Mr. Sregor. You told us about your brother's size. He weighed about 200 pounds?"

"Yes, sir," Seth responded.

"And you told us he was a strong man?"

"Yes."

"And you told us, too, something as to homeboys being on his farm?"

"Yes."

"Who are the homeboys?"

"Training school boys, I should say."

"And you told us you had occasion to intercede on his behalf because your brother was doing some flogging?"

"Yes, on the 45 acres. He had a training school lad there and was giving him a good beating, so I interceded there."

Leonard Karl said, "And throughout the period of time this sort of thing would be going on, the flogging of homeboys and your intercession on their behalf, was Billings working for you? Was Jasper Billings working for you during the time of these floggings?"

"Yes, I am sure that he was with me over the time I drew the hay off. He might not have been, but I think so, over the 45 acres when he beat up Teddy Brookes."

"I take it that the reputation of your brother would be something that is known in the community? And certainly known to your employee, Billings?"

"Yes."

"That your brother was a bully? Is that so?"

Seth replied, "Yes, that is true. After all, he is my brother, but blood is thicker than water."

"We are interested in fairness. I know your difficulty, him being your brother, but you have told us as well he had a temper?"

"We all have."

"All the Sregors have a quick temper?"

"Yes."

"They fly off quickly?"

"Yes."

"And that would include your brother Troy, would it not?"

"Yes."

"And when they fly off in a quick temper, I think it is also fair to say the Sregor clan sometimes resorts to violence pretty quickly? Is that not so?"

"Yes, sir."

"And that also would pertain to your brother Troy, would it not?"

"Yes."

"Now, your brother Troy knew of your lease from your brother Ted on this place?"

"Yes, sir."

"It had been read to him by your wife, Annie, I think you told us?"

"Yes."

"And you told us she went over to the Jennings', who were prospective tenants at some time?"

"That is correct."

"And in his presence it was explained that you were the owner, and you were the person who had the right to rent the place?"

"And Troy told the Jennings' that."

"So it would be clear from that, as you saw it that night at least, that Troy understood you were the person with the right to rent that place?"

"He told the Jennings' that," Seth said.

"So he knew it, and we are speaking now of the place where Troy was shot?"

"Yes, sir."

"So unless Troy asked your permission, so far as you know and so far as he was concerned on the night of the shooting, he would be a trespasser on that place?"

"At the time of the threshing he was there, and I told him I didn't figure he was there to do me any good, and I asked him to stay away."

"It was clear that he knew he had no right to be there?"

"Yes, and he knew I had put 'No Trespassing' signs on the house."

"Speaking of that, I am showing you a photograph. Have you ever seen that before?"

"Yes; I nailed that on the house."

"You are speaking of what you see in the photograph."

"Yes, sir."

"What is it, a sign?"

"Yes."

"What does it say?"

"'No trespassing.'"

"It says here, 'No firing, hunting, or trespassing. By order.' Is that right?"

"I signed that, and there is one in the car, too, that goes along with that."

"Is that a photograph you took yourself?"

"Yes, I put that on. That is no steel on the door, and that is before Dr. Magee rented the place."

"That is the picture you have told us about before?"

"Yes."

"And you told Mr. Barry you also took a picture showing your brother Ted outside the house with some cattle?"

"After I took the cattle, I put one on there and it was took off, and I signed both of them and I put one on the garage. I can show you nails pulled out and the nails on the side of the house—I have never been any closer to the side of the house than the driveway since Troy was killed."

"You are speaking of three signs?"

"Yes. One this side of the house, and one on the porch, and one on the garage."

"Four no trespassing signs?"

"Yes."

"And they were all torn down?"

"Yes, sir."

"And that was prior to the shooting?"

"Before the shooting—about June, I would say. I gave you a picture."

"Just to complete these pictures, is this other picture I am showing to you the picture you told Mr. Barry about, of your brother Ted?"

"Yes. My brother Ted took the one picture with him, so I got two pictures for that."

"Brother Ted didn't take the picture of brother Ted. Who took the picture you have in your left hand, of a man with some cows?"

"I took both the pictures."

Justice Butler was a little confused. "He took it with him? He didn't hold the camera?"

"No, he took the picture after it was developed, and I gave Mr. O'Neill the picture in his office," Seth replied.

Leonard Karl listened and then asked, "Could we identify them, sir?"

"And the steel down from the wood shed, two sheets of steel. Dr. Magee got some made; there was no steel on the door." Seth had been responding when Justice Butler interrupted.

"Just a second, I think they would be exhibits five and six."

Leonard continued questioning Seth. "Dealing with Mr. and Mrs. Jennings, you told us of a conversation with them very shortly before the shooting, with regard to them getting the place, when Troy was there?"

"Yes, sir."

"And you told my friend you left with the definite impression they were not going into the place? Was that the impression they left with you?"

"Yes, sir."

"Was that because of something they said to you?"

"Yes, sir. I told them they might better stop where they were, and I wasn't going to put electricity in somebody else's house."

"And you told them they would have to raise $75?"

"I think it was 72 or 75 dollars, one or the other."

"And they indicated to you they couldn't raise $75?"

"Yes, sir."

"And they left you with the definite impression they weren't going to move in?"

"Yes."

"But in fact, you did see them there shortly after the shooting?"

"Yes, with their car right up the corner of the entry, about two feet from the garage."

"And at that time it was pitch black, was it not?"

"Yes, sir, a very dark night."

"And it had been dark for some considerable time?"

"I would say it was quite dark when we left there—left the boys at the house."

"And that is before the shooting. When you left there, it was quite dark?"

"Yes, sir."

"And how was this place lit? You have told us there was no hydro?"

"Just a little lamp in the corner, just a little old lamp."

"Coal oil lamp?"

"A coal oil lamp."

"Now, sir, are there any places very close to this residence where the shooting took place?"

"Well, no, not right close. Maybe 500 feet away, maybe farther; I don't know."

"Five hundred feet. I want you to consider how long 500 feet is. I put it to you, first of all, going south, you go down a hill and up another hill before—"

"I would say that would be a good half mile."

"And the Booker's house would be, I would suggest, a quarter of a mile from that over a hill, as the crow flies?"

"Yes."

"Which direction is that?" questioned the Judge.

Mr. Karl chimed in. "In the northeast direction?"

"Yes," Seth replied

"And this place is on a hill where the shooting took place?"

"Yes."

"And as you go up the hill to the north, there is a house on the corner?"

"Yes, sir."

Karl said, "And I put it to you that would be considerable more than 500 feet. I would suggest about a thousand yards, at least?"

"It could be; I am not very well up on the measurements. It could be a thousand or two thousand."

"Were someone to be shooting at that place on the outside in the fields, if there was shooting going on, those shots could be heard at the Booker's place?"

"Oh, definitely, sir."

"If somebody was doing some shooting or yelling inside that house, those people would have no hope of being heard from any neighbour?"

"Oh, no."

"You agree with that?" asked Justice Butler.

"Yes, I would say no neighbour would hear any hollering," replied Seth.

Leonard Karl continued with his questioning. "Or any cries for help?"

"No."

"Now, sir, my understanding is these boys had some rifles with them on the Sunday as well as the Monday. I am speaking now of the Monday, the day of the shooting, and the previous day. They had the rifles there the day before?"

"I think they were down through the fields hunting."

"My understanding is on the Sunday they were down through the fields that day?"

"I don't know that; I won't say."

"But you do know there would be the sound of rifle shots on that property on the Monday, because they were there then and saw that shooting?"

"Yes."

"And this was harmless shooting, as one would expect from youngsters shooting at the old stove?"

"Yes."

"And pigeons?"

"Mostly pigeons on the barn. They have shot pigeons off the barn, and Ted, when he was there, used to shoot at old pails and stuff like that."

"It was the usual shooting that one gets from young people in the country?"

"Yes. The only gun I ever had was the old 10-gauge shotgun, but I couldn't hit nothing with a .22."

"The reason why the boys went there, you told us—the only thing told to them by you, as I understand it—was to go there and find out who was causing the trouble?"

"Yes, that is what we put the boys there for, to see who was doing the trouble."

"Because Mr. Hurman had told you, or some solicitor had told you, it was important to find out who was causing all this trouble around the farm?"

"That is right."

"Would that be with reference to somebody cutting the telephone wires?"

"No. That happened on a Sunday night, as Troy would be shot on a Monday sometime."

"Was it Sunday night the telephone wire was cut?"

"That is what Dr. Magee said. Well, he said Saturday night or early Sunday morning."

"The periods the boys were there was just to find out who was causing trouble?"

"Yes, sir."

"Did you give them any instructions to shoot anybody?"

"Not as I know of."

"You would know?"

"Yes, sir."

"Did you tell them to shoot anybody?"

"No, sir."

"Was anything said about using rifles on anybody?"

"No."

"And the only purpose was to find out who was causing the trouble?"

"That is right."

"All right, sir. Have you found out since who threw the stones that broke the windows there?"

"I have not, sir."

"Have you found out since who cut the telephone wires at this place?"

"No, I don't know."

"Have you found out since who stole the hay out of the barns?"

"No, sir, I don't know. There was a load of straw off the stack back of the house, north of the house, along the road. There was a load of straw and right off the top of the stack, and the rain comes in, and practically soused the rest of the stack."

"You have told us there was some question as to who properly had title and right of possession to this house. I understand you did consult a solicitor after these troubles broke out?"

"Yes, sir."

"And after your consultations with the solicitor concerning these matters, I put it to you it was still your view that you still had the right of possession of this place?"

"Oh, yes. I have had a letter. This is it, Mr. Hurman."

"That is all right; I don't want it. Thank you very much."

"There is a road that runs past this house?" asked Justice Butler.

"Yes," replied Seth.

The discussion continued between Seth and Justice Butler. Justice Butler put his pen to his chin and looked down at his desk. He was thinking and trying to visualize all the locations in his head. Then he turned to Seth as he sat in the witness stand. "And the Bookers live north of this house on the same road, Seth?"

Seth began using the ledge of the witness stand to give Justice Butler a visual idea of where everyone was located. He started pointing. "The road would be here, and you go up this corner and down here, Your Worship, and the Bookers would be down there."

The Justice leaned over to Seth's imaginary map on the ledge and pointed. "They live down there?"

"Yes."

"And it is this—"

Seth pulled a pen and piece of paper out of his pocket. He decided to draw out what he had been talking about to make it easier for Justice Butler to understand. He continued outlining, "And this road here is where you come down here to the other farm."

Justice Butler held out his hand for the hard copy of the map that Seth had now created. Holding it up so that Seth could see it, he motioned his pen as he spoke. "If you went from this house to Mrs. McKibbon's, how would you go?"

Seth leaned over and pointed with his pen. "You would go into town and back up again by Bookers, or back up this old side road."

"Which old side road?"

Seth gestured. "This old side road down past—"

"As a matter of fact, you went down the side road that night?"

"Yes."

"You didn't go past the Bookers'?"

"No, I went down the side road, and therefore the Bookers—"

"They didn't know you had been up there?"

"No."

"And you didn't turn your lights on until you got to the corner?"

"No."

"And the whole purpose was so the Bookers didn't know anybody had been there?"

"No, the Bookers when I went on by—"

"You just said you didn't go by the Bookers?"

"When I took the boys by Bookers."

"You didn't go back by Bookers?"

"I went down to see Mrs. McKibbon, and that goes straight through, and then you go across the fields and down to Mrs. McKibbon's house."

"But you came up this side road before you turned your lights on, after you left the house?"

"Yes. It was dark down the side road, and the Bookers or anybody could see the lights."

"You told Mr. Karl it was dark when you left the house?"

"Yes."

"Why didn't you turn the lights on?"

"When you come down there, this old roadway is covered with trees and bushes."

"That would be the normal way you go to get to Mrs. McKibbon's?"

"Yes. I have gone by the stack on down to Mrs. McKibbon's, and on up the road there and out to Warkworth and home."

"Why did you go to Mrs. McKibbon's this night?"

"After the stack had been molested at the other place, both places—"

"I don't want to get into all that, but it was dark when you left the house. When did you go to look at the stack?"

"I went down with my lights on the stack, which was in the field, and I went down to Mrs. McKibbon's and across the field."

"This stack was at the other place?"

"There are two, one on each place."

"One where you left the boys?"

"Where I left the boys."

"Is that the stack you looked at?"

"Yes. And then I went down to the Cassidy place, where the big stack was, to see if I could see if it."

"And is that on the way down to Mrs. McKibbon's?"

"Yes."

"Well, why bother going to see her?"

"Just to stop in and say goodnight and see how she was feeling, because she is an old lady. I was interested in my stacks, and the—"

"It wasn't that you wanted an alibi for where you were?"

"No. I didn't know anything of the kind what was going on, and I was very much surprised. I was never so much surprised in my life."

"This stove you took is a stove you found in there before Dr. Magee moved in?"

"Yes, sir."

"That was sometime in July or June?"

"It could have been May, could have been June."

"And you moved it out?"

"Yes, sir, I and my brother Ted moved it out. I left it there for a while until I seen my brother Ted, and I asked him if he put the stove there, because if he wanted it, it was okay."

"When was that?"

"Before Dr. Magee moved there—could have been June or July, I wouldn't say."

"You said you moved it out on a Monday morning in August?"

Ryder O'Neill interjected. "No, he didn't. I felt sure you were confused about that. He said a Monday morning in August that he shot at it. He didn't say it was the Monday morning he moved it out."

"I don't know what day I moved it out," Seth said. "The stove was out there for a month, anyways, before we shot at it. My brother Ted helped me move the stove out. I thought Ted set the stove in there, and I wouldn't put the stove out until I had seen Ted, and he said it didn't belong to him. So we went down and got a brand-new lock and put it on the door, and we locked the house up, and—"

"Were Billings and Blake with you the morning you put the stove out?" Justice Butler asked, trying to understand.

"I wouldn't say; I couldn't be sure. Could have been Jasper, or could have been Stanley. I don't know."

Something didn't seem right to Justice Butler. "Blake couldn't have been there, because he didn't come till August?"

"I didn't say that. There could have been Jasper, or some of my boys with me. I wouldn't commit myself to say who. All I know my brother Ted was." Seth was stern.

This concluded the cross-examination of Seth Sregor by Leonard Karl. Seth Sregor was then cross-examined by Ryder O'Neill.

Ryder O'Neill approached the bench where Seth sat, and he was scratching his head in confusion. "I think you are mistaken that Blake came first. When did Blake come to stay with you?"

"He had just been there maybe two or three weeks."

"When did he come to work on the pea-viner?"

"Well, the wife has the time down, and I couldn't tell you, because I don't—"

"My understanding was you said it was in July?" Ryder O'Neill said.

"And the peas would be ready then."

"Then he didn't come in August, he came in July?"

"He helped to do the threshing."

Justice Butler was also confused. "Blake was the one who said that he came in August."

Ryder answered, "He said he came in July."

"He helped to do the threshing." Seth was not good at remembering months; he was a farmer, and he went with the weather and the seasons. His wife was the one that was good with the attention to detail.

Leonard Karl was looking at his notes on the desk. With his finger pointed at the spot in which he found the answer in his notes, and with his reading glasses on the tip of his nose, he looked up. "Stanley Blake came to work on the pea-viner in July of this year".

Justice Butler acknowledged Leonard Karl. "Yes."

This concluded the cross-examination of Seth Sregor. Seth Sregor was then re-examined by BJ Barry, to follow up on some answers to previous questions regarding the route that he and his wife, Annie, had taken.

Again clarification was being sought as to the path taken on the night of Troy Sregor's murder. Seth could not help but think they were beating a dead cat—he had already answered these questions—but he continued to answer the questions as BJ Barry questioned him yet again.

"Mr. Sregor, in order to come from Ted Sregor's farm, which was rented to the McKibbon place by the route you followed, did you pass Sid Hartman's place?"

"Yes."

"Right past it?"

"Sid Hartman's is this side of the road, and you go—" He was interrupted again. No wonder they kept asking the same questions again and again; they were not even letting him finish a thought.

"And the Hartman house is the nearest house to this particular place?"

"I would say so."

"And does he have a phone?" BJ Barry asked.

"I don't know. I guess likely he has a phone."

"Do you have a phone at your house?"

"Yes."

This concluded the re-examination of Seth Sregor.

Twelve

It appeared the lawyers were trying to have their clients' charges dismissed based on reasonable doubt. It was as though their objective was to show that someone other than the boys had motive, or that they had in fact acted on behalf of Seth Sregor in carrying out the murder of Troy Sregor. When Dr. Whitman was examined, the cause of Troy's death added more confusion and opportunity for reasonable doubt concerning the boys' role in his murder.

Dr. Ashton Michael Whitman was the coroner. He was in his mid 60s, and he was a tall man with salt-and-pepper hair. His green eyes were hazy from the years of examining dead bodies. He had a three-piece, dark-gray suit on, and his pocket watch chain dangled from his vest pocket. He wore a white shirt with a bow tie. He had started wearing bow ties early in his career because he found regular ties would interfere with his examinations of a body if called directly to the scene. Dr. Whitman now strolled up to the bench, was sworn in, and was examined by BJ Barry.

"Doctor, you are a legally qualified medical practitioner, and you practise at the City of Peterborough?"

"That is correct."

"And you're also a specialist in pathology, as I understand?"

"That is correct."

"On the 28th of August of this year, did you make a post-mortem examination of the body of Troy Sregor at Roberts' Funeral Home, in the Village of Warkworth?"

"I did."

"And it is my understanding the body was identified to you by Corporal Beattie of the Provincial Police?" BJ Barry asked.

"Yes, sir."

"And what did you find as a result of your examination?"

"He had died of a bullet wound that had entered the left side of the back, passed through the left lung, through the lower part of the heart—"

"It had entered the back where, doctor?"

"Four and three-quarter inches from the middle line." Dr. Whitman was referring to his waist area.

"Four and three-quarter inches to the left of the middle line?"

"Yes, and 10.5 inches below the level of the top of the shoulder, and it was at the level of the eighth thoracic vertebra."

"From that point of entry, in which direction did the bullet go?"

"The track went downward, forward, and to the right."

"Doctor, from the track followed by the bullet, are you able to say anything, about the position? If you assume the bullet was fired from a rifle, are you able to say anything about the position of the rifle relative to the body of the man at the time the shot entered?"

"If the man was standing upright, it would have to be shot—"

"It would have to be in a position higher than he was, I take it?"

"Yes."

"And pointed somewhat to his right?"

"Downward and to the right."

"And if he was standing upright, in whatever position he was in, it would have to be higher than he was?"

"Yes," Doctor Whitman replied.

"And you say that bullet had done what damage?"

"It had passed through the lung, causing considerable damage to the lung on that side, and also tore both ventricles of the heart."

"And having regard to the nature of the wound found, how long would you suppose a man would live after having received such a wound?"

"No longer than a matter of minutes, very few minutes."

"And with such a wound, would he be likely to move around, or not likely to move around?"

"I think it would be unlikely he would move."

"Is it possible the he could, however?"

"Certainly not very far."

"If he moved at all?" BJ Barry confirmed.

"If he moved at all."

"I take it from your evidence the more likely thing would be, he would collapse and stay there?"

"That would be my opinion."

"Then did you find any other wound?"

"Yes, there was another wound on the front of the abdomen."

"At what height, Doctor? I am sorry—let me go back to this other wound for the moment. I take it that the puncture wound you found was an entry wound, Doctor?"

"Yes."

"There was no exit wound with relation to the bullet you found in the back?"

"No."

"Did you recover that projectile?"

"Yes."

"Where?"

"Under the skin on the right side of the upper abdomen."

"What was done with that?"

"I gave it to Corporal Beattie."

"And then you say you found another wound, and where was that one?"

"In the lower abdomen. It was a transverse wound—that is, horizontal. It wasn't exactly horizontal, but in relation to the vertical axis of the man, it was approximately half an inch higher at the entry wound than the exit wound."

"In other words, the shot was going somewhat down?"

"Slightly."

"And the entry wound was on what side of the body?" BJ Barry asked.

"On the left."

"And had entered on the left in what position? At what point in the abdomen?"

"I have a full description of that. Three and a quarter inches to the left of the midline, and in order to get line marks, we took four inches to the left of the umbilicus in the line of the spine and pelvis, which is a stationary line mark we took in order to fix a point—"

"And where was the exit wound?"

"The exit wound was to the right of the midline one and a half inches, and that was three inches from the umbilicus."

"How far underneath the surface of the skin was the path of travel?"

"It was just under the skin."

"What was the distance separating the entrance wound and the exit wound?"

"It would be four and three-quarters inches," Doctor Whitman replied.

"Such a wound would not be fatal, I take it?"

"No."

"Would it be painful?"

"Yes."

"Did you find anything else in your examination that is of moment in this matter, Doctor?"

"Apart from the hemorrhage. which was caused from the first bullet wound described."

"And that hemorrhage was where?"

"Mostly in the left chest. There was also some in the right."

The first shot had been at the front on the left side, and Troy would have been able to survive this wound, had it been the only one. The fatal shot entered the back on Troy's left side, and the Doctor testified that this bullet had actually come from a higher angle; the shooter would have to be pointing downward and to the right. Dr. Whitman was stating that one bullet entered the front, and the other bullet entered from the back. This concluded the examination-in-chief of Dr. Whitman. Dr. Whitman was then cross-examined by Ryder O'Neill.

Ryder was looking at his notes and looked up and approached the witness stand. "Doctor, I believe you also found a small bruise on the right upper eyelid?"

"Yes."

"Now, would it be possible, with this second wound you have described, that it was one in which the bullet entered from the right side and came out the left?"

"We did not think so, sir. The wound on the left was a round—we call it puncture wound—whereas the one on the right was a ragged hole."

"This was more of a creasing wound?"

"It wasn't creasing, it was beneath the skin."

"But not very much? Entered at a very sharp angle to the body, to the skin, that is?"

"It went from across just beneath the skin."

"And was at an angle considerably away from the normal—quite sharp angle at which it entered to the skin and which it left?"

"I don't know what you mean."

"It didn't go in at right angles; it came in one side at a sharp angle to the surface of the skin. Couldn't it have entered from the right and out of the left side?"

"From what I know of bullet wounds, sir, it could not."

"And the reason for that is you compared the wound you described as the wound of entry with the other wound, which you described as the wound of entry with the other wound, which you described as the wound of exit?"

"That is right."

"That is the only way in which you have of telling?"

"Yes."

"This man seemed to be a man in the prime of life; that is to say, it seemed to have been?"

"He was a well-built man."

"And you would say he wasn't very old?"

"In his 30s."

"And physically strong?" Ryder O'Neill asked.

"Yes."

"And capable of considerable feats of strength and so on, as far as you could see?"

"He was a fairly muscular man."

"I understand he weighed about 190 pounds?"

"That is our estimate."

"You didn't weigh him?"

"No; we had no way of weighing him."

"But you measured the height?"

"We did."

"Five foot six and a half?"

"Yes."

"Now, then, this wound in the back. If the bullets were fired from a rifle that was held by someone standing on the floor, standing on the floor on which the deceased man was standing, it would suggest that the man was leaning forward toward the muzzle of the rifle, well forward?"

"That would be, yes."

"As if he might have been forward, like this, well down?"

"My opinion from the way the wound was, the direction of the wound, is he was probably leaning forward."

"Quite far forward?"

"Yes."

"Now, then, with regard to where his body would come to rest when he fell, a good deal would depend on whether he was in motion, and in what direction he was in motion at the time he was shot."

"I would think so."

"The theory that he would collapse where he was standing would depend more or less on the assumption that he was standing still, would it not?"

"You mean if he just collapsed?"

"Yes. If he had been engaged in any form of motion with any velocity that would continue to be imparted to his body, and might carry him into the position not quite what my friend has described of immediate collapse."

"If he was in motion when he was hit, he would carry on further a certain distance."

"Is there any way in which you can tell from the position of the body what type of activity the person was engaged in at the time he was shot, whether he was at rest or in motion?"

"No," Whitman replied.

"You can't tell? That is all, thank you."

This concluded the cross-examination of Dr. Whitman by Ryder O'Neill, and then Leonard Karl cross-examined Dr. Whitman.

"Can you tell me what a petechial hemorrhage is?" Karl asked.

Dr. Whitman looked at Leonard Karl and responded, "A very small one."

"Did you find any small hemorrhage on the upper thorax, shoulders, and neck of this body?"

"Yes, there were."

"Could you tell us what you saw there? What did you actually see?"

"The skin was dark, what we call cyanosis, and there were these tiny, pinhead-sized hemorrhages over the upper chest and shoulders and the neck."

"Now, would that be—what things could cause the condition which you have described?"

"Lack of oxygen in the tissues."

"Which isn't traumatic in origin, then?"

"No."

"And I believe you have found hemorrhage and mucous in the nose and mouth again?"

"Yes," Doctor Whitman said.

"And what would cause that?"

"The wound in the lung."

"Did you examine to see if there was any traumatic cause for that hemorrhage in that area? That is, traumatic in that place? In other words, was he hit in the nose?"

"There were no marks on the outside, sir. I didn't examine inside the nose."

"But hematoma was present on the right upper eyelid?"

"Very small, a small bruise there."

"How big was it?"

"I haven't got the measurements of that, sir, but I remember it was very small."

"Would you assist me what you mean by 'very small'?"

"Probably less than a quarter of an inch in diameter. Just a small, bluish bruise mark."

"That would be something that would be from a blow that was traumatic in origin?"

"Probably traumatic in origin."

"Did you find the body? Where was the body when you first saw it?"

"In the funeral home."

"Did you see any marks on the body that would indicate the body fell on its face?"

"Yes. Well, I should not say that—there was indication the body had been lying on its face."

"What indication did you have that led you to that conclusion?"

"There was some post-mortem staining on the front of the body as well as on the back. It was on its back when I saw it, and when a body is lying in any position, the blood tends to settle to that side."

"So this would just be a matter of gravity, and not by reason of striking the floor?"

"A matter of gravity," Doctor Whitman confirmed.

"And the only thing you found traumatic in origin, apart from the gunshot wounds, would be this bruising of the right upper eyelid?"

"That is correct."

"One other thing, Doctor. The body had apparently two gunshot wounds?"

"Yes."

"One entering the back, and one passing through the forepart and abdomen?" Leonard Karl said.

"Yes."

"I put it to you the abdomen wound was what one would term a superficial wound?"

"Yes, it was."

"And the penetration limited to the fleshy part of the abdomen?"

"Yes."

"And this would be painful in the sense—well, how painful would it be?"

"I would estimate it would be quite painful."

"But although it would be painful, that would be something that would not incapacitate a person like an inner wound, and he would still keep going?"

"Yes."

"For a person in a rage and moving at the time, that wound would have no effect in stopping him, but it might enrage him further?"

"That is right."

This concluded the cross-examination of Dr. Whitman by Leonard Karl. Dr. Whitman was then re-examined by BJ Barry.

As Leonard Karl returned to his seat, BJ got up and walked toward Dr. Whitman. "I take it your opinion is that the wound in the back was when the man was leaning quite sharply forward, or have I stated that properly? What is your opinion in that again?"

"This is only an opinion, in trying to visualize how that wound would occur, unless the gun was fired from above, unless he was leaning well back or forward."

"If it was well forward, would he have to be leaning toward the gun or away from it?"

"You mean leaning somewhat toward it?"

"The bullet, as I understand your evidence, ranged upward?"

Ryder interrupted, "No, downward."

"Downward and forward," responded Dr. Whitman.

BJ Barry continued, "I see. You say he would be leaning slightly toward it? He would be at an angle to it?"

Dr. Whitman responded as he nodded his head. "He would be at an angle to it."

"I see."

Justice Butler interrupted the cross-examination. "Well, did the bullet enter at the back or the front?"

Dr. Whitman had now turned his head to look at Justice Butler. "Back."

"So the rifle would have to be above him if he were bending forward?"

"Yes, depending on if he was leaning over, and how far."

"Well, let us go one step further. If he was wrestling to get the rifle away from a person, is that compatible with your idea of the position the rifle was in? Could he have been wrestling with a rifle, and the bullet could enter where it did?"

"He would have to be holding the rifle back here."

"Above his shoulder?"

"To be wrestling."

"And where two bullets actually entered his body, it could have been the same one?"

"No, they were entirely separate."

This concluded the re-examination of Dr. Whitman, and Dr. Whitman was again cross-examined by Ryder O'Neill.

Ryder placed his hand on the ledge of the witness stand. "Arising out of your questions, I would like to ask the Doctor a question. If we could hypothesise two people engaged in struggling for a rifle, one man holding the rifle, as the one who would be the holder of the rifle, and the other one perhaps grasping the muzzle, and both pulling and then coming apart because the man's grip came off the muzzle, the other man, the deceased person, could both go downward and perhaps the deceased person leaning forward like this, and the other man going back? Could the round have been fired in that way?"

"He would have to fall back so his back was presented at a lower level than the muzzle of the rifle."

"If he had leaned forward and went back in this fashion?"

"He would have to go down."

"The rifle would—"

"The rifle would still be pointing down."

"But that could have happened?"

"I don't know. I can say that it could, but I think it would be difficult."

"But it could have happened?"

"If you were pulling back, you would tend to fall back."

"Suppose the man who was falling back fell back toward the wall?"

"He would tend to straighten up downward."

"But the rifle might be discharged sometime in the operation. I don't mean the deceased. My suggestion is the deceased might have been trying to take the rifle away from somebody else. The other man may have been holding the rifle as one would hold a weapon, and the deceased might have had hold of the muzzle and pulling away from each other. The deceased might have been pulled well forward, might have let go, and at that moment the rifle might have discharged, and the bullet in that way would go in over the back of the deceased, and enter as you have indicated it did."

"I think you would have to fall forward to get a wound at the angle it was."

"All you have to say is he was in a certain position?"

"I can't even say he was in a certain position."

"But he was in a certain position with relation to the line of the bullet?"

"With relation to the line of fire."

"I suggest that the sequence of events I have outlined is a possible one."

"Could you tell from the path of the bullet whether he was standing erect or bent over, or is it not possible to tell?" inquired Justice Butler.

"No, I don't believe I can," responded Dr. Whitman.

Ryder O'Neill continued. "It might have struck an obstruction in there, which diverted its course?"

"Well, actually the bullet was deflected slightly from its original course. The first few inches were further down to the right, but it deflected from the upper edge of the ribs so it came a little forward and further up than the original would have."

"So you couldn't tell if the man was standing upright or bent over?"

"No."

This concluded the cross-examination of Dr. Whitman. Ryder O'Neill was convinced that his theory was the right one, regardless of what the Doctor said. He had clearly stated, "I suggest that the sequence of events I have outlined is a possible one." But from what Dr. Whitman was suggesting, the first gunshot wound occurred as a result of Troy trying to take the gun from Stanley, and in the struggle, the gun accidentally went off, causing a flesh wound. This would not have killed him; the bullet entering his back was the one that ended his life. There was no questioning or discussion regarding the setup of the room, or where people were standing. As one entered the summer kitchen from the side of the house, to the left of the entranceway was a stairway. Stanley's back had been to the wall on the right, which meant he was facing the stairway, which in turn meant that Troy's back was to the stairway.

When Seth had arrived at the scene, he testified earlier that, "No, sir. I was going to go in the house, and I heard noises in the house, and it seemed to be upstairs." However, there was no questioning or investigation as to whether or not there could be another person standing on the stairway. Jasper had followed in behind the Jennings, so it would be hard for him to have been able to get to the stairwell and fire the shot without someone noticing. Something didn't make sense; there were a lot of pieces to this puzzle missing.

Thirteen

The next witness to be called to the stand was Mrs. Annie Sregor, the wife of Seth Sregor. Annie proceeded to the witness box and took a seat. She was wearing a light pink dress with black shoes and a low heel. Annie held her small purse in her calloused hands. She was a beautiful woman, but one could tell from her hands she was a hard worker. Annie was sworn in, and BJ Barry began the examination.

"Mrs. Sregor, you are the wife of Seth Sregor?"

"That is right."

"And I wonder if you would be good enough to look at the documents, exhibits one, two, and four in this matter, and tell Justice Butler whether those documents were written by you?"

"This exhibit four, that one is, and two and one."

"They were all written by you, Mrs. Sregor?"

"Yes."

"Now, then, on the 27th of August of this year, did you go to what is known and has been referred to as the Ted Sregor farm?"

"Yes, sir."

"What time did you go there, Mrs. Sregor?"

"Well, I wouldn't want to say for sure the exact time, but somewhere between seven and eight at night."

"And in order to go by road from your home to Ted Sregor's farm, do you pass through the Village of Warkworth?"

"Just the outskirts."

"Who went with you from your home to the Ted Sregor farm?"

"Seth and Jasper Billings and Stanley Blake."

"And on the journey from your home to Ted Sregor's farm, did you go into Warkworth for any purpose?"

"Not that I remember."

"Did you buy anything on the way to the Ted Sregor's farm?"

"I don't remember if I did or not."

"Did anybody in the car buy anything?"

"I am not sure whether we went into town that night or not. I am not sure."

"Do you remember seeing your husband give either Billings or Blake any money that night?"

"That was on Monday night?"

"That was Monday the 27th."

"I have—I couldn't say if he gave them any money or not."

"Did you give them any money?"

"I gave Jasper money later that night."

"That is Billings?" BJ Barry clarified.

"Yes."

"When was that?"

"After he was put under arrest."

"Now, when you left the farm to go up to Ted Sregor's place, did either of the two accused men have anything with them? I am referring specifically to firearms."

"Yes, I believe the two .22s were in the car."

"When were they put in the car, Mrs. Sregor?"

"I don't know."

"Were they in the car when you saw them?"

"I know they had them when we got up to the place."

"What .22s were they?"

"Just two .22 guns."

"Who owned them?"

"Well, as far as I know, I believe Ted owned the guns."

"Where were they usually kept?"

"Well, sometimes they were—we have a couple of guns in the house around, but they were never kept out in the kitchen part; we kept them in the front parlour and sometimes out in the barn."

"Where were these two particular guns kept?"

"Oh, I don't know. I just remember exactly where they were kept at the time."

"You want us to understand you to say that you don't know where these guns were kept?"

"I wouldn't want to say for positive truth the exact spot where they were."

"Were they in the house?"

"Well, I think . . . yes, they would be in the house."

"And did you all leave the house together on this day?"

"What do you mean, all of us?"

"You and Seth and Billings and Blake?"

"Yes, we went up together in the car," Annie confirmed.

"Did you leave the house to get into the car together?"

"Well, it is kind of hard for me to say if we went all out of the house together or not."

"Was anything said about the rifles?"

"I heard one of the boys saying—I don't know if both asked, Jasper asked, or one of them—if they could take up their .22s."

"Who did they ask?"

"They asked Seth."

"And what did he say?"

"Well, I couldn't—I wouldn't want to say definite what he did really say."

"I would like your best recollection of, as closely as you can remember."

"As near as I know, he said he didn't care."

"And how was the question put by the boys? Was it said, *could* they take them up, or *should* they take them up?"

"I wouldn't say. I don't know."

"In any event, on the way up did you meet anybody?"

"We met Simon Magee."

"And what happened when you met him?"

"Well, he was supposed to have gone over a little bit earlier that night than we did, but on account of the threshing, we were later going, and we met him at the top of the hill. He gave Jasper and Stanley the key to his house to go in."

"Was anything said at that time?"

"He just said to them, 'Hold the fort until I get back,' or something like that, and he told them where to put the key if they should leave before he came back."

"When you left home to go to the Ted Sregor's place, were you intending to go any other place after you had finished there?"

"Well, we went down through this way; we called it the old back road."

"Were you intending to go there when you left home?"

"I don't know actually whether we were or not, but we just went down through this back road to see if the straw stack had been molested."

"You left the boys, Billings and Blake, at the house, did you?"

"That is right."

"About what time would that be?"

"I don't know what time, but I know it was about dark, because when we started down through the roadway, Seth turned the light on the car."

"You drove from Ted Sregor's house up the old roadway without any lights on the car?"

"That is right."

"Did you or Seth Sregor go in the house before you left?"

"In Ted Sregor's house?"

"Yes."

"We were both in the house, I believe, that night."

"Was there any conversation between Billings and Blake and your husband or yourself before you left?"

"Oh, we were just talking. There was no particular conversation, not that I recall."

"Did your husband give either of them any instructions as to what they were to do?"

"What the boys were to do?"

"That is right."

"No, not that I know of," Annie said.

"Was anything said at all along those lines?"

"Oh, I wouldn't say so. We were just talking."

"And you left, and where did you go?"

"We went down through this back road, to Mrs. McKibbon's."

"When did you decide to go down there?"

"Well, I really can't say whether we had decided to go down before or not, and the straw stack at Ted Sregor's farm had some straw taken off. We thought we had better go down the back road and see if the other stack had been molested."

"When did you first know any straw had been taken off the stack at Ted Sregor's place?"

"I believe it was on the Sunday."

"It was the day before, was it?"

"I think so."

"You went down to Mrs. McKibbon's, did you?"

"That is right."

"Is there a phone down there?" BJ Barry asked.

"No."

"She has no telephone?"

"No."

"How long were you at McKibbon's?"

"It is hard to say how long we were there, because I never looked at my watch when we went there."

"Have you any idea how long you were there?"

"Well, we wasn't there too awfully long."

"Then what happened?"

"A rap came at the door, and Mrs. McKibbon asked Seth if he would go to the door and see who it was."

"And who was it?"

"It was Stanley Blake, and Seth said, 'I guess the boys were having some trouble, and I guess we had better go.'"

"Was anything else said at that time?"

"Well, I don't actually remember all that was said, because I was just—"

"What did Blake say when he came in?"

"He didn't go in the house; he was at the door."

"And your husband was talking to him there?"

"Well, it was just at the door."

"And you didn't hear the conversation between your husband and Blake?"

"Well, I don't know if there was any conversation, actually, because I know Seth said the boys were having trouble, and he would have to go."

"And what did you do?"

"We just got in the car and went."

"Went where?"

"Back up to Ted Sregor's farm."

"And in the car on the way down, was there any conversation?"

"No. I told Stanley if his gun was loaded to unload it, but I don't know whether there were any shells in the gun or not."

"Anything else?"

"Oh, I don't really recall, actually."

"I want you to recall, Mrs. Sregor. I want you to recall now, and not sometime later."

"On the way up to the house?"

"That is right."

"I don't remember if there was anything said in the car. We were only a few minutes going up."

"You have no recollection of anything being said?"

"No."

"What did you find when you got to Ted Sregor's place?"

"Jasper Billings was standing in the driveway, and Mr. and Mrs. Jennings and Liza Duberg were there. Mr. and Mrs. Jennings, I believe, were both in the car, and Liza was standing beside the car. Their car was right in front of the garage doors. Well, I don't know really who spoke first, but Seth told the Jennings they had better leave, and Mrs. Jennings said, 'What do you mean? This is my home.' Seth said, 'It doesn't matter whose home it is right now, but I think you had better leave.' So he started round behind the back of the car, and Mr. Jennings went to say something—I did not hear what it was—and Mrs. Jennings called him, and he got in the car and went away."

"While your husband and Mr. and Mrs. Jennings were talking, where was Blake?"

"Well, he was either in the—I wouldn't say if he was in the backseat of the car, or if he got out and standing beside me."

"Did he have the rifle in his hand?"

"He carried the rifle; I think I told him to keep it until the police came."

"If he was beside the car, he had the rifle in his hand?"

"Yes."

"Did he do anything with the rifle when he was out behind the car, when all the talk with Jennings was going on?"

"No," Annie said.

"Did he say anything?"

"No, Stanley never said anything at all, until after the Jennings left."

"And then what did he say?"

"Well, first as the Jennings were leaving, and Jasper said to Seth, 'This is awful, I think Troy is dead.' Seth said, 'He can't be dead, because listen to the noise in the house.' Seth wanted to go in, and I wouldn't let him because after the gang that had been there that night and all the trouble before, he had better stay outside the house."

"Did Blake say anything at that time?"

"No, I don't recall him saying anything right then."

"When you went up to the house, did you know Troy had been shot?"

"Yes."

"When did you learn that, Mrs. Sregor? The first intimation you have mentioned is just now, when Jasper Billings said he was dead. When did you learn Troy was shot?"

"Well, as I came out of the house at Mrs. McKibbon's, Stanley was saying something to Seth that—Stanley Blake was saying something to Seth about 'Tick has got it.'"

"Who is 'Tick?'"

"A nickname for Troy. He said, 'Tick got it,' or something to that effect; I wouldn't say the exact words used. It was then that he was telling us—no, on the way up. Well, I don't know, it all happened so quickly, but it was either right there or on the way up that Stanley said that Troy went to take his gun away from him and the gun went off. After the Jennings left, then Jasper told me that these seven people came and forced their way in and went to take his gun away, and then they grabbed for Stanley's gun—Troy grabbed for Stanley's gun."

"When you got there, did Billings have a rifle?"

"No."

"Where was it, then?"

"I don't know."

"Did you go in the house?"

"No."

"Did you stay outside?"

"No."

"When did you go in the house?"

"I haven't been in."

"Were you there when the police came?"

"Yes, sir."

"And the Doctor?"

"Yes, sir," Annie repeated.

"Who was with you?"

"Jasper and Stanley were with me."

"Did Stanley still have the gun when the police officers got there?"

"Yes, sir."

"What happened to it?"

"Mr. Beattie was the one that took it from Stanley."

"Was that the same rifle, so far as you know, as the one he had when he came to McKibbon's?"

"Oh, yes."

This concluded the examination-in-chief of Mrs. Annie Sregor. Then Leonard Karl began to cross-examine Annie.

"Just a couple of brief questions, Mrs. Sregor, dealing with Jasper Billings. How old a boy is he?"

"I'm not exactly sure. I believe he is 22 or 23 last July."

"And he lived with you for how long?"

"Well, it is going on five years."

"In that time you would get to know a person fairly well."

"I have."

"I put it to you: from your knowledge of this boy, he is of a very peaceful nature?"

"Yes, very quiet."

"Not the type of fellow to go round picking fights?"

"Oh, no, not during the time he has been at our place."

"And as to Troy Sregor, would Billings have any reason in the world that you know of to purposely go out and shoot Troy Sregor?"

"No, none at all."

"Or take part in any affray in which he might be shot?"

"No."

"And you got to the scene where the shooting had taken place that night, and he was still there?"

"Yes."

"Making no effort to get away?" Leonard Karl implied.

"No."

"And he told you that people had forced their way into the place."

"That is right."

"Did he tell you who those people were?"

"Yes, he did."

"Who were they?"

"Mr. and Mrs. Jennings, Liza Duberg, Henry Booker, William Booker, and Virginia Booker, and Troy."

"And even after the shooting, I take it from what you told my friend that the Jennings were still insisting they had the right to be there?"

"That is right."

Mr. and Mrs. Jennings were the proposed tenants to whom Virginia Booker had promised the lease of the farm. Liza and Joe Duberg were the sister and brother-in-law of Willy Booker, and Henry was his father. This concluded the cross-examination of Mrs. Annie Sregor by Leonard Karl.

Ryder O'Neill continued with a cross-examination. He approached the bench where Annie was sitting. "Mrs. Sregor, what state of mind was Stanley Blake in when he came to the McKibbon household after the shooting?"

"Well, he just—in plain words, I would say he was scared almost to death."

"But he told a story, I take it, that gave you to understand that Troy Sregor had been shot?"

"Yes."

"And then somewhere on the way, either then or in the car, he told you Troy had tried to take his rifle from him. and the rifle had gone off?"

"Yes, sir."

"And that was how Troy had been shot?" Ryder O'Neill asked.

"Yes, sir."

"And what state of mind was he in after he got up to the Ted Sregor's house?"

"Well, I talked to him and told him—that is, after Seth left, he seemed to be very nervous and afraid the Bookers would come. After the police cruiser came in, and the Doctor and they went in the house, it was chilly, and we were walking back and forth in the driveway. Henry Booker and William Booker and Joe Duberg walked in behind the cruiser, and he was frightened because the Bookers had come, and I told him he didn't need to worry because the police were here, and the Bookers wouldn't bother him."

It seemed odd that Joe Duberg was there because he had not come in the car of seven. There did not appear to be a car around that he had travelled in, yet nobody questioned how or why Joe Duberg was there. Joe Duberg was a tall, balding man with piercing blue eyes. He was very muscular and could be quite intimidating just from his appearance alone.

Ryder O'Neill continued. "Were you at home on the Saturday night before the shooting, when Stanley Blake came in?"

"No, I was downtown getting groceries."

"Did you see him after this incident?"

"Well, Sunday morning he told me that Marty Morgan and William Booker and Virginia had chased him home from town."

"And what attitude did he have then toward the Bookers?"

"He seemed to be afraid to meet them."

"Now, had you been at home on the previous Sunday, when Dr. Magee had come to report incidents at Ted Sregor's house?"

"Yes, I was."

"And did you hear a conversation in which Stanley Blake took part then about his going over to the house?"

"Well, Simon had told us about the telephone wire being cut, and the stones being thrown through the window very early Sunday morning. And he had to come away, and he wanted to know if the boys could or would go over and stay in the house while he was away."

"Did the boys receive any instructions about what they were to do?"

"No, only just to watch and see who was bothering the place."

"Did they receive any instructions on the following night or the following day about what they should do on Monday night?"

"Well, the purpose they stayed there was to stay in the house to see who came, if anyone else came back to do anything."

"Did they receive any instructions at all on either day about the use of firearms?"

"Not that I heard, no," Annie replied.

"Now, I presume that you have become aware and have become to some extent involved, from time to time, in this series of incidents in which the Bookers have done things on this farm?"

"That is right."

"Were you present when any of these incidents occurred?"

"Just on the Friday before Troy was killed, Simon came to our house and told me the Bookers were up there ploughing, and there had been a car around. He said, 'I just don't feel safe with them around there, because I have to go to Campbellford.' I said, 'Seth has gone to town, and I will go up and tell them.' So Seth and I went up, and we ordered them out, and they wouldn't go. Both of them raised the ploughs on the tractor, and Virginia came within two inches of hitting me with the plough, and I told her I wouldn't move."

"You mean she backed this tractor at you and gave you to fear she was trying to hit you with it?"

"That is right."

"Trying to run over you with it?"

"That is right, and then I was—I went up the next morning again, and they were ploughing in the other field."

"Virginia Booker and William Booker?"

"That is right, with two tractors."

"Well, did you see an incident involving your husband and Henry Booker?"

"No; I went just after that, because the truck had come to load grain, and I went up to see how long they would be."

"Now, you have identified exhibit one as a document you prepared. Did you ever read this over to Troy Sregor?"

"I did, sir."

"Under what circumstances?"

"I couldn't actually tell you the day, but we were driving down the back roadway to see if the young cattle were still on the pasture. Troy was sitting up on the line fence between that place and the Bookers', and he told us that he was watching the Bookers, and we started talking about our agreement. I said, 'I have our agreement with me today, Troy, and I will read it to you,' because Troy didn't read, and I took out the agreement and read it to him."

"Were you present on an occasion when your husband and Troy went to see Mr. and Mrs. Jennings?"

"Yes, I was."

"Was a copy of the agreement taken at that time?"

"I am not sure whether it was the original agreement or if it was a copy. I kept a copy of that because I had given them to Mr. Hurman a couple of times, so I wrote a copy for to have myself, and I am not sure whether it was the original or copy that I showed Mr. and Mrs. Jennings."

"Did you read it to them?"

"They read it themselves."

"And Troy was present?"

"Yes, he was the one that took us there, because I didn't know there were such people as the Jennings at Norham at that time."

"Was there any conversation in Troy's presence at that time about who was entitled to rent the place?" Ryder O'Neill asked.

"That is why he really came to our place that night, because he was sowing grain, and Mr. Jennings had stopped and talked to him. Apparently he had known the Jennings before, and he said Mr. Jennings had told him he had rented Ted's place from Virginia Booker. Troy told him he couldn't rent that from her because we had it, and he got us to go over that night to show him the agreement to prove that Virginia couldn't rent him the house."

"In that connection, on the Sunday before the shooting, did you go with your husband to see Mr. and Mrs. Jennings?"

"That is right."

"You had a discussion with them then about their renting the place?"

"Yes."

"And your husband explained he wasn't going to put in hydro?"

"Oh, yes, we told them the first time off we couldn't. They couldn't rent it from Virginia, and they said would we, and they had electric appliances in the house. Seth said we weren't in possession, and there would be no hydro. 'I am only renting the place,' he said, and they said Virginia had told them there was soft and hard water in the house. and Seth told them there could be, but there wasn't at the time, because there was no sink or pumps in or eavestroughs in the house. She wanted to know if they rented it from us, would we put it on, and Seth said no."

"On this Sunday before the shooting, did you have any discussion or come to any understanding with the Jennings about their renting the place?"

"Well, we were there and discussed the matter over, but when I left, I had the particular feeling they didn't want the house at all."

"What gave you that?"

"Seth told them in order for them to rent the house, they would have to pay back rent and expenses it had cost Simon in moving."

"Did he state an amount?"

"I believe it was either $62 or $72 or $75, right in there some place. They said they couldn't pay that, that is definite, and they said they just had a monthly cheque and could only pay their rent by the month. When we left, Mrs. Jennings said, 'We will have to see our landlord and stay on there.'"

Ryder O'Neill said, "Now, these two rifles, you say they were kept somewhere around the house or in the barn from time to time?"

"That is right."

"And I presume Jasper and Stanley used them from time to time?"

"Oh, yes. Well, before Stanley came, Jasper often took one the .22s and went hunting with it."

"Did Stanley go out with him?"

"Yes, I believe he did after he came."

"Did you keep a record of dates on which various incidents occurred?"

"Yes."

"Have you got it here?"

"Yes, in this book. I have a lot of things wrote down in the book."

"When did you make the various entries?"

"At the time they happened."

"Have you any record of an occasion in the fall of 1955, when the Bookers pastured cattle on the fall wheat Seth had sown on one of these farms?"

"I haven't that date here with me. The reason why I didn't write that date down is we got Mr. Hurman to write them a letter about it."

"I see. And have you a date of an incident in the Spring, when cattle were found in the barn?"

"Well, I don't know what day they were put in the barn, but it was Troy who told us they were in the barn."

"When was that, do you know?"

"That was . . . well, it was either the last few days of—"

"Your book doesn't show?"

"Not the exact date, but the cattle were put in either the last few days of April or the first few days of May. We went to Detroit and were in Detroit the 3rd or 4th of May, and Troy told us the day before we went."

"What entry do you have in that book indicating incidents?"

"Well, it was on May 13 that Seth took the cattle out of the stable and took them down to the Bookers, and on June 17 they took our cattle from pasture and drove them over home."

"You saw them do that, did you?"

"Yes, sir, I saw them when they got home. I didn't see them at the pasture."

"What took place at your home that day?"

"June 17?"

"Yes."

"Well, there were six or seven of them, I believe, seven or eight of them came over, and Seth was quite angry with them because they had molested our cattle."

"Did he do anything?"

"He was quite sore at them, and after they left we put the cattle in the barnyard, and they drove them along the road and left them."

"Did he doing anything about that?"

"No, he just talked—he didn't hit them."

"That was the 17th of June?"

"That is right."

"And what next?"

"June 24 the lock was broken off the house, and the 'No Trespassing' signs were torn down."

"When was the old stove put out outside?"

"Well, I think that stove was put outside when Dr. Magee moved in the house."

"All right, and the next entry?"

"July 13 we rented the house to Simon Magee."

"And at that time the stove would be put out?"

"Yes, and I haven't the date down because I didn't—Simon didn't tell me the exact date that he saw Willy and Virginia Booker coming out of one of the cornfields."

"Subject to that objection, how much is actual information of this witness and what has been told her by her husband and Simon Magee, or from any other sources?" asked BJ Barry.

"There has been a lot of hearsay so far, a great deal led by the Crown as well," added Leonard Karl.

Ryder O'Neill continued. "Well, this incident is one reported to you. You didn't take part in it?"

"No."

"Is there any entry of any incident which you recorded from your own knowledge?"

"Well, it was on August 18 that we saw Troy ploughing in some of the fields on the Cassidy farm."

"You saw that yourself?"

"Yes, and it was August 24 that Seth went up and told Virginia and Willy to get out when they tried to run me over with the tractor."

"On the 24th, right. That was the Friday?"

"That is right."

"And the next time you had anything to do with it was when? Monday?"

"Well, I was there on Saturday, but I didn't see anything that happened there."

"Did you notice that there was straw taken?"

"Yes."

"On Saturday?"

"No, I didn't notice straw taken on the Saturday."

"Did you notice that afterward?"

"I don't know whether I noticed it Sunday night or Monday night. I know I did Monday night, but don't know if I did before that or not."

"Were you there at any time when wheat was discovered with the bands cut?"

"No; that was the day they threshed, and I wasn't up for threshing."

"Did you see any damage done to your husband's implements?"

"Yes."

"What did you see?"

"Well, some pieces of the plough and some parts of the seed drill that I saw."

"Have you any personal knowledge about Troy's temper?"

"Well—"

"Not what you heard, but what you know yourself."

"No. Troy stayed at our place since we have been married, and Troy, Ted, and James, and Seth too, all have very quick tempers."

"They all have quite a temper?"

"Yes, I have had experience right when they were staying at our place."

"Just one question," said Justice Butler. "Where does Mrs. McKibbon live, on a farm or in the Village of Warkworth?"

Annie explained, "Ted's farm consists of two together on this, that Cassidy farm and the Old Home farm."

"Was this a house on a farm?"

"Yes, on one of the farms we had rented."

Ryder O'Neill rejoined the conversation. "How far is it from the road?"

"The house is just a few feet, you might say, from one road. We went down through the back road so we could go by the straw stack and across the fields to her house."

"Where did you leave the car when you stopped?" O'Neill asked.

"We drove the car all the way through."

"When you go to Mrs. McKibbon's?"

"In front of the house," Annie said.

"If you were going from your farm to this farm, would you pass by her house?"

"No."

"You wouldn't?"

"No."

"Well, Dr. Magee is not Simon Magee is he?"

"Yes."

"He is one and the same person?"

"Yes, the veterinarian."

"Why did he rent the house? Because he wanted to be there, or because you wanted him there?"

"Well, really, he had always liked the place, and he asked us about renting it."

"He wanted a place to stay?"

"He has a home in Campbellford, but living beside the water doesn't agree with him too well."

"He has asthma?"

"Yes, and we let him have the house cheap. We didn't charge him much rent on it, and we paid up the rent on the telephone in the house, so if any other things happened he could call Central and let us know about it."

"What relation is he to you?"

"Brother-in-law—well, Seth's brother-in-law."

"He married Seth's sister?"

"That is right."

"Where was he on the Sunday night?"

"Well, he sort of—on the Sunday night when he got the boys to stay in the house?"

"Yes."

"He was over to his own house. He has a service in his own house in Campbellford, and he was going over to this."

"He stayed at the farm in the daytime and at his own house at night?"

"Not all the time. Well, Sunday was the night they have, where everybody gathers in the front part of the house."

"Is it a religious meeting?"

"Yes."

"And that is why he was going home Monday night?"

"Sunday night."

"Why did he go Monday night?"

"He wasn't actually going to his own home. He was out on a professional call to Meyersburg or some place, and then he went to a book study at Trent River. When he came back to Campbellford, he was supposed to be at the Chinaman's and then come to our house after. Seth told him what happened, and he wanted to come to the house, and I advised him not to come to the house tonight but go back to Campbellford."

"When had you made arrangements with him about the boys staying on Monday night? When did you make that arrangement?"

"On Monday."

"When? During the day?"

"Yes, because he had brought the boys over—we went to Cobourg Monday morning, to see if Mr. Hurman had come in yet."

"Who do you mean 'we'?"

"Seth and I."

"The doctor didn't go?"

"No, because Mr. Beattie told us on Friday he would try to go to Cobourg on Monday to make some arrangements to keep the Bookers away from the place."

"Dr. Magee came to you sometime Monday and wanted you to have the boys there that night?"

"We were at his place, too, and we got the boys and took them over, and I got Simon some groceries."

"Got Simon some groceries?"

"Yes."

"When was that?"

"Monday forenoon. We took the boys' clobber and out to our place at noon. and then they threshed that afternoon."

"Did you go over with Seth when he went to get the boys at noon, or what was the situation?"

"When we came back from Cobourg, we went over to Mr. Beattie's because we didn't see him in Cobourg and didn't see Mr. Hurman until Tuesday morning, so we went back up to get the boys and tell Simon."

"They had stayed there all night and till noon, when you came back from Cobourg?"

"Yes, and told Simon we couldn't see Mr. Hurman until the next morning."

"What happened when you got to the house to get the boys?"

"At noon on Monday?"

"Yes?"

"Oh, I don't know as anything happened. We just talked away there and took the boys home to do the threshing."

"Did they take their guns with them, or what did they do?"

"Yes, I think they did take their guns back with them."

"Was any use made of the guns there that morning while you were at the house?"

"Well, Seth went over to get the boys earlier in the morning before we went to Cobourg to get their breakfast, because Simon wasn't there."

"So you don't know what happened when he went over that morning? You didn't go with him?"

"No."

"When you left the boys on Monday night, did you tell them where you were going or what you were doing?"

"We told them we were going down the back road way to Mrs. McKibbon's, to see if the straw stack had been molested."

"Just to stop—"

"To drive right by it."

"Did you tell them you were going to see Mrs. McKibbon?"

"Yes, we told them we were going down that way, and I never go in the yard without stopping in because she is an old lady, and I always stopped when I was there."

"What time was it Blake came to the door?"

"I couldn't really say what time exactly it was, but I know it was dark. We had the lamp lit in the house."

"You didn't tell Blake or Billings how long you were going to be there?"

"No."

"So far as you know, you were just going down the back road to see the straw stack and say hello to Mrs. McKibbon and go home?"

"As far as I know."

"Well, why did he go down that way?"

"Stanley? I don't know."

"Neither do I."

"We told him we were going down by the straw stack."

"And as far as he knew, you were stopping momentarily and going home?"

"Actually, we weren't there very long before Stanley came."

"Is it further than to your place?"

"Oh, yes, because we went down to see the straw stack, and that is the way we had to go."

"Were you surprised when he came in looking for you?"

"I certainly was."

"Rather than go home?"

"I asked him, and he said, 'I thought you might still be here, and I could phone you.'"

"Somebody said Mrs. McKibbon didn't have a phone?"

"She didn't."

"But apparently he didn't know it?"

"Apparently."

This concluded the cross-examination of Mrs. Annie Sregor by Ryder O'Neill. BJ Barry continued to re-examine Annie.

BJ Barry was walking back and forth in front of the Justice and witness stand. He stopped and looked at Annie. "Have you told us everything that is of importance about what occurred on the 24th, the Friday? Is there anything more you want to tell us about the 24th?"

Annie held her book of notes in her lap with her hands clutching the sides. "Well, on the Friday before that—well, when Seth and I went up to tell Virginia and Willy to get off the place and stay away, they just laughed at us and Virginia tried to run over me with the tractor, and then she set the dog on me. I told her not to do that if she wanted to keep the dog, because the dog wouldn't live very long. I don't know if it was before that or after that, or right at that time, that Seth took the shotgun. They were up the other end of the field, and he shot one shot in the air."

"Did you see the shot hit the ground?"

"No."

"You didn't see that, you say?"

"No."

"When you arrived at the house after the shooting and Blake was there, Blake didn't do anything unusual except seem excited?"

"Well, he wanted to take the gun to the barn and hide it, and I told him no, there wasn't any point in hiding the gun."

Ryder O'Neill wanted to confirm. "Are you speaking about Blake or Billings?"

Justice Butler knew the answer. "Blake."

Annie looked at BJ Barry. "I told him there wasn't any point in hiding the gun, but keep it till the police came."

"Did he threaten to do anything else?" asked Ryder O'Neill.

"No," responded Annie.

This concluded the re-examination of Mrs. Annie Sregor. Annie then proceeded out of the courtroom to where her husband was waiting. The preliminary hearing was closed, and only those testifying at the time were allowed to be present. Seth took Annie's hand and said, "Come on, Mother, let's go home for supper."

Fourteen

Mr. and Mrs. Michael Jennings were the proposed tenants that Virginia had promised could rent the premises come that September. Michael Jennings took the stand first and was sworn in and examined by BJ Barry.

"Mr. Jennings, where do you live, please?" asked BJ Barry.

"I live in Crammahe Township."

"And do you know Seth Sregor?"

"I do."

"And did you have any conversation with Seth Sregor with relation to renting a house?"

"He was up to my place on the Sunday before the accident, Sunday night."

"The Sunday before the accident?" interrupted Ryder O'Neill.

BJ Barry continued, "Then what do you say now? He came to your house and said what?"

Michael looked back and forth between the two lawyers. "He wanted us to give him $72, $60 for the guy and give the guy back his rent, $12, and I told him if that was the case, he could keep his house. He told me, 'Then you had better come up and see Doc Magee.' And that is why we were up Monday night."

"To see Doc Magee?"

"And talk it over with him."

"Before that occasion of the 26th, did you ever discuss this house with Seth Sregor?"

"Oh, quite a while ago, before."

"How long before, Mr. Jennings?"

"Oh, it was . . . I think it was around April, if I am not mistaken."

"You had another conversation then?"

"Seth, Troy, and Mrs. Sregor—that is Seth's wife—came up to my place and were talking about the house then. He told me he would give it to me for ten dollars a month. I couldn't move out then because I couldn't get out, and I had to give my own landlord notice, anyway."

"Before that, before Seth came up on that occasion, had you been in discussion with Mrs. Booker about the house?"

"Yes."

"You did discuss with her about it, too, did you?"

"Yes."

"And on the 26th, he came down to your place, and you had a conversation which ended with him saying, 'You had better come up and talk to Doc Magee about it'?"

"That was the night before the shooting."

"And did you go up to talk to Dr. Magee?"

"We went up Monday night."

"What were you intending to talk about?"

"To see if we'd have to give Seth $72 to move out or what he wanted. We couldn't afford to pay $72, or even $52."

Michael Jennings was then cross-examined by Ryder O'Neill.

"Who was the first one in the door?" asked O'Neill.

"Well, I think, if I am not mistaken, I think Virginia was the first one in the door."

"Did she push past the two young men?"

"Just by, not the two of them. Blake backed into the house himself, but the other fellow stayed out on the stoop, and they went by him."

"And Blake then went in the house, followed by Virginia. Who was next then?"

"Well, Virginia and the Booker girl and her husband, and I just can't tell you where old Mr. Booker came in, but Troy was next to them, and then my wife and then me."

"What about Mrs. Duberg, the other Booker girl?"

"She went in with Virginia and her husband."

"William Booker is the husband of Virginia?" O'Neill asked.

"Yes, a young fellow."

"And the father's name is Henry Booker, or do you know?"

"I don't know what none of their first names are."

"Now, you say you and your wife stayed for a minute or two, or a short time, talking to Jasper Billings, the older boy?"

"Yes."

"On the stoop after the others had gone in?"

"Yes."

"And nothing that you think of any importance happened inside until after you went in?"

"I couldn't see nothing that happened," Michael Jennings said.

"Were there lights in the house?"

"I can't remember. I don't remember any lights."

"Wasn't it dark enough that lights were necessary?"

"I don't think lights would be necessary. There was a blanket on the floor, I know that."

"What do you suppose that was for?"

"I guess they were going to sleep on it; that is all I know."

"When you went in, you were looking straight ahead of you, and Virginia was over toward the far wall? We can take it you were going in from the south, and Virginia would be toward the north wall?"

"Yes."

"Or was she out toward the middle of the floor?"

"In a line right across the room, in the middle."

"Where was Mr. Booker's daughter?"

"She was just next to young Booker."

"Where was he?"

"Next to Virginia."

"Virginia, her husband, Mr. Booker's daughter?"

"And Troy and the wife and I. That places him where he was."

"Then Troy and your wife and yourself and Billings?"

"He was . . . he stood outside before the shooting started."

"You mean he wasn't inside at all?"

"Not until the shooting started, and then he stepped inside the door."

"Was Mr. Booker Senior in the room at the time of the shooting?"

"Which one?"

"The father?"

"That is what I say: I can't place where he was."

"Everybody was inside except Jasper Billings?"

"That is right."

"And Troy was standing next to your wife, and on the other side of Troy would be Mr. Booker's daughter?"

"Daughter, and his son and daughter-in-law."

"And Blake then was standing up. He would be to your right, would he?"

"Troy was on our left, and Troy would be—"

"Were you standing facing toward Blake?"

"That is right."

"When you went in the door, did you turn to the right?"

"Right."

"And Blake would be over toward the east?"

"That side, yes, that is the right."

"You told us about these two shots."

"Yes, they come so quick," Jennings said.

"Just bang-bang, like that?"

"Just like an automatic."

"Not even a second interval?"

"You couldn't count them, they came so quick."

"And Troy fell right on the floor?"

"Just turned halfway and fell and moaned about three times."

"He didn't move again after he fell?"

"No, never moved."

"Blake ran into the other room?"

"Yes, after Troy fell Blake went into the dining room."

"Think of where Troy was lying after Blake went away."

"I know: right square in the middle of the floor, with his feet down toward the wall."

"That would be the east wall?"

"The wall where Blake was. His feet were down that way, and his head toward the dining room."

"His feet were very close to that wall?"

"About three feet from the wall, if I am not mistaken."

"Did anybody move Troy?"

"Not while I was there. The doctor came and examined him."

"And you are sure you have given an accurate history of what happened?"

"As near as possible."

"If it turns out, for example, that other witnesses say Troy stayed in the car while you went to the house . . . ?"

"He wasn't in the car, no. I told you the truth. If he stayed in the car, I don't believe there would have been any shooting."

"I agree. As a matter of fact, you called this an accident when you first gave your evidence?"

"An awful accident."

This concluded the examination of Michael Jennings by Ryder O'Neill.

Michael Jennings was then cross-examined by Leonard Karl. Leonard began questioning Michael. "And you say Sregor was standing still when he was shot?"

"Right."

"And two shots, bang-bang?"

"Yes, yes, just like an automatic."

"Have you heard an automatic, sir?"

"Yes, sir, shot them."

"You have been in the Army?"

"Just about 13 years."

"Would it be as fast as a Bren gun?"

"I never shot a Bren gun."

"Try a Lewis gun. As fast as a Lewis gun?"

"Not quite so fast. Them Lewis guns can shoot pretty fast, you know."

"And Sregor was facing him at this time?"

"Yes."

"And there were two shots?"

"Two shots."

"And after that he spun around and fell down?"

"Turned half around and fell down."

"After he was shot?"

"Yes."

"After both of the shots?"

"There wasn't another shot fired after he fell."

"He was standing facing Blake—two shots almost as fast as a Lewis gun, and then he turned round and fell?"

"Turned half round and fell, and moaned about three times."

This concluded the cross-examination of Michael Jennings by Leonard Karl. Michael Jennings had watched the gun closely; he was in the Army and was familiar with guns. He stated it was either a .22 rifle or a pump gun. A pump-action rifle is when the handgrip can be pumped back and forth in order to eject a round and to fill the chamber with a new bullet, and it does not require that the trigger hand be removed from the trigger to reload. The .22 rifle has a low recoil and lower power. Were one of these the guns that killed Troy Sregor?

—⁂—

As Malorie reviewed this part of the transcript, something didn't make sense to her. How could the shots be one after another, so close that they almost seemed like one as Michael Jennings had said, yet one entered the front and one the back? Was it possible there were two guns that went off at the same time? Jasper Billings was not in the room at the time, and his gun was not fired. Was there a third gun? Michael Jennings did not mention about a struggle in his testimony, yet others had said there was a struggle and the gun had gone off by accident. The evidence being presented wasn't matching up. Her grandfather Seth had stated in his testimony that he heard someone upstairs.

—⁂—

Stanley Blake had always wanted a family, especially a father. He had always vowed that if he had a father, he would do anything for his father. When Stanley worked with Seth, Seth had noticed that sometimes he seemed a little off. Seth had not known him for a long time, but he had noticed that when Stanley was with his boys Ken, Gary, Harry, and Rick, and Seth was present, Stanley was always competing for Seth's attention. If Seth was talking to one of his sons, Stanley would try to do something to get his attention.

Stanley also had a way of misunderstanding what Seth would say. Stanley could not tell the difference between serious statements and joking. One day, when they were sitting and having dinner, Seth had commented on his daughter Georgie's new boyfriend. He had told Georgie if he caught them kissing, he would shoot the pellet gun in his butt. They had all laughed at the time, because they knew Seth's bark was worse than his bite, and he was very protective of his children, especially his oldest daughter Georgie. But that night when Georgie's boyfriend had brought her home, as he gave her a kiss goodnight, Georgie let out a scream. Seth had fallen asleep in the chair in just his overalls. He had taken off his shirt and loosened the straps. When he heard the scream, he jumped out of his chair, pulled up his bib overalls, and ran to the door where Georgie was. Stanley was holding a pellet gun aimed at Georgie's date's butt. "What the heck do you think you are doing Stanley?" bellowed Seth.

Stanley replied, "Just doing what you told me to do. I thought it would make you happy."

"Well, it doesn't make me happy at all—quite the opposite. Are you nuts? Give me that gun and go to bed." Seth was shocked but didn't think any more of that. He just thought he was being protective or maybe even jealous of Georgie; Seth had noticed the way he had looked at her. That was not unusual, though; Georgie was the most beautiful girl in the world as far as Seth was concerned, and most definitely the most beautiful girl in Warkworth. Men, young and old, got whiplash walking past her. Throughout the trial, Seth had thought about this moment over and over again, and he wondered if it had been a sign. Should he have known better and phrased his words more carefully? How would he ever have known that when he said, "Hold down the fort," they would think they were on a battlefield? It was a saying, just a saying.

Maybe he should have kicked Stanley out then, but in his heart of hearts he didn't really think that Stanley was capable of hurting anybody intentionally. He did wonder if Stanley's mental frame of mind had led him to believe doing such a thing would make Seth happy, but how had Stanley not known that regardless of differences, family was the most important thing to Seth?

Fifteen

Mrs. Grace Jennings approached the stand and was sworn in. The examination began by BJ Barry.

"On August 27, what happened, Mrs. Jennings?" Barry asked.

"We were just finished up supper and watching television at the same time, and up comes Virginia Booker, her husband, and Troy Sregor, wanting to know if we wanted to go down to the house, but Dad said he didn't want to go, and I said, 'We don't get out, let's take a spin. We only want to see Doc Magee anyway.'"

"Did Mrs. Booker or her husband or Troy Sregor say why they wanted to go to the house?"

"No, they didn't."

"They just said they wanted to go there?"

"Wanted to know if I wanted to go there."

"Did they say for what purpose?"

"Not at all; that is what got me."

"And you said you wanted to see Doc Magee?"

"I said, 'We have to see him anyways and might as well go now.'"

"Where did you go?"

"Through Warkworth. We stopped at Booker's place outside, and they all got in our car."

"Who all got in your car?"

"Well, I am so mixed up I don't know half their names, to tell you the truth. Virginia Booker, her husband Mr. Booker, and his daughter—"

"Were either Mr. Booker Senior or his other daughter known to you before this occasion?"

"No, and I didn't even know Virginia was a Sregor until later on."

"Was Troy Sregor known to you?"

"Yes. Well, we got in touch with him because we needed a gander," Mrs. Jennings said.

"You had a previous business arrangement with him?"

"Only once."

"But you didn't know him?"

"No."

"And where did you go from the Bookers?" BJ Barry asked.

"Up to the Bookers, and we stopped outside."

"You drove up to the house and stopped, did you?"

"Yes."

"Will you look at the photograph, exhibit number seven, please, Mrs. Jennings, and indicate on that photograph where your car was stopped?"

"Yes, right here by the little opening here right on the road. There is a little opening here right on the road. There is a little gateway there. It is not a gate, but an opening into the house."

"Would it be opposite the walk that goes into the house, Mrs. Jennings?"

"Yes, it would."

"Exhibit number six, will you look at that photograph. Does that show the place where you stopped your car?"

"Right here."

"The witness indicates opposite the walk, as shown in exhibit six."

"By the gate."

Ryder O'Neill wanted to confirm. "What was the exhibit previously shown?"

Justice Butler stated, "Seven."

BJ Barry continued. "Your husband stopped your car there?"

"Yes," replied Grace.

"And did everybody get out of the car?"

"Yes."

"And at the time you drove up and stopped the car, did you see anybody in the area of the house?"

"You mean beside the boys?"

"Including the boys?" questioned Justice Butler.

"I am now talking about the time you stopped your car," confirmed BJ Barry.

"No, we didn't," advised Grace.

BJ Barry continued, "And then you got out of your car, did you?"

"Yes."

"And then what did you see?"

"The two young lads opened the door and walked out; both had guns."

"What do you mean?"

"The two little fellows here."

Justice Butler looked at the two accused. "Billings and Blake?"

Grace was looking directly at them. "Yes."

BJ Barry approached the witness stand where Grace was sitting. "They opened the door and walked out to where?"

"One of them stood on the step of the house at the door, and the other one stepped down on to the platform, the cement platform."

"In other words, one was more or less in the doorway?"

"Standing at the doorway, and the other one stepped down a bit."

"On to the surface of the porch or stoop?"

"Yes."

"Which was which?"

"The young lad stood in the doorway," Grace said.

"Which one?"

She pointed. "The one here. Well, Blake is the one that stood in the door."

"And Billings on the stoop?"

"Yes."

"And they both had rifles?"

"Yes."

"And at the time you saw them in that position, where were you, Mrs. Jennings?"

"Starting to walk up the walk."

"Were you yet inside the fence?"

"I believe so."

"And where were the other members of your party?"

"Coming behind me."

"You were the first, were you?"

"Yes."

"And what happened?"

"I thought it was a joke, and I went up to the boy—Billings, is it?"

"Yes."

"And I said to him, 'Look, Son, I am not looking for trouble.' And he said, 'No, Missus, but they have been all around all day yesterday throwing stones and breaking windows.'"

"You said you weren't looking for trouble, and he said, 'I know, Missus, but they were around all day yesterday breaking windows'?"

"Throwing stones."

"And what else did he say?"

"I said I didn't know anything about that, and just then Virginia Booker walked in she gave the Blake boy a touch on his gun, and she said, 'You wouldn't shoot me.' He said, 'No, I wouldn't, Virginia.'"

"Which one are you talking about?"

"The Blake boy."

"And where did that happen? Where was Blake when that happened, Mrs. Jennings?"

"Standing on the stoop at the door."

"And where was Virginia Booker?"

"She started to walk in and touched the gun to kind of give him a little shove, not hard but just enough to get herself in, and she said, 'You don't want to touch me,' and he said no."

"And did she keep walking in?"

"Yes."

"And where were Billings and Blake at the time she did that?"

"The oldest boy was still standing there talking to me."

"And where was Blake?"

"He followed in, and then the Booker girl—not Virginia, but the other girl—followed in, and then somebody else went in."

"Who was that?"

"I don't know; it was one of the men."

"And were you still outside?"

"No, the oldest boy turned around and walked in, and my husband walked in, and I walked in behind this fellow here."

"Where was Troy Sregor?"

"He came in after me."

"You were inside when he came in, were you?"

"Yes."

"Where was Blake when Troy Sregor came in?"

"Standing opposite us."

"Where were you standing?"

"We didn't get very far in the door, anyway. That is all I can tell you about that part of it."

"Well, would it be fair to put it you were just inside the door?"

"No, we were just a bit further over."

"I am only concerned about you personally, Mrs. Jennings."

"I don't really remember the angle of the house, to tell you the truth. I know when I turned around, the front room door was right at my other side."

"That would be on your left?" BJ Barry asked.

"Yes."

"And where was the Blake Boy standing?"

"Straight opposite."

"Well, if you take it, Mrs. Jennings—"

"That way, he was that way."

"You can assume that door there through which you came is in the south wall of the building."

"That is the one by which she entered?" asked Ryder O'Neill.

"That is right," BJ Barry clarified. "You came in through that door, and how far into the room would you say you went?"

"Well, there were three of them ahead of me, and then the Billings boy, and I followed up close behind him," responded Grace.

"And Blake, I take it was, from the gesture you made, to your right as you came in?" asked BJ Barry.

Grace hesitated. "I imagine so."

"I would like your best recollection of where he was."

"All it seemed to me was he was almost opposite."

"I don't understand what you mean by opposite. Was he directly ahead of you, or to your right?"

"I have to think about the boys Blake and Billings."

"The boy in the grey suit?"

"If you go in the door that way, he was kind of that way off a wall, over to the far corner."

"To your right as you go in the door?"

"Yes."

"And where was Troy Sregor?"

"I don't know. Right directly beside me."

"To your left?"

"To my left."

"And what happened?"

"Well, he said to the young lad, he said, 'Oh, put your gun down.'"

"Who said?"

"Troy Sregor."

"He said it to . . . ?"

Justice Butler answered, "Blake."

BJ Barry looked at Justice Butler and then back to Mrs. Jennings. "He said, 'Put your gun down'?"

"And that was all there was, two shots and that was it," responded Grace.

"Where was Troy Sregor when he said that?" asked BJ Barry.

"Standing beside me." Grace gestured as though someone were beside her.

"How far would he be away from Blake?"

"You have got me in the room—I can't tell you that. He never even moved."

"Can you point to anything in this room about the same distance from you as Blake was from Troy Sregor?"

"I don't think any more than that there seat. Not the boys but behind them, if the kitchen is as big as that. Is the kitchen as big as that?"

Ryder O'Neill interrupted. "That is up to you." *After all, she was the one that was there,* Ryder thought. *How could any of them answer that question for her?*

Grace was indignant. "Well, I don't know."

Justice Butler did not like the way this was proceeding. "Let us, for the sake of the record, agree on that distance."

Ryder O'Neill stood up and looked at Justice Butler. "I don't see how you can do that, Your Worship. She said it is not much more than as far as that, if the kitchen is as big as that."

Grace's voice was snarky. "I would have to go and see the kitchen to realize what it is."

"Is that what you want us to understand, Mrs. Jennings, that—"

Before BJ Barry could finish his sentence, Grace cut him off. "There wasn't very much between them."

"Do you wish to be understood as saying the entire width of the kitchen was between them?" BJ Barry was still seeking clarification from Grace.

"Yes, I imagine we weren't standing up against the wall."

"I understand that. Were you in a straight line from the door?"

"No, you go in—the first ones went in and kind of turned."

"To your right? You are indicating with your right hand?"

"Yes."

"To the right, you say. Then what was Troy Sregor doing when he was shot?"

"Standing beside me."

"Standing beside you?"

"Absolutely."

"Then what occurred, if you will say it again, please?"

"You mean from the time we stopped the car?"

"No, I mean from the point following the time Troy Sregor said, 'Put your gun down.'"

"Well, there were two shots."

"Where did they come from?"

"There was the only one collecting the gun."

"Who was that?"

"The boy Blake."

"Where was Billings at the time these shots were fired?"

"Just around from me."

"Did he have a gun?"

"He had a gun."

"Where was it pointing?"

"Down."

"Pointing to the floor?"

"Yes; he was standing with it in his hand."

"Who were you watching at the time shots were fired?"

"We weren't watching anybody, to tell you the truth, because I thought it was a big joke."

"You heard two shots fired?"

"Yes."

"And what happened?"

"Troy kind of bent over a minute and then dropped on the floor."

"Was anything said?"

"Not a word."

"And what happened then?"

"The young Blake boy ran in the other room there and told us to get out, or he would let us have it."

"What room?"

"In the front room."

"To your left?"

"Right behind. And the big boy ran in and told him to cut it out, and he kept yelling, 'Seth told me to do it, Seth told me to do it.' And all of a sudden he turned round and said he was going to get Seth."

"Whom do you mean by 'he'?"

"The Blake boy."

"You say he turned into the front room and said what to you first of all?"

"Told us to get out, or he would let us have it."

"And Billings went in after him and told him to cut it out?"

"Yes."

"And Blake said, 'Seth told me to do it, Seth told me to do it,' and then he said, 'I am going to get Seth'?"

"That is right."

"And what did he do?"

"He went out."

"Through the door you came in?"

"Absolutely."

"And what did Billings do?"

"He stayed there with us."

"Not a word."

"What became of Billings' rifle?" Barry asked.

"Well, Mr. Booker asked him—that is, Booker Senior—if the gun was loaded, and he said yes, and he put his bullets in his pocket and told him to fire it away."

"And what did Billings do?"

"He walked outside."

"What did he do with relation to his gun?"

"He emptied the gun into his pocket."

"And what did he do with the bullets?"

"In his pocket."

"And Mr. Booker said something else to him. What did he say?"

"'You don't want to get implicated in it.'"

"And what did he tell him with relation to the gun? You mentioned something about firing it?"

"Firing it?"

"Yes."

"That boy didn't fire it."

"I understood you to say Mr. Booker said something to Billings, for him to fire his gun?"

"No, he asked him if his gun was loaded, and he said yes. And he emptied his gun into his pocket, and he told him to get rid of his gun before he was implicated."

"That is what I thought you said. Booker told him to get rid of it?"

"Yes."

"And where did he go?"

"Just on the stoop and threw it," Grace said.

"Then where did you go?"

"I stayed there."

"How long were you in the room before anybody else came?"

"Just till the doctor came."

"Which doctor came?"

"Dr. Koffee."

"And he ordered you out of the room?"

"Yes."

"And where did you go?" BJ Barry questioned.

"Outside to the car."

"How long were you in the car?"

"Five or 10 minutes."

And then what happened?

"Then Troy Sregor and his wife—"

"I take it you don't mean Troy Sregor?"

"Seth Sregor and his wife and the Blake boy came back."

"How did they arrive at the premises?"

"Car, it must have been, as far as I am concerned."

"And where did they leave the car?"

"Right up against the fence."

"And what happened after they got there?"

"They got out of the car, and the Blake boy stopped a little bit on the opposite side of the walk—the south side of the walk, it would be, just behind our car—and Seth Sregor and his wife came up to the car and asked us what we were doing there. We told him that he had told us to see Doc Magee, and he left us without a name."

"I don't understand, 'and he left us without a name'?"

"Yes."

"And then what happened?"

"Well, the Blake boy turned around and told us if we didn't get out of there, he would let us have it, and I told Dad not to answer him but get going."

"Where was the Blake boy when he said that?"

"On the south side of the car, just behind it."

"Did he have the rifle still?"

"Yes."

"In what position was he holding it?"

"Pointing it."

"And then you left?"

"No, Mrs. Sregor brought him over beside her."

"She went over to whom?"

"To the Blake boy, and she brought him to the side where he was and told him to cut it out."

"Did he say anything?"

"No, he didn't say anything, and then we left."

This concluded the examination-in-chief of Mrs. Grace Jennings. Mrs. Grace Jennings was then cross-examined by Ryder O'Neill. Before Ryder O'Neill had a chance to speak, Leonard Karl, the defence lawyer for Jasper Billings, spoke, "There will be no cross-examination."

A dialogue began between Justice Butler and Grace Jennings. "Where was Billings when the shooting took place?" asked Justice Butler.

"Standing on the cement stoop."

"On the outside?"

"Yes."

"Outside the door?"

"No, standing just the other side of me."

"To your right?"

"Troy was on my left; he would be to my right. He went in ahead of me."

"Billings did? The fellow in the brown suit?"

"Yes."

"He went ahead of you?"

"Yes."

"The two of you walked in together? You were still talking to him?"

"No, not then. He turned and went in the house."

"And he went to your right?"

"I guess he followed in the rest of them."

"Well, he was behind you?"

"No, he went in first."

"Could you see him?"

"All the time."

"At what position was his rifle in when the shooting took place?"

"He just had it like this."

"Under his right arm with the barrel pointing toward the ground?"

"I wouldn't say his barrel pointing to the ground, because I wasn't paying that much attention, but he put it face down when he was talking to me, and that is the way it was."

"The medical evidence is that the shot that killed Troy Sregor entered the back."

"I know."

"Have you any explanation of that?"

"No, not unless you ask the youngsters if there was anybody else in the house."

"That there was a third party with a gun?"

"I am not sure."

"That is the only way you think it would happen?"

"I am not sure, because he was shot with the young lad in the front, and when he turned, there was a spot on his back before he even turned facing that kid, and that is why I don't know."

"Both shots had been fired before he moved, in any event?"

"Right."

"So it couldn't have been a case of receiving the first one in the front and getting the second one in the back?"

"No chance whatever."

This concluded the cross-examination of Mrs. Grace Jennings. Grace had testified that she saw a spot on Troy's back before he even turned. The gunshot had entered the back before Troy even turned, after being shot by Stanley Blake. Was there a third gun? Mrs. Jennings seemed to think that was the only answer. Ms. Jennings had been confused by the whole reason for going up to the farm house, and her only intention was to find a place for her and her husband to live that they could afford.

Although her husband may have trouble hearing when he was nervous, their testimonies were very similar in the fact that there had to have been a third gun. There was the gun that Jasper Billings held but never shot. There was the gun that Stanley Blake had accidentally fired while the gun was facing in the down position which slightly grazed Troy Sregor. The question remained, who held the gun that murdered Troy Sregor? It was clear from this testimony that it was not Jasper or Stanley. Who had been there but had not been accounted for by the testimonies? As Malorie read through the transcript, she knew the one person who had not been accounted for yet had showed up at the scene. How had he even gotten there? But more important, why was he there? What was his reason for being there that late in the evening? It made no sense.

Mrs. Jennings stepped down from the witness box and proceeded back outside of the courtroom toward the other witnesses who had either already testified or were waiting to take the stand. The courtroom still remained closed to witnesses, and only those testifying were allowed to enter, one at a time.

Sixteen

Seth and Troy's sister, Mrs. Virginia Booker, was then called to the stand. She was sworn in, and BJ Barry began the examination began. Virginia was familiar with Mr. Barry because he had been one of the lawyers present at the trial for the probating of her father' last will and testament. The two held eye contact for a few seconds. Virginia gave a small girlish grin, crossed her legs, and folded her hands in her lap as the examination began.

Mr. Barry began by asking Virginia some standard questions about where they lived in Oshawa, and if they also lived in Warkworth. Virginia had advised that her husband worked in Oshawa, and they had a home on Athol Street in Oshawa and an apartment in Warkworth; they usually spent their weeks in Oshawa and weekends in Warkworth. Virginia liked to go home to her roots. Despite the tragedies that had occurred there, it was still home.

Virginia confirmed that she was the sister of Seth, Ted, and Troy Sregor. Mr. Barry looked at Virginia and continued to ask her questions.

"And in the settlement of your father's estate, among other things, did you obtain a mortgage on the farm, which your father had previously sold to your brother, Ted?"

"Yes."

"When was that mortgage assigned to you, Mrs. Booker?"

"It was either in November—"

"Of what year?"

"That would be 1955."

"You think in November 1955, do you?"

"Yes, either November or December."

"And at the time the mortgage became yours, what was owing under it, Mrs. Booker?"

"About $4,500."

"And was the interest paid up to date on it?"

"No, it wasn't."

"How much arrears of interest was it?"

"Well, 1953 of April was the last payment made on it, so it was 5 percent."

"It was in arrears from 1953?"

"That is right."

"In what connection, Mrs. Booker, did you have any bargain with your brother Ted? Did you make a deal with your brother Ted?"

"You mean . . . ?"

"About what should happen to the farm?"

"In 1953?"

"No, in 1955 after the mortgage became yours."

"Yes."

"When was that deal entered into?"

"November 16."

"Of 1955?"

"Yes, that is right."

"And where was it entered into?"

"Edward Wolfe's office in Colborne."

"A lawyer in Colborne?"

"Yes."

"And what was the deal you made with Ted?" Barry asked.

"Ted gave me the deed for $5,000. It was a deal made out that I paid him $5,000."

"And he deeded you the property at that time?"

"Yes."

"And did you actually pay him any money?"

"Well, I figured $5,000 was the payment that he wanted it that way."

"What I am concerned about, in Mr. Wolfe's office, is whether you hand over $5,000 in cash to him, or you took if off the amount of the mortgage?"

"No, like interest on it."

"You took a quitclaim deed and wiped out the money he owed you under the mortgage?"

"Yes."

"And at the time you took that quitclaim deed from your brother Ted, had you any knowledge as to whether or not the farm was subject to lease?"

"I had knowledge it was subject to one lease."

"For what period?"

"It said that Ted and Seth—I think it said, 'made a bargain on this date for Seth to work land on shares one-third'—that was Ted's one-third."

"For what length of time was that lease to be in effect?"

"Well, I am not sure exactly whether it stated, but Ted said it was only for one year."

"Will you look at the document that is exhibit number two in this matter, Mrs. Booker, and read it and tell Justice Butler whether that or a copy of that is the document you saw."

"Yes, that appears to be," Virginia replied.

"And who produced that document, Mrs. Booker?"

"Well, there was a copy that Ted produced."

"And you say Ted said it was to be for one year?"

"Yes, that is right."

"And was that the impression you had at the time you made this deal on the 16th of November in Mr. Wolfe's office?"

"Yes."

"At that time did you have any knowledge of the existence of any lease affecting the property for five years, with option of renewal for another five?"

"No, I certainly never did."

"Was that disclosed to you by Ted Sregor?"

"No, it was not."

"Having taken over the quitclaim deed from your brother, what did you do with reference to the property, Mrs. Booker?"

"You mean as to . . . ?"

"Did you go to the property to go into possession of it at all?"

"Yes, when I came back, Ted and Troy took me up home, up to where I lived in Warkworth."

"From Mr. Wolfe's office?"

"Yes."

"Let us go back to that interview a little further. At the same time did your brother Troy make a deal with Ted?"

"Yes."

"In Mr. Wolfe's office?"

"Yes."

"And that deal related to what farm?"

"The Cassidy farm."

"And what deal did they make?"

"That Troy was to pay Ted one thousand dollars and a Chevy truck."

"In return for that, Troy was to get what?"

"The deed."

"To the Cassidy farm?"

"Yes."

"And did Troy get the deed for the Cassidy farm?"

"Yes, he did."

"Was there any conversation about the Cassidy farm being subject to any lease?"

"Only the same as that, for one year."

"Did Troy give Ted the thousand dollars?"

"He gave him a cheque for a thousand, and he gave the ownership of the truck."

"To Ted Sregor?"

"Yes."

"And you say Ted and Troy drove you from Mr. Wolfe's office to your home in Warkworth?"

"Yes, that is right."

"On that particular day, were you on the Ted Sregor farm at all?"

"Yes, I was on the farm that day."

"With whom?"

"Well, I walked up afterward to take a look around to see if everything was all right, and Ted said there was a linoleum up over the kitchen—there was a manhole there, and he put it over the kitchen part, and that was the balance for the rug which he said was from the kitchen, the new rug he had put on the kitchen. I wanted to know if it was there because I wanted to put it on the hall at home."

"And did you find it?"

"No, I didn't see it."

"And you were in the premises, were you?"

"Yes, I was."

"How did you get in, Mrs. Booker?"

"I was given a key at Mr. Edward Wolfe's office."

"Who gave it to you?"

"Ted gave it to me in front of Mr. Wolfe, my brother Troy, and my husband."

"Were you alone when you went up on that occasion, or was anybody with you, on November 16?"

"No, my husband drove me up."

"When did you first learn of the existence of a five-year lease in connection with this property?"

"Well, I didn't know anything until I had my brother-in-law's and my sister's cattle up there, and that was in May."

"In May of this year?"

"That is right."

"May of 1956?"

"Yes."

"You say in May 1956 you put cattle up there?"

"No, we were up before, but that is when I learned—"

"When did you put the cattle up there?"

"I put the cattle up there in April."

"Tell Justice Butler the circumstances under which you learned of the existence of a supposed five-year lease of the premises."

"Well, after my brother-in-law and my sister—they came to me and said to me, 'Will it be all right if we put the cattle up there in the barn for a while, until we find a place for them?' and he wasn't sure as to whether he would rent them to someone or sell them, as he had gone to Oshawa to live with his wife."

"That is Mr. Morgan?"

"Yes. And I said, 'Yes, sure, go ahead.' So he took them up there and they were there . . . oh, several weeks. So one weekend we came home and Mr. Booker said to me that Seth—"

"Mr. Booker, that is your father-in-law?"

"Yes. He let us know Seth said that he has this farm for five years and five years longer, or something like that, and I looked at him and said, 'What?' He said, 'He told me to tell you to get these cattle out of there.' I said, 'Well, that seems strange, now.' I said there is a lease for one year and with no buildings stated, that Seth had not the buildings to do as he liked or with anything else, and so—well, he said, 'He is coming up this Sunday, and they had better be out Saturday or Sunday.' I am not sure whether Saturday or Sunday, but they were supposed to be out that weekend. And so I think it was right at dinner time or right afterward—anyway, we saw

Seth come up, and pretty soon we happened to go out of doors, and these cattle are coming down the road. One of us said to the other, 'Those are Marty's cattle coming down.' Marty and Joan walked up, and I said, 'I don't know what to do about it; it seems strange.' He drove the cattle down, that is, Troy's boys—"

"Troy's boys?"

"I mean Ted's—excuse me, Seth's boys."

"They drove the cattle down to where?" Barry asked.

"To the farm."

"Was Seth with them?"

"No, Seth was up the road talking to Marty Morgan in his truck."

"Did you have any talk with Seth at that time?"

"No, I didn't know what to make of it."

"When did you first have any talk with Seth about it, or did you ever have any talk with him about it?"

"I should say at the time of the threshing, I thought I might get a chance to say something, but unfortunately I certainly never got a chance to say anything about the farm or about his lease or anything."

"Was that an occasion when you—"

"August 7."

"And what happened on August 7?"

"Well, on August 7—I believe it was August 7—do you mind if I look at my notes that I wrote down at that time?" Underneath Virginia's folded hands was a small black book that held her handwritten notes. It had not been noticed when she initially approached the bench, because she had concealed it until this moment.

"Did you make them yourself?"

"Yes."

"When did you make them?"

"At the time."

"Why did you make them?"

"Well, I made them so—I know that Seth always seemed to more or less never want to talk to me, and when I walked into the store one day, he looked at me, and I thought I would be better to have these notes to refer to."

"When did you propose to use them?"

"I thought I might use them before the time Seth threw the water on me."

"When did you start to keep them?"

"Well, it was before that time, before August 7," Virginia said.

"And you expected sometime in the future you would have a need for them?"

"Yes."

"Well, apart altogether from the date, whether August 7 or what it was, what occurred at the time of the threshing?"

"It was between two and three on a Wednesday—do you mean if I told you a little before?"

"Go ahead."

"Anyway, we drove past Seth's because we drove over by there and wondered whether they were going to thresh that day, and we saw them hitching the ploughs on the tractor. We thought they were going to plough, and we thought, 'Shall we go back to Oshawa and wait to see, to hear word if he was going to thresh or not?' So anyway, my husband said, 'These potatoes need scuffling,' and he and my father-in-law went to scuffle the potatoes, so I did the dinner dishes and I thought—"

Before Virginia finished, BJ Barry cut her off midsentence. He didn't want to hear about her husband loosening the soil around the potato plants and removing any weeds. "Well, I am sorry, we are only concerned with what *you* actually did."

"Well, I soon saw the two tractors go up with the ploughs on the back—"

"Go up in which direction?"

"That would be west."

"Toward the Ted Sregor farm?"

"Yes, and a little later I heard something sounding like a threshing machine, so I walked up the road and took a look to see if they were threshing. I went not quite to the top of the hill, and I came down and I said, 'They are threshing up there.' I thought they were—that it was just something to fool us."

Justice Butler interrupted for a minute. "We are quite prepared to give you every chance to explain why you did certain things, and there is a lot of evidence and a lot of details probably necessary, but I suggest you cut out the unnecessary details."

BJ Barry continued." Did you go up to where they were threshing?"

"Yes," replied Virginia.

"And did you go up alone or somebody with you?"

"No, my brother-in-law and my husband went with me, and they were going to go in, and I said no."

"They just came to the edge of the field?"

"Just outside the gate."

"And you went in alone?"

"Yes."

"And who was there?"

"There was Seth and Stewart Fine and Kenny—"

"That is Seth's boy?"

"Yes, Seth's boy, and Harry—"

"Another boy of Seth?"

"Yes, and Gary, another one, and I think it was Seth's daughter Ruth, and Seth's youngest boy."

"And what happened after you got up there?"

"Well, I walked in and said to Seth, 'I am here to see about my share of the grain.' He never said a word, and I took a look and started counting the bags, and he was there doing something with the threshing machine. Then he got up and kind of shut it down. Well, he said to me, 'Get out of here.' I said, 'Why should I get out of here? I am here to see about my share of the grain.' He said, 'I am ordering you off the place. Get out.' So I said, 'I won't get off. I am still here to see about my share of the grain.' He called Kenny over and whispered something to him, and young Kenny went and got the pail of water, and he brought it and threw it at me."

"Did you leave then?"

"No, I didn't, and so he said to him, 'Go and get another pail.' I said, 'Well, I can stand it as long as you can,' so I stood up on top of the grain. He said, 'If you get the grain wet, I don't know how to dry it.' And I said, 'Maybe you can—'"

"Did they throw another pail of water on you?"

"Yes, they threw five pails, and then Seth left. Before that he picked up the shovel and said to Stewart Fine, 'Will I hit her? Will I hit her?' and he said, 'Stewart is here to see about the grain. He is counting the bushels.'"

"In this incident you told us about, is it typical of the attitude and relationship that exists between yourself and your brother Seth?"

"Yes, I would say that he—"

"And there was no discussion of that occasion at all regarding the lease, except that he told you to leave?"

"And he wouldn't even come to the point and say, 'Have you got a lease?' He said, 'I have it rented for five years, and five years longer, and I am going to keep it.'"

"What did you do to try and get possession of the property, if anything?"

"Well, I went to see my lawyer, and he said to go on and plough, that I had the lease for one year, that I was given the lease for one year, and go on and plough."

"When was that?" Virginia did not respond. "In the meantime, had you had any letters written to Seth over this matter?"

"Yes, my lawyer had wrote a letter to say—"

"Do you remember when that would be about, that that letter was written?"

"I am not sure as to when it was."

"Did you see the letter before it went?"

"No."

"Did you ever see a copy?"

"The letter that he wrote to Seth?"

"Yes."

"No, I never did," Virginia said.

"In any event, you were instructed you had the right to go on and plough?"

"Yes".

"When was that?"

"That would be August the twenty—"

"Do you remember what day in the week it was?"

"Friday."

"The Friday before your brother Troy was shot?"

"Yes."

"That would be August 24?"

"Yes."

"Who went up to plough?"

"Well, I took my brother-in-law's tractor, and my husband took our tractor."

"And you and your husband went up to plough?"

"Yes."

"And did Seth come there?"

"Not while we were ploughing the first field."

"Did he come at all that day?"

"Yes. When we went up to the field where the straw stack was, he came down there, and Simon Magee came out up the road with the truck and stayed there. We didn't pay any attention, we went on ploughing, so about 20 minutes later, up came Seth."

"Do I understand that Simon Magee stopped first?"

"Yes."

"Was Seth with him?"

"No."

"Did Simon Magee stop and holler to you to stop ploughing?"

"No; he wanted us to stop so he could say something to us. He hollered, 'Stop,' and we kept right on ploughing and didn't pay no attention to him."

"And then he left, did he?"

"Yes."

"And about 20 minutes later, Seth came up?"

"Yes."

"Was he alone?"

"He was alone in the Dodge truck, and his wife, Annie, was coming behind in a Dodge car."

"And what happened on that occasion?"

"Seth drove in there to beat the bank, and he jumped out and pulled out this gun. My husband and I were going up one of the furrows and saw him aiming the gun at us, and it lifted the dirt right between my husband's tractor and mine."

"Did he fire the gun?"

"Yes."

"How far away would he be when he did that?"

"Well, he was just down at the end by the headland, four or five hundred feet; I'm not sure."

"What was the result of the shot?"

"It lifted the dirt right between the two tractors."

"The dirt spurted up between the two tractors?"

"Yes."

"How far were the tractors apart?"

"My husband had turned to make a new strikeout, because he was standing at the end of the one we had went up with the gun, and I had just got to the top of the headland when he lifted the dirt there nearer to mine."

"How far would it be away from your tractor?"

"Oh, not more than a yard, I would say, not much more."

"And what did you do when Seth did that?"

"Well, my husband started a new strikeout over to the right of the way he was standing, and I went over and followed behind him."

"Would that course bring you—were you driving toward Seth?"

"No."

"In the general direction of where Seth was standing, I take it?"

"Seth would be standing over toward the right, and we were to the left."

Ryder O'Neill began to speak. "They were going in a direction at a right angle."

"Is that correct?" questioned BJ Barry.

Virginia stumbled. "Would you say again?"

"Were you going at right angles to the course you had been following before Seth shot at you, or retracing your steps and going back over the opposite direction?" BJ Barry was seeking clarification.

"Contour ploughing," Leonard Karl said, also trying to understand.

BJ Barry continued questioning Virginia. "In any event, if you kept on going in the direction you set out in the new strikeout, would it have ended up nearer to Seth than when the shot was fired or further away?"

"Further away," replied Virginia.

"And what happened then?"

"Annie was arguing with him—she was there arguing with him to put the gun away, and he was kind of saying something to her, but I couldn't understand what she said because of the tractors. Anyways, she got him to put the gun away, and then he came over towards us again with the gun. He got the gun again and came over."

"Did you have any talk with him at all that time?"

"No, you couldn't talk with him."

"Why?"

"There was no reasoning with him."

"He seemed to be somewhat upset, did he?"

"He sure did."

"And you had no talk with him at all?"

"Well, he said to my husband, 'Get off, or I will put you off.'"

"Did your husband do anything to him?"

"No, he didn't, and he came right close to where he was with the tractor, and he made a grab at him and Willy spurted out of his road with the tractor."

"At any time, how close to Mrs. Sregor were these tractors?"

"She was standing closer to me and stuck her tongue at me."

"Was she close enough to hit you?"

"No."

"Was she close?" wondered Ryder O'Neill.

"How close was she to the tractor? What was the closest she ever got to the tractor?" asked BJ Barry.

Virginia, looked back and forth between Ryder and BJ. "Well, she would be about a yard away, anyways."

"Then did Seth and his wife leave?" asked BJ Barry.

Virginia had been looking down at her lap and looked up. "Yes, after—well, Seth put his gun in the truck, and they left."

"Now, were either Jasper Billings or Stanley Blake with Seth on that occasion?"

"No, they weren't."

"Then you continued to plough there, did you?"

"No, I didn't know what to do, whether to go down and call the police. And if we called the police and they came out and arrested him, if he got away with it, I thought maybe something else would happen."

"In any event, did you call the police, and they did come down?"

"Yes; I wasn't there the Monday they came."

"But you called the police, and they said they would be down?"

"Yes."

"And you were not there when they came?"

"No."

"Then had you previously entered into an arrangement with Mrs. Jennings in connection with this house on these premises, Mrs. Booker?"

"Yes, I had."

"When was that?"

"In March, I phoned her because Troy had told Mother that Mr. and Mrs. Jennings were looking for a place, and I wanted to get someone in the house so I could get insurance on it."

"And did you make a bargain with her at that time?"

"I phoned her on the Sunday night—"

"Please, I think that is what we are all concerned about, not to waste too much time. Did you make a bargain with her?"

"Yes."

"And the bargain was you were to rent her the house?"

"Yes."

"For how much money?" Barry asked.

"Twenty dollars a month."

"And when was she to go into occupation?"

"September the first."

"This year?"

"Yes."

"Was it an agreement in writing?"

"Yes, it was."

"At the time you entered into that agreement, had you any knowledge Seth was claiming to be entitled to occupy the buildings?"

"No, I was not."

"Were you ever on the premises with Mrs. Jennings prior to August 27 of this year?"

"Yes, I was."

"When was that?"

"Well, it was the day we made the agreement. We went up and took her into the house, but she didn't pay no attention to it. She just took a look in the kitchen and said, 'You go and look.'"

"To who?"

"To Mr. Jennings."

"And that was your agreement with her, that she was to be in occupation on the first of September?"

"That is right."

"Then when did you next see Mrs. Jennings in connection with the premises?"

"The next time I saw her, she came and said Mr. Jennings had been down the street and said he heard some rumour that Seth was going to rent the place."

"Do you remember about when that was?"

"No, I am not sure when that was. He came there one Sunday, I know."

"And what did you tell her at that time?"

"Well, I said, 'We will see. You have already got it rented, and we will have to wait and see what he does.'"

"And then did you learn that he put Dr. Magee in?"

"Yes."

"And when did you learn that?"

"In July, I think."

"And did you do anything when you learned Dr. Magee was in possession of the house?"

"Well, you mean then, or when?"

"How long after you learned he was in possession of the house did you do anything?"

"I didn't do anything for a month, I guess."

"And then what did you do?"

"Well, on August—may I look to see the date?" Virginia was referring to the little black book she held on her lap under her folded hands.

Justice Butler did not like the idea of this little black book. "No, I think you should give your evidence to the best of your recollection."

"Do you remember what day in the week it was you went to speak?" BJ Barry continued.

"Well, it was on . . . well, we saw Simon Magee once before. I went up one other time. Would you like me to add that first?"

"What you are about to tell us about is a conversation you had with Dr. Magee?"

"Yes, a conversation."

"How many times did you see Magee about it?"

"I saw him several times when he was up there with Seth, and the time that he threw stones at us in the field, and another time when we walked up to see how the grain was, if it was weighed."

"Can we take it you had a series of conversations with Magee about the occupation of this house?"

"No. I walked up, and we were just going down to the barn when he came out and said to me, 'Who are you?' I said, 'You know me, Simon.' After all, he was married to my sister, Alice. Then he said, 'Who is this guy?' I said it didn't matter, and so he kept on talking, and he said, 'I got this place rented.' and I said, 'Do you? For how long?' He said, 'I might for a year or for as long as I want,' and he had a document. Then he said, 'Do you know you are trespassing?'"

"Talk or question?" asked Ryder O'Neill.

"Simon said to me, 'Do you know you are trespassing?' I said, 'Trespassing on my own property? You know better than that.' Afterward he started preaching religion of Jehovah's Witnesses."

"Did you at any time tell him it was your own property?"

"I told him then that it was my own property."

"Did you tell him to vacate the property, to get out?"

"I said, 'You are here now, but maybe you won't be here that long.'"

"And what did you mean by that?"

"That—"

Ryder O'Neill interrupted BJ Barry and Virginia. "I don't think it matters what she meant by that."

Leonard Karl chimed in. "The statement is quite clear."

"Is that what you said?" asked BJ Barry.

"Yes," replied Virginia.

"What did you mean by it?" questioned BJ Barry.

Ryder O'Neill then stated, "The witness can prove what she said as a statement but not what she meant, if she didn't mean what she meant—"

Virginia said, "Well, I figured—" But before Virginia could finish, Justice Butler interrupted.

"Just a minute. What is the objection to telling?" Justice Butler was confused.

Ryder O'Neill talked in riddles. "First of all, there has been a good deal of it, and I admit a lot is not admissible, because the proof the statements are made is proof of the fact that the statements are made. That is proof of a fact, but the proof what she meant by a statement is not admissible against the accused, as I see it."

"I don't think it matters very much whether it goes in or not, but I think the witness is entitled to an explanation of what she said," BJ Barry commented.

Justice Butler did not agree. "She is only a witness, not the accused. No, I think she had better not. I would like to call a 15-minute recess, and we will reconvene at 10:30. I would remind the witness that she is not to talk to anyone other than counsel during this time." Justice Butler hit the bench with his gavel, and everyone stood. Justice Butler left the court room.

Fifteen minutes later everyone returned to the courtroom, and the pre-trial picked up where it had left off. The questioning continued about Doc Magee and obtaining possession. After that, Mr. Barry began questioning Virginia about August 27, 1956—the day that Troy Sregor died.

"So you came home with Troy and, acting on this advice, I take it, you went down to get the Jennings and bring them up?"

"Well, we kind of—Troy said something about it on the way home, and it was kind of passed off. So when we got down to where Troy lived, Nancy got out, and I said, 'Troy, take me up home; I have to get supper.' On the way up Troy said it would be a good idea to go out and throw Doc Magee out, so he said, 'It looks as though it is going to rain tonight.'"

"A good night to throw him out, you mean, in the rain?"

"No, it was sprinkling a little bit on the way down from Oshawa, and he said, 'It looks as if it is going to rain. How do you know, the house might go up in flames tonight.'"

"I wonder what would make it go up in flames?"

"That is the words he said."

"Somebody might go around after midnight and set fire to it?"

"I had no insurance on the house."

"That is why it wouldn't go up in flames?"

"There was no intention of it going up in flames on my concern."

"Not when it was uninsured," Barry said.

"And I wouldn't ask for it to go up in flames, even after it was insured."

"So Troy thought it was a good night to throw Dr. Magee out, and as a result of that you and he went and picked up the Jennings?"

"Yes, in Troy's car."

"Did he say why?"

"Yes."

"What did he say?"

"He said, 'Mr. Cosgrove says to take your prospective tenants.'"

"Mr. Cosgrove said what?" asked Justice Butler.

"To take your prospective tenants up and go up and see Simon Magee and move him out, and he also said," Virginia paused and then quickly continued as she could tell BJ Barry was getting upset, "so anyway, we went over and seen the Jennings."

"That is why you were at the Jennings?"

"Yes."

"To pick them up, and go up and move out Doc Magee?"

"Yes, and the Jennings said they wanted to see the place again anyways."

Justice Butler was getting confused with the dates. "What day was this?"

"The 27th."

"And you picked up the Jennings, and where did you go?"

"We came back to our place, and Troy—Nancy phoned, and wanted Troy to phone—"

"I don't think that matters particularly, but Troy made a phone call, did he?"

"Yes."

"And then you went to your father-in-law's place?"

"We were up there."

"And you left there to go to Ted Sregor's farm?"

"Yes."

"And who went up?"

"There was Mr. and Mrs. Jennings, my father-in-law, Mr. Booker, and Liza and Troy—"

"That is Liza Duberg?"

"Yes."

"Why did your father-in-law and Mrs. Duberg go with you? Was there any reason for that?"

"Well, Troy said, 'Maybe we had better all go, because Seth just went up, and he is just going to cause some trouble.'"

"And when you got up, where was the car stopped?"

"We stopped in front of the garage."

"And what happened when you got there?"

"Well, Mr. Jennings got out of the car first, and I got out and held the door for Mrs. Jennings. Oh, first we saw Jasper Billings' head in the window, and we said, 'That is funny, now.'"

"Which window did you see Billings' head in?"

"It would be the south window, the little window."

"I produce to you exhibit six in this matter, Mrs. Booker. Does the window appear there?"

"Yes, it does."

"The window at the right of the photograph, as you look at the photograph?"

"Yes, that is right."

"You saw Billings' head there?"

"Yes."

"Where was your car then?"

"It wasn't ours; it was the Jennings'.'"

"Your car was then in the driveway and stationary, was it?"

"Yes."

"And that struck you as funny, peculiar?"

"Yes, it did," Virginia said.

"And what did you do?"

"The men said, 'You go in and see.'"

"Who said?" asked Justice Butler.

"The men said—well, pretty well said it at the same time, 'You go in and see,'" replied Virginia.

"So what happened?" BJ Barry motioned with his hand for Virginia to continue.

"They thought it was funny—"

"You can't tell us what they thought. You can tell us what they said. They said, 'You women go ahead and see'?"

"Yes."

"So did you?"

"Yes."

"Who got out of the car?"

"Mr. Jennings got out of the left-hand side, and I got out and held the door for Mrs. Jennings as she got out, and Liza stayed in the backseat. They said, 'You go.'"

"Which side of the car did you get out?" asked Justice Butler.

"The right-hand side," answered Virginia.

BJ Barry continued to question Virginia. "And Mrs. Jennings too?"

"Yes."

"And Liza Duberg stayed in the car, and somebody said 'You go, too?'"

"Yes."

"And did she get out?"

"Yes."

"And where were the men?"

"They were in the car."

"And what did you do?"

"Mr. Jennings was ahead, because I waited a minute for Liza to come."

"Did Mr. Jennings stay out of the car or get back in the car?"

"No."

"He stayed out of the car?"

"Yes."

"Who was left in the car when you walked up to the house?"

"Troy and Mr. Booker."

"Your father-in-law?"

"Yes, and my husband, Willy."

"Did you say Mr. Jennings was ahead?" asked Justice Butler.

Virginia turned her head to look at Justice Butler. "Yes. He walked ahead, and she was right behind him."

"And you had more or less hung back for Liza Duberg?" asked BJ Barry.

"Yes."

"And when she got out of the car, what did you do?"

"We walked up to catch up to the Jennings."

"And where were they when you caught up to them?"

"We caught up to them when they were pretty well up to the steps."

"At that time where were Billings and Blake?"

"I only know Jasper Billings was in the house. I'd seen him in the window."

"By the time you got as far as the steps, the door was still shut, was it?"

"Yes."

"And what happened when you got that far?"

"Well, we went on up to the door, and just as we got to the door and I reached my hand to open the door—"

"At that time I take it you were ahead, were you, of the Jennings?"

"Yes, I believe. Well, we were all standing on this cement stoop."

"You reached your hand out to open the door, and what happened?"

"The door came open, and there stood the two boys with guns in their hands."

"Where were they standing?"

"Jasper Billings was standing to my right."

"And Blake?"

"Stanley Blake was standing to the left."

"And they had guns in their hands?"

"Yes."

"In what positions were they holding the guns?"

"Well, Jasper Billings had the gun pointed at me."

"So what did you do?"

"I took my hand and pushed the gun aside, and he said, 'No, Virginia.'"

"Which way did you push it? Toward your right?"

"Toward my right."

"That is, toward his left?"

"Yes."

"And Billings said, 'No, Virginia'?"

"Yes."

"And did you say anything to him?"

"No, I don't remember as I did."

"And what did you do?"

"So then he dropped the—put the gun down pointing toward the floor, and they backed up into the room. Jasper went around to the right, and I walked in the house and took a look to see if the linoleum was on the floor."

"To the right would be along the south wall, would it?"

"Yes."

"And where did Blake go?"

"Well, when I turned around from looking at the linoleum to see if they were there, he was standing in between the two windows."

"That would be in between the two windows of the east wall?"

"Yes, the east wall."

"Look at this photograph shown here, photograph number twelve. Are those the two windows you refer to in the background of that photograph? Those are the two windows where Blake went, are they, appearing in that photograph?"

"Yes."

"At that time, did he still have the rifle with him?"

"Yes, he did."

"And in what position was he holding it?"

"He was holding it about his waist."

"At about waist level?"

"Yes."

"At that time was your brother Troy in the room at all or not?"

"No. Let me see, he came in—I heard him holler to Stanley, 'The boys have guns.'"

"Who said that? Your brother Troy?"

"Yes."

"Where was he when you heard him shout or holler?"

"He must have been out in the car."

"And at that time were you inside the house?"

"Yes."

"And your brother Troy came into the room, did he?"

"Yes."

"And what happened after he got in the room?"

"He came in and gave Liza a shove, and she kind of knocked me off balance, and I—"

"You say your brother Troy came in and gave Liza a shove, and she went into you?"

"Yes."

"And it knocked you where?"

"A step. I was facing the east windows, and it knocked me a step toward the door that leads into the front room."

"That is, toward the west wall?"

"Yes."

"It knocked you toward the doorway that goes into the front room of the house?"

"Yes."

"And what then happened?"

"Well, he stepped over toward Jasper Billings."

"Who did? Troy?"

"Yes, and then I heard a shot."

"Where did the shot come from?"

"It come from Blake's direction."

"You say Troy had stepped toward Jasper Billings?"

"Yes."

"And the boy was where?" BJ Barry asked.

"Along the cupboards, along the—"

"The south wall?"

"Yes."

"And when Troy stepped over toward Billings, which side of him was toward Blake?"

"It would be his left side."

"It would then be toward Blake?"

"Yes."

"Was he in that position when you heard the shot?"

"Yes."

"And then what happened?"

"Well, Troy said, 'Oh, oh no you don't.'"

"And you made a gesture with your left hand just now, Mrs. Booker. Did Troy also do that? I am sorry, with your right hand."

"Yes, he put his hand to his stomach."

"And he said, 'Oh no you don't?'"

"Oh no you don't."

"And then what did he do?"

"He kind of went out a wee bit."

"What do you mean?"

"Apart."

"His legs?"

"Yes, he spread them, and he kind of bent over a little. He stooped over a little."

"Did he still have his hand across his stomach?"

"Yes, and then he kind of straightened up and took a step more into the room, and he stepped toward Stanley Blake, and then the next thing before I knew it, I heard another shot, and Troy twirled around and lay on the floor."

"In what position was Troy that you could see, when the second shot was fired?"

"Well, I think he was facing Stanley Blake."

"And where did the second shot come from?"

"Well, it was so quiet I am not sure where it came from."

"And then what happened?"

"Stanley Blake went into the—he went around toward the bathroom there and went around into the front room. I hollered to my husband; I noticed him in the doorway and said, 'Call the police and get the doctor.' Then I heard Stanley Blake going up the stairs, and I said, 'Wait a minute, he is going upstairs.' Then I said, 'Go on and hurry.' Then I remember Stanley came out, and Jasper came out toward the front door—well, the room that led off the kitchen. And Jasper Billings went over and said to Stanley, 'Put that gun away; you have done damage now.' Stanley Blake said, 'Well, Seth told me to do this. I am going to get Seth.' And then he stuck the gun out of the door post and said, 'If anyone follows me, you will get the same.' So he went out of the kitchen door, and I don't know where he went then."

"What did Billings do? Did he stay there?"

"Yes, he was there."

"Did he say anything after Blake had left?"

"Well, they were talking, and he was pretty well upset over seeing the blood. Then I said, 'Is the doctor coming?' I was wondering too about my husband, and I skinned out and went to see if they were coming or not."

"You left and went to where?"

"Sid Hartman's."

"That is the next place to this house?"

"Yes."

"And they have a telephone there?"

"Yes, they have."

"And you stayed there, Mrs. Booker?"

"Yes."

"Until when?"

"I stayed there and said, 'Did you call the police and the doctor?' They said yes, and my husband turned around and said, 'Don't they seem a long time coming. I am going to phone the Brighton police.' So I think he phoned Brighton police then, and I said, 'I am going back down.'"

"And did you go back down?"

"No, they wouldn't let me. They said, 'You stay here.'"

"And you were at Sid Hartman's?"

"Yes."

"In this whole matter at the house, I take it from what you say that at no time, so far as you were aware, was Billings' rifle fired?"

"No."

"And after you had brushed it aside with your right hand when you came in, in what position was he carrying it?"

"After I walked in?"

"After you walked in and pushed it to one side."

"He had it pointing toward the floor."

"Did it stay in that position, so far as you are aware?"

"So far as I am aware."

"You said that Troy, after the first shot, grasped his stomach with his right hand and said, 'Oh no you don't.'" Justice Butler was referring back to earlier in Virginia's testimony.

"Yes."

"And then he bent over?" Justice Butler wanted to be clear on the sequence of events as he continued to clarify.

"Yes."

"And then he straightened up?"

"Yes."

"Before the second shot was fired?"

"It seemed to me it was."

"It was before the second shot?"

"Yes."

"He was standing upright when the second shot was fired?"

"Oh, yes, when he straightened up, he took a step towards Stanley."

"And he was in an upright position when the second shot was fired, as near as you can remember?"

"Yes."

This concluded the examination-in-chief of Mrs. Virginia Booker.

Seventeen

Ryder O'Neill began his cross-examination of Virginia Booker.

"Mrs. Booker, first of all what was the date of your father's death?"

"June 23, 1953. Or June 24, I mean."

"Thank you. Going to the time when you arrived in the Jennings' car at this house where the shooting took place, I understand that Mr. Jennings was driving the car?"

"Yes."

"And who was sitting beside him?"

"His wife, Mrs. Jennings."

"And who was sitting beside her?"

"I was."

"You were both in the front seat?"

"Yes."

"And in the rear seat would be left your sister-in-law, Mrs. Duberg?"

"Yes."

"And your husband, William Booker?"

"Yes."

"His father, Henry Booker? And Troy Sregor?"

"Yes, that is right."

"When the car stopped, Mr. Jennings got out on the left, I take it?"

"Yes."

"And you and Mrs. Jennings out on the right?"

"Yes, that is right."

"And shortly afterward Liza Duberg got out from the rear seat?"

"Yes."

"And you approached the house. Who was leading?"

"Mr. Jennings."

"Followed by Mrs. Jennings?"

"Yes."

"And then you and Liza Duberg caught up to them?"

"Yes."

"And you stood together, or more or less together, on this cement stoop before the door was opened?"

"Yes."

"And as I understand it, Mr. and Mrs. Jennings were standing toward the right?"

"They were standing toward the left of me, I am pretty sure."

"And you reached out your right hand with the intent of opening the door?"

"Yes."

"And you saw the door open in front of you, and you saw Jasper Billings and Stanley Blake standing in the doorway."

"Yes, when we opened the door, there stood the boys."

"Did they come forward after the door opened?"

"They might have taken a step; I'm not sure about that."

"The reason why I asked that is because the door opened inward?"

"Yes."

"So one of them would be back from the door at least?"

"Stanley Blake was standing back."

"And he stepped forward, did he?"

"No, he was standing back of Jasper Billings, to the side and back."

"I see, and it was Billings' rifle that was pointed toward you?"

"Yes."

"Blake's wasn't pointed toward you?"

"No."

"And Billings said, 'No, Virginia,' and that is all that was said at the time?"

"As far as I can remember."

"You didn't say anything at all at that moment?"

"No, not that I remember."

"You just pushed Billings' rifle aside with your hand?"

"Yes, my right hand."

"And you went in, followed by Mrs. Duberg?"

"Yes. Jasper stepped around to the side of the cupboards with his gun down, so I stepped forward, more into the house, and took a look around to see if the linoleums were on the floor."

"You stepped in, and where did you look for the linoleum?"

"I could see in the kitchen when I went in."

"Did you look on the kitchen floor?"

"I kind of glanced down and kind of stepped over to the door that led into the front room. I took a look, and I could see off the kitchen into the front room, because there is an archway that leads into the far room. I could see near the kitchen door, the door that leads into the front room, right straight—"

"To the very front room of the house?"

"Yes."

"And then you felt yourself being pushed from behind? Is that it?"

"Yes."

"Pushed with some force?"

"Oh, just as if you went and hit me like that with your fist, or your elbow or something."

"What happened, then, is Troy had come into the house and bumped into your sister-in-law?"

"He gave her a shove."

"And that pushed her into you?"

"Yes."

"And you were pushed forward about a step?"

"Yes."

"And I take it Troy came in with some speed. Is that correct?"

"He came in fairly quick."

"Running in?"

"Well, he sure wasn't walking. He came in quite fast."

"As fast as he could go?"

"No."

"And then he ran into, or pushed, your sister-in-law, and that pushed you. And the effect of the whole thing, even after she had absorbed some of the blow, was that you went forward about a step?"

"Yes."

"Meanwhile, I take it that directed your attention to Troy?"

"Yes," Virginia said.

"And you looked around and saw him turn over toward Jasper Billings?"

"Yes. He went toward Jasper Billings. He turned to Jasper."

"And Jasper was standing near the cupboard near the south wall?"

"Yes, he was standing alongside the cupboards."

"Did he take a hold of Billings' rifle?"

BJ Barry interrupted for a second. "You are now talking about Troy?"

Virginia stated, "He was facing Jasper, and I couldn't say for sure if he got a hold of Jasper's rifle or not."

Ryder continued asking Virginia questions. "Was there any action as if they were wrestling?"

"No."

"Were they engaged at all?"

"No, I didn't see any movement from the two of them, but I couldn't say if Jasper moved his gun or not."

"But he was between you and Jasper Billings?"

"Yes."

"Troy was?"

"Yes, with his back toward me."

"Troy was quite a substantial obstacle to the view, wasn't he?"

"I could see him clearly."

"But you couldn't see through him?"

"No, of course not."

"He was quite a big man?" Ryder O'Neill asked.

"Yes."

"A big man, strong and active?"

"Well, I would say as active as any man of his age."

"You don't know of anybody who would be more active or any stronger, do you?"

"Well, there are men stronger than he is."

"Do you know any?"

"Sure."

"How many?"

"I think his brother is stronger than he is."

"Seth?"

"Yes."

"That is one, all right. Now, then, at that moment you say you heard a shot?"

"Yes, I did."

"And do you know, of your own knowledge, where that shot came from?"

"I would say it came from Stanley Blake's direction."

"What makes you say that?"

"Because I noticed Stanley kind of—I glanced, I was kind of watching Troy, and I took a glance at Stanley, and Stanley had the gun pointed at him, anyway."

"Did you hear Stanley say that was a warning shot?"

"No, I didn't."

"You didn't hear that?"

"No, I did not."

"And Troy turned, and after he had put his hand to his stomach and bent over, he straightened up and made a move toward Blake?"

"Yes. After he put his hand to his stomach, he took a step more into the room and stepped toward Stanley Blake."

"You thought—you took it from what you saw that he was going to go to Blake? Is that right?"

"Yes, he was making a step toward Stanley."

"To take some action with regard to Stanley?"

"Yes, if he could get the gun away from him."

"That is what you thought he was going to do?"

"Sure, who wouldn't?"

"And he was going toward Stanley with that apparent intention, as far as you could see, at the time the second shot was fired?"

"Well, as far as his intention, I couldn't say, and neither could you."

"As far as you could see, from what you observed, you took it he was going to take the gun away from Stanley Blake?"

"Yes. He stepped forward and kind of made a grab out like that for the gun, and I heard a shot, and he spun around."

"You say he spun around?" Ryder O'Neill asked.

"Yes."

"And then he spun around until he faced you?"

"Yes."

"And then he fell toward you?"

"He just turned around and fell toward us."

"Did he spin right around in his tracks where he was standing and fall toward you?"

"I believe he did."

"From your recollection, then, when he had fallen toward you, where would you say his feet were?"

"Well, that night after—I don't think I could say exactly, that I could tell you exactly where his feet were. It didn't seem too far, but I can't tell you exactly how far from the wall they were."

"His feet seemed to be not too far from the east wall?"

"Yes, but I can't exactly tell you how far."

"They seemed to you to be quite close to the east wall?"

"Well, fairly close, but—"

"I won't tie you down to a few inches, but they seemed to be fairly close to the east wall?"

"Yes."

"And that, then, was where his body came to rest after it had spun around and fallen toward you?"

"Pardon?"

"That is where his body came to rest after it spun around? That is, toward you with his feet fairly close to the east wall?"

"When he was lying on the floor, they were close to the east wall."

"That is right, and he wasn't moved, or he didn't move after he fell down, did he?"

"No, he didn't move," Virginia confirmed.

"And nobody moved him that you saw?"

"Well, when the blood started coming from his mouth, I said, 'He is bleeding to death, and he is going to smother,' and I went to turn his head."

"Somebody turned his head?"

"Yes, I think I did."

"I don't want to pursue this any further. I just want this to be clear, that he fell down and remained in that position, except somebody perhaps turned his head? Is that correct?"

"Yes."

"Now, you have said that before being shot, Troy reached out, and you took it from what you saw that he went out to grab the gun from Stanley's hand?"

"Yes."

"Do you know if he did grab it?"

"I don't, because I couldn't see."

"You don't know whether he actually grabbed it or not?"

"No, but it appeared to me as though he didn't. But as far as knowing, I don't."

"Immediately before the shot, you say he was going toward Blake with his arm reached out. His right arm or left arm, or both arms?"

"I can't say whether he had both arms reached out. I know he put a hand out, anyway."

"And from what you saw, you took it his hand was out to grab the gun at the moment the shot was fired?"

"Yes."

"Up to that time, had you heard Blake say anything?"

"Yes, he did say something, but I am not just sure what he did say."

"Could it have been, after the first shot, 'That is a warning shot'?"

"No, I know he didn't say that. I would remember if he said that."

"You would remember what else he said before the shots were fired."

"I know he said something. Would you say again . . . ?"

"Whether Blake said anything before the shots were fired."

"Before the shots were fired, I am not sure if he said anything."

"I take it from your manner, your recollection is that he didn't say anything before the shots were fired?"

"No, I don't think so."

"Now, would you say at the time the second shot was fired that Troy was quite close to Blake?"

"I couldn't say how close he was for sure. He seemed a fair distance."

"I see. Well now, when Troy fell, Blake moved into the next room, didn't he?"

"Yes, he went around—"

"He went around Troy?"

"He walked around to the north, toward the north wall, and around and into the front room."

"When Troy fell, was he right in front of Blake?"

"No, I don't believe he was."

"Was Blake to the north side of Troy when Troy fell?"

"I believe he was to the north."

"Had Blake moved at all between the first and second shots?"

"Yes, I believe he did move a step or two."

"To the north?"

"You mean . . . ?"

"Between the first shot and the second shot?"

"After the first shot, when Troy reached out, I think he stepped to the—like, when I would be facing him to the left, that would be to the north wall."

"As if away from Troy?"

"Yes."

"Now, did you observe Blake's manner when he was in the room before the shooting?"

"No. You mean when he was standing?"

"From the time the door was opened until the moment before the shooting, did you observe Blake's manner?"

"I didn't pay too much attention to him."

"Would you say from what you saw that he looked frightened?"

"No, I wouldn't say exactly that he looked frightened. But I didn't pay too much attention, and I couldn't definitely say anything."

"You couldn't say that he was or he wasn't?"

"No."

"The only time you actually paid any attention to Blake, I take it, was after the first shot. Is that correct?"

"Yes, I took more notice."

"Of him then?"

"Yes."

"I take it before that—first of all, you gave your attention to Jasper Billings?"

"Yes, when Troy was kind of standing over toward him."

"Then you went in and looked for linoleum? You weren't looking at Blake?"

"No."

"Did you have a good look at Blake between the first shot and the second shot?"

"Yes, I was watching him fairly close."

"What would you say about his manner then? Did he seem frightened then?"

"No, I wouldn't say that he seemed frightened then."

"What did he seem?" Ryder O'Neill asked.

"He seemed to act kind of calmly."

"Did you see anything in what happened that would induce him to shoot?"

"No, I didn't."

"Do you know what the word 'induce' means, Mrs. Booker?" asked BJ Barry.

"To frighten him," Virginia answered confidently.

"To lead him to shoot, to bring about this shooting," answered Ryder O'Neill.

"No, I didn't see anything like that." Virginia was looking at Ryder O'Neill again as she continued to answer.

"Now, I think Mr. Barry showed you this document?" Ryder O'Neill held it out in his hand so that Virginia could see it better.

"Yes."

"That is exhibit two you are referring to?" asked BJ Barry.

"Exhibit two," Ryder O'Neill confirmed. He then turned to Virginia and continued. "And you say your brother Ted had showed you a copy of that?"

"Yes."

"At the time in November when you made an agreement with Ted?"

"Yes."

"This farm where the shooting took place was one that had been conveyed to your brother Ted by deed by your father in his lifetime, subject to a mortgage?"

"Yes, there was."

"At the time of his death, your father held a mortgage on the farm?"

"Yes."

"And the date of your father's death was June 24, 1953?"

"Yes, that is right."

"In your father's will, did he provide as follows, 'I release and forgive to my son, F. T. W. Sregor'—that is, Ted?"

"Yes."

"'—or his representative if he should die in my lifetime, the principle sum owing on certain registered mortgage given by him to me on the farm property in lots 13 in concessions two and three, Township of Percy, except only the amount of $500, provided that he pay the said sum together with accrued interest on the said mortgage within three years after my death.' Was a provision to that effect in your father's will?"

"That was in there, something like that, but there was a codicil."

"What did the codicil say?"

"The codicil read in it that it was to be left to me, the mortgage."

"The mortgage was to be left to you but still subject to this clause, was it not? If Ted paid $500 within three years after your father's death, the mortgage was to be discharged?"

"What did you say?"

"That if Ted paid $500 within three years after your father's death, the mortgage was to be discharged. Wasn't that the provision of your father's will?"

"No, that wasn't stated in the codicil."

"What did the codicil say?"

"The codicil said the mortgage was left to me."

"I suggest to you the mortgage went to you as part of the residue of your father's estate, and not under any codicil?"

"Pardon?" Virginia asked, confused.

"I suggest the mortgage went to you as part of the residue of your father's estate, and not under any codicil. What do you say?"

"I still don't get what you mean."

"Do you know what 'residue' means?"

"No."

"It means the undisposed of remainder of an estate. Do you understand that? In other words, if a man leaves a will and deals with certain things by name or specifically, and then leaves the rest of his estate without any specific mention, the remainder is the residue of the estate. Do you understand that?"

"I still can't get what you are getting at."

"What I want is this—what I have suggested is on November 16, 1955, Ted still had the right, and had the right until June of 1956, to pay off the mortgage by paying $500."

"Or what?"

"Well, those are all small, simply words. On November 16, 1955, Ted had the right, and still had the right, and would have it until June of 1956, to pay off the mortgage on the farm by paying $500. Is that correct, or is it not?"

"I don't understand that."

"Is there anything hard to understand about the words I have used?"

"I still don't know—"

Justice Butler asked Virginia, "Do you want the question repeated? Do you know what the question is?"

"I still can't understand what he means by this $500 he is speaking about." Virginia was confused.

Ryder O'Neill tried to explain it in another way. "I am suggesting to you under your father's will, as it was provided, Ted had the right to pay off that mortgage by paying $500."

"You mean by paying $500 that would cover the whole mortgage?"

"Yes."

"How could it be?"

"By the provision of your father's will."

"It states in there I was supposed to have the mortgage."

"You were supposed to have the mortgage, perhaps, but subject to the provision that Ted could pay it off by paying $500."

"That was to my mother."

"It wouldn't matter if it was your mother or you."

"Why wouldn't it?"

"It wouldn't matter who held the mortgage—"

BJ Barry could sense the difficulty that Virginia was having answering the question. "I think what my friend is asking the witness to answer is a legal question that Your Worship would have to determine on examination of the document."

Ryder O'Neill mentioned, "I think Seth Sregor said in his evidence that he understood all Ted had to pay off on that mortgage was $500?"

"Seth Sregor certainly swore that," added BJ Barry.

O'Neill continued. "And I suggest it is a matter of common knowledge to anybody: if I take an assignment of the mortgage, I take it subject to the mortgage account, and if I am a testator and hold a mortgage in my will, I can forgive all or part of the mortgage money, and if the executor assigns the mortgage, it is subject to the forgiveness clause under the will, and if there was such a clause, I would like to know."

"My friend has apparently a copy of the will. The witness says there is a codicil that changes that copy, and I don't suppose we can get a solution until we see the codicil, if there is such a document," said BJ Barry.

"Well, I think my mother has a copy of the will," answered Virginia.

"Your mother has a copy of the will?" asked Ryder O'Neill.

"Yes."

"And the codicil?" Ryder added.

"Yes, I believe she has."

"May we have that produced, then? Has your lawyer or solicitor a copy of the probate or copy of the will and codicil? Mr. Cosgrove?" Ryder O'Neill requested.

"I don't know for sure whether he has or not. I don't think so," answered Virginia.

"He said no," mentioned Justice Butler.

Ryder O'Neill surrendered to this question but continued on with the others. "All right, I will leave that document. Now, that document beside you, Mrs. Booker, exhibit two. That contains your brother Ted's signature, does it?"

"It appears to look like it." Virginia glanced at the document to which Ryder O'Neill was referring.

"This document, exhibit one, does it contain your brother Ted's signature, too?"

"May I compare?"

"Yes. What is this you are comparing it with?"

"A cheque."

"May I see it, please? May I have that put in as an exhibit?"

"Is it cashed or uncashed?" asked BJ Barry.

Ryder O'Neill looked at it. "Paid, Royal Bank at Warkworth."

"Have you any objection to it being filed, Mrs. Booker?" asked BJ Barry.

"If I can get it back after," Virginia said with a smile.

"You can get it back," promised BJ Barry.

"That will be exhibit 19," noted Justice Butler.

Ryder O'Neill continued. "Have you the other copy of exhibit two?"

"Have I the other copy with me?"

"Yes."

"No, I haven't the other copy with me."

"Has your solicitor?"

"Yes."

"Would you produce it, please? What Mr. Cosgrove has is not an original document, but a copy made by somebody else. Having compared the signatures on exhibits one and two and that on exhibit 19, what do you say about the signature of Ted Sregor, comparing on exhibit one?"

"This is exhibit one?"

"Yes, the longer agreement. Based on your knowledge of your brother's handwriting, what do you say?"

"It appears to be the same."

"All right, thank you. I show you a photograph, exhibit six. Can you tell me who is shown on that photograph? It is rather small, I admit."

"Well, it looks to be Ted."

"Do you know where Ted is now?"

"No, I certainly don't know; I heard that he was at Sutton."

"Sutton, Ontario?"

"Yes."

"A place south of Lake Simcoe?"

"I don't know exactly where he is, except I heard it was Sutton."

"When did you hear that?" asked BJ Barry.

"It was my sister-in-law, Troy's wife, who told me she saw on the boys' shirts, and they were either at Sutton, Ontario, or passing through," replied Virginia.

"On the boys' shirts?" asked Ryder O'Neill.

"The boys' shirts, little sweatshirts, Glen and James.'"

"When did she tell you that?" asked BJ Barry.

"Oh, I can't say for sure when she told it to me," said Virginia.

"Recently or months ago?" Ryder O'Neill asked.

"It would be about a month ago."

"Now, this trouble between you and Seth developed shortly after your father's death, didn't it, when he contested your father's will?" asked BJ Barry.

"Trouble between Seth and I?"

"Yes," responded Ryder O'Neill.

"Well, I wouldn't say it was trouble between Seth and I, but it was trouble over the will, anyway."

"But you were on one side of that will contest, and he was on the other? Is that right?" asked BJ Barry.

"Yes."

Ryder O'Neill added, "And he got some benefit out of the settlement, which ultimately comes out of your side of the contest? Isn't that right? He got some money, $5,000, or $5,000 was paid? Isn't that right?"

Virginia responded curtly, "There is a settlement made."

"And what were the terms of the settlement?" asked BJ Barry.

"The terms of the settlement?" repeated Virginia.

"Yes," Ryder O'Neill said.

"I think you would have to ask my mother what terms," responded Virginia.

"Virginia, were you not a party to the settlement?" asked BJ Barry.

"No, I certainly had nothing to do with the settlement."

"It didn't affect your property in any way?" asked Ryder O'Neill.

"Yes, it was something to do with the place where we lived there, with Mr. and Mrs. Booker. There was something to do with that."

"In what way?" asked BJ Barry.

"Well, if mother didn't make her payments on a certain time or something, he was to take over."

"'He' is Seth?" Ryder O'Neill was clarifying.

"Yes, Seth. My husband would have to make payments to Seth."

"Now, it was in Mr. Wolfe's office in November 1955 that Ted gave you a deed, a quitclaim deed. Is that right?" asked BJ Barry.

"November 16, 1955."

"And now, following that, did you pasture cattle or cause cattle to be pastured in Ted Sregor's farm?" asked Ryder.

"No, we certainly didn't. We didn't put cattle on there where Seth was working," responded Virginia.

"Virginia, did your father-in-law put cattle there?" asked BJ Barry.

"No, he certainly never did."

The questioning continued for a while about the pasturing of castle and the destruction of Seth's wheat. It seemed like the same question-and-answer period went on for hours. BJ Barry continued to focus on their visit to their lawyer.

"You went to your solicitor, and he said to go on and plough?"

"Yes, he told me to go on and plough."

"And you were to go on and plough, regardless of what attitude Seth took? Is that it?"

"Well, if he should come popping around with any guns, we were to get out of there."

"Did your solicitor say what you were to do if he came around with a gun?"

"Well, if there was any happenings, we were to run and call the police."

"Did he say you were to go on and see if Seth would shoot at you?"

"No."

"How big a field is it? Ten acres?"

"I think Mr. O'Neill could tell you how big the field would be. I believe I happened to see him there, but my brother-in-law—"

"Would it be approximately twice as long as it is wide? If you are not sure, just say so."

"Well, it would be around a five-acre field, and that is as long as I can tell you. One side would be longer than the other, but I don't think it would be twice."

"Seth stood at one end and fired this shotgun, and you and your husband were almost at the other end?"

"My husband had just turned the corner, and I was almost at the other end."

"You turned and were going away at a right angle, I take it, and going still further away from Seth? Both you and your husband?"

"When he shot us?"

"After the shot was fired?"

"Yes, we swung to the east and came down over, further toward the south."

"You were both on tractors. What kind of a tractor were you driving?"

"A Ferguson."

"How big?"

"You mean how long?"

"What model was it?"

"A '49 Ferguson."

"What kind of an engine?"

"Well, I don't know what kind of an engine it would be."

"Gasoline or diesel?" asked BJ Barry.

"Gasoline."

Ryder O'Neill continued. "Would it be as silent as a '56 Cadillac?"

"I hardly imagine so."

"And Annie and Seth were at the other end of the field?"

"Yes."

"Which would be the long end too, wouldn't it?"

"Well, just depends—yes, it would be."

"How do you know what Annie was telling Seth?"

"Well, she acted as though she was telling him—"

"You are guessing what she told him, aren't you?"

"She was making motions for him to put away the gun."

"I thought you were driving the tractor?"

"Sure, I was driving the tractor, but she was making motions."

"How could you see if you were driving a tractor?"

"You can take your eyes off a tractor."

"That is why tractors go over on people, isn't it?"

"Not on level land."

"You were driving away from them, weren't you?"

"Driving toward them when he was putting the gun away."

"He didn't fire any more than once, did he?"

"That is, towards them on the other side," responded Virginia.

"He didn't fire any more than once, did he? Just one round?" Ryder O'Neill wanted a clear answer from Virginia.

"No, he didn't fire any more shots."

"My friend asked you how close you came to Annie Sregor when you were driving. She was behind you, was she?"

"You mean behind the tractor?"

"Yes."

"No, she was standing—well, behind me when I was sitting on the seat. She would be about the back wheel, about a yard away from it."

"Did you back the tractor up?"

"No."

"Did you lift the plough up?"

"Well, we stopped the tractors, and Seth walked toward us—"

"Did you lift the plough up?"

"Yes."

"And back the tractor towards Mrs. Sregor?"

"No, I did not."

"Did your husband?"

"No, he did not."

"Neither one of you?"

"No. Seth made a grab for my husband, but he spun on."

"You say you reported the incident to the police?" Ryder O'Neill asked.

"Yes."

"Did you think it strange that Seth wasn't arrested?"

"I didn't know that I was supposed to draw a warrant up or what to do, something for his arrest. I guess that is why he wasn't arrested."

"You didn't do anything more about it after phoning the police?"

"Well, I didn't see the police until . . . I didn't see them Monday, when they came there, because I was away."

"Now then, were you downtown with your husband on Saturday night not long after supper?"

"When?"

"The day after his ploughing?"

"That would be . . . ?"

"The 25th."

"Yes, I was down the street."

"With your husband?"

"No, I wasn't." Virginia was being very vague, it was unclear if her husband was with her.

"Did you see Stanley Blake down the street?"

"No, I didn't see Stanley Blake down the street."

"Did you see him Saturday night at all?"

"No, I didn't see Stanley Blake on Saturday night."

"Who cut the telephone cables on this house on Saturday night and threw stones through the windows?"

"Telephone wires?" Virginia asked.

"Yes."

"Well, I know about that, but I didn't do it."

"Who did it? Someone associated with you, was it?"

"A friend of ours."

"Who was acting, or thought he was acting, in your interests?"

"Well, I guess he thought he was acting a little bit of interests of his own," she admitted.

"Who was it?"

"It was my brother-in-law."

"That is Mr. Duberg?" Ryder O'Neill asked.

"No."

"Mr. Morgan?"

"Yes, Mr. Morgan."

"Did you know before that he was going to do it?"

"They said something about they were going to go up."

"This was part of the collusion to get rid of Dr. Magee, was it?"

"No, I wouldn't say that."

"Who were 'they'?"

"My husband and Marty Morgan."

"They said they were going up to cut the telephone cable?"

"Yes, because they got tired of Simon Magee running over and throwing stones at us or shooting at us."

"And your solicitor had told you to get rid of Dr. Magee, to put him out, didn't he?"

"That was on Monday, the 27th."

"He told you that earlier, didn't he?"

"No, not to move him out."

"The idea of cutting the telephone wire and throwing stones through the window originated in your own party, and didn't follow any advice from your solicitor to put Dr. Magee out?"

"We didn't intent to put him out that night."

"But you knew Seth had put him in as a tenant?"

"Yes," Virginia admitted.

"And you had spoken to him on a number of occasions, hadn't you?"

"No, I hadn't. I had seen him, and he had hollered at me at the time of the ploughing up there."

"And he told you that you had no right to be there, didn't he?"

"He said something about trespassing."

"What does that mean? Do you know?"

"Well, you are not supposed to be on a place or something."

"He told you that you were trespassing?" Ryder O'Neill asked.

"But I didn't figure I was."

"You knew Simon Magee was in there as tenant, and he was taking the position you were trespassing?"

"Because I didn't know nothing of what kind of an agreement he had."

"You knew he was there as tenant?"

"Yes."

"And that he took the position you were trespassing if you went on the farm? Is that correct?"

"I don't know. Actually—"

"I didn't ask you what else you knew. Do you know what I asked you? You knew that he took the position if you went on the farm you were trespassing. Is that correct?"

"Well, I can't say what he thought."

"You know what he said?"

"Yes."

"That is what he said, wasn't it?"

"Yes."

"Well, this idea of throwing these stones and cutting the cable was to frighten Magee, was it?"

"We didn't intend to break any windows."

"'We didn't intent to break any windows!' You were a party to this arrangement, is that right?" Ryder O'Neill pressed.

"Not at the time my husband and brother-in-law went up and cut the wires."

"When was it you intended to do something else? When you say you didn't intend to break any windows, what did you intend to do?"

"Well, we intended to throw some stones at the cement. That is what they intended, to scare him."

"Scare Magee?"

"Yes, so he wouldn't be running around talking."

"And in the hope he would get out, I take it?"

"Yes."

"And the idea of cutting the telephone wire was so that he couldn't call for help?"

"So he couldn't call Seth and say we were spouting."

"Or throwing stones?"

"Well, you'd better wait a minute until I tell you the story."

"All right, go ahead."

"They went up around . . . it must have been ten o'clock or a little later."

Justice Butler interrupted to get clarification. "On Sunday night?"

"No, Saturday night. and Marty got up with his little vice grips, and he cut the wire."

Ryder O'Neill continued. "Just as simple as that. Go on, Virginia."

"And so later on I came home from down the street, and we went up and we got a load of straw."

"You knew Seth claimed the straw?"

"I expect I have a third of the straw."

"You knew Seth claimed the straw, didn't you? Take a look at exhibit one. What does it say about straw? Tell us what it says about straw."

"It says, 'Seth Sregor to have all straw and hay.'"

"And you had seen a copy of that in June, hadn't you?"

"Yes, I had seen a copy of that in June."

"And you knew Seth claimed all the straw, didn't you?"

"I don't remember that part reading in there about the straw."

"You took this straw on Saturday night after dark?"

"Yes, because we needed bedding for the pigs, and I certainly got no grain or anything else out of it."

"That was the same night your husband and brother-in-law threw stones through the windows?"

"My husband didn't throw stones. He wasn't there, and he didn't know we were up there."

"You were there too?"

"Yes, I was standing back."

"Who threw the stones?"

"Marty Morgan and my brother-in-law Joe."

"Joe who?" Ryder O'Neill asked.

"Joe Duberg."

"They threw stones through the windows and one cut the telephone wires? They threw stones at the house, with no intention to break the windows. They threw stones through one window?"

"And somehow they hit the glass and broke it."

"It was thrown through the window. It didn't jump up and hit the window?"

"A person can't say how close it will go."

"Let us try to be accurate and brief. They threw a stone through one or more windows?"

"A stone went through the window."

"It was thrown through the window, wasn't it?"

"I wouldn't exactly say. It was thrown at the house, not with the intention of going through the window."

"It was thrown through the window, wasn't it?"

"Yes, there was a stone that went through the window."

"And at the same time you took a load of straw?"

"Before."

"When did you take the straw?"

"The straw was taken before the stones," Virginia said.

"How long before the stones were thrown?"

"Well, we were all on the wagon, on the back—"

"You were just leaving with the straw?"

"Just leaving with the straw, and they went out and had neared toward the top of the little hill by Sid Hartman's. We jumped off, and Marty said, 'Let's go and scare Simon Magee. He thinks he is so smart, running around and tattling so much, so we will have a little fun with him.' And we went up, and Marty and Joe picked up a stone and threw it over toward the house."

"How old are you, Mrs. Booker?"

"I am 21."

"How old is your brother-in-law?"

BJ Barry confirmed which brother-in-law. "Morgan."

"I think he is 19."

"How old is Joe Duberg?"

"Around 25, I think."

"That is your idea of fun, is it?"

"Well, we thought that this way he wouldn't be running around and tattling. By throwing a few stones at the house, he would be scared and move out."

"Up to this point you hadn't thought of moving him out?"

"Yes, I had thought it."

"But you hadn't done anything about it up to this point?"

"No, I hadn't," Virginia admitted.

"Did it occur to you that you had made an agreement that required you to give vacant possession of this house on September 1? When did that occur to you? Or was it on September 1?"

"Yes, it was on the first of September."

"Not the first of November?" Ryder O'Neill asked.

"No."

"When did it occur to you that you had made a contract in writing that obliged you to give vacant possession of this house on the first of September?"

"Mr. and Mrs. Jennings came over and wanted to know if Simon Magee was in the house, and I said yes."

"Mrs. Jennings asked you whether Simon Magee was out?"

BJ Barry interrupted, "No, he asked her if he was in the house."

"Yes," responded Virginia.

"Or did she say Doc Magee?" Ryder O'Neill asked.

"No. I couldn't be sure if she called him Doc Magee, or what she called him."

"How old is Dr. Magee?"

"I couldn't say how old he is."

"Considerably older than you?"

"Yes, I imagine he is older. I don't know how much older."

"And he is a veterinary surgeon?"

"I understand that he is."

"He is your brother-in-law, isn't he?"

"Yes, he is my brother-in-law."

"Did you ever discuss him with Mrs. Jennings?"

"I don't remember right now whether I did or not," Virginia stated.

"Do you know for sure if Mrs. Jennings knew who he was?"

"I don't know whether she knew who he was or not."

"Now then, before I leave Saturday night, who chased Stanley Blake down the street toward Seth Sregor's on Saturday night?"

"What did you say?"

"Who was it that chased Stanley Blake down the street from Warkworth to Seth Sregor's place on that Saturday night?"

"I certainly don't know."

"You don't know?"

"No."

"We will leave Saturday, and did Mrs. Jennings come to you on Saturday or Sunday of that weekend?"

"Yes, they were there on Sunday."

"Sunday afternoon?"

"Yes, it was Sunday afternoon."

"Do you know how they came and went toward your place?"

"They came up to—driving from the town's way to our place."

"Driving from town, would they go past this house?"

"They came from the town."

"From Warkworth?"

"From the east to our place."

"And going from the east, would they go past this house where the shooting took place?"

"No, they wouldn't."

"Which way would they go? Past a metal door of some kind?"

"Well, there are only three houses from the school on the left-hand side, and that is—that would be counting our house where we live, and Artie Hartman, and my mother's."

"All right, do you know whether they had gone past this house they were to rent from you?"

"It seems to me she said she was up there and that there was a steel door on the house."

"She said she was up there, and there was a steel door on the house?"

"Yes."

"That was Mrs. Jennings who said that?"

"Yes. She said to me, 'Did you put that on?' and I said no."

"Was that the first time you knew it was on?" Ryder O'Neill asked.

"I didn't know it was a steel door, but I knew it was a silver door."

"A metal door of some kind?"

"Yes."

"And that was on the Sunday afternoon?"

"Yes," Virginia said. "You mean when she said what was on Sunday afternoon?"

"When Mrs. Jennings came up and said there was a steel door and asked you who put it on."

"Yes, it was on a Sunday."

"She spoke to you as having been there that afternoon?"

"Yes, I think that she spoke as if she had been there that day. I don't know if it was that afternoon or not that she had been there."

"That is fine. Now, did you tell the Jennings you were trying to scare Dr. Magee and get him out?"

"No."

"Did you tell them you were going to put Dr. Magee out?"

"Yes, when we went over to get them on Monday."

"You didn't tell them before that time?"

"No."

"Did anything go on at night up or near Seth Sregor's place, any exhibitions by you or your husband or brothers-in-law, to scare Seth or do something to Seth or Seth's property or Seth's cattle?"

"No, not that I know of."

"What about Sunday night? Did anybody go around this house on the Sunday night?"

"No. My husband and I took Marty Morgan down to the post on Sunday night, and it was late when we got home because we stopped at our mother's."

"Were you there at all on Sunday night?"

"No, I was not."

"Were you there at all on Sunday night?"

"No, I was not."

"Were you there Sunday at all?"

"Yes. Well, Sunday, it would be two minutes after twelve when we went up there, early Saturday morning."

"To get the straw?"

"Yes."

"To bed down the pigs?"

"Yes."

"And you discovered just before midnight that the pigs had no straw?"

"No."

"Were you at home on Monday?" O'Neill asked.

"Monday when?"

"Monday the 27th, at any time in the morning."

"Yes, I was home. Well round half past three or right in there, I went down to my brother Troy's."

"Troy lives the other way, doesn't he?"

"Yes, his farm—you go down to the school, yes."

"Did you hear any shooting near Ted's house on the Monday?"

"No."

"Or Sunday?"

"No, we didn't."

"Did you see Stanley Blake or Jasper Billings around this house on Saturday or Sunday or Monday?"

"The only time we saw them there was—you mean—"

"Around Ted's house."

"I was up there on Saturday. I saw Jasper and Stanley Blake because they were up there on Saturday throwing stones at us."

"Where were you?"

"We were ploughing."

"And they were throwing stones at you, and you continued to plough?"

"Yes, only in a different field from where we were shot at."

"How far were they from you when they threw the stones?"

"They were right close—close enough to break the spark plug wire off the tractor I was driving."

"Did the tractor stop?"

"The plug was certainly missing, and I thought it was going to stop."

"Was this the time your father-in-law had a club or a stick?"

"My father-in-law had no stick or club I've seen."

"Was he there?"

"Yes, he was there. He was, I don't know . . . oh, round the side of the farm."

"Did he not go on the other farm?"

"No; Seth threw stones over the fence at him."

"Your father-in-law never crossed the fence?"

"No."

"That was the Saturday, the 25th?"

"Yes, that would be the 25th, on Saturday."

"The Saturday before the shooting?"

"Yes, it would be on the Saturday before the shooting."

"Now then, you went to see your solicitor on Monday the 27th?"

"Yes, I did."

"And he told you to put Dr. Magee out?"

"Yes."

"Had you made any plan for the way in which you would put Dr. Magee out?"

"No, I don't think there was anything actually thought of as to the way."

"But in any case, they got in the car. They drove their car up to your father-in-law's place?"

"Yes, that is right."

"And then you wanted reinforcements, so you got your father-in-law and your sister-in-law to go with you?"

"Troy, he ran down to the barn and said to Mr. Booker, from what I understand, 'Come on, and let's all go up.'"

"And put out Dr. Magee?"

"Because Seth had just went up. We were told Seth had just gone up."

"And there might be trouble, he said?"

"Yes."

"That is, there might be trouble if you tried to put out Dr. Magee?"

"Yes."

"He heard Seth was there?"

"Yes."

"So in order to be prepared for trouble, you took seven people in all? Is that correct?"

"Well, we all went up, and we were hoping not to have trouble."

"But you were prepared for it if it came?"

"They all stayed in the car."

"You had prepared yourself for trouble if it came, when you left your father-in-law's place."

"Yes, that is what Troy said."

"If Dr. Magee would be alone, he would be confronted by seven people?"

"No, only confronted with us ladies that went to the house, and Mr. Jennings."

"Seven of you in the party?"

"Yes, but they were in the car."

"They would be very close within call?"

"Yes."

"How would Dr. Magee call for help if he needed help?"

"We certainly wouldn't intend—"

"When you cut the phone wire, you had made sure that he wouldn't call for help, hadn't you?"

"Well, he had his truck."

"Suppose he said, 'I am rightly in possession, and I will stay,' and you put him out. He couldn't call for help?"

"Nobody would be stopping him with his truck."

"But if he wanted to stay?"

"If he stayed and didn't open the door, I don't think we would have bothered."

"But you went with the object of putting him out,"

"He always kept the padlock on the door and was always prying out of a window."

"The arrangement you had made before you left the Booker house was that you were going to put him out. Was that right?"

"I don't know exactly what the definite thing was. When we went up, there was more or less—"

"Did you go up there with any other object?"

"Well, after Seth went up, Troy said—well, Mrs. Booker, that is my mother-in-law, came out and said, 'Seth has gone up, and you are just asking for trouble if you go up.'"

"So you knew when you went up that you were asking for trouble? Is that right? You had already been warned of that, hadn't you?"

"I didn't see how we were going to come to any decision over the farm, because he said—he had me scared. He said if I took him to court, I wouldn't be around to tell anything the next day."

"Was there any greater risk in taking him to court than going up at night with seven people to take the place at night by force?"

"We would go out and tell Magee what we thought, and get Doc Magee out, and if he didn't get out, we would throw him out."

"Let's be honest to the court: you didn't tell—" Ryder O'Neill did not get to finish his sentence.

"Did you hear the last part of her answer?" asked BJ Barry.

"I heard enough," responded Ryder O'Neill as he walked away.

"If you heard—"

But before Barry could finish his sentence, Justice Butler joined in. "And if he didn't get out, they would throw him out."

After hearing what Justice Butler had said to Virginia, Ryder O'Neill quickly turned back to face the witness, "Did she say that too?"

"Yes."

"Well, I apologize. You are honest, and that is why you took seven people?" Ryder O'Neill could not help being sarcastic. "And he was the one who made the plans and issued instructions, more or less, wasn't he?"

"Well, Seth always had a big—"

"That is why you took seven people, wasn't it?"

"Well, we—"

Ryder O'Neill was raising his voice. He was frustrated with this cat-and-mouse game. "Yes or no? That is why you took seven people?"

"Well, Liza said she would go—"

Justice Butler could tell this discussion was getting rather heated. "Look, look, don't quibble; you are not charged with any offence. You may have some moral responsibility, but all you have to do is answer the question."

"That is my—she could have been charged with forcible entry if she had carried out her intention," said Ryder O'Neill.

"We didn't intend to break any locks off the door if it was locked," Virginia said.

Ryder O'Neill continued, "All right, leave it at that. When you got there, you could see Dr. Magee's truck wasn't there?"

"Yes, his truck wasn't there."

"So you knew he wasn't there, didn't you?"

Virginia replied. "Yes, with his truck not being there, but it doesn't explain a person isn't there."

"And you didn't see the car either?"

"No."

"Nor Seth?"

"Well, maybe the car was hid down around the barn."

"All right, you went up prepared for trouble, and prepared to put out Dr. Magee if he wouldn't go? That is a fair summary of it?"

Virginia started, "Well, I would say after Seth went up—"

"I won't question you any further. It was Troy's idea you should go up that night, was it? He was the one who suggested you go up that night?"

"Yes, he said to me, 'Let's go up.'"

"And it was also Troy who suggested that you—that Mr. Booker Senior go, because there might be trouble?"

"Yes, Troy went down to the barn and jumped over the ditch, and he went to see Mr. Booker—"

"There might be trouble?"

"Yes, there might be trouble, and he said, 'I will go along, too, for fear Dad gets in trouble.'"

"Now, Troy was really the leader of this expedition?"

"Well, we kind of all talked about it, but Troy was the one who really suggested we go."

"And he was the one who made the plans and issued instructions, more or less, wasn't he?"

"Well, I didn't see there was very many instructions really issued."

"You all knew pretty well what you intended to do?"

"No, I guess we didn't know, only that what we were supposed to do in regard to knowing—"

"Tell me, can your brother Ted read and write?"

"He can read a little, and he can write the odd words."

"You said you had nothing to do and weren't around on the night of the chasing of Stanley Blake, on the Saturday night. Do you know who chased him?"

"I know nothing at all of the chasing of Stanley Blake whatsoever, and I never heard anyone else say it until you did now," Virginia replied.

"If he was terrified on the Saturday night, it was no fault of yours?"

"No, it wasn't."

"Where were you on the Saturday night?" asked Justice Butler.

"On Saturday night?"

"Around eleven o'clock."

"On Saturday night between 10:00 and 11:00, or somewhere right there, I couldn't exactly tell you what time—because I went down the street, but I know it was fairly late—downtown I met Seth's wife, Annie, in the lockers at McKee's."

"Around eleven o'clock?"

"Between 10:00 and 11:00."

"Where was your sister-in-law and the rest of the Booker family?"

"I went down with Joe and Liza in Joe's car."

"You were all downtown that night?"

"Joe and Liza and myself."

"In Warkworth?"

"Yes."

"Not Norham?"

"No, Warkworth."

"But you didn't see Blake?"

"No."

"So if Blake came running home saying he was chased by the Bookers, that is wrong?"

"That is wrong."

"You didn't say where your husband was that night, did you?"

"When I left, he was home."

"You don't know where he went?"

"Yes."

"Of your own knowledge?"

"Yes, I know where he and Marty went."

"Because they went over to the farm?"

"Yes."

"I see. You don't know where they went from there?"

"They came back home."

"You don't know that."

"I was there when they came there."

"You weren't with them."

"They came back home and said—"

"You weren't with them," O'Neill repeated.

"No, I wasn't with them, but they came back home and said where they were."

"They could have chased Blake?" Justice Butler asked.

"No."

"Why not?" asked Ryder O'Neill.

"Because I saw them coming across the yard. The pole light was on from the other place. They can angle across to our place from the turn or cut away toward the lane into the house."

"You mean that is the opposite direction?"

"Yes, from up to the farm known as Ted Sregor's farm. That is the way they came."

"Mrs. Booker, did you know that Jasper Billings and Stanley Blake spent Sunday night at this house?"

"No, I did not."

"Did you know that Dr. Magee was scared by what you had done?"

"No, I didn't know he was scared."

"You only hoped he would be?"

"Troy said he saw Dr. Magee over to the police that night around seven, or a little later."

"Presumably reporting the damage; that is why you had interest in it," O'Neill said. "You would only be interested in his visit to the police if he was reporting the damage done on the previous night."

"Well, all Troy said is he saw him over there."

"Was it daylight or dark or dusk, or what was the condition of light on the 27th, when you went up?" asked Justice Butler.

"I would say it was just getting dusk. It wasn't dark at all, I wouldn't say; it was just getting dusk when you start to need a light."

"Was there a light any place around the place?"

"Yes, I think there was a light, but it wasn't turned up very high. It was sitting on a chair, I believe."

"A kerosene lamp?"

"Yes, but you could see plain toward the front room. I could see the linoleum wasn't on the floor."

"When you drove up, was any comment made by anybody in the car when they arrived there? Did anybody make any comment that Dr. Magee was or wasn't there, or anything like that?"

"I may have said it didn't look as though he was there, but I definitely remarked about not seeing Seth's car there."

"What I was getting at—"

"Yes, I might have, because we drove up a while before that and turned around at the gate and drove back down, and his truck, it seems to me, was there then and out in the yard."

"You drove up to the gate before?"

"Yes."

"How long before was that?"

"Before we went to get the Jennings."

"And his car was there?"

"Simon Magee's truck."

"It was there then?"

"Yes."

"So you thought he would be there and went to get the Jennings and move him out, because he was there, and now would be a good time to move him out because you could talk to him?"

"Yes."

"That isn't right."

"You wanted to find out?" asked Justice Butler.

"Yes," Virginia said.

BJ Barry continued, "You wanted to see him?"

"Yes. Doc Magee. Of course we did."

"When you came back, was any comment made that his truck wasn't there then?"

"I think there was."

"His truck wasn't there when you came back?"

"No, his truck wasn't there, no."

"And you don't know whether or not any comment was made?"

"I think there was some kind of comment, but I wouldn't say for sure what it was."

"When you went back to the Jennings, did you tell them you had seen his truck there and knew he was there?"

"We may have. I don't know exactly what was said."

"The reason I am asking you this is that Mrs. Jennings said she didn't know whether either Billings or Blake might be with Dr. Magee. Is that possible she didn't know that, or—"

"I don't know," Virginia said.

"Or do you know whether she knew Dr. Magee or not?"

"I don't think she knew him."

"But you don't know if anything was said to lead her to believe Dr. Magee wasn't there, and neither of these were Dr. Magee?"

"Well, I said something looked like Billings in the window. I think it was me. I said, 'There is Jasper Billings in the window, poked his head out of the window.' But I don't know if she knows Dr. Magee or not."

"She said she didn't, but there was no difficulty in seeing when you got there?"

"No, no difficulty at all."

"Did you drive with the lights on or off?"

"Off."

"And Seth wasn't there when you got there?"

"No."

"If he had been there any time that evening, he had been there before you were there?"

"Well, he just went up a few minutes before. We followed right up."

"I should have asked one question. When you first went up toward the steps, or when the door was opened, did Mrs. Jennings say, 'We didn't come to make trouble, we just came to talk'?"

"Yes, she did."

"Did she say, 'We came to see Dr. Magee?'"

"Yes, she spoke something about Dr. Magee. She said, 'Put your guns away, boys; we didn't come to make trouble, we are here to talk.'"

"That wasn't why you were there at all."

"She said something about how Seth told her to go up and see Doc Magee, anyway," Virginia said.

"Did she say that to the boys?"

"No."

"She said that to you?"

"Yes."

"But you didn't really go to see Doc Magee. You had come to make trouble."

"We thought he was supposed to be up there when we started out, so we were going to go up and tell Seth what we thought."

"At that stage, you didn't think Doc Magee was there?"

"We didn't see his truck."

This concluded the cross-examination of Virginia Booker by Ryder O'Neill.

The testimony about the stone throwing was not clear to BJ Barry, and he needed to understand the situation more clearly. "Virginia, just a couple more questions, please. On the Saturday when Blake was throwing stones at you, how did he participate in that?"

"He jumped up on the tractor and tried to pull me off."

"Blake did?"

"Yes, and my hat blew off."

"Was he frightened then?"

"No; he tried to pull me off the tractor."

Justice Butler could not make sense of the reason. "What for? Just fun?"

"I don't know what for. He was there with Seth, and they were having a merry time throwing the stones at us, at the tractor and at us."

Stanley Blake could get carried away and lose perspective. He looked up to Seth as a father and wanted to do whatever he could to make Seth happy. Stanley was more often than not in a fantasy world; he was a lost boy. Virginia uncrossed her legs and got up from the witness box, still clutching her little black book, and she left the courtroom. As she exited the courtroom her husband, Willy Booker, was being escorted into the courtroom by the bailiff. They glanced at each other and smiled, but no words were spoken.

Eighteen

William Booker, Virginia's husband, approached the bench and was sworn in. BJ Barry began the examination.

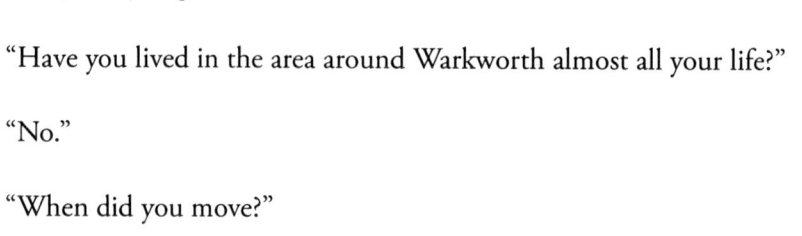

"Have you lived in the area around Warkworth almost all your life?"

"No."

"When did you move?"

"In 1953."

"Where had you lived previously?"

"Port Hope," William Booker replied.

"Then when were you first present at any conversation with the Jennings relating to a property your wife owned?"

"The first time, I guess, when they were up to our place on a Sunday."

"What time of year?"

"In the spring."

"Was some agreement entered into by your wife with them to rent them a house?"

"Yes, I think it was."

"And do you know the details of that agreement?"

"Yes, I know a little bit about it."

"You did have some knowledge of that score?"

"Yes."

"Then when did you first become aware that Seth Sregor was claiming to have a five-year lease on that property?"

"This was when my brother-in-law's cattle was up there."

"Morgan's cattle?"

"Yes."

"Do you remember when that was?"

"I think that would be in April; I don't know."

"Who said something about it at that time?"

"Well, Dad told us when we came home at the weekend."

"Told you and your wife?" Barry asked.

"I think he told her, but I don't know whether he told the wife."

"You had some understanding—"

"He told Dad something when he was talking to him, that he had an agreement or something."

"And there was evidently a disagreement between your wife, Virginia Booker, and Seth Sregor as to who was entitled to possession of this place?"

"Pardon?"

"There was evidently a disagreement between your wife and Seth Sregor as to who was entitled to possession of this place?"

"You mean at that time?"

"Well, following that."

"Yes, I think so."

"And do you remember an occasion when you went up there to plough with your wife?"

"Yes, I remember that."

"And there was some trouble on that occasion?"

"Yes."

"And that would be, as I understand it, on August 24, the Friday?"

"Yes, that is right."

"And were you up there on the Saturday ploughing?"

"Yes, Saturday morning."

"And what occurred on that occasion?"

"That is when Seth and his boys came down the field there and started throwing stones at us."

"Who was with him?"

"His own boys, and Stanley Blake and Jasper Billings, and I think Doc Magee was there, too."

"What did they do on that occasion?"

"Well, when I came down to the bottom of the headland and turned around, they were picking up stones and throwing them along the field. I went to turn the other way, and they chased up. The wife went up the other side too, and one of Seth' boys went to jump on her tractor, and I made him get off her tractor. He was going to grab her tractor, and I came behind him then to get him away then."

"What part did Blake play in that?"

"He was on her tractor."

Justice Butler wanted to clarify to whom William Booker was referring. "That is what you meant by 'one of Seth's boys'?"

"Yes."

"One of his sons?" asked BJ Barry.

"No, one of his boys, Stanley Blake and Jasper Billings."

"Was one of his boys on the tractor?"

"They tried to get on the tractor, and I kept them off."

"What part did your wife play?"

"I guess she came on the other side. I don't know."

"You say Blake tried to get on her tractor?"

"Yes, and he tried to pull her off, and that is all I know because Seth was running after me."

"Did you see whether Blake threw any stones that time?"

"No, I couldn't say whether Stanley threw any stones."

"How many of Seth's boys were down there on that occasion?"

"I think they were pretty well all there."

"And he has how many?"

"I think there were four there, anyway."

"Four of Seth's own boys; these two, Billings and Blake; and Seth himself?"

"Yes."

"And there was trouble that day?"

"Yes."

"Did you go back up to the premises that night, with Marty Morgan on Saturday night?"

"Yes."

"And what did you do up there that night?"

"We cut the telephone wire."

"Who cut it?"

"Marty Morgan."

"What was the reason for doing that?"

"We were going to take a load of straw out, and we didn't want trouble when we were getting the straw, so we cut the wire."

"And about what time would it be when you did that?"

"I imagine it was getting pretty late, because we had all our chores done, and the wife and my sister and brother-in-law went down the street, and while they were down the street, we cut the wire. I couldn't say what time it would be—somewhere between 10:30 and 11:00."

"Did you go back and get the straw later?"

"Yes."

"What time would that be?"

"I don't know what time it would be. It would be close to midnight."

"On that occasion were any windows broken in the place?"

"I don't know, because I left with the tractor and the straw."

"On Saturday night, August 25, did you see Stanley Blake at all?" Barry asked.

"No."

"At Warkworth or any other place?"

"No, I don't think I was down the street."

"You don't think you were down the street at all?"

"Not that I know of, from the early part of the evening."

"On Sunday the 26th, were you up around the premises at all?"

"I can't remember that."

"You can't remember if you were around the premises?"

"The 26th, must have been . . . We must have finished ploughing that field on the Sunday, because the field was done before Monday."

"Was there any trouble on the 26th?"

"No."

"And on the 27th, did you go back up again?"

"No," Booker said.

"On Monday, the day the shooting occurred?"

"Only when they came home, and then we took a drive by."

"When who came home?"

"Virginia and Troy."

"What was your purpose in doing that?"

"Well, they said something about going up to see about getting Doc Magee to move out, so we took a drive to see what was going on, because Dad was putting a fence up that day, and he heard a lot of hammering going on."

"Could it have been shooting going on?" prompted Barry.

"Well, if it was, it was short-range because there was no echo at all about it."

"And you took a drive up there. About what time in the evening would that be you went up there?"

"I don't know . . . Might be around six o'clock. I don't know what time it was."

"Could you tell whether Doc Magee was on the premises at all at that time?"

"I didn't see his truck."

"Then where did you go?"

"I'm not sure. We went down home after that, or right out to the Jennings."

"When you got to the Jennings, what was said?"

"They talked about going up to Doc Magee's."

"Who said?"

"Troy and them."

"What did they say?"

"They wanted to go up and see about getting Doc Magee to move out, so they said they would go up with us, and we all went."

"And you stopped and picked up your father and sister on the way up?"

"Yes."

"And when you got to the premises, was it daylight or dark?"

"Just kind of getting dusk," said Virginia.

"Did you have lights on your car or not?"

"No, we didn't. We may have had the lights on; I can't remember."

"Whereabouts did the car stop?"

"We stopped in the driveway."

"And what happened?"

"Well, we took—Mother told us Seth Sregor had went up, and when we got in the yard, we didn't see Seth Sregor's car, and then we saw Jasper Billing's head in the window."

"Which window was that?"

"The kitchen window, southeast window."

"The little window?"

"Yes, and I don't know if we saw Stanley at that window at that time or not."

"And what happened after your car stopped?"

"Well, the door opened up, and we saw Stanley and Jasper."

"Who got out of your car?"

"Mr. and Mrs. Jennings, and sister Liza, and my wife, Virginia."

"Where did you or your father—"

"We were all in the backseat."

"Yourself, Troy Sregor, and—"

"My dad."

"In the backseat?"

"Yes."

"What was the reason for you staying in the car?"

"We didn't see anybody around, didn't see Seth Sregor, and didn't see no reason to get out."

"If Doc Magee had been on the premises, who was going to talk to him?"

"I guess they were, Virginia and them."

"And where did the other group of people go? That is to say, your wife and your sister?"

"They walked toward the house."

"How close to the house did they get before anybody appeared?"

"I don't know whether they hardly got out of the car or not before the door opened."

"Who did you see?"

"Jasper and Stanley."

"And where were they when you saw them?"

"Just in the doorway."

"Did they have anything?"

"I didn't see they had anything."

"And what did you see happen?"

"They went up—"

"Who is 'they'?"

"Mr. and Mrs. Jennings and Virginia and Liza went up to the door, and Troy said, 'They've got guns, let's go.'"

"And did you see anything?" BJ Barry queried.

"I didn't see anything at that time, no."

"So Troy said, 'They've got guns, let's go.' And what did he do?"

"He got out of the left-hand side of the car, and I got out of the right."

"And what did your father do?"

"He stayed in the car."

"What did Troy do?"

"He ran up to the steps there, into the house, and when I was getting out, I got caught in the backseat, and he was in the house. I was coming up through the little gate there, and just as I got to the door, I heard a noise, you know, and I took a look and seen a muzzle flash from Blake's gun."

"What kind of a noise?"

"Just like a gun."

"And you looked and saw a muzzle flash from Blake's gun. Where was Blake at that time?"

"Over at the east side of the kitchen, between the two windows pretty well."

"Over between the two windows?"

"Might have been a little more to the right; I don't know."

"And you saw the muzzle flash, and what did you see happen?"

"I took a look next time and saw Troy turned the other way with his hand up to his stomach, and he said, 'No, you don't.'"

"Troy had his hand to his stomach, in what fashion?"

"Like that."

"His right hand, was it?"

"I'm not sure which hand it was. I know he had his hand to his stomach."

"He had his hand to the middle of his body?"

"Pretty well, I think."

"And he said, 'Oh, no, you don't?'"

"Yes."

"Where was Troy standing at that time?"

"Well, he would be standing a little bit to the—maybe the right of the door in the front part of the house."

"Was Troy in where the door goes into the front part of the house?"

"To the south."

"To the south side of the front door, where the door goes into the house?"

"Yes."

"And how far would he be away from the west wall of that room?"

"Oh, maybe three feet, might have been four, I don't know."

"And you heard him say, 'Oh, no, you don't,' and he grabbed his stomach?"

"Yes."

"And then what did he do?"

"Well, when I turned around, he was kind of turned the other way."

"Which way?"

"Facing east, and I seen him take a few steps forward then toward where Blake was."

"Toward where Blake was?"

"Yes."

"And then what happened?"

"I noticed a spot on his back after he got pretty well across the floor, and I was watching them, and he kind of turned a little bit then. I think I heard Virginia say to get help, and I didn't think then he was shot. I thought they were using blanks, and I saw him put his hand up, and I think it must have come in here and out of his back."

"How many shots did you hear?"

"I heard the one, and the other one didn't make very much noise at all. I can't remember hearing that one at all."

"Have you any recollection of hearing two shots?"

"No. The other one I wasn't sure of."

"When did you notice that blood stain on his back?"

"When he was fairly close to where Stanley was. I noticed that."

"How close would he be to Blake at that time?"

"I don't really know how close he would be."

"And then what did you see happen?"

"I just saw him turn."

"Who?"

"Troy. He turned, I think it was, and somebody said something about Troy being shot and to get help."

"When you last saw Troy, where was he?"

"After I got down to the step, he was laying on the floor."

"When you left he was standing up?"

"Yes, when I turned to leave, but after I got to the step, I turned and he was lying on the floor."

"Somebody said to get help, and you went to get help?" BJ Barry asked.

"Yes."

"And where did you go?"

"To Sid Hartman's."

"What did you do there?"

"I phoned the police, and I think it was Dr. Koffee I phoned. I couldn't get the Campbellford, police and I phoned for Brighton."

"Did you wait at Hartman's until they came there?"

"Yes, that is right."

"Did you see your wife later?"

"Yes, she came up."

"How long after you got to Hartman's did she come up?"

"Well, she came in just as I was phoning the police again, and I was going to tell them what it was when she was there."

"When you went into the kitchen, did you see Billings?"

"Yes, I did."

"Where was he?"

"Standing to the right of the door."

"Did he have his rifle?"

"Yes."

"What was he doing with it?"

"Slanting down a little bit. I noticed the barrel of the gun first; I didn't know there was anybody there until I looked."

"At the time you saw this muzzle flash from Blake's gun, in what position was he holding it?"

"Pretty well waist level, I imagine. About here some place."

This concluded the examination-in-chief of William Booker.

Ryder O'Neill began his cross-examination. "Now, Mr. Booker, I don't want to go into too much detail, but you have helped your wife and assisted her, I take it, from sometime this spring or even earlier, in her efforts to claim and obtain possession of this farm, have you?"

"Yes."

"Did you have anything to do with pasturing cattle on this farm in the fall of '55?"

"Yes, in a way."

"In what way?"

"Well, the cattle had been over on this wheat, but it wasn't our fence."

"Did you take them away?"

"I took them away a good many times to keep them going back, and once there Seth said they were all right on the north end of Cassidy farm, and he said, 'Will you tell Ted to get the fence fixed?'"

"At that time you knew Seth had some right on the farm, did you?"

"Yes, some, I guess. He said he had the right. He told me there it was his farm and just waiting until the estate was cleaned up and he could pay it off."

"The estate was cleaned up at the time the cattle went on the wheat?"

"Yes, the wheat, but on the north farm when he was doing the ploughing—"

"Did you have anything to do with putting cattle in the barn in the spring of this year?"

"No, I didn't."

"Did you have anything to do with driving Seth's cattle from the farm to his own farm in June of this year?" O'Neill asked.

"Yes, I helped."

"And that was done, I take it, as a means of claiming the right to possession of the farm and saying Seth wasn't entitled to possession?"

"No, according to the agreement she had, he had no right to have cattle there."

"Did you get a letter from Mr. Hurman in the fall of 1955?"

"Yes, I did."

"You haven't got that letter, have you?"

"No, but I have it at home."

"To what did that refer?"

"It stated there Seth wanted $100 for damages to his wheat."

"Did you do anything about it?"

"No, I didn't."

"Did you have anything to do with cutting the bands on the grain Seth harvested this year?"

"No."

"Do you know anything about it?"

"No, I don't," William Booker stated.

"Did you have anything to do with damaging the plough of Seth's on the farm?"

"No."

"Do you know anything about it?"

"No, I don't."

"Or damaging the seed drill?"

"No."

"You don't know anything about that either?"

"No, I don't."

"Did you have anything to do with . . . Well, you did have to do with ploughing on August 24?"

"You mean we were ploughing?"

"Yes, you with one tractor and your wife with another?"

"That is right."

"Can you back one of these tractors up?"

"Yes, you can back them up."

"You lift the plough?"

"Yes, you can lift the plough."

"And back up that way?"

"If you put it in reverse."

"It is quite a formidable instrument if it comes to a person in that manner, if backed toward someone with the plough up?"

"What do you mean?" Booker asked suspiciously

"Would you like it come to you backward with the plough up?"

"No, I don't think so."

"Did you back it toward Mrs. Seth Sregor on August 24?"

"No."

"Did your wife back hers up?"

"No."

"Did you drive the tractor toward her in any way?"

"No."

"Or toward\ your wife?"

"No, because she was behind me."

"All right, now, on Saturday there was this incident of the ploughing and the stone throwing, and you said you cut off Seth's boys with the tractor?"

"I cut off one because he was going to jump on her tractor. I ran up so close he couldn't get in where her tractor was."

"You drove your tractor at him?"

"No, just drove it to keep him off, so he couldn't get on her tractor."

"And what did you do to Blake?"

"I didn't do anything to Blake."

"You said you did something to him."

"No, I don't know how he got by me, but when I went to the corner, he went to my left. I didn't do anything with Stanley Blake at all."

"I think you did something with your tractor toward him."

"No."

"Did you say you went down town early that evening?"

"No."

"Did any of your family or relatives or connections?"

"It wouldn't be very early."

"When was it?"

"I don't know what time it would be. I guess after they got the chores done, and my brother-in-law came home from work."

"What brother-in-law?"

"Joe Duberg, he and my sister and my wife went down the street."

"And the Morgans?"

"Marty was up with me."

"And his wife?"

"I can't tell you what about her. Maybe she went back down the street with them."

"Mrs. Duberg went back down the street?"

"Mrs. Duberg may have gone down the street with them."

"Her husband?"

"No, Joe and Liza and Virginia."

"Did you know who chased Stanley Blake that night?"

"No, I don't."

"Did you hear about it?" O'Neill asked.

"No, I never heard about it."

"As far as you know, he wasn't chased at all?"

"No."

"But you did go sometime around midnight and take a load of straw from the stack near the house on the Ted Sregor's farm?"

"That is right."

"Why did you go at midnight?"

"Well, it is the only time we had, and we had done the chores and waited for them to come back from down the street."

"And why were the phone wires cut?"

"We didn't want no trouble when we were getting it."

"You didn't want to scare Dr. Magee?"

"What do you mean?" Booker asked.

"You didn't want to frighten him?"

"I had no reason to frighten him."

"Had your wife?"

"Not that I know of."

"You didn't want to frighten him?"

"Well, I wasn't going down. I wasn't around there, only to get the straw."

"But you were there along with the party consisting of your wife and Morgan and I guess Duberg, weren't you?"

"What was that to do . . . ?"

"I don't know. I want to find out."

"I wasn't there, not when they went down there."

"You went down to get the straw?"

"Yes, I took my truck, but we weren't down to the house to get the straw."

"It is not far from the house?"

"I don't know how far it is. A little piece."

"What do you mean, 'a little piece'?"

"A fair distance."

"You go past the house to get it?"

"No."

"How do you go to get it?"

"There is a gap alongside two fields; it's off the road."

"Did you know your wife and the party were going down to scare Dr. Magee?"

"Well, they said something about it."

"Who said it?"

"I don't know who it was."

"What was said?"

"I don't know, because I was on the truck."

"What did they say something about?"

"I just heard them say something about going to scare Doc Magee or something."

"Who were they?"

"I guess Virginia and Joan and Marty Morgan and my sister and Joe Duberg."

"Five of them were going to scare Dr. Magee? That is what they said?"

"Five? Six, wouldn't it?"

Well, I don't know. Virginia and the two Morgans and the two Dubergs?

"Yes, five."

"This was around midnight?"

"Yes."

"And you were getting the straw, because you couldn't get it earlier?"

"No, we couldn't get it earlier."

"What was the straw for?"

"For the stock."

"What stock?"

"Pigs."

"What for, for the pigs?"

"Bedding."

"When did the pigs need bedding?"

"Well, we were out that night."

"They didn't have any that night?"

"We had some there, but not straw."

"Did they have to wait until after midnight for their bedding?" asked O'Neill.

"Well, we couldn't go up Sunday."

"Why not?"

"We had to go up ploughing again."

"Did you take the straw right to the pigs when you got home?"

"I don't know, because Dad finished up the chores."

"After midnight?"

"Dad does most of the chores, so if he bedded the pigs, I don't know."

"You didn't bed the pigs?"

"No, I don't bed them out very much."

"You got straw for them?"

"Yes."

"Every midnight?"

"No."

"Just this midnight?"

"Yes."

"Did you ever go out at midnight before?"

"No."

"Now, the next day did you see Mr. and Mrs. Jennings?"

BJ Barry interrupted Ryder O'Neill to get clarification. "You are now talking about Sunday or Monday?"

Ryder O'Neill answered, "Well, say Sunday. Did you see Mr. and Mrs. Jennings, Mr. Booker?"

"Yes, I think they were there," Booker replied.

"At your place?"

"Yes."

"What were they talking about?"

"I don't really know, because I left them when they were there."

"Did you hear any conversation between them and your wife?"

"Yes. I heard them saying something about Seth having an agreement or something, five or ten."

"Did you hear Mrs. Jennings ask your wife who put the metal door or steel door on the house?"

"No."

"Did you hear Mrs. Jennings say she had been up around the house during the day?"

"No, I can't recall I did."

"So you went away while they were still talking, did you?"

"I don't know whether I left them there or not."

"You have already said you did."

"No, I said I didn't know."

"You don't know?"

"I am not sure."

"Did you hear of any agreement or arrangement made between your wife and Mrs. Jennings that day?"

"I don't know whether it was that day or not, but I remember Mrs. Jennings saying Seth wanted the agreement she had, to get it back from Virginia, but I don't know whether or not it was that day. Seth wanted Mrs. Jennings to get the agreement that was between Virginia and Mrs. Jennings to rent the house."

"He wanted her to get that back?"

"Yes."

"Mrs. Jennings told your wife that?"

"Yes. I don't know whether it was that day."

"The following day you went to Oshawa with your wife?"

"On Monday?"

"Yes."

"No, I didn't."

"You stayed home, did you?"

"Yes."

"What was the first you had to do with this visit, this expedition?"

"When Virginia and Troy came up and said something about getting Doc Magee to move out."

"Who told you what they were going to do? Troy or Virginia?"

"I don't really know; they were both talking there."

"Between the two of them, they told you that you were going up to get Doc Magee to move out?"

"Yes."

"Did they say they were going to get the Jennings for that purpose?"

"No, they said about just getting the Jennings to go up with us. I don't know who said that."

"So you got in the car with your wife and Troy, and drove to the Jennings?"

"Yes."

"When you got to the Jennings, did you go inside?"

"Yes."

"And did you hear what someone told the Jennings, your wife or Troy?"

"I remember them talking, but I don't know what it was about."

"The subject matter of the conversation was going back to this house, was it?"

"Yes, it was."

"And they wanted to go with you back to the house?"

"They were asked if they would go, and they said they would."

"And you and Virginia and Troy got in Troy's car again, and drove back to your father's place?"

"No, Troy and I came back in his own car."

"Troy and you came in Troy's car?"

"Yes."

"And did you make plans, as you came with Troy, about what you would do when you got over to the house to where Dr. Magee was?"

"No. He was talking with me about getting machinery between us and getting the farms together."

"All right, you were planning what to do with this farm when you got possession of it?"

"Not that one, just our own. We were just talking about farming in general."

"And weather and crops?"

"We were talking about machinery."

"You got to your father's house, and Seth got a phone message from his wife? I'm sorry—Troy got a phone message?"

"I don't know."

"Your mother gave him a message, or else Troy was called to the phone, or something like that?"

"I don't remember that."

"Did you get there first, or did your wife and Mr. and Mrs. Jennings get there first?"

"Troy and I got there first."

"You waited a while for your wife and Mr. and Mrs. Jennings, did you?"

"Yes."

"Or was it just a matter of minutes?"

"Just a matter of a few minutes."

"Was there any discussion during that interval about what you were going to do when you got to the other house?"

"No. What did you mean by a message? I know—"

"Did someone tell Troy that Seth was at the other house?"

"Yes, he and I went round to my Dad's and Mother's part, and she said, 'Seth just went up.'"

"That is what I meant by a message."

"Oh, I didn't know."

"Did Seth then go down to the barn to get your father?"

"Not Seth."

"I'm sorry, did Troy?"

"Troy and I both went down. He went down to see Dad, and he came behind me. He wanted Dad to go up because Seth was up there."

"And he thought there might be trouble?"

"Yes."

"And that is what he told your father?"

"Yes."

"And Mr. and Mrs. Jennings also appeared at your father's farm somewhere?" O'Neill asked.

"Yes."

"And you all got in the Jennings car?"

"That is right."

"What was your objective in going over to the other property, where Dr. Magee was staying?"

"To see about getting him to move out."

"And if he wouldn't move out, what then?"

"Well, I guess we would have to put him out."

"Your object, first of all, was to get him to move out, and if he wouldn't, to put him out?"

"Yes."

"And if he resisted, what were you going to do?"

"I don't know; I never thought about it," Booker admitted.

"You would have to use force?"

"I don't know. I never thought about that."

"That is why you had seven people in the car?"

"Not for him. Because Seth Sregor was up there."

"If Seth used force, you were going to use force."

"Yes."

"You thought it might come to the use of force by your party against another party."

"We figured he might jump us."

"You knew you were heading for trouble."

"I didn't see Seth's car when we moved in."

"You knew you were heading for possible trouble when you got in the Jennings' car at the Booker home. Is that right?"

"I don't know, because—"

"Did your mother say, 'Don't do this, you are only making trouble?'"

"No."

"What did she say?"

"I don't know what she said."

"Did she say something about that subject?"

"She just said something about, if we had to move them out, she didn't know if we could do it, because it was getting too late."

"Too late?"

"Yes, in the evening."

"Was it raining that evening?"

"No."

"It wasn't?"

"No."

"Did you hear Troy state it would be a good night to put Dr. Magee out?"

"I don't know whether I did or not."

"Well, at any rate it was a night when you knew he couldn't telephone for anyone if he needed help?"

"Yes, but we didn't know if he had the wires fixed."

"You didn't know that?"

"No."

"But you knew the wires had been cut on Saturday night?"

"I don't know whether we noticed them the first time."

"But you knew they had been cut?"

"I didn't know whether the telephone company had come down and fixed."

"I suppose that was possible. Now, going back to this business of the ploughing. At the time when you did this ploughing on Friday the 24th, you knew Seth claimed exclusive right to possession of the farm, didn't you?"

"Where we are ploughing?"

"Yes."

"Yes."

"Before you went there?" O'Neill asked.

"Yes."

"And you also knew it on Saturday morning."

"Yes."

"If you knew it on Friday, you must have known it on Saturday, too."

"Yes."

"And you knew what you were doing was going in there, and disturbing the possession of someone who claimed to be entitled to possession?"

"Yes, he claimed possession."

"And you were disturbing that possession?"

"Yes, because it didn't agree with the contract she had."

"But he claimed he was entitled to possession?"

"Yes, he claimed to."

"And you were disturbing that possession?"

"Yes."

"And you would be making trouble by doing that, wouldn't you?"

"Yes. If he was going to stick to us, we might as well give up."

"Did you know on the Monday night that Dr. Magee claimed to be entitled to possession of the house?"

"Pardon?" Booker said.

"You knew on Monday night, August 27, that Dr. Magee claimed to be entitled to possession of the house?"

"Yes."

"And you were going there to put him out, by force if necessary?"

"Yes, if he didn't cause too much trouble."

"You were going to use force to put him out, if the force you used was sufficient?"

"It depended what it was."

"In other words, if you were strong enough, you would put him out?"

"Not that way."

"Well, what way?"

"Well, if we had to put him out and there would be no trouble over it, we would."

"If he couldn't bring up reinforcements. Is that what you meant?"

"Yes."

"If you were strong enough, you would put him out. That was right, wasn't it?"

William Booker did not respond.

This concluded the cross-examination of William Booker by Ryder O'Neill. Willy Booker stood there looking a little shell-shocked. Mr. O'Neill advised Willy that he was excused. Willy got up and left the courtroom.

Nineteen

In the summer of 2008, Malorie had decided she needed to know more about the dreams she used to have. Since her grandmother's passing, she had not dreamt at all, but she use to have dreams that she believed were giving her messages from those that had passed on. Malorie signed up to visit a group to learn more about mediumship. It was very interesting, and Malorie really liked the medium to whom she was speaking. After leaving, Malorie looked into the medium's website and noticed that there was going to be another group session held at the woman's home, and Malorie hoped she could learn more. Malorie and her daughter Rorie ventured out one Saturday afternoon near the end of September. They had a great time, and Rorie also felt very comfortable with Lynn, the medium. Lynn was also from Newfoundland, where Malorie's husband was from, so there was that bond in itself. Because the spirits were not coming through well that day, many of those attending got free reading cards. Rorie and Malorie were both disappointed and happy at the same time. They decided that they would try and book something for November, when Rorie came back from university.

Lynn started by reading Rorie. The person coming to talk to Rorie was a father figure on Malorie's father's side. At first Lynn thought it was Malorie's father, but Malorie didn't think her father was dead, even though he had not been part of her life for over 12 years; she assumed she would have heard. Malorie figured it must be her grandfather Seth, because Lynn said she did not give bad news, so if Malorie didn't know her father was dead, then it wouldn't be him. Malorie was thrilled to think it was Grandpa Seth; he was just the person she needed and wanted to talk to. Malorie was on the edge of her seat and couldn't wait for Lynn to finish with Rorie's reading, as selfish as that sounded. Lynn's message proved later to be eerily dead-on for Rorie.

It was now Malorie's turn, and though normally she could never remember her questions, this time she had. She felt as though she had hit another roadblock in her investigative work, and she hoped that perhaps the other side could help. She wondered if that was what had led her to Lynn that Saturday afternoon in November. Many of those that had been present at the actual murder had passed on.

Lynn first started talking about Malorie's husband and the muscle spasms behind his heart; she said there was no concern and not to panic. Anthony did get muscle spasms, but he always thought it was his back. His heart looked fine, Lynn confirmed; it was just muscle spasms. *Thank goodness,* Malorie thought, because he was her strength and the love of her life. Malorie would make sure she made a doctor's appointment for Anthony as soon as she got home. She had done it before, and Anthony's doctor was always great. One time Malorie had been given a reading about a special blood problem that her husband had, which could only be detected by a specific blood test not normally done. Malorie had sent a note with Anthony the next time he went to his doctor. His doctor very kindly did the test, and sure enough, there was a problem. It was easily corrected by medication. Since then, there had always been an unspoken trust between Malorie and the doctor.

Lynn then asked Malorie if the name J or Jake came up around her, as someone who had passed. Lynn reminded her it could be from her husband's side, too. Malorie chuckled and said, "I forgot about that; it is suppose to be about me." The only Jake she could think of was her cousin's horse. Stupidly Malorie had not even thought that the "J" could be referring to her great-grandfather, James. She could be so dense at times. Malorie had still not remembered when Lynn moved on to another spirit.

Lynn then focused on someone from Malorie's husband's side that was connected to his mom and had Alzheimer's prior to passing. Was it possibly Anthony's grandmother? Malorie had thought she had passed from cancer. Lynn said she was vacant, and though she may have died of cancer, she thought she had Alzheimer's too.

Now it was time for Malorie. "Is there anything you would like to know about?" Lynn inquired.

Here it was. "I'm not sure if you can tell me this, but I would like to know who really murdered my great-uncle, Troy." Malorie could feel that her entire body was tense.

Lynn explained her vision. "As soon as you said murdered, I got the image of a stabbing. Is that what it was?"

Disappointed, Malorie answered, "No, gunshot. There were two."

Then Lynn moved on. "I feel like you are of the family, but not of the family. What does that mean? Were you adopted?" Lynn explained how her mom had a baby out of wedlock that was still raised within the family, and actually she grew up knowing this baby girl as her cousin.

Malorie had been frequently reminded of how she was a mistake. Her parents had only been married three months when her mother became pregnant. It was not Malorie's fault that her parents chose to use the rhythm method with a menstrual cycle that was completely out of whack. Malorie focused back to the question at hand. "My mom has the scars from her C-section which she is more than willing to display, because I don't think she was too thrilled to have me."

Lynn was focused on what the spirits had to say. "I have to ask you, are you one of four?"

"Technically I am, as my mother lost two boys. But really I should be one of five, because my mother had an abortion. I felt largely raised by my grandparents. But knowing my father, there may be more of us; it is hard to know. I have always felt like the black sheep, like I didn't belong. I never felt even my mother and sister were family; I was just very much alone. I have never been close to my cousins. But I was close to my grandparents.

With my parents, I always felt that I was the parent." Malorie was confused by the "one of four" question.

"Okay, I just don't feel you are part of that family. Your dad seems to have an alcohol issue, or does he?" asked Lynn.

Malorie knew he did at one point, but she was not sure if he still did. She was pretty sure that with his new health-freak girlfriend, the only alcohol he came close to would be rubbing alcohol. "He did have a drinking problem when I was young; he had suffered a nervous breakdown and tried to commit suicide." Malorie was 12 or so at the time, and the next morning when she asked her dad why he had tried to kill himself, he had told her it was because he had a horrible daughter like her. Malorie had carried that with her until she was about 21, and only after the birth of her son did she realize one should not blame those types of things on a child.

Lynn tried to go back to Malorie's original question, but she said she really wasn't pulling anything up on Malorie, other than the fact that she didn't belong to the family she was born into. "I don't feel anybody here, and yet with you, Rorie, there was a very strong pull. Yet I don't feel that with you, Malorie. Even aside from the questions that you have asked, I am not getting a sense of anything. Are you really fixated on this?"

Malorie began to cry. She felt like such a fool and began to apologize. Her father had raised her to believe that crying was a sign of weakness. Not only did Malorie feel all alone, but she felt ashamed for being so weak and crying. Lynn was so kind and said not to worry at all, and she made her feel so comfortable. Malorie told them that she just felt so alone at that moment. She did not belong in the present family world, and even her relatives in the other world did not want to speak to her. She was all alone and on a mission that seemed like a waste of time. She was heartbroken.

When they were all done, Malorie and Rorie thanked Lynn and went to get their coat and boots on. They were having company for dinner and still had to pick up some things at the grocery store. It was already after five o'clock; they had been there for over two hours. Time had flown by, but Malorie didn't feel any further ahead on her quest.

Rattlesnake Fever

As Malorie went to leave, she thanked Lynn and apologized again. Lynn put out her arms to hug Malorie. Malorie was extremely touched, especially because she had never thought of Lynn as the touchy-feely type. Her outreach to Malorie made Malorie think that regardless of how the reading went, she hoped Lynn would always be a part of her life.

It was a sad drive home, but as always, Rorie was great and kept her mom's spirits up. They began to focus on the evening ahead with friends and family.

On the following Monday, when Malorie arrived at work, she remembered that the information she had requested from the archives had not come, and she had not received any further e-mails. She contacted the archivist and discovered that they had everything for her and had e-mailed her the invoice, but they had not heard from her. When Malorie confirmed the e-mail address, she realized they had sent it to her old e-mail address. They could not mail the hard copy until they received payment. Malorie pulled out her credit card and paid for it over the phone. The archivist said they would send it out as soon as possible. Malorie thanked the archivist again for all his help.

The large brown package arrived three days later. Malorie had a lot of work to do, but she was too tempted by it and couldn't resist. She sat down and realized that not only had the archivist been able to find James Seth Sregor's last will and testament, but also Troy Sregor's. In addition to James' will was the transcript documentation from the probating of the will. Malorie was so excited! Once she started reading, she couldn't stop.

Anthony cooked dinner as she read. When he came in to the family room where Malorie was curled up in her comfy chair reading, he could see how pale Malorie had gone. "Are you okay?" Anthony asked.

"I don't think I am. I think I am going to be sick." Malorie held her stomach and started to cry. This was not what she had expected to find at all. Not only was it about finding out her family history, but she was also confirming her own dreaded past. She needed to step away from all this research for a while. It was too overwhelming for her, and she felt as though she was in a very dark place.

Twenty

It had taken about six months for Malorie to be able to think about looking at the transcript again. She picked it up and began reading the three expert testimonies by Corporals Brown, Beattie, and Wagner. BJ Barry began examining Corporal Brown.

"In addition to your work as a photographer, do you also specialize in fingerprint identification work?"

"Yes, I do, sir."

"In connection with this matter, did you make an examination of two .22 calibre rifles?"

"Yes, I did."

"When?"

"On the Thursday following this incident, sir, as near as I can recall."

"Where did you examine them?"

"At the Campbellford Provincial Police office."

"Corporal Beattie, what was your purpose in examining them?"

"To ascertain if there were any fingerprints on the barrel or the butt belonging to either of the accused or Troy Sregor."

"And what did you find?" Barry asked.

"I did not find any fingerprints at all, sir. There were two smudges on one—I don't recall which one—that bore no ridges whatsoever except an indication that fingers had been placed on the butt."

"Is that finding at all common in regard to the material you were examining, Corporal?"

"Yes, sir."

"That is the usual finding?"

"Yes, sir: minute portions of oil and the steel being cold; very little indication of fingerprints found on the barrel."

This concluded the examination of Corporal Brown. As Corporal Brown left the bench, he nodded to Corporal Beattie out of professional courtesy. Corporal Beattie approached the witness box to testify, and then BJ Barry began his examination.

"You are a corporal of Provincial Police stationed at Campbellford?"

"Yes, sir."

"And on the evening of August 27 of this year, did you receive a telephone call in this matter?"

"Yes, I did."

"What time would it be you received that?"

"At 8:50 p.m."

"And who called you?"

"I got the call from my wife."

"And what did you do when you got the call?"

"Constable Bigelow and I proceeded to a farm west of Warkworth approximately two miles, known as the Ted Sregor's farm. We arrived at 9:25 p.m. As I drove into the driveway of the farm—"

"Let me stop you there. Did Dr. Burger, the coroner, also follow you down?"

"Yes."

"And you got there at 9:25 p.m., and as you drove in . . ."

"Three persons stood just south of the driveway. I knew two of them: Mrs. Annie Sregor, Jasper Billings, and another youth."

"And what did you do?"

"I went into the kitchen at the rear or east of the house, and I saw a person known to me as Troy Sregor lying face down on the floor, his feet to the east, his head to the west. There was a pool of blood at his face on the floor, and the blood stained his shirt on the back."

"Did you make a search of the premises?"

"I stayed in the kitchen part of the house, and Constable Bigelow went into the other part of the house."

"For what purpose?" Barry asked.

"To search the house."

"Was anyone found?"

"He didn't find anyone."

"And what followed?"

"A sketch of this portion of the house was made, and a few minutes later William Booker came into the kitchen, or came to the kitchen door, and I had a conversation with him."

"Following that conversation, where did you go?"

"I went to a garage south of the house, where Jasper Billings, the accused now known to me as Stanley Blake, and Mrs. Annie Sregor stood. As I walked up to these three, the two accused stated they had nothing to say. I noted that Stanley Blake held a rifle in his hand next to his leg, which I took. The rifle was a .22 calibre Cooey bolt-action repeater, which was empty."

"Empty at the time you got it?"

"Yes."

"What did you do with that rifle, Corporal?"

"I held it in my possession."

"You say both accused said they had nothing to say?"

"That is right, sir."

"Up to that time, had you said anything to them?"

"Nothing up to that time."

"What followed after you took the rifle from Blake?"

"I asked Stanley Blake his name, to which he stated he had nothing to say, and Mrs. Sregor stated his name was Stanley Blake. I asked him if Stanley Blake was his full name, and he again stated he had nothing to say. Mrs. Sregor advised me that was his correct name. I then asked him how old he was, and he stated he had nothing to say. Mrs. Sregor advised him to tell me his age, to which he stated he was 18. At that time I placed Stanley Blake under arrest, and I advised him that he would be charged with either wounding or murder. I warned him in the following words: 'Do you wish to say anything in answer to the charge? You are not obliged to say anything unless you wish to do so, but whatever you say may be given in evidence.' He made no remark."

"Then what occurred, Corporal?"

"I searched Stanley Blake, and nothing was found other than tobacco, and he was placed in the cruiser."

"Then were both men taken to the County's gaol?"

"They were, sir."

"And did you return to the scene of this shooting?"

"Yes."

"And what occurred with relation to the body of the deceased?"

"The body was in the same position as when I had been there previously, and Inspector Fancy arrived shortly before I had returned from Cobourg. I found and picked up two cartridge jackets, .22 calibre, from the floor. One was north of the body beside it, and one was lying between the legs."

"With relation to this jacket to the north of the body, Corporal, in what condition was it?"

"It was partially flattened."

"As if somebody might have stepped on it?"

"Right."

"And the other one between the legs, was it cylindrical shape, the ordinary round shape for a fired case?"

"Yes, sir."

"You took possession of both of these articles, did you?"

"Yes."

"And then what happened?"

"The body was removed by Roberts' Funeral Home, and I took a sample of blood from the floor and placed it in a test tube. I accompanied the body to Roberts' Funeral Home in Warkworth where, at approximately 11:00 a.m. the same date, Dr. A. M. Whitman arrived and commenced a post-mortem."

"Did you identify the body to the doctor?"

"Yes, sir, I did."

"And the body on which the doctor made the post-mortem examination was the body of Troy Sregor?"

"Yes, sir."

"I take it Troy Sregor was known to you before this?"

"Yes, sir, I knew him."

"On the same morning of August 28, did you go to the County's gaol with Corporal Lowe of the Ontario Provincial Police at Brighton?"

"Yes, sir."

"And what occurred there?"

"Corporal Lowe interviewed the accused, Jasper Billings."

"And following that interview, what did you and Corporal Lowe do?"

"We returned to the farm known as Ted Sregor's farm, and I took possession of a second .22 calibre Cooey bolt-action repeater rifle lying on the ground at the gate in the southeast corner of the barn yard."

"Will you look at the photograph, exhibit number nine in this matter, and tell us if that is a photograph of the rifle before it was moved?" BJ Barry said.

"It is a photograph of the rifle, sir."

"Before it was moved?"

"Yes, sir."

"Can you indicate in the photograph exhibit number eight where it was in the barn?"

"The rifle lay on the ground at the east, which would be the left side of the larger barn, the larger structure."

"In connection with the post-mortem examination, did you receive any material there?"

"Yes, I received a Blake outer shirt, a Blake undershirt, and a pair of trousers."

"And did you receive anything from the body itself?"

"I received a sample of blood taken from the heart from Dr. Whitman, and a lead slug removed from the body."

"And what did you do with these articles?"

"The blood was placed in a best tube and the slug put in a metal box."

"And kept in your possession?"

"And kept in my possession."

"And what other material did you receive in this connection, Corporal?"

"I removed from the west wall of the kitchen of the farmhouse a second slug, a lead slug, that I also retained in my possession."

"And then what was done with all these materials you had taken—the rifles, fired cartridge jackets, the two lead slugs, and the clothing?"

"These exhibits were delivered to Constable Wagner at R. C. M. P., Rockcliffe, on August 31, 1956."

"Who delivered them?"

"I did personally, sir."

"And at the time they were taken in your possession, were they in anybody else's possession?"

"No, sir; they were locked in a metal vault at our office in Campbellford, and I retained the key."

"How many fired jackets did you take to Constable Wagner?"

"I took three."

"Where had the third one come from?"

"From the cement stoop at the kitchen door of this farmhouse, outside the building."

"And the two slugs you say and the empty jackets—was one of the slugs one you obtained from the body of Troy Sregor, and the other you took out of the wainscoting?"

"Yes, sir."

"And the two rifles you delivered, what were they?"

"They were both .22 calibre Cooey bolt-action repeaters."

"And were they the rifles you had obtained from Blake and the one you had found in the barn yard?"

"That is right, sir."

"Then I take it you took the sample of blood to Professor Rogers?"

"The two samples of blood were delivered to Professor Rogers in Toronto on August 29, 1956."

"I will have to recall this witness, Your Worship, to identify exhibits when Constable Wagner gets here."

This concluded the examination of Corporal Beattie, and BJ Barry proceeded to have Constable Wagner sworn in before he commenced his examination.

"Mr. Wagner, you are a Constable of the Royal Canadian Mounted Police?"

"I am, sir."

"And you are presently stationed where?"

"In Ottawa, sir."

"How long have you been a member of that force, Constable?"

"I'm in my ninth year."

"And presently what work are you engaged in?"

"I'm presently employed in the Firearms Identification Section of the R. C. M. P. Crime Detection Laboratory in Ottawa."

"And how long have you been specializing in that?"

"Approximately three years."

"And what experience have you in it?"

"I have been employed in that particular field of work for the three years. I have studied under the firearms examiners, who have been recognized as expert witnesses in criminal trials across Canada. I have written examinations on the subject."

"Set by those examiners?"

"Yes, sir."

"And have you made examinations of bullets and jacket cases of your own initiative?"

"I have, sir."

"Have you given evidence as a result of your examinations in other cases?"

"Yes."

"Where?"

"In the Provinces of Quebec, Ontario, and New Brunswick."

"In connection with this matter, did you receive the materials Corporal Beattie identified as having been given to you?"

"Yes, sir."

"And what did you do with these materials?"

"May I refer to my notes made at the time?"

"Yes."

"After having received the exhibits in this case, it was my purpose, firstly, to determine whether or not exhibit bullets were fired from either of the exhibit rifles. It was also my purpose to determine whether or not the exhibited expended cartridge cases were fired in either of these two exhibit rifles. My third purpose in this examination was to examine the undershirt, the over-shirt, and the pair of trousers submitted as exhibits for evidence of close range firearms discharge effects."

"Dealing first with the matter of whether the exhibit bullets were fired from either of the exhibit rifles, what conclusion did you arrive at in that connection?"

"As a result of my examination, I concluded the exhibit bullets—I don't know what they are marked now . . ."

"Exhibits 23 and 24."

"Exhibits 23 and 24 were fired from the exhibit .22 Cooey rifle."

"And for the sake of clarity of the record, it is exhibit number 22, not the calibre?"

"Yes."

"And what conclusion did you arrive at in connection with the fired cartridge jackets?"

"The result of my examination is that the exhibit cartridge cases, exhibits 25, 26, and 27, were fired from the exhibit 22 rifle."

"And what conclusion did you arrive at as to the range or probable range at which the two bullets had been discharged?"

"I was unable to come to any conclusion as to range, but my examination disclosed no evidence of close-range firearm discharge effects."

"And when you are referring to a firearm of that kind, what do you mean by short range?"

"Actually firing this weapon, I found partial burn up to as far as 46 inches—that is, partial burn and unburned grains of powder."

"And what kind of material was used?"

"We used absorbent clean white paper. We have found it to be the best material for our purpose."

"You found that up to 46 inches. you would find residual powder stains on the paper or absorbent?"

"Yes."

"And did you find any such evidence on the garments you examined?"

"I found none."

"What sort of tests did you do to determine the presence or otherwise of powder burns, Constable?"

"There are a number of tests we do. Our first examination, of course, is a visual examination. Our second examination is microscopic examination. Then we go on to normal photography, infrared photography, and soft X-ray. Our last test is the chemical test."

"And as far as you are concerned, are those tests exhaustive? Are there any other tests you haven't mentioned?"

"Actually, if we found nothing on these articles microscopically, it is unlikely we will find anything by any other means. However, these tests are conducted to be sure we overlook nothing."

This concluded the examination-in-chief of Constable Wagner. Constable Wagner was then cross-examined by Ryder O'Neill.

"Constable Wagner, What is a soft X-ray?"

"It is an X-ray that is not as penetrating as the normal, hard X-ray. If there is any metallic particles on the object we are X-raying, powder grains will also show up if they are there."

"This paper you use is the most receptive material, I take it, for these powder grains?"

"Yes, sir, it is the best material to see what we want to see on, and it also will retain the powder particles, which will stick to the white absorbent paper."

"More than, for example, to a white shirt?"

"I wouldn't say that, sir."

"You say this other absorbent paper is the best material. Do I take it the white cotton shirt is not as good a material?"

"We can't expend cotton shirts for our test, sir. We found for our purpose it is the best material we have."

"And as I understand it, however, as a general rule when you say there is no evidence of close-range discharge, you mean within 36 inches, don't you?"

"That is a more or less arbitrary standard we have. It is beyond a man's reach."

"All right, thank you."

Justice Butler had a question. "In finding that these bullets were fired from exhibit number 22, did you find they could not have been fired from the other rifle?"

"Yes, sir. The characteristics are the same, the number of lines of grooves and widths are the same. They are the same Cooey rifle model, but the signature—that is, the marks left on the bullet—can be attributed to one particular weapon."

"So you are satisfied none of these bullets were fired from exhibit 21?"

"No, sir."

"Are you an expert in firearms in other ways than identification? Could you tell me, for example, whether a hard jolt on the butt of a .22 rifle might cause it to be discharged?"

"No tests were made in that respect, sir, but when I was firing it, I found no unusual condition."

Ryder O'Neill continued, "I see. But in order to load it, as I understand it, you lift up the bolt lever and pull back the bolt, which draws a round from the magazine?"

"Yes, sir."

"And twist the bolt forward and down?"

"Yes, sir."

"And the rifle is now cocked?"

"Yes, sir."

"I am suggesting a sufficiently hard jolt on the butt might cause it to be discharged."

"I couldn't say, sir, but we can try it." Constable Wagner took the rifle and tried it.

Ryder O'Neill was watching, "Not that one, no. I see, all right."

"No actual test was made for that," responded Constable Wagner.

"It is a characteristic of bolt action rifles, is it not, that on occasion they can be discharged in that way?"

"It depends on the weapon, sir, the condition of the weapon."

This concluded the cross-examination of Constable Wagner by Ryder O'Neill.

Twenty-One

Malorie felt strong enough to again review the material she had received from the archivist. She had always thought that the death of Troy Sregor was over greed and her great-grandfather's estate; even the front page of the August 29, 1956, newspaper had suggested that. It had referred to the fact that there was no liquor involved at the time that Troy was murdered. BJ Barry had stated it was the result of a family feud that began when James Sregor died.

The will was a standard will and only one page long. He had left to his wife Elizabeth the following.

> 3. I bequeath to my wife, Elizabeth Sregor, all my furniture, furnishings, pictures, plate, household equipment, and other household effects, which at the time of my death shall be in, about, belonging to, or used in connection with my home; and also all livestock, farm machinery and equipment, crops growing or gathered, automobiles, cash on hand or in bank, and all securities for money, for her own use and benefit, absolutely and forever.

To his son Ted Sregor, he wrote,

> 4. I release and forgive to my son Ted Sregor, or his representative if he should die in my lifetime, the principal sum owing upon a certain registered mortgage given by him to me on the farm property in Lots 13 in Concessions 2 and 3, Township of Percy, excepting only the amount of five hundred dollars, provided

he pay the said sum, together with accrued interest on the said mortgage, within three years after my death. If he pays the said sum and the interest within the stated period, he shall be then entitled to receive a discharge of the said mortgage without being compelled to make any further payment thereon.

All Ted had to do was pay $500 over three years, and the property was his to keep. That was a pretty fair deal for Ted; surely he would be able to accomplish that.

For his son Troy Sregor, James wrote,

> 5. I give and devise my farm lands in Lot 14, Concession 3, Township of Percy, together with the adjoining three acres which I bought from Joe Shotz, to my wife Elizabeth for the full term of her natural life, but she shall permit my son Troy to continue to reside thereon, to continue to work the lands and take any profits therefrom arising, so long as he continue to so remain. But if he should abandon the lands during the lifetime of my said wife, then she shall be entitled to the rents and profits therefrom during the remainder of her lifetime; and after the death of my said wife, I give and devise the said lands to my son Troy, absolutely and forever.

For his daughters Virginia and Joan he wrote,

> 6. I give and devise my home property consisting of parts of Lot 14 in Concession 2, Lot 18 in Concession 5, Lot 19 in Concession 6, all in Township of Percy, to my wife Elizabeth for and during the full term of her natural life, and upon and after her death, I give and devise the said lands to my daughters Virginia and Joan, in equal shares, share and share alike.

That meant that if Troy was not around, his property would also become Virginia and Joan's.

For his other six children he wrote,

9. I make no provision in this my will for my other sons Seth and Daniel, nor for my other daughters Alice, Ethel, Victoria, and Bethany, as they have already received from me material benefits and assistance during my lifetime.

Although it all seemed quite straightforward and somewhat unfair, there was a codicil that had been added dated March 22, 1951, which stated,

> I hereby revoke the entire Paragraph #4 in my said will, regarding release to my son Ted Sregor of certain principal moneys, which may at my death be owing by him to me under a registered mortgage given by him to me on farm property on Lots 13 in Concessions 2 and 3 of Township Percy, and I now substitute in place of the said Paragraph #4 the following:
>
>> I give and bequeath to my daughter Virginia, in addition to any other benefits provided for her in my will, all the principal sum under a certain mortgage made to me by my son Ted Sregor on a farm property on Lots 13 in Concessions 2 and 3 of Township of Percy, with all securities collateral thereto and all interest accrued thereon, which may be owing to me at the time of my death.

It was signed James Seth Sregor. But within the file that Malorie had received, there were other copies of James' wills; some had been ripped up. It was as though James Seth Sregor had an idea in his mind but then kept changing it. Was he blackmailing his children by holding his will over their head? Something clearly wasn't right.

When the will was finally read, Seth Sregor, the eldest son of James Seth Sregor, knew that something was not right. He retained a lawyer and probated the will. The proceedings were held in the Surrogate Court of the United Counties of Northumberland and Durham. The parties were represented as follows for the probating of the estate of James Seth Sregor, deceased.

Mr. Potter was the lawyer for Seth Sregor and Daniel Sregor. Mr. Hurman appeared on behalf of Victoria Gerrard, Ethel Edwards, Bethany Woodrow,

Alice Magee, and Ted Sregor; they were probating but did not make an appearance. Mr. Thompson and Mr. Stein was for Elizabeth Sregor and Mr. Johnson was for Joan Sregor and Virginia Sregor, as represented by Official Guardian.

Thus began the examination of Seth Sregor, before G. D. Robertson, Examiner, in Victoria Hall in the Town of Cobourg, on Monday May 30, 1955. After the general information had been completed (name, address, number of brothers and sisters, etc.), Mr. Thompson began questioning Seth Sregor deeper.

"And you filed a caveat against your father's will?"

"Yes, sir."

"To prevent it from being admitted to probate and you have made certain grounds of undue influence?"

"Yes, sir."

"And misrepresentation?"

"Yes, sir."

"Would you tell me, please, what is the nature and what are the details of the misrepresentation alleged by you?"

"Just how do you mean by that, now?"

"The copy of the order that is set up to find the issues between the parties sets out that you—Seth Sregor, Daniel Sregor, Victoria Gerrard, Ethel Edwards, Bethany Woodrow, Alice Magee, and Ted Sregor—affirm, and your mother and two sisters as represented by the official guardian, deny that the making of this will was procured by misrepresentation and undue influence. Now, just in general terms, from your knowledge of the word 'misrepresentation' that you are stating took place with respect to the making of this will, what is it you are getting at, in your own language?"

Mr. Potter, Seth's lawyer, interrupted. "First of all, you should make it clear this man can't read or write. He may or may not understand what 'misrepresentation' means."

"Misrepresentation means that someone has made statements, misleading statements, to your father with respect to the situation with his family, prior to the making of this will. Now, tell me what you are alleging are the misrepresentations you complain of." After explaining, Mr. Thompson looked directly into Seth's eyes.

Seth was a big man, and he leaned back in his seat and crossed his arms. "Well, the best thing would be for you to ask me questions from now on."

"I am asking you, what are the misrepresentations you are alleging took place with your father in making this will and codicil? Just tell me in your own words of what you are complaining."

"Well, we have other brothers and sisters."

"Other brothers and sisters than what?"

"That helped to make the estate."

"And what happened to them in the will?"

"They got nothing, and they were always promised something."

"Tell me who are the brothers and sisters that were promised something. Is that yourself?"

"Yes, sir."

"What do you feel should be left to you?"

"I figured we should all be given equal shares. We were promised something."

"All 10 children should have equal shares?"

"Yes."

"And your mother?"

"No, I figured—"

"What did you figure your mother should have?"

"She should have more."

"How much more?"

"It's not for me to say."

"How much do you say your father promised you?"

"My father always told me that I stayed to home, and which was better to have, an education or money? He said education would only make you money."

"What was your answer to that?"

"He said, 'You stay home and work, and I'll fix you up at the time of my death.'"

"When was it that conversation took place?"

"When I was home working."

"That is over a long period of time, I suggest, Mr. Sregor."

"Yes, sir."

"And how old are you today?"

"I'm 37."

"How long were you at home working with your father?"

"I was married in January '39 or '40."

"The early part of this last war?"

"Yes."

"What month were you married?"

"January, on the 11th."

"After your marriage, did you leave home, or had you already left the family farm?"

"I was home at that time."

"Did you subsequently get your own place?"

"Yes, sir."

"Shortly after marriage?"

"Yes, sir."

"These conversations you speak of with your father—had they been going on over a period of time prior to your marriage?"

"Yes, sir."

"Over a period of some years."

"Mostly when he was trying to keep me from going to school, keeping me at home from school."

"How long would that be before your marriage?"

"That would be when I was 13 or 14."

"How old were you when you were married?"

"I would have been 22."

"At the date of the marriage?"

"In May, as I was married in January."

"Twenty-two in May of '40?"

"That's '39 or '40."

"But in a period from approximately the age of 14 to 22, some seven or eight years, you were working with your father?"

"For seven or eight years," Seth confirmed.

"You stopped school at 14?"

"Yes, sir."

"And you were working at home?"

"I never went to school full time at any time. I would go to school for a week. I will bring the record."

"I'll take your word on that. You weren't going to school full time and stopped at 14?"

"Would go maybe a week, and be out maybe two weeks."

"What you say is there was a general agreement with your father: he recognized the fact that you stayed home those years when you might have been going to school?"

"I heard him tell my younger brothers the same thing."

"You heard him tell them the same thing?"

"After I left home."

"Do you feel your father should have given you the same share, or a greater share than he did?"

"Well, the same share would be nothing."

"Because you don't receive any benefits under this will?"

"I don't think that you can show any place that I received any benefits at any time."

"Did you and your father have any partnership dealings? Were you in business at any time after you were married and away on your own?"

"I have helped him several times back and forth."

"Has he also helped you?"

"No, I wouldn't say that he has helped me back and forth, when we changed work as much as I helped him."

"Your father did quite a bit of business with cattle, did he not?"

"Yes, sir."

"And he put cattle out on farms and shares, that sort of thing?"

"He rented the cattle out off and on."

"Did you have anything to do with any of that business, any cooperation with your father at any time?"

"No, sir. The only time I had anything to do with that business was when someone wouldn't give the cattle up. My father would say, 'Will you come with me and get the cows?'"

"He wanted help on those occasions, and you went with your father?"

"Any boy would help his father."

"What I am getting at is that your relationship with your father was quite good, was it?"

"Oh yes, I would say it's not too bad when he wanted something."

"Not too bad when he wanted something—you are going to put it that way. Were they quite bad sometimes, when he didn't want anything?"

"No."

"Did you have any real fights?"

"No, I wouldn't say real fights. We have had arguments as family affairs, but outside of that—"

"Well, tell me, Mr. Sregor, as far as misrepresentations, you are not able to give me examples except in the most general terms. In connection with the making of this will, in which you were left out, is there anything particular you can tell me? Whom are you suggesting made the misrepresentations to your father?"

"Well, it is like this: when I'd go to see my father, he would be right in the house. I'd ask for Dad and would be back to Cye Johns'. I come from Cye Johns', and my father would be lying upstairs in bed. Ma didn't want me to see him."

"You are making an implication that your mother was preventing you from seeing your father on occasions, by giving misleading answers as to his whereabouts. Is that the total of the basis you can tell me of your misrepresentations made against your mother, Mrs. James Seth Sregor?"

"I made a bargain with my father—"

"When?"

"During the day you were down there, and the roof burned off my brother Troy's house, and he was fixing the fence."

"What would that be?"

"That was on my birthday, and you came down to see the fences."

"What year was that?"

"I would say approximately 1950. I wouldn't commit myself."

"But at that time, fixing that date as 1950, what do you say happened between you and your father that has anything to do with this will?"

"In '50 the roof burned off my brother's house in Warkworth. I was to get the tractor. I was to help put the roof on the house. I filled in an old back well, and I was supposed to get the tractor to put in my spring work. After I got the roof on the house, I went to get the tractor. He says, 'You can have the tractor tonight.' So I used the tractor that night. The next morning he was over to get the tractor."

"He wanted it back very quickly?"

"Yes, very quickly."

"What has that to do with misrepresentations that you are alleging against the making of your father's will?

"Well, that's to show that when I went to get the tractor the next day, my mother says, 'He's not here. He is back to Cye Johns'.' That's the story to that. I couldn't see him. The next day or so, Dad said, 'You were over yesterday.' I said yes. 'I was upstairs in bed,' he says."

"That was the second time your father was up in bed, and you couldn't see him?"

"Yes, sir."

"What has that to do with the alleged misrepresentations in the making of your father's will?"

"How do you mean?"

"Just the question. You are alleging that misrepresentations have been made, that this will has been made due to misrepresentations and undue influence. You said that your mother has made statements to you as to your father being somewhere else, when you say he was at home. There might be some differences within the family at times, but what has that to do with this question you are alleging of misrepresentation in the making of your father's will?"

"I don't understand."

"All right, if you don't understand, I'll leave that. Do you understand the general words when you allege that undue influence has been used to your father in the making of this will? Do you know what the words 'undue influence' mean? That somebody has used influence to get your father to make a will that cut you out? Do you understand those words?"

"Yes, sir. Now I do."

"Whom are you alleging used undue influence in the making of your father's will?" Seth did not reply. "I think the order speaks for itself. This is a situation somewhat similar to fraud. We have no information as to what was said or what was done, but the result of the will might speak for itself. But can you answer the question, please, as far as you can: who are the members of your family, if you are alleging there are members of your family, that exerted undue influence on your father to make the will that he did make?"

"Well, it would be my mother."

"It would be your mother, and anyone else?"

"And Virginia. These are embarrassing questions." Seth just wanted what was owed to him. He didn't want to have to answer all these questions.

"Now, anyone else?"

"Well, I presume that they are the two."

"They are the two, you say, so far as you know?"

"Well, Joan was used, too, but as a minor girl, I wouldn't say that as far as her influence would—"

"Wouldn't be as great as the mother's or Virginia's, because she was a minor, a younger girl; is that right?"

"No, it wouldn't be."

"Now, you have told me this is a very embarrassing question, this conversation. We will have to get rid of these embarrassing questions, so let us have it. On what grounds are you alleging there was undue influence, so far as your sister Virginia is concerned?"

"We'll take it at the time of his death. I have yet to find out the truth," Seth said.

"Have you any specific ground for alleging undue influence by your sister Virginia?"

"Well, my father came to me a short time before he died, at my home, and he told me that he wanted to make a will. My father told me—"

"We are clear on this, Mr. Sregor. This is a short time before he died?"

"Yes, sir."

"Do you know the date of his death?"

"The 24th of June."

"Of what year?"

"Of '53"

"The 24th of June, 1953?"

"I presume that's right."

"This is a short time before his death?"

"Yes, sir."

"He came to your home. Proceed."

"He said—my father said that he wanted to make a will, that he had made other wills, and he wasn't satisfied and he tore them up, for, he says, 'As you know, Seth, Ma had me over a barrel when I made the will—the wills.'"

"The wills, plural?"

"Yes."

"He said, 'Ma had me over a barrel when I made the wills'?"

"He said, 'She had me picked up, taken to Cobourg and questioned, and she told me she would not press charges,' if he made the will to her—made the will in her favour."

"Did you know the nature of the charges that she was not to press?"

"I said to my father, 'Why do you do these things?' He says, 'Seth, times of the month that I cannot help myself.'"

"Did you know to what he was referring?"

"Yes, sir."

"And to what was he referring?"

"Sexual."

"And what is the implication in your talk with your father? The implication was what?"

"I said, 'You have had trouble with Alice, you have had trouble with all the girls, and you shouldn't ought to do that kind of work.'"

"So what your father in substance said was he wanted to make another will?"

"He wanted to make a will."

"And this was in what month of 1953 that you had this conversation with your father, as nearly as you can say?"

"I'd say it was in June."

"That is the month of his death?"

"Yes, sir."

"How many days before his death?"

"I'd say approximately around . . . I wouldn't say definitely. Say, approximately around the 16th."

"And it took place at your home?"

"Yes, sir."

"What time of day?"

"Between seven and eight o'clock."

"At night?"

"In the morning. Maybe nine o'clock. It would be in there someplace."

"Were you alone?"

"No, sir."

"Who was there?"

"Some other people."

"You had this conversation confidentially in the presence of some other people?"

"Yes, sir. I asked him about Joan. I says, 'You have been picked up about Joan. Did you do that?' 'Yes' he says, 'I done it.' She was picked up and taken to Dr. Koffee."

"When was this supposed to have taken place? That is, what year?"

"I would say that would be in . . . I couldn't commit myself."

"Would it be the same year as your father's death?"

"No, I don't think so."

"It was somewhat earlier in time than '53, in respect to Joan?"

"Yes, sir."

"Are you making a similar allegation in respect to any other beneficiary to this will?"

"What's the use?"

"Are you making any similar allegations about Virginia?"

"Yes, on the night of his death, definitely."

"The night of his death?"

"Yes, sir."

"That is the only occasion on which you are making allegations of this nature with respect to Virginia Sregor, now Virginia Booker, that some event that happened on that night of your father's death?"

"No, there is more, but I'm not telling it today."

"This examination is for the purpose of explaining what these issues are about."

"Well, the night of my father's death, I met my father along the road by Vince Pike; my sister Virginia was driving. I was drawing hay that day. The next morning or around six o'clock, the phone rang. My wife, Annie, answered the phone. My father was dead, she said. I immediately drove to my father's place. My mother was not there at six o'clock that morning. I met Virginia at the door and asked her what happened. She told me that Father had a heart attack on some ridge and died there. My wife was present. After his death, or after he was buried, I drove out to the place where he died, and where the car was parked, or backed into the ditch, was nine-tenths of a mile by my speedometer."

"Nine-tenths of a mile from where?"

"From where the car was parked to where he had walked."

"How do you know it was to where he had walked?"

"My brother showed me. My brother Troy showed me where he died. 'Right here, Seth,' he says, and the grass was all lying down. So my brother Troy told me that she had called—Virginia had called him, and Troy said my mother answered the phone, so he got her in the car and struck out to where he died. Troy started to drive fast."

"Your mother got in the car, is that it?" asked Mr. Potter.

"Yes, Mother got in the car with Troy. Troy started to drive fast, and Mother says, 'Troy, don't drive so fast. It's too late now.' We have his statement to that effect. Troy says when she got to the body, she took out his purse, which there was $500 in it. She took $25 out, or put $25 in and took

$475 out and shoved it down the neck of her dress. I have yet to know from my family, from their part, how my father died."

"This episode the day of your father's death, which you have given us, was on the 24th of June, 1953. That's the correct date of your father's death, June 24, 1953, and that is the date of the episode you related here between your father and your sister Virginia. Is that right?" confirmed Mr. Thompson.

Mr. Potter turned to look at Mr. Thompson. "He says it happened on some evening, and he didn't know until six o'clock the next morning."

Mr. Thompson looked away from Mr. Potter and toward the witness bench, where Seth Sregor was sitting. "Whatever the date of your father's death, the day preceding, that was the date this episode happened?"

"Yes, sir," replied Seth.

Mr. Thompson continued with his examination of Seth Sregor. "Do you know, of your own knowledge, there is a will of your father dated March 22, 1951?"

"Yes, sir."

"And I am producing to you the will that has been filed for probate. Would you look at that signature and tell me, to your knowledge, is that your father's handwriting?"

"Well, I have seen his handwriting a lot of times, but I have never seen it look like that."

"You are suggesting it isn't his handwriting?" Seth did not respond. "Mr. Sregor, I will leave that for a moment. The will can speak for itself."

"You ask me my opinion. I have seen his handwriting a lot of times."

"You are not prepared to say that is not his handwriting?"

"I wouldn't commit myself on that."

"That was two years before your father's death, that this will was made?"

"Yes, sir."

"Will you look at this codicil, which is dated the blank day of February, 1952, which is the next year? Would you look at that, please?"

"He is a better writer there than he was on the other one."

"Would you say that is his signature?"

"If that is his writing."

"He is a better writer on the codicil than he is on the will, if it is his writing; so both the will and the codicil are both signed by your father, Mr. Sregor?"

"I couldn't say. I didn't see him sign it."

"That's a matter of evidence. Assuming they were signed by your father, one was signed more than two years before his death, and the other more than a year before his death."

"Well, he has signed other wills and tore them up, and if he was satisfied with the wills, why would he make more wills?"

"Exactly. You are not seriously suggesting that your father, if he wished to, couldn't have made another will in that time?"

Mr. Potter interrupted Mr. Thompson on his questioning. "Mr. Thompson, I suggest this is a question hardly proper on discovery."

"Very good," answered Mr. Thompson then he continued. "Now, are those statements that you have made with respect to your two sisters the grounds on which you are alleging undue influence against your Father?

Are those the grounds on which you are making it, the evidence you have just given us?"

"My father told me, 'I had to make a will for her.' He said, 'I'd have went to jail. He would have pressed the evidence, and every time I get into a jam, I make a will to Ma. She wants to run things. She thinks she will get to run things. But I have come to your place today to make a will.'"

"Did he make the will at your place?"

"No, sir, I didn't have time."

"You weren't going to make the will yourself?"

"I didn't have time to go with him."

The transcript read that the examination was adjourned until later, but for Malorie she had read enough.

After reading this transcript, Malorie had remembered when a medium had told her that her great-grandfather James was actually dead before he left the car, and a woman had actually pushed his body out with her feet. She had described the car as a 1949 black, four-door Studebaker, and that the woman was young with blonde hair and very beautiful. The medium had felt this woman was a daughter and that it was done out of self-defence.

Aunt Georgie had often mentioned to Malorie how Virginia would drive by in her car with Grandfather James and never even stop to pick them up. There could be a blizzard outside, and they would just keep driving, not even so much as a wave of the hand to say hello.

During one of Malorie's visits with Grandma Annie, she had mentioned what the medium had said. Grandma Annie was most upset about the fact that Mrs. Landon, a nearby neighbour who was driving by at the time, had put a blanket from her car over the dead body, because it was hot. She wanted to keep the flies and buzzards away from the corpse until help arrived. Grandma Annie was appalled that Virginia had not had the decency to wash the blanket first before she returned it to Mrs. Landon. "It was full of gravel and dusty when she returned it," was all Grandma Annie could say as she shook her head. She was not concerned about the fact that James Sregor may have been killed and his body dumped, rather than dying of natural causes due to heart problems.

Twenty-Two

Troy's death was not because of greed—it was far deeper than that, It was because of a scorned woman. She now realized why her father had told her, "Don't poke your nose where it doesn't belong." He had warned her, but in a way that had felt more like a threat at the time. She now understood.

Malorie received the information on Thursday evening and tossed and turned all night. She was angry about her past and the past of others. When she got to work the next morning, she called her mother first thing. It was probably a discussion that should have been in person, but Malorie couldn't wait. She was worried about her nieces because they lived with her mother, and she knew that they were still in contact with her father, Ken. Malorie asked her mother if the girls ever spent the night with him, and her mother confirmed that the oldest niece had once, but she was bored and didn't want to go back. When Malorie was about 11, her father had touched her inappropriately. At the time Malorie had been so confused. She had told her mother, but her mother had told her that her father would never do anything like that. She had even confronted her father, but his reply had just been, "What are you talking about?" and then he walked off.

Malorie had convinced herself it was a bad dream. But she now knew that was not the case. Malorie told her mother, "You didn't protect me, and you didn't believe me when I told you. Do you believe me now?"

"Yes, I believe you, Malorie, and I'm sorry." Malorie's mother was always ignoring things, and this had been another example of that.

"Just make sure you protect those girls, and don't let anything happen to them. That is all I ask," replied Malorie. But Malorie knew in her heart of hearts that she would never forgive her mother, and she couldn't possibly forget.

Malorie hung up and tried to focus on the day's work. The weekend was nearly here, and that would give her time to reflect and get strong again. She had spoken to Anthony and told him, not knowing how he would respond to her. He was so supportive and loving. She had honestly been afraid, but he let her know it was okay, and she felt safe in his arms.

She thought about it all weekend and kept to herself. This was heavy-duty information, and she wasn't sure what the next step was. She wanted to talk to Aunt Georgie, but what if she stirred up bad memories for her, too? Who knew how far these secrets ran. So Malorie decided she would call Grandma Isabella, who always had words of wisdom for her.

The following Monday at lunch, Malorie finally got the courage to call her grandma. Malorie told Grandma Isabella everything, including when she was a child. She was not sure where to go from there; should she leave it or call her Aunt Georgie? She told Grandma Isabella she was worried it may open more skeleton closets. Grandma Isabella convinced her to call and said she wished Malorie had of come to her when she was younger. Malorie was shaken up, but she had survived, and she would again. What didn't kill her made her stronger. Malorie told her grandma she loved her and thanked her.

After Malorie hung up, she decided to call Aunt Georgie right away. She told her aunt that she had received more information, and that it was quite shocking and quite bad.

"Oh I don't care. That don't matter none to me," Aunt Georgie said, and she stated she would be over that night. Malorie told her she would have dinner ready for her.

Malorie called her husband to let him know that Aunt Georgie was coming for dinner. When Malorie got home, she was pacing. It was almost eight o'clock at night, and Aunt Georgie had not yet arrived. All of a sudden the phone rang; it was Aunt Georgie. She had fallen asleep on the couch and just woke up. There was a big storm out her way, and she didn't think she should venture out.

Malorie was disappointed but completely agreed; she didn't want any harm coming to her aunt. She adored Aunt Georgie. She thought about telling her over the phone for a minute, but it was definitely in-person material. They agreed that Aunt Georgie would try for the next night.

The next day at work seemed like a long one. Malorie still could not get all of this overwhelming information out of her head. Aunt Georgie arrived about seven o'clock the following night, and after they ate dinner, everyone else seemed to disappear from the dinner table. It was rather odd, but it allowed Malorie and Aunt Georgie to sit and talk.

Malorie pulled out the material that she had received from the archivist. Malorie explained that she had thought that if she got the last will and testament of James Seth Sregor, this would help her find the real murderer of Troy Sregor. Malorie explained that her father had warned her not to dig, and now she understood why. She began going through the material and read parts of the transcript to Aunt Georgie. Malorie could feel her hands shaking and her voice quivering, but she hoped her aunt would not notice. Then she began to read a crime report dated October 1, 1949, and completed by Constable Zachary Kraft from the Hastings Detachment. The first report read as followed.

1. A call was received at this office at 7:00 p.m., September 29, 1949, from Mrs. James Sregor, who stated she wished me to come at once because they had trouble at their home. I proceeded to the scene at once and now wish to submit the following.

2. On my arrival at the home of James Sregor, which is on the county road and about three-quarters of a mile west of Warkworth, I interviewed Mr. Troy Sregor, a son. He first met me on the road just outside of the house and advised me that there was no trouble there and to continue on my way. Thinking better of this, I went into the home and

was met by Mrs. Sregor, who had marks on her face and distinct finger marks on her throat. She was very excited and appeared to be suffering from shock. She advised me that on this date when her daughter, Joan, came home from school, Joan had complained about her back hurting her. Mrs. Sregor states that she was looking over-tired; her reason for this was the appearance of Joan's face. Mrs. Sregor has been suspecting that Joan was being mistreated by her father for some time. Up until this date, when she questioned Joan about this, she had always denied it. On this date, however, Mrs. Sregor questioned her very closely. After considerable questioning, Joan told her mother that her dad, James, had intercourse with her the previous evening when they went for the cows on the tractor. According to Joan, this had taken place in the small woods adjacent to the pasture field. Mrs. Sregor further advised that she suspected this going on for some time, because she had noticed blood stains on Joan's panties on three or four occasions during the past summer. And on one occasion, Joan had washed her panties out herself and placed them with other dirty laundry. Mrs. Sregor believed that these stains must have come from having intercourse, as Joan had not started to menstruate.

After the supper was finished in the home on this date, James Sregor got up from the table, walked around to where Joan was sitting, and attempted to kiss her. Joan had avoided the kiss and gave her dad a short nasty remark. Joan then got up, left the table, and went with her brother to get an animal that had broken out of the pasture field. Her father left and stated he was going to feed the pigs. After he left the kitchen, Mrs. Sregor thought she was alone with her daughter Virginia, and she started talking to Virginia about what had taken place with Joan. After talking a few minutes, Mr. Sregor opened the kitchen door suddenly and stated, "You two are making up a lot of lies about me." He then slapped Virginia severely. He let Virginia go and then beat his wife up. According to Mrs.

Sregor, this beating appeared to last at least 15 minutes, and she shouted for help. Her son Troy heard her across two fields. Just as he arrived, the father quit beating her, went upstairs, and changed his clothes and left.

Mrs. Sregor stated that she was of the opinion that this had been going on for the past 8 or 10 years. On one occasion, about 8 years ago, she had caught her husband having intercourse with her daughter Bethany, who at the time was about 13 years of age. She stated that Bethany was a sullen person and had a sulky disposition. It was very difficult to obtain an admission from her. On this account of the affair with Bethany, the mother had given her consent for Bethany to get married when she was 15 years of age. After Bethany was married. she warned her sister Virginia about their dad, and she also told her never to trust her dad with either Virginia or Joan. The only statement made by Mr. Sregor, which would verify Joan's statement, was made just as he was leaving the house. At this time he told Mrs. Sregor, "I did not do any more to Joan than Hughie Hartman did to you." Mrs. Sregor advised me that he has always accused her of having intercourse with Hartman.

3. Joan Sregor was next interviewed. This child was 11 years of age on August 10 this year. In my opinion she is small for her age, appears to be retarded mentally, and goes to the public school at Warkworth, in Book 2. In talking to her, I formed the opinion that she was very truthful and frank. She advised me that she attends church but has never attended Sunday school. Her mother advised me that the stoppage in her speech and being mentally retarded was caused from Joan having scarlet fever when she was around 5 years of age. Joan advised me that her daddy had been dirty with her on at least 6 occasions. When questioned what she meant by this, she said that he put his thing in her. The first few times he did this, she bled after. She also told me about the time she had washed her panties. She did this so that her momma would not see them all

stained. She states that the first time her daddy did it to her, it took place in the hen house; on another occasion in the horse stable; another in the alley-way in the hog pen; and the last occasion took place in the woods the previous night, September 29, 1949.

I then took Joan to Dr. Koffee's office at Warkworth. I informed him of what Joan had told me. He questioned her, and she gave him the same story with only a few minor changes. After he examined Joan, he advised that her hymen had been broken, and it would be possible for her to have intercourse, although it would hurt her terribly. Further, he had heard rumours and had reason to believe that this had been going on for some time. Little Joan told me on the way home from the doctor's that every time her dad did it to her, he told her, "If you tell, I'll slap you up good." She said, "I was always afraid to tell until tonight." I have no reason to believe that this child told me nothing but the truth throughout to the best of her ability. It was a very pitiful story to listen to.

4. Virginia Sregor, age 14 years, was next interviewed. She is a well-developed girl and seems to be above average in intelligence. She was reluctant to talk about her father. She told me how her married sister, Bethany, had warned her about staying clear of her father for fear he would be having intercourse with her. She also told of how, in the early part of this past summer, her dad would come into her bedroom and endeavour to feel her breasts. She resented this. It continued, so she then would get out of bed before her dad got up, dress, and be doing her morning chores when her dad came downstairs. These occurrences only took place in the mornings. She advised that on August 12 of this year, her dad came to her room, and she was still in bed, having failed to hear him getting up. He had come in and started feeling her breasts, when she woke up suddenly and struck her dad in the face. She could not get out of the bed past him, so she rolled to the far side next

to the wall. He then jerked her out of bed and gave her a severe beating. Her mother had witnessed the latter part of this occurrence. I asked Virginia how she remembered the date, and she told me, "At the time I was going to tell the Children's Aid Society at Port Hope, and I recorded the date on a calendar." She showed me where she had marked it on a calendar.

5. I then left the Sregor home and began a search for Mr. James Sregor. I was assisted by Provincial Constables Baker and Lumins of Brighton Detachment. We searched and checked all known relatives until 2:15 a.m., when the search was given up. The next morning, September 30, I located James Sregor at his son's (Ted). He was arrested and taken to Cobourg. He was warned and told what the charge was. I did not enter into conversation with him as we went to Cobourg. He started making one excuse after another and suggested some other persons who would have had intercourse with his daughter Joan. I then advised him to stop this, or I would confront him with the person he was naming. We arrived at Cobourg at 9:10 a.m., and Provincial Constable Fancy and I then questioned Sregor until 2:30 p.m.

During the questioning the lies that he told were pitiful. As to the fight with his wife, he explained that he had never heard them talking about him, but he slapped Virginia on account of her having the radio too loud, and he beat his wife because she interfered while he was punishing Virginia. He had dressed and left home because they treated him so mean. As to having intercourse with his daughter Bethany, he said she was just framing him along with her mother so they could get his money. When informed that Joan had been ravished and her hymen was broken, he explained this by hearing Virginia tell Joan to put her fingers up herself, and they would fix the old man. He told how ridiculously silly he was making a statement like this, and he then offered the excuse that Joan had lost her virginity from continuously riding horseback. He was also told that his actions were not that of an ordinary parent, who would be nearly frantic on finding out what had happened. He would brush nearly all our questions aside by saying the girls were lined up with their mother, and she was trying to frame him to get his money because he had destroyed his will a week or two ago. This will had been made out leaving everything to Mrs. Sregor.

At one point during the questioning, he requested me to draw up an agreement where he would give his wife and daughters, Virginia and Joan, all he had. We advised him that we could not be a part to any such arrangement. Once when I was questioning him alone during the noon hour, he let on that his memory was just a blank, and he asked who was this Joan I was talking about. This man has been known to me from the very first day I came to this detachment. I was warned never to talk to him alone by one of the inspectors in our department. He is very sly and noted for his evasiveness. He has got quite well off financially, having got the most of his money through crooked deals with old people. He is known around Warkworth by the name of Honest James, for always pretending to be honest. We were unable to get any admission from him.

6. I have kept in touch with Crown Attorney Barry throughout this investigation. Owing to our being unable to get an admission from Mr. Sregor, we had to allow him to go, as we did not have enough evidence to substantiate a charge of incest. There is no doubt in our minds that he is guilty of the offence and has done it several times. I would request that this file be kept open, because we are going to take some other action, as well as some action will be taken by the Children's Aid Society. Mrs. Sregor may lay assault charges also.

7. Copies of this report forwarded to Crown Attorney Barry at Cobourg, with extra copies for the Children's Aid Society.

Respectfully submitted,
Zachary Kraft

On October 26, 1949, Provincial Constable Zachary Kraft had followed up on this matter and found out that Mrs. Sregor had separated from her husband and was living in the Village of Warkworth with her two girls, Virginia and Joan. Crown Attorney Barry had told her that as long as she remained separated from her husband and the girls were with her, no further action would be taken.

Constable Kraft also found out that James Sregor was living with his oldest son. The son had advised Constable Zachary that he had warned his father about his actions, and further, he has told him that should there be any recurrence of the same thing, the son was going to take steps to place the father in an institution.

When Malorie was finished reading the information, she told her aunt about how her father had touched her inappropriately when she was young. She had been lucky enough that it had not been as bad as what had happened to Great-Aunt Joan and her sisters, but it was still unacceptable and had left a very deep scar on Malorie. Malorie looked up at Aunt Georgie. "Statistically children that are sexually abused usually repeat the pattern."

Aunt Georgie looked up from the pages that she had been reading. "But as adults you can make it stop; you have that control."

It had started with Malorie's great-grandfather James sexually abusing his daughters. Malorie's mother had told her that her father and his two brothers had sexual intercourse with their aunt Joan when they were younger, but at the time they had thought it was one of her father's silly stories. Joan, being a victim, in turn had sexually abused Malorie's father,

Ken, as well as his two brothers, Rick and Harry. It was a sickness that kept affecting every generation.

When Malorie was finished going through everything, she looked at her aunt and could see something in her eyes. Her aunt had gone silent. Malorie thought that maybe she had thought badly of her for what she had told her about her father. She already felt dirty, as though it was her fault anything had happened in the first place. But when she looked at Aunt Georgie again, she could see that her eyes were watery.

"Aunt Georgie, what's wrong? Did something happen to you?" Malorie had said it before she could stop the words from leaving her lips. Even though her aunt had not responded, she knew there was something wrong. "I am so sorry. I was afraid this might stir up bad memories for you—I should have left it alone." Malorie looked away, embarrassed that she had caused her aunt pain.

Aunt Georgie looked at Malorie with her eyes moist with tears that she was strongly trying to keep from falling. In a gentle and soft voice she said, "I can't tell you."

"Was it Grandpa Seth?" again Malorie wanted to kick herself. Why couldn't she just shut up and leave it alone? Her aunt just told her she couldn't tell her. Why was she pushing? It was like she had no control over her mouth. Malorie feared that Grandfather Seth, whom she had always placed on a pedestal, was about to make a huge crash to the ground. She felt sick at the thought.

"No, my father was my protector." Aunt Georgie paused and tried to keep from choking on the lump in her throat. "I always begged my father to let me go with him. I would rather be out working in the field than left at home. At least when I was with him, I knew I was safe." She hesitated and then continued. "I have never told a soul," and then Aunt Georgie began to sob. "I never thought anyone would love me for who I was."

Malorie didn't know what to do. She put her arm around her aunt's shoulder, and they both cried for themselves and for all those lost souls who were victims.

Aunt Georgie's brothers Harry, Rick, and Ken had each sexually abused Aunt Georgie. Malorie felt sick, not only for her aunt's pain and suffering, but that Malorie's own father had caused it. She was disgusted. She held her aunt and apologized profusely. She was sorry for drudging up bad memories and for what her father had done to her.

"Aunt Georgie, should I just let this go now and forget about the book?" Malorie was so upset.

"No," Aunt Georgie replied in a gentle, soft voice. "The story needs to be told. It needs to stop."

The bond they shared as black sheep of the family was even stronger now. They both took a deep breath. They were very strong women, and this was only going to make them stronger. Malorie gave her aunt a big hug and told her how much she loved her. Aunt Georgie went home after that, and the next day Malorie called to make sure she was okay. Aunt Georgie was tough, and she was her hero.

Twenty-Three

On Monday, November 5, 1956, at two o'clock in the afternoon, the matter resumed. Justice Butler began the closure of the preliminary trial. "You have appeared before me last Wednesday and Thursday at Brighton on a charge that you, Jasper Billings, together with Stanley Blake, on the 27th day of August, 1956, at the Township of Percy, in the County of Northumberland, did unlawfully murder Troy Sregor, contrary to Section 206 of the Criminal Code. The evidence was taken on the preliminary hearing, and on Thursday the matter was adjourned to today for argument." Arguments were then submitted by counsel for the defence and the Crown.

Justice Butler then looked out at the courtroom. "Stand up, Billings and Blake. You are charged before me that you, Jasper Billings, together with Stanley Blake, on the 27th day of August, 1956, did unlawfully murder Troy Sregor. There has been a preliminary hearing, and the evidence has been given. Having heard the evidence, do you, Billings, wish to say anything in answer to the charge? You are not bound to say anything, and whatever you do say will be taken down in writing and may be given in evidence against you at your trial. You must clearly understand that you have nothing to hope from any promise of favour, and nothing to fear from any threat which may have been held out to you to make any admission or confession of guilt. But whatever you now say may be given in evidence against you at your trial, notwithstanding such promise or threat."

Jasper looked at Justice Butler. "No, Your Worship."

Justice Butler then asked the same thing of Stanley Blake. He too responded, "No, Your Worship."

Justice Butler then advised, "I will reserve my judgment on the committal and ask Mr. Reed to transcribe the argument, and you will be remanded in custody until Monday, November 12, at 10:00. If by any chance I am ready on Friday, I will let you know, but I don't think so."

—m—

On Monday, November 19, 1956, at ten o'clock in the morning, the matter resumed at the Cobourg courthouse.

Justice Butler said, "You have appeared before me previously on a charge that you, Jasper Billings, together with Stanley Blake, on the 27th day of August, 1956, at the Township of Percy, in the County of Northumberland, did unlawfully murder Troy Sregor, contrary to Section 206 of the Criminal Code. The evidence was heard, you were warned and given an opportunity to say anything you wished to in your own defence. You had nothing to say, the argument of counsel was heard, and judgment was reserved to determine whether you should be committed for trial on the charge. I have read and re-read the argument of counsel submitted, as reported by the reporter, and when I got through I was in greater doubt than when I started—that is, with all respect to counsel—so I started all over again from the beginning. My judgment is as follows: The two accused are charged with the murder of one Troy Sregor on the 27th day of August, 1956. The facts which came out in the preliminary hearing were, I suggest, as follows.

1. That Blake and Billings were, at the time of the offence, employed as farm hands by Seth Sregor.
2. There is a dispute as to the title of certain land between Troy Sregor, Seth Sregor, Ted Sregor, and Virginia Booker, the sister of the first three named.
3. Due to certain happenings on the various properties, and participated in by Billings and Blake, along with members of the Sregor family, I am convinced, and I suggest the evidence discloses,

that Billings and Blake were aware of the situation between the parties.
4. There is no evidence, so far as I can find, to warrant a conclusion that either Billings or Blake knew or should have known anything of the merits of the various cases of the parties concerned.
5. Both Billings and Blake knew, by having witnessed certain incidents, that Seth Sregor was prepared to go to great lengths to get his own way and resolve the situation in his favour. But nowhere can I find any evidence in the acts of Seth Sregor to entitle Billings or Blake to believe Seth Sregor would resort to murder, nor do I believe that was the opinion of Billings or Blake.
6. On the night in question, I am convinced the evidence only discloses an intent, so far as Seth Sregor, Billings, and Blake are concerned, to ascertain who was causing damage to the house in question and, if possible, to scare away those responsible.
7. On the night in question, the seven persons who make up what might be termed the "invading forces" arrived at the house where Billings and Blake were. The door was opened, and they walked in. I cannot find any evidence to suggest forcible entry, except it might be suggested, from the size of the opposing forces, that they overwhelmed the defenders by their numbers.
8. As a result of their presence there, Troy Sregor was shot and died as a result.
9. The bullets that caused the death of Troy Sregor were, according to the evidence, fired from the rifle in the hands of Stanley Blake.
10. There is evidence that none of the bullets found came from the rifle in the hands of Jasper Billings.

The law, in Section 194 of the Criminal Code, defines homicide as follows: "A person commits homicide when. directly or indirectly by any means. he causes the death of a human being." I must find there is evidence to indicate that Stanley Blake caused the death of Troy Sregor and is therefore guilty of homicide.

Section 194(5) of the Code states, "Culpable homicide is murder or manslaughter." Further it says, "A person commits culpable homicide when he causes the death of a human being (a) by means of an unlawful act and (b) by criminal negligence." Going back to (a), "by means of an unlawful act," and referring to the Criminal Code again, the only two sections which pertain to the discharge of a firearm—Section 160, which is the disturbance section of the Code, and starts with "not being in a dwelling house," and is therefore not applicable. The only other section is Section 216 of the Code, which reads, "Everyone who with intent (a) to wound, maim or disfigure any person, (b) to endanger the life of any person, or (c) to prevent the arrest or detention of any person, discharges a firearm at or cause bodily injury in any way to any person, is guilty of an offence." I cannot find from the evidence that there is any evidence that discloses Stanley Blake or Jasper Billings, but Stanley Blake mainly, did discharge a firearm with intent to wound, maim, or disfigure any person endanger the life of any person or prevent the arrest or detention of any person, and going to subsection (b) "by criminal negligence," and referring to Section 191 of the Code, "Everyone is criminally negligent who, in doing anything, shows wanton or reckless disregard for the lives or safety of other persons." I suggest there is evidence to warrant Stanley Blake, in discharging the firearm, did something which showed wanton or reckless disregard for the lives or safety of other persons. Therefore, I suggest there is evidence to warrant the committal of Stanley Blake on the charge that he did commit culpable homicide by criminal negligence.

Turning to Section 201 of the Code, "Culpable homicide is murder (a) where the person who causes the death of a human being (i) means to cause his death, (ii) means to cause him bodily harm that he knows is likely to cause his death and is reckless whether death ensues or not." Returning to (i) "means to cause his death," I cannot find any evidence to warrant the conclusion that Stanley Blake meant to cause the death of Troy Sregor. Part (ii) "means to cause him bodily harm that he knows is likely to cause his death and is reckless whether death ensues or not"—again I find there is no evidence to come to any such conclusion.

Again, "Culpable homicide is murder where a person, for an unlawful object, does anything that he knows or ought to know is likely to cause death and thereby causes death to a human being, notwithstanding that he desires to effect his object without causing death or bodily injury to any human being." Turning to the beginning of that clause, "Where a person for an unlawful object," what was the object of Blake in discharging the firearm? I suggest his object in discharging the firearm, so far as the evidence is concerned, was to keep Troy Sregor away from him, and to prevent Troy Sregor from taking the rifle away from him. Is that an unlawful object? True, it wasn't Blake's own personal property or Troy Sregor's, but as between Troy Sregor and Blake, I suggest Blake had the greater interest in the weapon, and I do not feel that Blake for an unlawful object did something that he knew or ought to have known was likely to cause death. Further, I suggest the evidence goes no further than to warrant the conclusion that what Blake did on the night of August 27, he did on the spur of the moment and without meditation. I cannot find, therefore, that in discharging the firearm on the night in question and causing the death of Troy Sregor, there was any evidence to warrant the conclusion that he committed murder, and when culpable homicide is not murder, it is manslaughter, according to the provision of Section 205 of the Code.

Insofar as Billings is concerned, turning to Section 21 of the Criminal Code under the heading of "Parties to Offences," (1) "Everyone is a party to an offence who (a) actually commits it, (b) does or omits to do anything for the purpose of aiding any person to commit it, or (c) abets any person in committing it." I cannot find there is any evidence to warrant the finding that Jasper Billings did anything on the night in question to bring him within that subsection of Section 21.

Subsection (2) states, "Where two or more persons form an intention in common to carry out an unlawful purpose, and to assist each other therein and any of them, in carrying out the common purpose, commits and offence, each of them who knew or ought to have known that the commission of the offence would be a probably consequence of carrying out the common purpose, is a party to that offence." As I have already said, the only purpose of these two boys in the house in question on that night was to ascertain who was causing the damage and to scare them away. I cannot find that was an unlawful purpose, and I cannot find, therefore, that there is any evidence to warrant a conclusion that Billings was party to the offence. I discharge Billings.

Stand up, Blake. I have therefore found there is evidence that would warrant me in finding a probably case of guilt insofar as you are concerned on the charge that you, Stanley Blake, on the 27th day of August, 1956, at the Township of Percy, in the County of Northumberland, did cause the death of Troy Sregor and did thereby commit manslaughter, contrary to the provisions of the Criminal Code. I commit you to stand trial on this charge before the next court of competent criminal jurisdiction.

Stanley Blake proceeded to trial and was found guilty of manslaughter by Justice Winston, the trial judge. The headline of *The Warkworth Journal* dated January 23, 1957, referenced that Stanley was to serve two years in jail for manslaughter. During the trial Stanley Blake had undergone a psychological assessment. Stanley was considered pleasant and well-mannered, but only a grade four level of intelligence. Dr. Gilday had testified that Stanley Blake was a follower and could easily be lead by a strong character. Due to the loss of his parents at an early age and being raised by foster parents from the age of 12, he was always looking for parents to accept him and love him. The Judge had believed that this had led Stanley to see Seth and Annie Sregor as the parents for which he had yearned.

Justice Winston stated in his verdict that although Seth Sregor was not on trial for the murder of his brother, he was the one who had caused it in the Judge's eyes, and the Judge felt Seth had a moral responsibility for the crime and hoped that Troy's death would haunt him for years to come. However, the Judge continued to advise Stanley that he was the one who had ultimately pulled the trigger and was therefore guilty in the court's eyes for the murder of Troy Sregor. He encouraged Stanley to get as far away from Warkworth as possible when he was released from prison, and to not return to Seth Sregor's farm or have any contact with him going forward.

Annie and Seth Sregor had been at court every day to support Stanley Blake. They wished they could have done more to help Stanley. The words from the Judge had cut Seth like a knife. He would never do anything to hurt his family. They may have harsh words and disagree about things, and yes, it was true he could have a bad temper, but family was very important to Seth.

Twenty-Four

On July 2, 2009, Malorie arrived home to find a piece of paper on the counter by the microwave. Within other scribbled notes she saw a phone number and her cousin's name. Despite it being so small and difficult to read, it seemed to pop out at her. She asked her son Seth, "Did Ronnie call?"

"Yes; she called to tell you her mother died." Then Seth went back to watching television. Virginia Sregor Booker was dead.

It had been a couple of months since they had last seen each other. Ronnie had arranged for all of them to go to Aunt Ethel's farm. Ronnie was really hoping to get some pictures of her mom and the family on the Sregor side. Malorie had gone to spend time with her cousin, but also with the hope maybe she would find out something that would help her with her research. Nothing had come up. Seth and Rorie and gone with Malorie, and on their way back they had stopped at the Warkworth Cemetery. This was the first chance that Malorie was able to travel to the cemetery since she had spoken to the caretaker's wife. The orange peg was long gone, but oddly enough her son was able to find Troy's resting place right away, as though he had been there before.

Malorie called Ronnie right away, and Ronnie seemed so together. Ronnie advised Malorie that her mother, Virginia, had been in the Bowmanville Hospital and had now been transported to the Bowmanville Funeral Parlours. She and asked that Malorie let Aunt Georgie and Uncle Gary know as well. Ronnie was making arrangements for a graveside funeral, to

Rattlesnake Fever

have Virginia buried with her parents and baby John, who was her older brother and who had died of scarlet fever at the age of 7.

This really bothered Malorie, knowing what she knew about Virginia's father, but it was none of her business. Who was she to say anything?

Malorie called Aunt Georgie to see if she wanted to go, and she replied, "Oh, yeah," but it didn't sound like a true yes, so Malorie said, "Is that a yeah no, or a yeah yes?" Malorie told her it was okay if she did not want to go, because she knew there were many bad memories. Aunt Georgie said it would depend on which day, because she had some appointments that week. Malorie told her she would let her know as soon as she found out. Aunt Georgie mentioned letting Uncle Gary know. Malorie thought it might sound weird coming from her, but she would get the information, and then they could go from there. Uncle Gary would wonder how Malorie knew about Virginia; Nobody had heard of or spoken of Virginia in years.

Virginia Sregor Booker died on July 1, Canada Day, and it was one year, one month, and one day to the date that Malorie's Grandma Annie had passed away. Things had been quiet for Malorie in terms of receiving messages in her dreams or people entering Malorie's path of life, except for the wedding invitation that Ronnie had sent to Malorie and her family. Malorie had hesitated about going to the wedding until the very last day, because she felt awkward. Family was important to Malorie, and she wanted to support her cousin, but on the other hand they had been taught over the years to never trust a Booker.

Malorie couldn't help but think that now that Virginia was gone, she may never know the answers to her questions. Virginia was the one person that might have the answers, and now she was gone too. Malorie felt as though she was driving herself crazy with all this information, and she had all but given up. Malorie's main focus now was to be there for her cousin Ronnie.

On July 6, Malorie, her son Seth, and her daughter Rorie drove to Warkworth for the funeral of Virginia Sregor Booker. Malorie had called Aunt Georgie and Uncle Gary; they were going to meet her there. When

Malorie arrived in Warkworth, she really needed to find a bathroom. As she entered the main street in the small town, the first thing she saw was the hearse that had been carrying Aunt Virginia. Malorie returned to her focus of finding a washroom. She first tried the bank at Rorie's suggestion. It was a Monday, yet everything seemed closed. Malorie then saw a little coffee shop, and as she was walking toward it, she thought the man in front of her looked familiar. It was Ronnie's soon-to-be husband, Donny. Then Malorie noticed her cousin Ronnie and her half-sister Julie. She gave them a big hug and apologized for her one-sighted vision—a bathroom. Malorie gave Rorie and Seth some money to buy a pop; she didn't feel right just going in to use the washroom.

When she came out, she saw Ronnie and Julie walking up and down the sidewalk. Ronnie looked completely together with no signs of being distraught, but Malorie could tell from her constant puffing of the cigarette in her hand that it was not an easy day for her. She had not seen her mother in over 18 years, and her last memory of her mother was of her mother laughing; she wanted it to remain that way. Malorie told Ronnie that Aunt Georgie was coming with Uncle Gary, and he always had spoken well of Virginia. Both Donny and Ronnie were happy that someone would be coming with fond memories. Malorie followed Ronnie to the cemetery. When they got to the cemetery, Ronnie got out with some pictures of her mom and some flowers. Donny and Julie were right beside Ronnie, and they all walked toward the gravesite.

Malorie saw her Georgie, and as they were walking, she realized everyone was looking their way. Malorie realized she was leading the way. This was Ronnie's day, and Malorie pulled back to let Ronnie lead the way. As Ronnie went to talk to the minister and gave the pictures to display, Malorie went over to see Uncle Gary and Aunt Georgie. As she stood back watching, she could tell right off who Aunt Joan was. She was there with her husband and son, as well as her daughter with her husband. Aunt Joan began to give Ronnie a hard time because she had not seen her in such a long time. Her son David said, "That is my mom, giving someone crap at a funeral."

Aunt Joan then began to say, "There is nothing more important than family and sticking together." Malorie couldn't help thinking about the transcripts that she had read. Sticking together at all costs had been very apparent. Keeping those closets locked had affected many lives and many generations.

Virginia's brother Daniel was there with his wife, Joan. He had not seen Virginia in years, but he appeared to be quite close with his sister Joan. When she was a young child Malorie had remembered him looking very much like Grandpa Seth. As she looked at Uncle Daniel, she wondered if that was how her Grandpa Seth would look if he was still alive.

The woman minister was very kind and spoke of Virginia when she was a hairdresser. Aunt Joan, Virginia's sister, had requested to say a few words. The minister introduced Joan, who went up to the front by the coffin. With her lip quivering, she spoke to those attending. It was short and sweet. "Virginia was a good sister until she got sick, and then she wasn't such a good sister."

Then Ronnie gave her Aunt Joan a hug and traded places with her at the front. Ronnie began to recite a poem she had chosen. A small tear fell from her eyes, and she took a deep breath and began to speak. Malorie shed her own tears; they were tears for Ronnie, for the mother she had lost way before this day, and for Virginia, who had spent her life institutionalized and fighting the demons in her head—the demons that her parents had caused rather than protected her from. Malorie felt bad that Virginia's final resting place would be with her parents and wondered how she would have felt about that.

After the service, they went back to a coffee shop in town to chat and get to know each other again after so many years. There were first cousins, second cousins, and third cousins—quite a range, but it felt like they were strangers.

As they sat around chatting, Malorie's Great-Uncle Daniel mentioned how, when he came back from Korea, he was supposed to get the land, but when he went to the homestead, it had been given to Virginia. Uncle Daniel said he never went back. But on this day, when they were all going to the coffee shop, Uncle Daniel had turned the opposite way. He had gone to see the old homestead that he had not visited in over 50 years.

As they all sat and had coffee, they shared tales and memories and asked about family members that were not there and their paths, some of which were unknown. As Malorie went to pay for their drinks, the waitress advised that it had all been paid for. Malorie asked Ronnie, and she said she thought that the man in the suit had paid for it, and she pointed to Malorie's Uncle Gary. That was just like him; he was such a sweet man. Malorie said she wished he was her dad, and they had a chuckle.

Malorie went out to the car and thanked Uncle Gary, and though he denied it, she could tell by his mouth. Malorie laughed and said she knew it was him; she could tell for sure if he was fibbing if she could see his eyes under his glasses. He took them off, and as soon as she looked she knew, and they both began to laugh. Malorie asked that if she won a lot of money, if she could pay for him to adopt her. She told him she didn't want any of his possessions; she just to be able to say she had a great dad. He said she didn't have to be adopted to say he was her dad. They both knew the DNA would say different, but it was so kind of Uncle Gary to agree to let Malorie live in her own little dream world.

Malorie told Uncle Gary that she was going to go and put some flowers on Grandpa Seth's and Grandma Annie's graves. Uncle Gary mentioned that Aunt Georgie had been telling him about her family tree searching, but she didn't think much of it. Aunt Georgie came out, and they all decided to go to the gravesite together. As Malorie pulled up behind Uncle Gary on Church Street in Campbellford, she went past the cemetery and pulled into the first farm on the left-hand side. This was the farm that her parents had owned when she was younger. The owners were outside fixing it up, and it looked really good. They had done a lot of work on it. However, it always bothered her over the years to see that they had taken the big wrap-around porch and closed it in. That had been her favourite part of that farmhouse. She showed her children and then drove down and parked by Uncle Gary's car.

They all walked to the headstone, and Malorie placed her flowers by the headstone. She had brought pink roses and daisies from her garden. The roses smelt beautiful. As they began to walk away, Uncle Gary made mention of his conversation that he and Aunt Georgie had in the car on their way to the cemetery. Malorie was not sure how much Aunt Georgie had told him. As Aunt Georgie walked closer, Malorie felt it was okay to tell Uncle Gary about what she had discovered. He had no idea and seemed shocked that he had not seen any signs of the abuse. But back then, he was always in the kitchen helping his mom. Uncle Gary had always been the type of person that only saw the good in people; he had a heart full of love that he was more than happy to share. Malorie told him he was too good and pure; he only wanted to see the good and refused to believe there was anything else. No wonder both his grandmas always called him their boy. He had not been touched by the evil.

Uncle Gary said he would show Malorie where Great-Uncle Troy was killed, but first Malorie knew she needed to feed Seth and Rorie because they were about to drop. They all decided to go to Tim Hortons in town, and Seth treated everyone to treats. They sat around chatting, and Malorie was loving the time she was spending with those she loved. Malorie then followed Uncle Gary, and when they got to the place where Great-Uncle Troy had died, she realized that what she thought initially was the place he was killed was the wrong place. It fit the transcripts, but the roads had been changed since that dark day in 1956. Looking at this house made sense. The one that she thought it was looked beautiful and bright, but this house was dark and dreary.

Malorie thanked her Uncle Gary, and he drove Aunt Georgie home while Malorie and her kids got in their car and returned home. As Malorie drove, Seth and Rorie fell asleep, and she began to reflect on the day's events. She was thinking about Ronnie and her family. She would be seeing Ronnie in two weeks at her bridal shower, and then the following week at her wedding. She felt awkward, but she couldn't very well go up and say to her, "So by the way, your mother was molested by her father, and that is probably why she was sick for so many years, among other things."

The wedding was on a beautiful summer day in July. The bride wore a beautiful, long, blue dress, and her father, Willy Booker, walked her down the aisle. This was an opportunity not only to be there for her cousin Ronnie and support her, but also to put faces to the names in the transcripts that she had only read and heard about for many years. The one person Malorie had quite often wondered about was Joe Duberg, Willy's brother-in-law. When she had gone in and introduced herself to Willy Booker as Seth Sregor's granddaughter, Willy had seemed confused and thought she was Gary's daughter. But while he tried to remember, she had noticed out of the corner of her eye the way that Joe Duberg was looking at her; it had made her feel uncomfortable. Later that night, when she was sitting and chatting with some of the other guests, she had an uneasy feeling, and when she looked up, she could see Joe Duberg staring at her from around the corner of the entrance. She suddenly felt uncomfortable in her surroundings, and she told her husband Anthony that she thought they should leave. They gathered Seth and Rorie and said good-bye to the newlyweds, wishing them all the best.

Malorie did not see much of Veronica and her family after the wedding. It may have been her imagination, but she felt an awkwardness. Veronica had actually called Malorie at one point to see who in the family was trying to dig up family history; she had seemed angry. Her father Willy had told her about a letter he had received from a "M. Sregor." She said the letter was asking questions about Troy's death, but he refused to respond to it if he didn't know who had sent it. She had wondered if it was Aunt Georgie, because her full birth name was really Mabel Georgia Sregor. Malorie said that her uncles had married women whose first name started with "M," so there were quite a few people who those initials could belong to. In fact, Malorie said, "It could even be me, as I was Malorie Sregor." Ronnie seemed to calm down. When Malorie asked her if her father had told her anything about that day, she was cautious but mentioned that he had said it was an accident, and that Troy had come out to the driveway, and it had scared them, and the gun went off. But Malorie knew that his testimony was very different from what Ronnie was telling her.

Twenty-Five

When Malorie had set out to find the answers to the murder of Troy Sregor, she had wanted to know who really killed him. Time and time again, she had heard the story of Jasper Billings and Stanley Blake, but like others, she never believed they were the reason Troy was dead. She thought her purpose in life was to find the real murderer or murderers who took Troy away from his wife and young family much too soon. It was clear that Stanley's gun had gone off, accidentally shooting Troy—but was that the bullet that had killed Troy? Witnesses had testified that the shots were so close that they sounded like one. One witness said they saw the blood on the back before he turned around from his struggle with Stanley. A gun was found in the barn, and a third casing from a bullet was found on the landing off the kitchen . . . yet only two shots were heard.

After finding out all the new information from her research, there were a lot of suspects and a lot of motives, but no answers and no confessions. The testimonies had holes in them, and many witnesses were fed their answers, and then, when an answer seemed like it was going somewhere, it was dropped.

It could have been any one of Troy's brothers or sisters because of anger and greed over their father's will, but that didn't make sense, because it was Virginia who got the majority of their father's estate in the end. So why kill Troy?

Perhaps it was one of Seth's three boys, Ken, Harry, or Rick, because Troy had found out about their sexual relations with their sister Georgie. Or maybe it was because Troy knew of their relationship with his sister Joan.

Maybe Marty Morgan had lashed out because of all the indecencies that had happened to his wife as a child, and he wanted someone to pay regardless of whether they were guilty or innocent.

Joe Duberg had been at the scene of the murder when the police arrived, but there was no mention of how or why he was there. He had not gone with the rest of them in the car, according to the transcripts. He had also seemed oddly uncomfortable when Malorie met him.

Possibly Virginia and her husband, Willy Booker, had plotted to try and get everything in the will. They had found a loophole with Ted, and the only person left who stood to inherit something of value was Troy. If that was the plan, it backfired when her mother transferred the land to his widow and children for a mere $100. Was that out of guilt?

Some of the family stories had insinuated that the bullet was not really for Troy, but for his brother Seth, who drew a strong resemblance to him. In the dark, had someone thought they were shooting Seth Sregor, not realizing it was actually Troy until it was too late?

Had Virginia been so hurt and distraught at the thought that their father had sexually molested and abused his daughters while her big brothers stood by and did nothing? Big brothers were supposed to protect their little sisters, and they had not done that. The only thing that they were interested in was land, to the point where their dirty laundry had been exposed in court. Had Virginia hoped to get them where it hurts? Why not take the one thing away from them that they wanted—the land? In those days the amount of land a man had was considered a reflection of his success. A man felt he was a man because of what he owned. But Virginia and her sisters would never be able to feel like successful women; they only felt dirty.

Did Virginia have her husband disconnect the telephone lines and set the stage for her brother Seth's murder—only to discover she had made a grave error and killed the one brother who had been there for her when she needed him? Despite the fact that when the police initially came because of his father's abuse to his sister Joan, Virginia didn't know that Troy had tried to turn the police away . . . Had he really been there for them? And if Virginia didn't know about that, had she accidentally killed the one big brother that tried to protect her in his own way?

Seth Sregor died from diabetes and heart problems, 14 years after his brother Troy's death. He dropped dead at the kitchen table just before dinner. Many said he had pined for his children after the youngest got married and left home. Family was very important to Seth. Had the pining started long before, with the death of his baby brother? Justice Winston had made it sound like Seth had set up Stanley Blake and Jasper Billings to commit this crime. Given Seth's education level, although he was smart, he would not know that Stanley's psychological imbalances would lead him to think that killing would make Seth happy and accept him as a son. Did Stanley plan it with the hope it may win him his own sense of belonging in a family? If that was his thought, he had to know that no matter what, in the Sregor family blood was thicker than water.

Ted ended up in a mental hospital in Western Canada, and nobody heard anything about him other than he had since passed away. He had suffered greatly. He knew what his father was doing, and Malorie believed that when he tried to come forward, that was when his mother had Ted committed to the mental hospital and requested electric shock therapy on him. Although it had kept him quiet about the family secret, she couldn't erase his memories of guilt and pain.

Malorie's Uncle Rick had died young of cancer, but not before it was discovered he had other women on the side and approximately 14 other kids somewhere. Malorie's family was always hitting the front page of the newspaper, but not for being good Samaritans. Rick had destroyed and hurt many people. Was it as a result of him being molested at such a young age? Was he always trying to find love, but he never felt worthy of it.

Malorie's Uncle Harry lived in western Canada somewhere, still believing in wrestling but now a widower at a young age. He was living off the money of his mother's house, which he had taken out from under her. No matter how he wanted to slice it, he stole it.

Malorie's estranged father, Ken, was suffering from prostate cancer and still living in a fantasy world. He had cried wolf about dying so many times, even attempting suicide at one point, so that Malorie no longer believed him. She didn't trust him and had no wishes to open that door again. Yet she couldn't help but feel sorry for him. If things had been different for him as a child, maybe he could have made a better life for his children and grandchildren.

Grandfather Seth's brother Daniel and sister Joan lived near each other, close to where they grew up in Warkworth. Life was simple but full of love with the families they had. That had been clear when Malorie had seen them at the funeral.

Willy had divorced Virginia and remarried, and he now had a farm in the Durham Region with his new wife, two daughters, and a son whom he adored. He had grandchildren, and life was good for him. He still kept in touch with his sister Liza and her husband, Joe Duberg.

Virginia had ended up in a mental institute at a very young age. She had even undergone the painful shock treatment. Her mother had instructed this for both Virginia and her brother Ted, perhaps as a way to make them forget. Virginia had died all alone in a hospital; nobody really knew her. Her only daughter had ensured a loving send-off with family members and stories of when she was a young girl. The good memories of Virginia were the ones that Ronnie wanted to hold close.

Bethany had committed suicide. Many said it was because she was promiscuous and was trying to play two men against each other by pretending to commit suicide, but her plan backfired and she ended up dead. Was that the truth, or were the effects of what her father had done to her more than she could bear? Maybe she had never felt worthy of anyone's love, much less a man's. Was the pain so unbearable that she no longer wanted to live, and it was in fact no accident? She left behind two beautiful children.

The truth had been buried with all those lost souls. But now Malorie knew what the reason for all her research was. It wasn't to find the real murderer, because in essence the true murderer was James Seth Sregor—their father.

Malorie's purpose was to let the truth be known. Her grandfather had always said that those present at Troy's death would take the truth to their graves. She believed she was meant to set the story straight so that history would no longer repeat itself. The incest and abuse had affected several generations because nobody spoke up. Malorie was no longer going to continue the silence. The story needed to be told because, as Aunt Georgie had said, the adults can make it stop.

Virginia had appeared to be like a rattlesnake in the middle of gold rush fever. She would bite with her tongue and then run with the gold after her victim was paralysed by the poison. Aunt Georgie had told Malorie about how Virginia would drive right by her when Georgie was walking home from school and never pick her up. But was it to be mean or to protect her? After all, Georgie was approaching the age that James Seth Sregor would strip her of her innocence. Things may not always be as they appear. Perhaps she did not want Georgie to endure a fever from the poison of incest as she had for many years from the guilt and anger.

In the end, the poison had destroyed all of them. As strong as Grandma Annie was, she had come from a generation where certain things were to be seen but not spoken of. She had not been strong enough to save the others, especially her daughter Georgie, and she would always regret that. She had gone to her grave afraid to speak the truth, and afraid to tell her daughter Georgie she was sorry she did not protect her. By giving the transcript to Malorie many years before, she knew that in time, Malorie would ensure the truth was told, and that those innocent souls that had gone on before her could now rest in peace, as Malorie hoped her Grandma Annie would now, too.

BIBLIOGRAPHY

Archives of Ontario. RG 22-191. File # 19709 [1956 to 1963]. Estate File for Roy Rogers.

Archives of Ontario. RG 22-191. File # 19461 [1949 to 1956]. Estate File for John Wesley Rogers.

Cobourg Court Office—Preliminary Trial Transcript, In the Magistrate's Court of the Province of Ontario. In the matter of *Clifford Brough and Robert White*, And in the matter of Section 206 of the Criminal Code. The preliminary hearing into this matter before R.B. Baxter, Esquire, Magistrate for the Province of Ontario. At Brighton , Ontario Wednesday, October 31, 1956.

CPSIA information can be obtained at www.ICGtesting.com
Printed in the USA
LVOW050113190213

320624LV00002B/379/P

9 781475 930016